# GILBERT-AUGUSTIN THIERRY

# THE BLONDE TRESS
# AND THE MASK

## TRANSLATED AND WITH AN INTRODUCTION BY
## BRIAN STABLEFORD

THIS IS A SNUGGLY BOOK

ISBN: 978-1-64525-058-6

# THE BLONDE TRESS
# AND THE MASK

GILBERT-AUGUSTIN THIERRY (1843-1915), the son of the writer Amédée Thierry and the nephew of the historian Augustin Thierry, was a novelist, poet and journalist, who published extensively in the *Revue des Deux-Mondes*. In 1875 he debuted with the intensively-researched historical novel *L'Aventure d'une âme en peine*, followed in 1882 by *Le Capitaine Sans-Façon 1813: épisodes de la contre-révolution*. His subsequent works, which include *Marfa* (1887), *La tresse blonde* (1888), *La Savelli* (1890), *Le masque* (1894) and *Le stigmate* (1898), often dealt with the occult and the supernatural.

BRIAN STABLEFORD'S scholarly work includes *New Atlantis: A Narrative History of Scientific Romance* (Wildside Press, 2016), *The Plurality of Imaginary Worlds: The Evolution of French roman scientifique* (Black Coat Press, 2017) and *Tales of Enchantment and Disenchantment: A History of Faerie* (Black Coat Press, 2019). In support of the latter projects he has translated more than a hundred volumes of *roman scientifique* and more than twenty volumes of *contes de fées* into English. He has edited *Decadence and Symbolism: A Showcase Anthology* (Snuggly Books, 2018), and is busy translating more Symbolist and Decadent fiction.

His recent fiction, in the genre of metaphysical fantasy, includes a trilogy of novels set in West Wales, consisting of *Spirits of the Vasty Deep* (2018), *The Insubstantial Pageant* (2018) and *The Truths of Darkness* (2019), published by Snuggly Books, and a trilogy set in Paris and the south of France, consisting of *The Painter of Spirits*, *The Quiet Dead* and *Living with the Dead*, all published by Black Coat Press in 2019.

SNUGGLY BOOKS

# CONTENTS

# INTRODUCTION

This is the second volume of fantastic fiction by Gilbert-Augustin Thierry to be published by Snuggly Books, following *Reincarnation and Redemption*, which contains translations of "La Rédemption de Larmor" (*Nouvelle Revue* April 1882; tr. as "Larmor's Redemption"), "Rediviva" (*Nouvelle Revue* November 1883; tr, as "Rediviva") and "La Bien-Aimée" (*Revue des deux mondes* December 1891; tr. as "The Beloved") The present volume contains translations of "La Tresse blonde" (*Revue des deux mondes* July 1888; book 1889; tr. as "The Blonde Tress") and "Le Masque" (*Revue des deux mondes* January-February 1894; book 1894; tr. as "The Mask"). The third volume, *Stigma and The Pompeiian Fresco* contains the final two items in the series, "Le Stigmate" (*Revue des deux mondes* July-September 1897; book 1898; tr. as "Stigma") and "La Fresque de Pompéi" (*Revue des deux mondes* March 1912; tr. as "The Pompeiian Fresco").

The first two stories in the sequence were identified as the opening items of a series entitled "Histoires de Mort et de Vivants, récits étranges" [Accounts of the Dead and the Living: Strange Stories], but no further items appeared in *La Nouvelle Revue*. Two further novellas that the author published in the *Revue des deux mondes* in the 1880s, "Le Palimpseste" (March 1887; reprinted in book form in the same year as *Marfa, ou Le Palimpseste*; tr. as *The Palimpsest*) and "La Blonde Tresse" can be seen as continuations of that series, recapitulating and elaborating themes introduced in the two novelettes in the *Nouvelle*

*Revue.* The remaining three novellas also carry forward the theme of expiatory redemptions, but only "Le Masque" does so in the context of reincarnation; although the last two items reproduce the basic theme and story-arc of "Le Masque," they alter the context in which that fundamental narrative is worked out quite considerably, transforming the tacit metaphysics of the events thy depict considerably. By that means they complete a remarkable evolution in the series as a whole, which is only clearly visible and fully appreciable if all seven of the works continued in the present trio of volumes are read successively.

Gilbert-Augustin Thierry (1843-1915) was given his second forename after his uncle, the noted "Romantic historian" Augustin Thierry (1795-1856), who was more scrupulous in his consultation of documentary evidence than many historians of the era but who routinely adopted a colorful style of narrative reportage that affiliated him strongly to the French Romantic Movement. Augustin Thierry's enduring fame eventually encouraged his nephew to transplant the hyphen in his signature and begin to sign himself "Gilbert Augustin-Thierry"; both the novellas in the present volume bore that signature in all their French versions, but I have retained the baptismal version of the author's name in order to maintain continuity with the first volume in the present series of translations.

Gilbert's father, Amédée Thierry (1797-1873), was also a historian, and was also significantly associated with the Romantic Movement, but he obtained his principal reputation as a journalist—a profession that he was initially obliged to adopt because he was dismissed from the chair of history at the University of Besançon for being too liberal in his expressed opinions during the repressive reign of Charles X. His bold opposition to absolute monarchy guaranteed him favor after the July Revolution of 1830 issued in a new era of constitutional monarchy; he was appointed prefect of the Haut-Saône, and he held various other administrative posts before and after the 1848 Revolution, before becoming a Senator in 1860. In the meantime, he was a regular contributor to the *Revue des deux mondes*, which began as a Radical Romantic publication but shifted considerably to the right in response to changes in the political climate after Louis-Napoléon's 1851 *coup-d'état* launched the Second Empire and a new era of stern censorship.

Gilbert followed in his father's footsteps, publishing extensively in the *Revue des deux mondes* and enjoying a successful career in journalism, but he was also heavily influenced by his uncle; he became an assiduous researcher and employer of documentary sources, and he followed the example of the Romantic writer of flamboyant historical fiction S. Henry Berthoud in labeling many of his works of fiction "historical studies" in order to emphasize their scholarly underpinnings. Gilbert's work might, however, also be held to illustrate that an assiduous interest in dubious documentary sources can easily tempt a historian, however scrupulous he might be, to fanciful conclusions. It is also arguable that his intellectual scrupulousness became somewhat questionable when he became very interested in, and temporarily involved with the French Occult Revival, which had begun as an offshoot of the Romantic Movement in the movement's decadent phase. Much of his fiction was written under that influence, including his first novel, the intensively-researched *L'Aventure d'une âme en peine* [The Adventure of a Soul in Pain] (1875).

As a result of his occult research, the supernatural became much more explicit in Thierry's works in the 1880s, including the two novellas translated in the present volume, but both the items included herein also exhibit a burgeoning interest in new interpretations of phenomena previously considered purely in a religious context by pioneers of the nascent science of psychology. Both of the novellas in the present volume introduce a measure of ambiguity into the interpretation and representation of the supernatural events that they feature, in which the notion of "mental alienation" provides an alternative explanation for the experiences of the protagonist. In "La Blonde Tresse" the religious implications of the events of the story retain their hegemony, but in "Le Masque," in spite of a scathing hostility to alienists and to the treatment of patients interned in mental hospitals, the balance of interpretation is more even, and the suggestion is clear that if the phenomena of reincarnation are, in fact, to be construed literally, then the unlucky individuals subjected to them would, indeed, have to be reckoned quite mad as a result.

"La Blonde Tresse" is interesting in the context of the series as a whole because it addresses more directly than its predecessors and its immediate successor, "La Bien-Aimée," the question of the fundamental morality of a metaphysical system by which individuals are doomed by fate to expiate sins that they have not committed. It introduces an extra twist—taken from the Old Testament—in which people are not even required to compensate for alleged misdeeds of their own immortal soul but for sins committed by their forefathers. It also raises the question of whether the person to whom repayment ought to be made in the present for crimes committed in previous generations would actually welcome the partial redemption offered. The continuation of that train of thought helps to sharpen the moralistic element of "Le Masque," too, although the principal focus of attention therein moves to new ground in its examination of the possible psychological side-effects of inherited karmic burdens.

Although "Le Masque" certainly qualifies as an important and intriguing contribution to the late nineteenth-century boom in fantasies featuring Egyptian mummies, therefore, its intense interest in the psychology of reincarnation, taking up themes first broached in "La Blonde tresse," gives it an extra dimension of complication that differentiates it markedly from the majority of the thrillers and "karmic romances" employing the same motif that followed hot on its heels. It is a much more sophisticated and intriguing story than such English developments of the theme as Clive Holland's *An Egyptian Coquette* (1898), Guy Boothby's *Pharos the Egyptian* (1899) and Bram Stoker's *The Jewel of Seven Stars* (1907), and is certainly entitled to be considered the most interesting work exploring the theme produced before the Great War.

Although the author's perennial interest in the metaphysical context of his stories, and his use of his fiction to explore those notions in a new way did not help him to gain great popularity or a lasting reputation among aficionados of fantastic literature, it is worth noting that their appearance in the *Revue des deux mondes*, supported by subsequent publication in book form, certainly obtained them a wider initial readership than many more downmarket products, and deservedly so. Both stories are horror stories, but the element of horror within them is more intellectual than visceral, and its full appreciation requires a more sophisticated turn of the imagination than most stories that appeared in more downmarket publications. Their proper appreciation also requires a more subtle appreciation of ambiguity than unsophisticated readers routinely bring to the consumption of supernatural horror stories. It is not so much that Thierry does not offer definite answers as to what happens in the stories as the tendency he has not to give the reader any insistent advice as to how to feel or what to think about what happens. Because of the way he routinely filters his narratives through unreliable and unsympathetic narrators, there is very rarely a voice in his fiction with which the reader can or ought to identify with wholeheartedly.

The essential subjectivity and bias of the reports rendered to the reader in Thierry's works by different viewpoints sometimes cause problems of narrative construction—particularly evident in "Le Masque," where the reader, who has access to the full range of documents, ends up knowing far more than any of the individual reporters—but that too is an aspect of the work in which the author took an intense and inquisitive interest, and which he tried to develop meticulously in a fashion that allows him to set up tense and dramatic climactic confrontations. If his narrative constructions sometimes seem a little awkward, that is because they are sometimes ground-breaking, working without much in the way of useful precedents and exemplars. When his climaxes arrive, however, they always carry a substantial impact by virtue of their careful preparation. Although the conclusion of "Le Masque" can be seen as a stepping-stone to the more elaborately melodramatic climaxes of the two works contained in the final volume of the present series of translations, helping considerably to pave the way for "Le Stigmate"—unquestionably the author's masterpiece—it is a very estimable work in its own right, and "La Blonde tresse," although simpler and a little slighter, is also a very effective story.

Many of the writers associated, even peripherally, with the Occult Revival, have been considered with some suspicion by aficionados of fantastic fiction because of their presumed propagandistic element, which was certainly a notable feature of the three stories contained in the first volume of this series. The two stories in the present volume, however, are far more dubious in their metaphysical assertions, and clearly reflect the fact that Thierry has become much more suspicious of ideas that had previously attracted him, and is trying to explore and analyze them in a more open-minded fashion, while not forsaking his fundamental fascination. He becomes suspicious, too, of his potential literary affiliations; while retaining an obvious fondness for the Romantic tradition of French fiction he is decidedly uncertain as the merit of its more recent developments, and it is very difficult to assign him a definite place in the literary spectrum of the *fin-de-siècle*. He was a maverick who would surely have rejected all the labels conventionally applied at the time, very reluctant to think of himself as having any connection with the Symbolist and Naturalist schools whose perceived opposition seem to many observers to set the agenda for the evolution of French fiction as it moved toward the twentieth century, but he was not a stubborn traditionalist either, and his work certainly does not hark back to any earlier phase of that evolution.

The particular emphasis of Thierry's occult fiction differs markedly from the work of such contemporary literary participants in the Occult Revival as Joséphin Péladan, Jules Bois, Édouard Schuré, Victor-Émile Michelet and Jane de La Vaudère, not just because of its preoccupation with philosophical corollaries of the notion of reincarnation, but also because of its reluctance to embrace any but a very broad mysticism, and an insistence of retaining doubts even about that. Of all the writers of that genre of fiction—if it has sufficient commonality to be considered a genre—he is the one who seems to have moved furthest, in ideological terms, in the course of his work than any other, and he seems to have made that move largely as a result of the thought-experiments carried out in his work.

In terms of the particular spectrum of Thierry's works contained in the present series of translations, the two novellas herein are pivotal, not only in the sense that they fill in the gap of what would otherwise be a very marked difference of attitude between the *Nouvelle Revue* novelettes and the two intense amorous fantasies in the third volume of the series, but also because they show how that change of direction was achieved. "The Masque," in particular, involves a complex ideological shift of perspective that provides an intricate but smoothly-operated joint. Few of Thierry's contemporaries were capable of that kind of mental flexibility, or managing the necessary mental and artistic maneuvers to achieve it, and that is why he remains a fascinating and admirable writer.

The two translations herein were almost entirely made from the relevant issues of the *Revue des deux mondes* reproduced on the Bibliothèque Nationale's *gallica* website. The BN's scans of the early pages of "Le Masque" are, however, very poor, and several paragraphs on the first page of the story are illegible. Fortunately, the scans of the relevant pages contained on JSTOR are much better, and I was able to fill in the text from that version, accessed via the London Library website.

—Brian Stableford

# THE BLONDE TRESS AND THE MASK

# THE BLONDE TRESS

. . . . . . . . . . . . . . . . . . . . . . . . . . . . . . . . . . . . . . . . .

. . . Here commences the first fragment of the memoirs of Professor Victor Rameau.

## I

. . . It was on the twenty-sixth of December 1865, the day after Christmas, that I gave a reading at the Académie de Médecine of my Essay on *The Simulations of Second Sight among the Ancients and the Moderns.*

About that work I do not want to say anything except that I believed it to be destined to procure its author some reputation and a little glory in my homeland. I was not disappointed in my hope, and my learned sallies amused the illustrious assembly while edifying its members. From the first phrases I sensed that it was as if I were enveloped by the sympathies of my listeners. Soon, my explanatory dissertation on the sacred furies of the prophets of Israel, the raptures of Saint Francis of Assisi and the nine ascendant steps toward seraphic amour, earned me flattering murmurs, followed by the most profound silence. But when I arrived at my conclusions, I dare to affirm that my success became a veritable triumph.

Scarcely had I pronounced the words "animal magnetism," with a smile, than little mocking sniggers immediately made a chorus with my epigrams, and "Good, very good," resonated in the hall while I reproved the "criminal farces" of Mesmer and deplored the "candid reveries" of the likes of Faria and Puységur.[1] Finally, when I came in my peroration to request of the Prefect of Police an effective, continuous, severe and moralizing surveillance of all magnetizers, fascinators, hypnotists, mediums and other charlatans, unanimous *bravos* proved to me that the conscience of the Académie was speaking, that day, in unison with mine.

That was a very fine victory for me. My head on fire, but my heart swelling, I quit the hall for the Rue des Saints-Pères and, descending toward the quais, began walking at random; I needed to refresh the fever of my brow. Night was falling—a snowy December night—and the passers-by were fleeing under the bite of the north wind, plunging into the fog. Having reached the first houses of the Rue du Bac, I stopped in front of a small newsagents' shop and went in to peruse the evening newspapers.

Only one gazette was on sale as yet, a legitimist, ultra-royalist, ultra-Catholic and even slightly literary paper that has since disappeared, *Le Croisé*. I bought it. Perhaps it would make mention of the Académie's session, perhaps even of my humble person . . . ? No, nothing yet: banal articles on the routine events of the day; a few retrospective insults addressed to the hideous Voltaire; a rea-

1 Abbé Faria (José Custodio de Faria, 1756-1819) was an important pioneer of the scientific study of hypnotism, abandoning Franz Mesmer's theory of a "magnetic fluid" introducing a somnambulistic trance, and arguing that it worked entirely by means of suggestion, including autosuggestion, all the productions of hypnotism originating in the imagination of the subject. The Marquis de Puységur (1751-1825) had previously introduced the notion of 'artificial somnambulism" as a description of the hypnotic state, and founded the Societé Harmonique des Amis Réunis in order to train "magnetizers," and his techniques for inducing artificial somnambulism displaced Mesmer's own methods, becoming standardized before falling into disrepute after the 1789 Revolution; when they were revived in the late nineteenth century, Puységur's writings had to be rediscovered, but his contribution to the theory of the unconscious mind was then recognized by neuropsychologists.

soned analysis of the recent miracles accomplished by the soutane of the Curé d'Ars[1] . . . but of the Académie de Médicine and of his adversary, Victor Rameau, there was no question.

I was about to take offense and throw away that insipid prose when I shuddered suddenly; my eyes had just perceived the following note:

> *Sad news. We have just learned of the death of Claude-Charles Le Prégent, Marquis de Mauréac, Commander of the Royal and Military Order of Saint Louis, Lieutenant-General of the King's armies, former colonel of the Catholic armies of Bretagne, d'Anjou, etc., deceased in his house in the Rue Saint-Dominique after a long and cruel illness.*
>
> *All those who have conserved in their soul the sacred cult of honor will want to render the supreme duties to that valiant man, who was once a champion of his God and a knight of his sovereign. Heroes of that stature are rare, alas . . . God help us!*

I knew the Marquis de Mauréac slightly, having been a comrade at college of his son, who had become one of my dearest friends. He was an octogenarian grand old man, haughty of manner and still superb in his visage, the heir of an old family of the Parlement de Bretagne: good nobility, albeit *de robe*. For several generations the Prégents de Mauréac had occupied, by hereditary right, one of the four charges of the presidency of investigation, almost always "*ordonnés pour tenir la Tournelle*"—a redoubtable honor that was justified by successive labors of criminal prosecution, the consequence of a hereditary knowledge of rascally soul and a family practice of "the question" in accordance with

---

1 The "Curé d'Ars" was Jean Vianney (1786-1859); the present story was written prior to his beatification in 1905 and canonization in 1925, but the campaign for that sanctification was already under way.

"the usage of Rennes"—which is to say, torture by burning the feet and the legs. Nowadays, they were mostly members of the legal fraternity, but he, Charles de Mauréac, had been a soldier, a glorious soldier, and it could be said that the fortune of his household was the work of his sword.

An ardent royalist, he had fought obstinately and hard for his prince and his God during the emigration, especially in the last days of the Empire. The government of the Restoration had heaped him with its favors. Recognized as a colonel in 1825 he had become soon afterwards a Maréchal de Camp and lieutenant of the Royal Guard. Much favored by Madame la Duchesse d'Angoulême and pampered by Monsieur, the king's brother, he had then mingled actively with all the petty conspiracies of the Pavillon de Marsan against the Château, considering Duc Decazes[1] as a *sans-culotte* and willingly referring to Louis XVIII as "the foremost Jacobin of the realm." Thus, the succession of Charles X had inevitably made such a right-thinking man a Lieutenant-General and a Marquis.

Between two favors, Monsieur de Mauréac had married, and married very nobly. He had received his wife from the hands of Monseigneur de Quélen[2] himself: a very gentle, very pious young woman somewhat subject to ecstasies, and also very rich. "Soldier of France, which is to say, soldier of God," the prelate had cried, in giving the nuptial benediction, "the hand of the One who Recompenses is extended over you! The Eternal is already contemplating with amour an entire lineage of born knights, for the merits of the father are continued in his children."

---

1 Élie-Louis Decazes (1780-1860), later Duc de Decazes et Glücksburg, was the Prefect of Police in Paris before embarking on a successful political career. As Minister of Police he suppressed the ultra-Royalist insurrections of the "white terror," in which the fictitious Monsieur de Mauréac would obviously have played a role, before emerging as the leader of the liberal Doctrinaires during the later years of Louis XVIII's reign.
2 The Breton Churchman Hyacinthe-Louis de Quélen was installed as Archbishop of Paris in 1821.

One day, however, misfortune had fallen upon that fortunate of the earth. While still young, Lieutenant-General de Mauréac had been struck by a sudden apoplexy in the middle of a ball one Christmas Eve, and had only recovered consciousness to find himself permanently paralyzed. Death soon entered his household and had ravaged it pitilessly for twenty years. By turns the marquis was obliged to wear mourning for his wife, a young daughter and two sons, killed in the ranks of the Carlists at the same moment in the same battle. The end of those young men, captains in Cabrera's guerillas, had been lamentable; surprised with their partisans by Maria-Christina's troops, they had been burned alive in a chapel where they had taken refuge.[1] Today, of all that superb line, only the last child remained standing, a naval officer far from France at that moment, in the rice-fields of Cochinchina, in the pestilential mud of the Mekong: my dear friend René de Mauréac, a gentle soul, feeble and beautiful in the unhealthy body of a neurotic corroded by anemia, exhausted by his long sea voyages in the torrid regions, by fever and delirium. Alas, how long would that one have to live?

And while death filled the house of Mauréac with funerals, striking it without mercy in its dearest hopes, it seemed, as if in jest, to spare its head. The marquis had been able to attain his eighty-sixth year—more than five times the "grand span of human existence" of which Tacitus speaks—but for a long time, Monsieur de Mauréac, an old man belated in life, had been little more than a lamentable cadaver. Paralyzed in all his

---

1 What is nowadays known as the First Carlist War was a civil war in Spain that lasted from 1833-1840, in which the reformist widow of Ferdinand VII, Maria Christina, representing her daughter, Isabella II, as regent, was opposed by the late king's brother, Carlos de Borbón, who wanted to retain an absolute monarchy. Numerous French monarchists who had lost out in the July 1830 Revolution in France, volunteered to fight for the Carlists. The Carlist general Ramon Cabrera had the upper hand for a while, and held out long after defeat was inevitable, returning to the conflict again in the Second and Third Carlist Wars; he was frequently accused of committing atrocities, so the reference in the present story is consciously ironic.

limbs, incapable of the slightest movement, having even lost the use of speech, he no longer had anything living within him but thought. And that thought escaped the inert body through two black eyes that shone, sometimes desolate and moistened by tears, sometimes sinister and charged with hatred; there must have been despair, and also blasphemy, in that gaze. In truth, why had it fallen, that hand extended over "the soldier of France and God"?

My intimate relationship with René imposed a duty of politeness on me. I headed for the Hôtel de Mauréac in order to inscribe my name in the concierge's lodge. While I was walking toward the Rue Saint-Dominique, memories of the past rose up in a host before me. I saw the old marquis again clearly; I remembered every detail of my introduction to that strange invalid.

That evening, a winter evening, I had dined at the Hôtel de Mauréac with René. Throughout the meal, my friend had only talked to me about his father, and with what respectful affection! What enthusiasm there was in his voice when he recounted the past life of the former leader of partisans, the audacity of his prowess and the temerity of his actions. When dinner was over he had introduced me into the invalid's bedroom, and for the first time I had found myself in the presence of the glorious soldier. I perceived an old man collapsed in an armchair, very pale, entirely white-haired and utterly exhausted, whose bleak eyes were staring fixedly at the logs burning in the fireplace. Next to him, a mastiff was asleep on a chair.

"My Father," René said, "may I introduce to you Monsieur Victor Rameau, the college friend about whom I have spoken to you very often."

Monsieur de Mauréac raised his gaze upon me, examined me, and smiled with a slightly haughty benevolence. In the meantime, René, coming and going, had opened a newspaper placed on the table, still in its rubber band.

"Oh, my dear father," he said, suddenly, "here's something that will interest you: an article on the armies of Bretagne and the Maine, on your former companions in arms and their noble deeds of war."

"The combats of giants," I said in my turn, saluting the marquis.

But the flame in his eyes was already extinct, and the smile on his lips had already contracted into a grimace.

"Victor," René continued, "since God has deigned to endow you with a sonorous voice and lavished the gifts of eloquence upon you, sit down at this table, my friend, and read us this chronicle."

He went to place himself beside his father, placing his hands gently on the two inert hands. I opened the newspaper and commenced reading. The article was nothing but a long dithyramb in honor of the Chouanerie of the year VII, and enthusiastic praise of the likes of Frotté and Cadoudal.[1]

"Bah! Bah!" cried René, interrupting me. "Overrated glories! Their Monsieur de Frotté was never worth as much as Sans-Pareil, and Cadoudal would certainly never have dared to steal the *Albatros!* Isn't that true, Father?"

A shrill plaint, the cry of a bird of prey, replied to him. The old marquis, that paralytic nailed to his armchair, had straightened up stiffly; and he laughed: a savage insensate, frightening laugh. Abruptly, however, he fell back, collapsing on himself. I thought he was dead. Soon, however, he returned to life, in order to bury himself once again in silence and to contemplate with a stupid gaze the flames and embers of his hearth.

After that evening, I noticed that my friend never spoke to me about his father again.

---

1 The principal leaders of the "Chouan revolt" against the Republic, which petered out in year VII (i.e. 1796) were Louis de Frotté (1766-1800) and Georges Cadoudal (1771-1804), but Chouanerie had a brief resurgence thereafter when Napoléon's empire began to totter after the Russian campaign. The nickname of Sans-Pareil given here to Mauréac, and the background of the story's crucial incident, recall Thierry's earlier account of an "episode of the counter-revolution" in his historical novel *Le Capitaine Sans-Façon 1813* (1883).

✳

The coaching entrance of the house stood ajar; I went in. In the courtyard, in spite of the chill of the night, which was now profound, a man was walking bare-headed, smoking a cigar. I approached him and recognized him as one of my pupils, young Doctor Cordier, who had been living with Monsieur de Mauréac for several years, as his personal physician. He came toward me making grand gestures.

"Oh, my dear master," he cried, "what a bizarre end and what a curious death! It's the return of his son that has killed him!"

"What! Monsieur René has returned?"

"He has returned. Yesterday, in the night, at about one o'clock, as I was about to retire, René de Mauréac suddenly entered his father's bedroom. No one was expecting him. He headed toward the marquis, gripped him with his hands and, holding him upright, he looked at him without saying a word. In his turn, the old man raised his eyes and extended his head toward his son. For a long time—a very long time—they looked at one another like that, face to face, in silence.

"Suddenly, cries and songs rose up from the street: a band of students who were reveling passed under our windows. Then—oh, dear master, it's incredible, and yet absolutely true—the paralytic raised his head and from his lips, mute for so many years a word emerged: 'Noël!' he said.

"'Yes, Father, Noël,' Monsieur René replied, in a tremulous voice.

"And suddenly, the old man stood up; he took three steps forward, and, uttering a burst of laughter he cried: 'France and honor!' Then he fell heavily to the floor. He was dead. Truly strange, isn't it? Very strange!"

"Certainly! And what did Monsieur René de Mauréac say and do?"

"Oh, you ought to go and see. He worries me. He has been shut away with his father's corpse for twenty-four hours, refusing nourishment, having not taken any repose . . . yes, he worries me!" added young Monsieur Cordier, who touched his forehead with an expressive gesture.

I went into the house, desirous of going to shake the hand of my friend and to bring him a few consolations. I went up the great stone staircase and penetrated into the completely obscure drawing room. At the far end of the room I perceived a closed door, beneath which a thin streak of light filtered. Behind that door was the bedroom of the marquis. I headed in that direction and I was about to knock to announce my arrival when I stopped, gripped . . .

Someone was talking in that bedroom—and one might even have thought that someone was replying; it was like the sound of a conversation, of a dialogue.

"No, oh, no . . . !" murmured a supplicant voice, that of René. "You're calumniated, Father . . . ! For pity's sake, extract me from doubt . . . spare me that ordeal!"

I knocked gently. Immediately, the voice fell silent and there was a profound silence in the room. I knocked more loudly: no response. I tried to open the door; it resisted, sealed by a bolt. Then, very emotional, I listened. The voice rose up again, no longer supplicant this time, but irritated and vibrant with indignation:

"Oh! Oh!" it cried. "That's horrible, Monsieur! That's infamous . . . yes, infamous!"

What happened within me? I'm ashamed to admit it, but fear seized me, and, fleeing from the drawing room, I left in haste.


## II


The next day, the obsequies of the Marquis de Mauréac were celebrated at Saint Thomas Aquinas; a very simple ceremony in good taste. A gentleman of the Faubourg Saint-Germain cannot go toward God without the vainglorious apparatus customary in the Chaussée-d'Antin. There were not many people, but it was a very noble, very pious and very edifying society; in order to grant the absolution there was even a prelate with a little Roman collar, a bishop *in partibus* and a papal chamberlain. There was no cortege of troops for that lieutenant-general, doubtless in order to avoid shading his coffin with the folds of the tricolor flag that he execrated so much and had combated so fervently—a pious filial attention.

I was late, retained at home too long by the imperious care of correcting my proofs; my memoir on *The Simulations of Second Sight* was, in fact, due to appear in a few days in one of our medical gazettes. When I arrived outside the porch of the church, the mass had concluded and the funeral convoy was setting forth. The little Place Gribeauval was overflowing with curiosity-seekers and the mourning carriages were already full. Where could I be accommodated? War-weary, I was about to abandon the game and return, desolately, to my labor, when I heard my name pronounced.

"My dear doctor! Good Monsieur Rameau! Here . . . a place for you!"

At the same time, the face of Corentin Le Barze appeared at the portière of a mourning-carriage. I accepted his invitation and climbed up beside him.

I did not know Corentin Le Barze very well, although he had called me "his dear doctor" and "good Monsieur Rameau." I knew that he was closely linked with my comrade Mauréac and the father of a pretty young woman, Marie-Thérèse. René had once even made me the confidence of certain quietly-caressed projects of marriage, and I had thought that I divined a profound amour hiding mysteriously in the depths of my friend's heart.

Resident in Bretagne, where he possessed vast domains, Monsieur de Barze was reputed to be rich, possessing millions, as well as being a man of the best society and very erudite, but a trifle naïve and reeking somewhat of his province. A Celtic enthusiast, not to say a Celtomaniac, he was occupied with Druidic archeology, and abandoned himself to a passion for dolmens and menhirs. He was also a poet, a spiritualist and Christian poet. He ordinarily sent me each of his works, profane or sacred: sometimes two fat volumes, a dissertation on two skulls discovered under a galgal—one per volume—and sometimes a finely-bound small volume of Breton and French verses singing the praises of Saint Cornely, the curer of cattle and the patron of the town of Carnac. Finally, a political candidate and a member of the General Council of his département, Monsieur Corentin Le Barze was an ardent legitimist, posing willingly as a Monsieur de la Vielle Roche, blazoning his letter-paper, and very proud of the article that preceded his name, a disconnected and noble article: all in all, an excellent fellow.

He was not alone in his carriage. Another person was installed facing him, whose face was not unknown to me. Where had I encountered him before? He was a man about fifty years old, tall of stature and clean-shaven, with dark eyes plunged beneath thick eyebrows. A clergyman's frock-coat and a white cravat completed the ensemble of the individual. On seeing me climb aboard he inclined his head, and smiled at me amicably. I returned his salutation.

And we went silently along the muddy pavement, under the falling snowflakes, in the great busy rumor of the city. At each street-corner I perceived the head of the convoy, and, marching alone behind the hearse, bare-headed and curbed by his dolor, poor René de Mauréac. How changed he seemed! The pallor of his face and the expression of his despair wrung my heart with an immense compassion. I pointed him out to my neighbor, Monsieur Le Barze.

"Yes," he said to me, sadly. "A model of filial piety! But also," he exclaimed, emphatically, "what a loss for him, what an incommensurable mourning! You messieurs of Paris don't know what Colonel Le Prégent de Mauréac was in his time, in the great days of our giants: a Homeric hero! Oh, our peasants know his story, and our heaths still resound with the noise of his exploits. They still sing it out there, in the lands of Vannes and Auray.

How many ballads and complaintes there are in his honor! I have added my own humble contingent to those hymns of glory and consecrated a few verses to that valiant man.

The man sitting facing us took a notebook from his pocket, and a pencil, and began to write

"Charles de Mauréac," Monsieur Le Barze went on, "was a knight of olden times. At sixteen years of age he fought at Quiberon; soon a companion of Cadoudal, his friend and counselor, he wanted his share of all dangers as well as all glories; at thirty he was a colonel, a colonel for the king, and when Bonaparte had finally wearied the clemency of God, in 1813, the affair of the *Albatros* . . ."

"Aha . . . your Monsieur de Mauréac was a Chouan," interrupted the baritone voice of the individual who was making notes. "A man of blood and rapine! His redemption will be difficult. He has great need of our prayers."

"Do you know this fellow?" my red-faced neighbor whispered in my ear.

I shook my head to reply in the negative. The impassive individual continued writing.

"You're a journalist?" I asked him. "Doubtless a reporter charged with rendering an account of the funeral ceremony."

He started to laugh. "No, Monsieur, no; I am not subject to that ordeal. My mission is quite different. Yes, my mission," he declaimed, filling his mouth with that grandiose word. "I keep the archives"—he paused for effect—"the archives of Death."

Monsieur Le Barze turned to me, alarmed. He did not understand. Nor did I.

"Yes, Messieurs," the unknown man added. "Archivist of death! I ordinarily attend the obsequies of every deceased individual of note; I listen to the judgments rendered on the defunct; I collect the eulogy or the criticism; I establish my dossier of Good and Evil. It will serve my successors in the mission, in due course, to discover certain souls lost in the crowd of reincarnates."

He closed his notebook, put it back in his pocket, and, still smiling broadly, said: "Thus, Messieurs, we say: the late Marquis de Mauréac, man of rapine and blood, opener of civil wars, traitor to his country! Ha ha! The reincarnation of the poor soul will be hard. Perhaps that fine colonel will one day carry the musket of a simple soldier and fall under the bullets of the Prussians or the English, his former good friends. Amen!"

A traffic jam had just brought the cortege to a halt; the macabre individual opened the door and launched himself into the street.

"What was that?" Monsieur Le Barze asked me, stupefied.

I shrugged my shoulders. "Paris is full of madmen," I replied.

"A sinister madman, my dear doctor!"

I approved the remark, and a profound silence was established between us.

At the cemetery, another surprise was reserved for me. Corentin Le Barze made a speech. Speaking "in the name of the Breton fatherland," he saluted with an adieu full of tears the remains of the Marquis de Mauréac. A superb oratory morsel, in truth, in fine poetic prose: a dithyramb in which affliction was expertly expressed by means of all the known tropes of rhetoric. The peroration, above all, in the form of a prosopopeia, moved the audience.

"Repose peacefully, blissful soul, and we, your friends, we, your family"—the orator addressed an affectionate glance to René—"will live in the contemplation of your virtues . . . what am I saying? . . . in the certainty of your immortality next to God! Yes, your life was a model and your death an instruction; in order to express myself as a poet, your last sigh was an illustrious sigh! 'Noël! . . . France and honor!' you repeated—the thrice-sublime cry of a soldier, a Frenchman and a Christian! France and honor! Oh, Messieurs . . ."

At that moment, René de Mauréac, who had seemed sunk in dolor, his head bowed, motionless and mute, straightened up with a start.

"Enough! For pity's sake, enough!" he stammered. And with a brutal gesture, he snatched the speech.

A painful emotion took possession of us all; everyone inclined, as quickly as possible, before that somewhat intemperate despair. Then everyone returned, either to his business or his pleasures.

<br>

## III

I had regained the gate to the exterior boulevards when I heard precipitate footfalls in the fog. Almost immediately, someone tapped me on the shoulder; it was René.

"I was looking for you," he said. "Come—I need to talk to you."

A coupé was waiting for him, and twenty minutes later we went into the house in the Rue Saint-Dominique. Preceding me then, he went up the stairs and stopped in the drawing room. An ardent fire was burning in the fireplace and a lamp, already lit, was illuminating the vast and somber room with its discreet glow.

A veritable ice-house, that great drawing room of the Hôtel de Mauréac, uninhabited for a long time, oozing damp and reeking with the insipid odors of closure; in the style of Louis XVI, it was entirely paneled in sculpted and white-painted wood. The furniture that garnished it dated from the early days of the Restoration: armchairs and chairs upholstered in red satin with silver embroidery, sofas with gilded copper trimmings, and Greek stools. Near the fireplace, under the gleam of the old Carcel lamp, a large table with the heads of sphinxes was covered in papers, visiting cards, letters and newspapers. Around the room, suspended from the panels, I noticed an entire gallery of family portraits: the Messieurs Le Prégent de Mauréac, presidents of investigations, wearing wigs with three tassels, scarlet togas and spotted ermines, very dignified, extending one hand over their velvet caps with gold braid.

To the right of the fireplace I also perceived a portrait of my friend René's mother, a young woman of about thirty, brunette, stiff, rather ugly and insignificant in appearance. But to the left, making a pendant with it, was a remarkable canvas signed Prud'hon: the marquis. Sitting in an armchair and dressed in the mode of the beaux of 1815: a high muslin cravat, a polonaise jacket with Brandenburg fastenings, pearl-gray culottes and Souvaroff boots, Charles de Mauréac was shown smiling, his pale and superb face illuminated by two large black eyes. I went to place myself in front of that portrait and contemplated it for a few moments.

"What are you doing?" René asked me, brusquely. "Come on, my dear friend, and leave that."

With his hand he designated a sofa near the fire, and came to sit beside me.

"Victor," he said to me, after a brief silence, "this morning's newspapers are full of your name; I congratulate you on yesterday's success."

"My success?" I had understood, though.

"So," René went on, "you don't believe in the phenomenon of second sight?"

"Of course not! You can read my memoir; it's being printed at present."

He drew closer to me and looked me full in the face. "You don't believe in it, Victor?"

"No, certainly not. I've formulated the adage: Second sight: impudent charlatanry or cerebral derangement."

"And you're sure of what you're advancing? Absolutely sure?"

"Sure? One philosopher has said: what certainty cannot be touched by doubt?"

He stood up and started marching back and forth with agitation. Soon, however, he came to sit down again. He took a packet of letters and cards from the table and began opening them, while talking: "How many friends! Good God, how many friends! No, I'd never have believed myself so pampered. Ah! A letter from the Ministry of Marine."

He broke the seal and scanned the missive with his eyes.

"That's good," he said. "They've accepted my resignation."

"Your resignation?"

"Yes, my dear. I'm weary of traveling the world; in any case, it's necessary for me to remain in France henceforth."

"Your resignation . . . at your age?"

"My age? Thirty-five years, at the last count, Victor, and I'm weary of so many things. Fatigued by equatorial *comitos-negros* and polar scurvy, the dances of bayaderes and the kisses of negresses . . ." He seized my arm and squeezed it forcefully. ". . . Even the voluptuousness that opium procures!"

I shuddered, quite bewildered. "Opium? You're not committing such a suicide, I suppose."

René released my arm and resumed the examination of his correspondence.

"Oh, good God!" he cried, suddenly. "What does this want of me? Look."

The object that he held out to me was a large card, glossy and goffered, like a commercial advertisement containing a trade name, an indication of merchandise and the merchant's address. The strange prospectus was thus drafted:

*OCCULTISM—SPIRITISM—VISION OF INFINITY*

*ELIAS*

*Celebrate the mysteries of the Eternal Now—put terrestrial humanity in communication with the Spirits and Perispirits of the Ether—soften and abridge proofs—reveal the great secret of Life and Death.*

*O Death destroyed forever!*
*O Death where is thy victory!*
*O Death, where is thy sting?*

*In Paris, 24 Rue Rousselet, fourth floor.*
*Visible every evening.*

"Well," I said, returning the card, "it's Monsieur Elias, a well-known fraudster. He's unhinged many brains, and he's recently had to serve six months in prison."

"What did he do?" interrogated René, his eyes suddenly gleaming.

"Dangerous tricks. He evokes specters and recalls the souls of the dead to earth. A charlatan and a practical joker."

"Get away! And he finds imbeciles to lend themselves to such a game?"

"My dear, as the late Solomon said very wisely: the number of fools is infinite. The name of that kind of imbecile is Legion."

René seized the prospectus, crumpled it, folded it up and threw it in the fire. The cardboard rebounded from one of the firedogs and fell to one side, into the ashes.

"Oh, certainly," cried Mauréac, "such a wretch merits perpetual hard labor!"

Again he stood up and resumed the course of his feverish march. At times he stopped and lowered his gaze toward Elias's circular, scintillating in the firelight.

A domestic came in, bringing us the evening papers. René took possession of them and scanned them rapidly.

"Ah!" he said, smiling. "Monsieur Le Barze's speech! Pronounced at three o'clock and printed at noon! Depend on poets to know the price of glory!"

I was slightly shocked by his persiflage and his jesting manner with regard to such a dolorous subject.

"What an excellent man, Monsieur Le Barze!" I said. "I'm told that his daughter is charming."

A slight blush spread over René's face. "Yes, charming," he murmured. "Poor Marie-Thérèse! Pretty, distinguished, well-educated—charming, indeed. How many times I saw her again during the long insomnias of my life of adventure." He lowered his voice. "Above all, during my terrible nights in Cochinchina! Absent, but always so present!"

"Well, aren't you going to marry her?"

"Me?"

"Yes, you, René de Mauréac. Her father desires that alliance, and her too, I believe."

"Her too, I know."

He leaned back, languidly in an armchair, closed his eyes and put his hands together. "Oh, the noble and tender companion I would have in her. What a fine day that of such a marriage would be! Dear beloved, I can see her already, kneeling at the altar; I . . ."

A crack of the woodwork cut short his sentence and filled the drawing room with a strange, dolorous plaint exactly like a sob.

"What's that noise?" René demanded, raising his head abruptly.

I could not help smiling. "Too many nerves, my poor friend. This drawing room has been uninhabited for a long time; the heat is making the panels dilate, and some woodwork cracked . . . that's all."

A brief silence followed my explanation.

"Yes," Mauréac went on, abandoning himself to his thoughts for a second time. "I shall quit Paris; I'll sell this house and go to my dear Bretagne. There, fleeing society, far from the imbecile crowd, I shall shelter my happiness in her arms. Oh, the happiness, the great happiness, finally found in great forgetfulness!"

For the second time the crack made itself heard, more prolonged and even more lamentable. Mauréac got up and ran to the place from which the noise had come.

I was not mistaken; under the action of the heat, the old woodwork of the drawing room had shifted; a gap had been produced to the juncture of a panel, near the fireplace, almost beneath the portrait of the Marquis de Mauréac. That panel must once have formed a cupboard, but it had been sealed a long time ago, for I saw that it had been carefully nailed shut.

René rang.

"Quickly, a hammer and a chisel."

Soon, he set to work, pulling out the rusty nails one by one. The cupboard opened, René plunged his arms into the depths of the hiding-place, groped momentarily, and, suddenly uttering a cry, pulled out an object, which he brought to the table.

It was a dainty little casket, the work of the First Empire: a casket of mahogany wood, embellished with gilded copper ornaments: two Amours enlacing one another on a garland of roses. The key was not in the lock, but a violent thrust of the chisel lifted the lid. Then, leaning over the jewel-case, this is what I saw:

In the box, lined with red satin, was a black velvet cushion, and reposing on the cushion was a long tress of blonde hair.

René de Mauréac had also seen it, and he had gone very pale.

"God! My God!" he stammered, distraughtly. "It's true, then!"

He took possession of the tress, folded it carefully and put it in his jacket pocket. Then he threw the casket back into the hiding-place.

"It's true, then," he murmured, again.

He went to stand in front of the portrait of his father, and for several minutes he looked at it in silence. Suddenly, I saw him head for the fireplace, bend over the ashes and seize a piece of cardboard that the flames had not yet consumed.

"Elias . . ." he said in a loud voice, ". . . reveals the secret of Life and Death."

This time, he tore up the prospectus and dispersed the fragments in the hearth. The clock chimed five.

"Come on," he said to me. "My head's on fire; I want to get some air. Let's get out."

# IV

The snow was no longer falling, but the winter wind bit us in the face, and we walked along the muddy pavement cutting through the damp opacity of the fog.

"Where are we going?" I asked.

"Straight ahead . . . at random."

René leaned his arm on mine and, drawing me along, went down the Rue Saint-Dominique. When we reached the corner of the Rue Bellechasse, he seemed to hesitate; soon, however, he turned left and plunged into the bleak solitude of the Babylone quarter. Sometimes he stopped and took deep breaths.

"Oh, winter," he said, "the bitter cold . . . what voluptuousness! When an unfortunate like me has been writhing for years under the furnace of the sun of Indo-China, how he loves a snowy sky and icy ground! The great freeze of December!"

"A frightful climate, the lands of Indo-China?

"Atrocious! Heatstroke by day, the tortures of insomnia by night! Oh, the absence of sleep, the sinister thoughts, the regrets for what one loves, the doubts, the suspicions! Then, oh, then . . . !"

He stopped, and disengaged his arm. "It's here," he said.

We found ourselves in a narrow street bordered by high walls, where a few sparse street lights had great difficulty puncturing the darkness with their ruddy glow.

"This is definitely the Rue Rousselet," Mauréac continued, "and there's number 24. For a mariner who has never sounded the depths of Paris, that little exploration wasn't bad. Dare, then, to deny second sight!"

The house that he designated was a five-story building of poor appearance. The door was open.

"Oh!" I cried. "You're not going to see that man, I suppose?"

Without replying to me, Mauréac went in. Bewildered, even anxious, I consulted myself momentarily, and then I entered in my turn. From his lodge, the concierge, a veritable Gael who was mending old socks, called to us: "Who do you want? Elias? He won't see you today."

René went on, and I followed him. At the end of a narrow corridor a wooden stairway with dirty steps rose up, snaking; René went up. From the upper floors a strange noise reached us, all the discordant sound of a concert in which the sound of an organ was soon combined, sometimes with joyful singing and sometimes with groans. Having reached the landing of the entresol I abused my companion: "Come on! This isn't serious! You can't be visiting that charlatan!"

He bowed his head in silence.

"Is this really the day for such folly, René?"

"It's the day," he said, simply, and continued climbing.

I stopped, hesitating to continue the adventure; I experienced some shame. However, my doubt only lasted for an instant. Curiosity prevailed over my scruples. I too desired to know the excessively famous Elias and surprise the secret of his impostures. I climbed the stairs at a run and caught up with Mauréac.

On the third floor we halted. By the smoky light of an Argand lamp I saw a white-painted door on which hieratic signs stood out in red: a coiling serpent formed an omega, and in that circumference was the image of the Egyptian Isis. An iron chain terminated by a little copper sphinx was the bell-cord. Rene tugged it violently; the hymns immediately ceased. He waited for some time, and then agitated the chain for a second time. Finally, a key grated in the lock, and one of the battens of the door opened timidly. The head of an old woman extended toward us, and suspicious eyes examined us.

"What do you desire, Messieurs?"

"Elias."

"He isn't here."

"I'll wait for him," riposted Mauréac; and, pushing the old woman, he penetrated into the antechamber.

The woman tried to bar our passage. "Don't go in!" she cried. "The priest is celebrating a mystery; don't go in!"

But at the same moment, another voice made itself heard: "Let them come in! And you, whom the arm of the Eternal Now has conducted here, souls thirsty for the Truth, come without dread!"

# V

A man had just appeared abruptly, and I had recognized the person glimpsed in the morning at the lieutenant-general's obsequies: it was Elias. He bowed, but with a slightly arrogant politeness.

"What!" he said. "Professor Victor Rameau among us! Science will deign to interrogate Faith?"

Then he bowed to Monsieur de Mauréac, while observing him with an attentive curiosity. René soon turned his eyes away, while Elias repressed a smile.

"You, Monsieur le Marquis," he said then, "be welcome also. I was expecting you."

And he took us into another room.

"You'll excuse the poor welcome, Messieurs," he said, when we were seated, "but you surprised me in mid-worship. I was initiating a neophyte into our mysteries: a poor soul who is subject to a dolorous reincarnation, a wretched sinner whom I am trying to extract from sin."

He had pronounced those insensate phrases with the risible assurance of a thaumaturge. He continued: "Besides which, my good old maidservant lives in a sacred terror of the police. Monsieur Louis Bonaparte's police are very tyrannical, and his acolytes, Messieurs Boitelle and Piétri, seem to me to be rather poor philosophers.[1] Did they not throw me in prison among the crooks and the thieves? They intended to diminish me, but I

---

1 Symphorien Boitelle (1813-1897) was the Prefect of Police in Paris from 1868-1866, when he was succeeded by Joseph Piétri (1820-1902), who held the position until 1870.

was magnified. *Cum infirmor, tunc potens sum . . .* Saint Paul saw many others!"[1]

Elias paused, still keeping his gaze fixed on René de Mauréac.

"In any case," he went on, "What do their houses of detention matter to me? I have been condemned to death. Oh, don't be alarmed—condemned to death for a political crime. You see in me an old insurgent: one of our revolts against social infamy. In June 1848 I was picked up, holed by bullets, behind the barricades of the Faubourg Saint-Antoine. I was hungry, Messieurs, and I hoped to find bread at the end of my rifle: the illusion of a young man! My penalty was commuted, however; clemency was shown. They contented themselves with sending me to rot in the silos of Lambessa;[2] sixty of us were deported in my squadron . . . more than forty went to colonize the cemetery. Finally, I was granted mercy. Oh, how I detested then! What bile there was on my lips and what venom in my heart!"

He fell silent momentarily; his forehead was bathed with sweat, and his mouth was grimacing in a savage rictus. He quickly recovered possession of himself, though, and his voice became very soft and utterly penetrating.

"But today those rages of a tatterdemalion, those hatreds of a ragamuffin, have gone from my soul. At present, I believe; I know now! Yes, I know the great secret of mortal life, the secret of the apparent injustice of God, the primal cause of poverty, as of fortune. All wealth is merely a proof, all misery merely an expiation. Without the redoubtable law of hunger, which obliges us to submit to labor, and without labor, how would human beings be able to raise themselves above brutality? From incarnation to incarnation, a human being purifies himself under dolor and

---

1 The Latin quotation is slightly modified from the Vulgate version of *2 Corinthians* 12:10. The A.V. has "when I am weak, then I am strong."

2 Lambessa was the French name of an army camp in Algeria; Elias must have been sent there as a member of a criminal battalion of the Foreign Legion.

by way of suffering; thus, from crucible to crucible, a precious metal is refined. Yes, yes, wretched are the rich and very fortunate the poor—for they are closer to the supreme liberation. Oh, Messieurs, when will the blessed day shine, the imminent day of the triumph of my ideas, what harmony, what love, what fraternity between humans! Dare, then, evil rich man, to deny Lazarus his part in your feast—you who are condemned to beg in your turn for the crumbs from his table! In truth, I say to you: we alone can cure the great social cancer!"

The illuminate stood up, and started walking back and forth, excited and utterly convinced. Abruptly, however, he stopped in front of René, and addressed himself to him.

"Others, too, Monsieur Mauréac, ought to run to us: those who are suffering, and whose tears we alone have the secret of drying up. Once, the voice of which the prophet speaks made itself heard lamentably: the sob of Rachel calling her children in vain. But Rachel can smile henceforth amid her tears, for those who were no more are again! How many mothers come here every day to rediscover the beloved they believed lost, to receive their kisses and shiver under their caresses! And we are persecuted, we who can give such consolations to desperate hearts and transform blasphemy into an ecstasy of happiness!"

Suddenly, he interrupted his mystical homily, and beneath the pontiff the charlatan appeared. A convulsive tremor agitated his body; his voice became hoarse and his terrified eyes rolled.

"Oh God!" he cried. "What is this, then? God! Spirits fluttering around us. I sense them, I hear them, I see them. There is going to be a communication! Formidable being, what do you demand of me?"

Then, staggering like a drunken man, Elias headed for one of the doors of the room, pushed the two battens and invited us to enter with a theatrical gesture.

"Messieurs, the Eternal Now commands! Let your formed eyes open, then, to the light! Let them see!"

## VI

The room that we had just entered was a pretentiously-furnished drawing room: chairs and armchairs of sculpted wood; the new-antique of cheap Gothic. On the mantelpiece, decorated like an altar, stood a statuette, between two perfume-burners of the Greco-directoire style and horrible gas candelabra. They were lit and their smoky light vacillated in the demi-obscurity of the room.

I turned round. Elias was no longer with us.

Rene de Mauréac, however, had collapsed heavily into an armchair. A bizarre somnolence had begun to overtake him. His eyes remained open, however, and his dilated pupils were staring straight ahead.

"Look over there," he said, suddenly, "against the wall . . . isn't that ridiculous?"

With his finger he pointed at various gilded frames shining in the gaslight. I went to see what he was indicating to me. It was, in fact, ridiculous. In the frames and under glass, numerous texts were displayed imprinted on vellum, and a few drawings of a truly monstrous fantasy.

For the most part, the texts had been taken from the theurgical work of the Alexandrines: here, the demi-Christian Origen; there the demi-pagans of neoplatonism, a Porphyry, an Iamblichus, a Proclus and other adepts of "metemsomatosis," the reincarnation of beings. Certain modern authors were also cited: Swedenborg, Henri Martin, and above all the prophet Jean Reynaud, the mild and naïve dreamer, an exile from Heaven on earth.[1] Those vari-

---

1 The Romantic historian Henri Martin (1810-1883), a disciple of Augustin Thierry and an associate of Paul Lacroix ("Le Bibliophile Jacob") considered the Gauls and their supposed Druidic religion to have been the cardinal representatives of the "primitive tradition" of France; Monsieur Le Barze would undoubtedly have admired him. Another of Martin's friends, the Saint-Simonian philosopher Jean Reynaud, (1806-1863) published *Terre et ciel* in 1854, which begins as an odd exercise in the popularization of science but metamorphoses into a mystical treatise in which he proposes that the souls of human beings will be reincarnated on other worlds and offers a new ac-

ous theosophers[1] affirmed their robust faith in the progressive ascension of the animate creature from the formless organic cell to the human being, toward the great Good, the great Beauty, the great Truth, the infinite and finite All, the Impersonal of the radiant Personality, the Ever-present in the past and future . . . toward the Eternal Now.

Stranger still were the images that covered the wall. Alongside the hypothesis the proof—and what a proof! Portraits of errant souls and perispirits in pain! A notice, sinister more often than not, declared the name and the destiny of those vagabonds of space.

Firstly, the design of a palace in all styles, the cupola and the marabout as well as the bottle-top rococo, mingled in a surprising assemblage. The hand of a medium had written beneath it is a caption: "House on the planet Mars, the habitation of a fortunate soul—Victorien S. *fecit*."[2] Alongside his palace was the fortunate soul itself: a kind of human form, clad in a long floating robe, an endless body surmounted by an enormous head with a glabrous face and cow-like eyes, a hydrocephalic cranium with the hair of a romantic poet. Beneath the portrait was another legend: "Soul liberated from the earth. First sidereal migration. Stage toward God. V. S. *cidit*."

Other drawings depicted the postmortal features of certain creatures condemned to expiatory reincarnation; each, with its name, bore an order number of apparition. There were sinners of both sexes, among them a number of people of note: a

---

count of the nature of angels. The book is frequently mentioned in Thierry's works.

1 I have used this translation of "theosophes" because "theosophist" might be taken to imply a follower of Madame Blavatsky's "theosophy", which Thierry was not.

2 Best known as a dramatist, Victorien Sardou (1831-1908) participated in séances hosted by the astronomer Camille Flammarion—a great admirer of Jean Reynaud—in which he participated in early experiments in "automatic drawing" under hypnosis, producing numerous images of human souls reincarnated on other planets.

Nero, a Louis XV, a Robespierre . . . Napoléon! His legend was frightful:

"No. X. Napoléon Bonaparte: Spirit swollen by pride. Refuses to submit to reincarnation among the humble. Turning in space for half a century, the plaything of winds and tempests, driven from the south to the north and brought back from the ice of the Berezina to the sands of Egypt. When, flagellated by the wind, he traverses one of his battlefields, every blade of grass born of human dust stands up against him and cries toward God."

The collection had no lack of female sinners as well: queens and royal favorites, courtesans and daughters of the theater.

"No. XXVII. Comtesse du Barry. The scaffold of the Place de la Revolution has not purified her sufficiently. Clung to life and did not understand death. A second baptism of blood is necessary to her."

Finally, in the midst of a confused mass of draperies, I glimpsed the ignoble figure of a gnome with a hirsute face, a hooked nose and a nutcracker chin—a fantastic and grimacing apparition— and beneath the image, the words: "Iscariot. Origen has prayed, Swedenborg has begged; even this soul will go toward the light. The Just is not implacable."

At that moment a slight sound made me turn my head. Elias was there. He was standing in the middle of the room, one arm leaning on the shoulder of a young woman clad in white, doubtless the "reincarnate soul," the neophyte whom he had been initiating into his mysteries at the moment of our arrival. She seemed to be scarcely twenty years old, frail and small, rather dainty, although frankly ugly, and of a vulgar ugliness: an overly large mouth and the nose of a grisette; but large dark eyes, very shiny, and admirable blonde hair gave by their contrast, a bizarre expression to her face; and that loose hair fell in broad undulations over her shoulders. The woman's face was also covered with white make-up and the edges of her eyelids, marked with bistre, made her an enormous gaze. She was camped before us without any embarrassment, staring at us brazenly. René, in particular, seemed to captivate her attention. Outside, the organ-harmonium began to play mutedly, alternating with child-like voices; its melody reached us as if from a distance, very suavely.

A gesture from Elias interrupted those songs.

"This is the seeress," he said to us, in a solemn tone. "A seeress, Messieurs, the like of whom I have never encountered during my long priesthood. No medium has ever equaled her power of lucidity. Sometimes, she duplicates herself and, retraversing death, can relive one of her anterior lives. Soon, she annihilates herself entirely. Then she ceases to be herself; another spirit comes to inhabit her body, and her soul gives way to the evoked soul. Anne-Yvonne, Mademoiselle Gallo, sit down here!"

Elias extended his hands over the shoulders of the subject, pressed down forcefully, and moved his face close to the young woman's.

"Sleep!" he said.

The woman let her head fall backwards, exhaling a profound sigh. She was asleep. Again, the organ made its harmonies sound, cut off by the magnetizer after a few notes.

"The seeress is ready. Monsieur de Marquis de Mauréac, what do you have to ask of her?"

I looked at René; he was very pale. His head extended toward the golden-haired woman, he was contemplating her with a haggard gaze, as if fascinated. At that appeal he stood up, took a step toward the prophet, stopped, seemed to hesitate, and finally handed him an object that he was gripping with both hands. I recognized the blonde tress.

"Monsieur de Mauréac doubtless desires to know whose hair this was?" said Elias. "He shall know!"

Deploying the tress then he ran it over the forehead of the subject, over her eyes and over her lips, to deposit it and attach it over the heart.

"Anne-Yvonne," he said, in an imperious voice, "describe to us what you see."

A frisson ran through the limbs of the dormant your woman, whose breast heaved, breathlessly.

"See!" ordered Elias, again. "I command it!"

Immediately, she straightened up. Her face, trivially ugly a little while before, was transfigured; now, the young woman was truly beautiful. An immense joy, an unspeakable wellbeing, illuminated the vulgarity of her features. Her mouth smiled amorously, her eyes were radiant with a long passionate gaze. She marched toward Monsieur de Mauréac, her arms open, in a rapturous ecstasy.

"The beloved!" she murmured.

"Anne-Yvonne," said Elias, "describe to us what you see."

A violent emotion contracted the face of the somnambulist; her respiration became more uneven, and even more wheezy; with a chilly gesture she brought her arms up over her bosom, and shivered.

"What cold and what snow! How lamentably the waves are breaking over the strand; one might believe one were hearing a sob! A dull rumor is rising from the river: the great murmur of ice-floes; and there, down there, behind the fearful blackness of the fir-wood, the pontoon beaten by the waves is groaning. The terrible night! Let's hurry! Let's hurry! Ah . . . ! The sound of a bell . . . the Christmas bell! Noël! It's the good and joyous Noël today! Oh, what a sin to flee like this, far from the church! And the poor child who is ill . . . so sick, the fear and tender child! Oh . . . ! Oh . . . ! Oh . . . ! But no! Even with him, the beloved!"

She knelt down slowly before René de Mauréac, and, taking his hands, she deposited a long and passionate kiss on them.

Suddenly, she threw her head back, and a shrill screech emerged from her mouth: "Wretch!"

And she fell full length on the floor.

Then a terrible scene was played before me, a drama of agony and death. The woman struggled as if in an embrace, writhing as if she had been burned. Tears flowed from her eyes; she put her suppliant hands together; her savage howls filled the silence of the night.

Gradually, however, the cries became fainter and the convulsions less frequent; a rattle caught in her throat; I heard a dolorous sigh; finally, everything ceased.

"She's dead," said the thaumaturge, leaning over the body. "Does the Marquis de Mauréac want to know more?"

René, very pale, only uttered a single word: "Charlatan!"

Under the shock of that insult, Elias straightened up. "So," he said, coldly, "you have nothing more to ask, since you're insulting me now?" He paused briefly, and became very solemn. "Marquis de Mauréac, a crime was once committed against this soul."

"Impostor!" René retorted.

"Marquis de Mauréac," the prophet shouted, in a thunderous voice. "I have seen the blood on your blazon!"

A burst of furious laughter replied to him.

Elias marched toward René; the latter stood up. Extending his head, his eyes haggard, his mouth open, sticking out his chest, he started retreating step by step, and step by step the other followed him. It was truly terrible to see. One might have thought him a ferocious beast writhing under the gaze of a tamer. Finally, the prophet's fists fell heavily upon Mauréac; he fell, helplessly, to his knees.

Outside, everything was silent: no more organ with alternating hymns; no more voices singing canticles. Elias broke the lugubrious silence; he was talking to himself, seemingly addressing some ejaculatory prayer to an invisible being that was nevertheless hovering above us.

"O you," he said, "who wanted to create the rich for the proof and the poor for the expiation . . . is it necessary to obey you? Dare I oblige his rebellious conscience to do good . . . ? Yes, I hear you . . . you're ordering me to apply your holy law . . . I submit!"

In the speech and gestures of the man there were all the mannerisms of an actor, and also all the fanaticism of a sectarian.

"Marquis de Mauréac," he said, "your eyes desired to see and they have seen. Your heart wanted to know; it must know now."

"Alas!"

"Listen, then, dear son, listen and comprehend. My God, the Eternal Now, has impelled you here in order to constrain you to duty. A mysterious bond unites you in ages past with the reincarnate who was writhing as she expired before you. Poor creature, she is running to her perdition again; her heart is so weak, her conscience so wretched! Save her, my son, in saving yourself. In the existence of adventures and temptations that is hers, she will succumb fatally. Preserve her from her fall; give yourself entirely to that work of redemption. She is alone down here; be her family, then, become her honor. You and her; she and you—so long as you live your days of passage on the earth! Perhaps the prejudices of the world will condemn you; perhaps it will reprove you in accordance with human morality. No matter! But he, the Eternal Creator, will smile upon you, because you will have kept one of his creatures for your amour."

He seized René's hands; René was immediately agitated by a long shudder.

"Marquis de Mauréac," the prophet continued, "I command! You see this woman, whose name today is Anne-Yvonne Gallo? I want her to become your terrestrial proof, as you ought to be her redemption; that you will suffer for her, as she will for you. You will follow her step by step in her life. You will feel for her all the despair of disdained passion, all the bitter tortures of unsatisfied desires. You will love her, you will love her, pitilessly rejected by her . . . until the day, my son, when, vanquished in your familial pride but victorious over that very pride, you will choose her for a companion, for a wife; when, before everyone, you will give her your name, thus testifying and proclaiming that God has made her your equal, Marquis, by the laws of childbirth, malady and death."

Then, bending over the woman, who was still inanimate, he placed a finger on her forehead. Instantly, she raised her head, then her upper body, and stood up, like an automaton moved by a spring.

"And you," the thaumaturge said to her, "poor creature whom the pity of my God has sent to me, I do not know whether I shall be able to watch over your weakness for much longer, for I do not know, alas, what tomorrow the malignity of men has in preparation for me. But today, my daughter, I can protect you from yourself. You see this man here; he is rich, he is noble ... he will doubtless seek to induce you to temptation; you will reject him. You will flee his pursuits; you will be disgusted by his desires, terrified by his amour. If your arms open for him, it will only be tremulously and in the nuptial chamber. Then, but only then, having become yourself again, you may act in accordance with your will, or in accordance with your mission. I have spoken!"

Elias fell silent for a few seconds, observing both of them. Suddenly, anger turned his face crimson; once again, his voice resonated in the silence, but vibrant, imperious, full of menacing inflections:

"Oh, I hear," he cried, "yes, I hear the revolt that is already growling in your hearts! Well, I will master your rebellion! Slaves of my will, it is necessary that you believe yourselves to be free ... that you think, you, that you are freely obeying the impulsions of your amour and your conscience, and you the repulsions of your flesh and your honor! So, I am taking away your memory. I forbid you—understand me well, I forbid you—even to remember me. I demand that you forget my very name ...

"Go, and let everything be accomplished!"

At those words, the strident sound of a gong rang out abruptly; the lights were suddenly extinguished, and I was plunged into a profound obscurity. For rather a long time I groped in that darkness, searching for a way out. At the same time I called out to René, but he did not reply.

Finally, a door opened, and the prophet's old maidservant appeared on the threshold, a candle in her hand.

"The mystery is terminated," she said to me. "It's necessary, Monsieur, that you retire now."

I looked around: no more Elias; no more "seeress," and no more Mauréac either. I was alone, quite alone, in the room.

"Well, where is my friend?" I demanded, very astonished.

"Your friend?" replied the old woman. "He's already left."

"Left?"

"Yes, Monsieur, doubtless through the door reserved for the officiant." And she pointed with her finger at a tapestry that I had not perceived, which masked an opening made in the wall.

"Hurry up!" the woman continued. "He can't be far away, and you can still catch up with him."

I launched myself into the stairwell. In the street, in the gleam of the snow, I glimpsed a shadow fleeing at a run. It was definitely René. He seemed to be chasing a carriage that was drawing away rapidly. I called to him, but he increased his pace and soon disappeared, plunging into the fog of the December night.

## VII

On the evening of that day I was the witness—I was going to say the hero—of an adventure, banal in itself but which was subsequently to lead me to strange suppositions.

Having returned to my apartment in the Rue de Bac, furious at René's casual behavior, I found a letter waiting for me in my study, and in that letter, a theater ticket. It was a gracious gift from my colleague, Doctor Lantz, the physician of five or six Parisian theaters, a specialist in diseases of the larynx, the Providence of all sopranos and contraltos with sore throats, a slightly superficial scientist but an excellent fellow. He was sending me his own armchair for the third performance of a new play, an end-of-year Revue, the "day's great vogue," as certain newspapers said: *Pékin à Paris*.

The evening was well advanced; nevertheless, enervated by the funereal emotions of the day and desirous of distracting myself, I dined promptly and got dressed. I have in any case, always liked little dramatic farces, vaudevilles, operettas, and the like. In my estimation, they do not fatigue the brain, and are a good preparation for sleep. That one was being played on a stage situated a long way from my beloved Faubourg Saint-Germain, the Folies-Comiques, out in the turbulent vicinity of the Boulevard du Temple. It was after nine o'clock when I arrived outside the brilliantly-illuminated façade of the theater.

"Hurry up," the usherette said to me. "The second act has already begun. First armchair to the left as you go in, near the orchestra." And the lady with the pink bonnet added: "You're alongside the authors, Monsieur."

I went to take my place, discreetly and without making a noise; the second act had, indeed, just begun.

My long habitude of synthesis and analysis permitted me to reconstruct the exposition of the dramatic work rapidly. The pretext for the folderol chosen by the authors was our glorious recent expedition to China.[1] In the previous act, a mandarin, Monsieur Pékin—how inventive!—had fallen in love with a canteen-waitress of the zouaves, an audacious personification of my country, had abducted her, and, having conquered her too by means of his conquest, had come to Paris to initiate himself into civilization in the dazzle of the City of Light.

To begin with, the Mentor in skirts had taken her Telemachus to the Bal Mabille. That was the place of delights that I had before my eyes, with its forest of zinc palm trees and girandoles of coconuts. In the hall, the orchestra was playing furiously, and behind the footlights, a disheveled bacchante was quivering. Dancers in short crinolines were lifting their legs loosely, exhibiting all the beauties of the cancan—the national dance

---

1 The conflict nowadays known as the Second Opium War (1856-60), French involvement in which spread southwards to what became known in France as the colony of Cochinchina (now Vietnam).

of France, the Germans have always claimed. Next to me, the authors were sitting still: a very old monsieur, a septuagenarian with white hair and spectacles; and a very young monsieur who still had the down of the twentieth year on his chin. They were savoring the literary delicacies of their work silently.

Meanwhile, that first scene, a skillful preparation for the entrance of the mandarin, came to an end. Chorus-girls, dancers and figurants were grouped to the right and left of the stage; the large door at the rear opened, and the hero of the play, Monsieur Pékin, appeared in the background. Almost immediately, there was a hesitation among the actors, and the leader of the orchestra stood there with his bow suspended; someone had missed their entrance.

The septuagenarian author agitated in his armchair and leaned toward the twenty-year-old author. "Another hitch!" he said to him. "Now the Bal Mabille is delayed!"

The young monsieur let his monocle drop, and riposted: "The little Mignon-Chérie? You know, Bon Papa, that one can never count on her. A snag! You were the one who imposed her."

The good papa replied: "It's necessary to encourage youth. Doubtless she's been celebrating Christmas to excess. Here she is!"

The arm of the leader of the orchestra came down, and the music resumed its rigadoon. Mademoiselle Mignon-Chérie came on stage. I aimed my opera-glasses at the new star, and perceived a thin young woman in a very short skirt and a Folie bonnet on her head. But I started suddenly; stupefied, I had recognized Elias's neophyte, the reincarnate soul, the seeress, the expiatrice. Was it possible? Of what carnivalesque farce had I been the dupe?

I shrugged my shoulders, confused by my credulous emotion of a little while before.

The folderol had recommenced. The Bal Mabille gave a welcome to the "noble foreigner." Paris saluted Pékin in manufactured couplets.

"As long, my God," muttered the septuagenarian author, "as she can carry those couplets!"

"One of the nails of the piece," murmured the young author.

"A little ditty, young man, that ought to make its tour of France."

In a blank falsetto voice, Mademoiselle Mignon-Chérie warbled:

> *I've attracted to the vaudeville,*
> *Me who is the Bal Mabille . . .*

She stopped abruptly, rolled frightened eyes, and her gaze remained fixed on one of the corners of the hall. There was a moment of surprise. There were already murmurs from the stalls: "Uh oh! She doesn't know her role!"

The young actress made a visible effort to resume possession of herself.

> *. . . Monsieur the Chinese . . .*

She interrupted herself again. "*The Cochinchinese . . .*" the prompter shouted.

A further silence of the Bal Mabille; more mocking laughter in the hall. Next to me, the white-haired author lowered his head all the way to the pommel of his cane; the other, the young one, stood up to the storm impassively, very handsome . . .

Finally, very upset and stammering in an unintelligible manner, Mademoiselle Mignon-Chérie finished her famous couplet—a couplet in the grand style, then very much in fashion, of the *Roi barbu . . . bu qui s'avance*:[1]

> *. . . Monsieur the Chinese,*
> *You whom pleasure will restrain,*
> *Enter my do . . . my dodo . . . my domain.*

---

1 The line is from Jacques Offenbach's comic opera *La Belle Hélène* (1864).

A volley of whistles departed from the upper galleries; the *paradis* was not content. And then, uttering a cry of fright, waving her arms and tumbling backwards, the poor girl collapsed on the boards. Immediately, the curtain came down; and shortly thereafter, the stage-manager, a neat monsieur in a white cravat wearing the rosette of Nicham[1] in his coat, showed himself at the front of the stage.

"Mesdames et Messieurs, our colleague Mademoiselle Mignon-Chérie has just been taken ill. Is there a doctor in the house?"

He turned in my direction, to the chair where Doctor Lantz ought to have been sitting. A moment later I was in the wings.

A truly comical confusion reigned on the stage. Mademoiselle Mignon-Chérie had been picked up in order to be placed in an armchair. I approached her. The syncope was complete; I even observed a contraction of all the limbs: a bizarre case of catalepsy. I prescribed a few remedies, hastily. The comrades surrounded the invalid, and the director, a short, bearded man, David Hertzog, strode back and forth furiously.

"Receipts of four thousand francs!" he howled. "We'll have to return the money! No, no! Carry her to her dressing-room, and let's continue!"

But the stage-manager decorated by Nicham, who was following the master, hat in hand, replied: "Impossible, Monsieur de directeur! It's the first of the three and the fifth of the four."

"Cuts and links."

"Impossible! Impossible! Who will do the imitations of Mélingue and sing the rondeau of the *Vénus aux navets*?"

"The whole attraction of the play!"

And the director resumed his feverish pacing. A sensible improvement had, however, taken place in the invalid. She opened her eyes and extended her arms toward the auditorium.

"There . . . ! There . . . !" she stammered. "He's there!"

---

1 The Order of Glory, or the Order of Nicham Iftikar, was founded by the Ottoman Bey of Tunisia in 1835. Numerous French officers were among its recipients

David Hertzog ran to the gap in the curtain.

"Who's there?" he demanded. "And where's . . . there?"

Mademoiselle Mignon-Chérie sat up weakly, and in a strangled voice, still in the grip of fear: "There! At the back of the theater! In a floor-level box . . . the man!"

David Hertzog called the stage-manager. "Monsieur Guzman! You who know no obstacles, go and see who the fellow is who frightened that child so much." Then he added: "All the same, these girls! One quarrels with her good friend and fears the blows . . . of despair!"

"By the way, Hertzog," asked a newspaper reporter, a curly-haired fellow with an insolent face, "What's the name of her shareholder?"

"Anonymous society, Seigneur Arlequin!"

"A joyful laughter saluted that directorial joke. Even the young woman started to giggle. Mademoiselle Mignon seemed entirely cured now, for she got up and approached the impresario.

"No, no . . . it's over. On with the music!"

The stage-manager decorated by Nicham, the handsome Monsieur Guzman, came back.

"I didn't notice anyone," he said. "All the floor-level boxes are full except one, number seven. A gentleman came into it during the second act, but he's just left."

"To the curtain!" cried Monsieur Hertzog, agitating a hand-bell. "Receive our thanks, Doctor."

During that brouhaha, I had not ceased examining the sick woman. I was beginning to doubt my memory. In truth, I seemed to recognize her, but so vaguely. No, she had neither the appearance nor the expression of the somnambulist I had glimpsed a short while before. And yet, that gaze, that provocative ugliness, and above all—yes, above all—that blonde hair? Very anxious, I wanted to clarify the matter. I leaned over the shoulder of the actress and said, in an insinuating voice: "I've had the pleasure of seeing you before, Mademoiselle?"

She turned round and looked me up and down, surprised, and even impertinent. "Me, Monsieur? Where?"

"Today, in the Rue Rousselet, with Elias, the prophet Elias."

The young woman burst out laughing. "Rue Rousselet? Elias? A Prophet? Don't know him! What are you saying? Elias? Oh la la, there's a name!"

And laughter overcame her again.

Very good! I was fixed; an uncertain resemblance had induced a momentary error, but the illusion had just dissipated of its own accord.

I returned to my place, and the revue concluded without encumbrance. Mademoiselle Mignon reappeared in the "first of the three" and the "fifth of the four," she imitated Monsieur Mélingue and sang the praises of the Venus of the Turnips.[1] It was a resounding revenge for the child, a veritable success, a triumph. The audience in the stalls stamped their feet; the gentlemen wearing gardenias extended their gloved hands and applauded with four fingers. In one forestage box demoiselles were convulsed with laughter, and a Moldavian prince sent bouquets with his visiting card. The play, however, was utterly inept.

That night, I slept without bad dreams.

The following day, I received sad news. My brother, a consul in Egypt, was ill and in danger of death; he was appealing for me with desperate cries. Very emotional, I hastened to depart the same day, and at seven o'clock in the evening, the express train bore me away to Marseilles. I quit Paris without being able to visit my friend Monsieur de Mauréac.

## VIII

My voyage was prolonged more than was reasonable, and I was away for nearly seven months. I had the good fortune to return my brother to health, but his convalescence was slow, and I was obliged to install myself by his bedside for many a night. Finally,

---

1 "Turnips" is the literal translation of *navets*; in argot, the word is also employed to mean tripe, or rubbish. Étienne Mélingue (1807-1875) was a famous actor most famous for performing in plays by Alexandre Dumas

when all danger was past, I abandoned myself without constraint to the study and contemplation of marvelous Egypt. I went up the Nile as far as the second cataract, rummaging in the hypogea, handling the mummies, and brought back a nice collection of the little good gods in usage among the ancient people.

When I returned to Paris, in the last week in July, I shut myself away at home. I was in haste to resume the printing of my work, the *Essay on the Simulations of Second Sight*, interrupted for such a long time. The book, in any case, had increased considerably in my thought; the plan had been modified on a larger scale. The original pamphlet would now fill two solid volumes. My conclusions, however, remained the same: war upon charlatans, scorn for charlatanism. French, I wanted to write a book for France, the nursery of common sense and pondered imagination. Such work certainly ought to open the road to the Institut to me.

During the first days after my arrival I had gone to lift the knocker at the door to the house in the Rue Saint-Dominique. There, Monsieur Baptiste, a model concierge, had apprised me of René's absence.

"Where is he?"

The discreet Monsieur Baptiste replied, with a vague gesture: "Monsieur le Marquis is traveling."

I had, therefore, been in my voluntary reclusion for a fortnight, in the sole company of my proofs, when the post brought me a letter one morning bearing the postmark of the town of Auray in Morbihan. The letter in question was addressed to me by Mauréac:

> *My dear comrade,* he wrote, *our Sieur Baptiste— as a King of France would have said—has informed me of your return to Paris; it appears that you have come back from Egypt. So, you have been able to tear yourself away from the seductions of mummified women and the embraces of dog-headed deities! Never, I confess, would I have supposed you to have such cour-*

*age. But a truce on nonsense; let's talk about serious matters.*

*I'm getting married. I'm marrying the most adorable of young women, a woman of great heart and high intelligence, loving and good. You've already named her, haven't you? It's Mademoiselle Le Barze. I'm happy, profoundly happy. A week still separates me from the blissful moment when the beloved will be entirely mine—a week . . . alas, an entire eternity for my impatience. Oh, how many times I have caught myself declaring, with the poet (the poet in question is named Corentin Le Barze and he is my father-in-law): "Rapidity of days, how slow you seem to me!"*

*Yes, I'm happy, for I'm in love and sense that I am loved. But you, Victor, can you not take part in my happiness? You, my oldest friend, my dear comrade? Without a doubt! In any case, your precipitate flight to Egypt, without even bidding me adieu, merits a punishment, an expiation, according to the priests of Isis.*

*"So, on receipt of this, you'll take the train to Bretagne; having arrived at the station at Auray, you'll descend from the carriage; from the station platform, you'll be taken away, willingly or by force and brought to the Château de Bruyère, the property of Monsieur Corentin Le Barze. There, you'll be sequestered, and in a week, you'll appear before Monsieur Le Maire as a witness to the marriage of Sieur René de Mauréac, your childhood friend. Come! Come!*

*P.S. Great archeological rejoicings are going to take place at Bruyère before, during and after the betrothal. Galgals will be excavated, sepulchers violated, skulls will be discovered, perhaps dolichocephalic. Once again, come!*

My first impulse, on receiving that letter, was assuredly not a good one. I cursed the importunate fellow who wanted to snatch me away from my work. Unfortunate book, so often interrupted, when, alas, would you appear? Reflection soon came to calm an excess of ill humor. Yes, I ought to go; everything made it an obligation. It was not permissible, after my "flight to Egypt," as René put it, to refuse his affectionate request; that would be to fall out with him forever. In addition, the announcement of "archeological rejoicings," was calculated to lighten the ennui of such a chore. What, galgals were about to be excavated and skulls exhumed—perhaps dolichocephalic!

I hastened to send a telegram announcing my imminent arrival.

Two days later, in the morning, I climbed into a railway carriage; I arrived in Nantes in the evening, and the locomotive soon carried me along the track to Vannes, Auray and Quimper.

Oh, the wild sadness of the landscapes of Morbihan! The vast heaths bristling with furze; the green heather dappled with yellow; desolate cultivations from which the granite protruded like reefs in an ocean at repose.

And while I contemplated the undulations of those plains in the moonlight, I composed a preface. Gradually, however, the monotony of the spectacle, the swaying of the carriage and perhaps also the cadence of my phrases threw me into a languor; I closed my eyes and dozed.

At the halt in Vannes I was extracted from that demi-slumber. On the station platform a band of young officers was laughing, talking loudly and causing a scandal. One of them opened the door of my carriage and called to one of his comrades: "Henri! An almost empty compartment . . . only one passenger, and a monsieur . . . you can smoke at your ease."

Then, adopting the notes of a shrill falsetto, imitating a woman's soprano, he sang: "Enter your do . . . your dodo . . . your domain, my captain!"

"What ineptitude!" cried the whole band.

"And what hams!" added a loud voice, joyful and sonorous.

At the same time, a monsieur decorated with the Légion d'honneur climbed into my carriage.

"*Au revoir* and *à bientôt!*" his friends said to him.

He saluted them with a familiar gesture while the train set forth again.

He was a man of about thirty, short and thickset, already a trifle stout, with an ugly sun-tanned face, but very energetic; his short-cropped hair and brush-shaped moustache denounced an officer. He sat down in a corner of the compartment, stretched his boots out on the banquette, and then took a cigar from his case, without addressing a word of politeness to me, and commenced smoking. And while he filled the compartment with the odors of his nicotine, the monsieur sang.

Divine bounty! I recognized them all, those tunes, those refrains, those folderols—the musical and literary horrors heard at the Folies-Comiques! Yes, the septuagenarian author, the "Bon Papa" had been a prophet; the poetry of *Pékin à Paris* was making its tour of France; at that moment, the epidemic must be rife in Vannes.

Half an hour later the train pulled into a station; I had arrived at Auray. Monsieur de Mauréac was waiting for me at the barrier. I fell into his arms.


# IX


"Oh, wicked man," he said, while clasping my hands. "Flighty soul, forgetful heart, I finally hold you!"

"Salutations, Monsieur de Mauréac!" said a baritone voice behind us.

I turned round and perceived my melomaniac smoker.

"It's you, Henri?" said René, dryly, and immediately introduced us to one another. "My dear Victor, Captain Le Barze, my future brother-in-law . . . Monsieur le professeur Rameau, the best of my friends.

"Aha! Here he is, then, the famous Monsieur Rameau, about whom the Marquis de Mauréac speaks to us so often!" cried Captain Le Barze, in a jovial tone. "Delighted by your visit. We have, I believe, traveled together just now. I ought to have divined your name. A scholar! That stands out a mile, and I've been a customer of one who resembles you greatly, also a professor, Monsieur Durand. Oh, a true scholar, decorated with the violet ribbon, the boot-puller, as we call it in the regiment. He lived in Souk Ahras, near Guelme, when I was a lieutenant in the third zouaves . . . oh, the worthy fellow!"

I declared to the captain that I had been unaware thus far of the existence of his Monsieur Durand, and had never visited Souk Ahras.

"Oh, too bad, Monsieur Rameau. A wretched hole, but a nice little garrison. I was there ten years ago. In those days, once could still amuse oneself a little, beat up the Jews, harass the mercanti and raid the low dives when one had debts. But today . . . ach! A fortnight in the stockade if you so much as give a bailiff a flick. In Paris, they call that colonizing!"

"Victor," said René, "let me have your luggage ticket; I'll have your trunk taken to the caleche. In the meantime, my brother-in-law will tell you about his adventures in garrison; that might take a long time."

He had pronounced those few words in a bantering tone, on a mocking note, but Henri Le Barze did not take offense at the joke. He took me by the arm in a familiar fashion and we left the station.

"Do you know Monsieur de Mauréac well?" the captain asked me, abruptly.

"Yes, very well, for many years."

"Ah! An honest man, is he not? Oh, pardon that ludicrous question. I'm not a monsieur of the salons of Paris myself, I haven't frequented the Jockey Club. I'm a soldier, and my boudoir has never been anything but a barrack-room. Enlisted at eighteen, Monsieur, always in Africa in the midst of the Arbi or on campaign in the Crimea, among the Kabyles, in Italy. Now I'm thirty-six and have just been promoted to captain. That's very fine, undoubtedly . . . yes, but I'm a little rude, a little rough at the edges, a true savage, but a good fellow nevertheless. Would you like a cigar?"

I refused, having always nursed a prejudice against nightshade nicotine. He took from its case a superb Meerschaum pipe, stuffed it and lit it. For myself, I armed myself with patience; evidently, he was going to narrate his amours with Kadidja or his feats of arms against the beni-whatever.

"You see, my dear Monsieur," the cruel chatterbox went on, "it's a matter of my sister's happiness, and I love my sister. A soul so candid, so sweet, so charming: a little saint of paradise. I've been a true papa for her although I'm only ten years her elder. It was necessary! My poor father, the best of men, has all the naivety of a child. Without me, the poor child would already have entered into religion. But what means is there of watching over the welfare of a young woman when one's a captain in the turcos and one lives six hundred leagues away from her under the gourbi in the middle of Tugurt?"

"Tugurt, Captain? You've gone as far as Tugurt? An ancient Roman colony; the fatherland of Saint Augustine, I believe."

He looked at me askance, muttered a few oaths between his teeth, and, adopting a jocular tone, said: "I don't know, Monsieur Scholar. But for want of a saint, there's a Cadi out there who's a famous customer; he steals and gets drunk; he's been made an officer in the Légion d'honneur. In Paris they call that civilizing. Please, let's remain serious. I'm talking seriously, myself."

He fell silent momentarily, and then went on: "In sum, you affirm that he's an honest man, your friend? When I received the letter from my father announcing my little Marie-Thérèse's marriage, I asked for a leave, and I've been here at Bruyère for a few days. Do you know that I find him a little strange, your comrade, Monsieur René de Mauréac, and that I would have

61

preferred for my sister someone less noble, less distinguished, less naval officer, and less marquis? A worthy fellow like me, for example, a son of his works, and—as the canteen waitress who married a Maréchal de France said—only having himself for ancestors. But bah! They met at Lorient, at the soirées of the maritime prefect, they met again in many local excursions; words were exchanged, they've already been engaged for a long time. Anyway, my excellent father, although a simple bourgeois, is a fervent royalist besotted with nobility. 'My son-in-law, the Marquis de Mauréac' is a sentence that resonates well in these parts, a 'Sesame!' that opens the doors of the most tightly-closed châteaux. And then, Marie-Thérèse loves him, your marquis . . . but does he truly love her?"

While speaking, the captain had dragged me outside the confines of the station toward the first houses of Auray. Imminent celebrations were evidently in preparation for the little Breton town, for the walls were covered with posters announcing a grand fête and "a concert given with the collaboration of the principal artistes of the capital."

"Yes," exclaimed Henri Le Barze, continuing his interrogation. "Does Monsieur de Mauréac truly love her, my dear and sweet Marie? Look, Monsieur, in the week that I've been at Bruyère I've already received several anonymous letters. Certainly, I despise an anonymous letter and the scoundrel who can write one, but it's a question of my sister; they recount certain amours of Monsieur de Mauréac and the scandal of an almost public liaison. My God! I'm a man and I'm an officer, not very rigorous and not at all prudish. I thought it a duty, however, to talk to your friend; I wanted a chat with my future brother-in-law. Well, instead of laughing and confessing, he got carried away. He played me the comedy of the man who doesn't want to understand. Why? Myself, I don't like these hypocrisies; they always hide a secret desire not to break with the mistress!"

He was still dragging me, raising his voice, irritated by his own discourse. "Then, I wanted to clear things up. I had myself introduced to the Dulcinea. She's in Vannes right now, a few leagues from Bruyère. Why, again? And I saw her. Oh, my dear Monsieur, what ignominy! What . . ."

"Victor!" cried Monsieur de Mauréac, who had been looking for us for some time. "Where were you? The luggage is in the carriages; let's go."

"We'll resume this conversation," the captain said to me. "I want to clear up this mystery."

A caleche harnessed to two horses advanced toward us.

"Climb aboard, my dear friend," René said to me, opening the door.

"Pardon me," said Captain Le Barze, dryly. "Permit me to do the honors in my own home."

He invited me to take my place with a gesture. Mauréac sat beside me, Monsieur Le Barze facing us; soon we were rolling over the pavement of Auray. The vehicle crossed the old bridge built over the Loch and, turning right, took a side road, rugged and bumpy, snaking in accordance with the meanders of the river, sometimes cutting through meager arable land, sometimes plunging into the obscurity of fir-woods.

An icy constraint reigned between us. Henri Le Barze was the first to break the awkward silence.

"Has the Englishman finally gone?" he asked.

"He'll never leave," replied René. Addressing me, he said: "How content you'll be, my dear friend. We're going to serve you an Englishman! Oh, but what an Englishman! A passionate lover of skulls, tibias and femurs, the Reverend J. K. W. Cotter-Powell, fellow of Oxford, vicar of St. Edward's, Kidderminster, broad church. M.A.C.L.—which is to say, a member of the Anthropoid Club of London:[1] an Anglican pastor by profession, and a Darwinian philosopher and theist by conviction. It will

---

1 The author has in mind the Linnean Society of London, founded in 1788, and dedicated to the study of natural history and taxonomy. Charles Darwin was a member, as was Thomas Henry Huxley, the most ardent popularizer of his theory of evolution; the first exposition of the theory of evolution by natural selection was made at a meeting of the society in 1858.

soon be a month since he's been taking his gin in my father-in-law's château; a devotee of Celtic studies; you probably know him—the reverend J. K. W. Powell is a fervent anti-Celticizer. The member of the Anthropoid Club professes the theory of tertiary man. Dolmens and galgals are, in his belief, the primordial expression of the civilization of the transformed ape. He goes everywhere, scratching, excavating, digging the earth in quest of prognathous jaws: ape he'd like to be and ape he is. So, the days and evenings at Bruyères are spent in formidable controversies; one argues, one disputes, one insults almost as much as in the Institut de France! You're lacking that pleasure party, my old comrade."

I listened to Mauréac painfully. He was animated, overdoing the pleasantry and forcing his laughter, very nervous. I noticed his eyes, which were gleaming strangely in the night.

Finally, the caleche turned, penetrated into the avenues of a park and came to a halt before the façade of a charming country house. I was at Bruyère.

# X

Corentin Le Barze was waiting for us. He ran to meet us and welcomed me in a very amiable fashion.

"Be welcome under my roof, my dear doctor. Your visit is doubly precious; it permits me to know better a distinguished scholar and to claim from him a little of the amity that he has for my new child, Monsieur le Marquis de Mauréac."

He had pronounced his "Monsieur le Marquis" with an emphasis that was slightly comical in a man who did not want to understand the egalitarian aspirations of his homeland. I felt slightly wounded in my liberal convictions; nevertheless, I did not let anything show.

"And Marie-Thérèse? Where is she?" asked René, searching for the absentee.

"My daughter, slightly fatigued," Monsieur Le Barze told us, "has retired to her room; you'll excuse her, Messieurs. In any case, it's late; two o'clock in the morning will soon chime. Would you like something, Monsieur Rameau?"

I thanked him, but protested that I was neither hungry nor thirsty.

"Father," said René, "my friend needs repose most of all; I'll take him to his room."

Showing me the way then, he drew me away rapidly. Through the open door of the dining room I perceived, sitting at the table, a monsieur of about sixty years of age, very tall, very stiff and very bald: the reverend clergyman of the broad church, J. K. W. Powell. He was sitting with his head bowed between two bottles: brandy to the left, whisky to the right, very red-faced and seemingly asleep. Perhaps he was evoking in a dream the vision of his grandfather the gorilla, or perhaps he was preparing a sermon.

The room that had been destined for me, very elegant with its fresh cretonne wall-hangings, overlooked the park, and the perfumes of honeysuckle and syringa came in through the open window, mingled with the acrid odor of maritime pines. In the distance, on the river, the murmur of the rising tide could be heard, the monotonous plaint of which awoke the great slumber of the night.

"Are you fatigued?" Mauréac asked me. "Would you like me to leave you?" He continued, without waiting for my response: "Oh, my friend, how happy I am! In five days, she'll be mine—you understand?—entirely mine, the beloved. You don't know her? Tomorrow, you'll see her. How she'll please you! She's brunette, Victor, brunette with great blue eyes, velvet eyes . . . and so tender, so soft, so sad! Admirable hair! A slim figure, a graceful stride. Such small hands and feet, with such dainty wrists and ankles. She's charming . . . she's charming . . . And in the body of that pretty Breton fay, the soul of a saint. Modest, and yet learned, almost a scholar; full of intelligence, sometimes even malice, but without malevolence; having the cult of Beauty, the religion of God—a noble creature! Yes, yes, I love her . . . and I'm loved by her! Me, me, beloved by her!

"Oh, what a strange suffering amour is! When she looks at me, I go pale; my heart stops; something within me makes me feel ill. When she smiles at me I close my eyes, for fear of seeing; I dread that I might faint! Oh, the dear evenings that I've spent with her. Yesterday evening, again, we were both sitting in the garden. Her hand was abandoned in mine, and, only letting our gazes speak, we remained silent in the silence of the night. The flowers-beds were exhaling all the perfume of their blooms; frissons were passing through the branches of the trees, and the moon was enveloping us with its serene light.

"Then, turning toward my beloved, I perceived tears running down her face. 'What! You're weeping, Marie?'

"'Yes, I'm weeping,' she said. 'I feel too happy,'

"Then, oh then, drawing her to me in a passionate embrace, I placed my lips over her eyes and I drank her tears . . . You're smiling, you skeptic; you think I'm mad . . . well, yes, I'm mad, my friend . . . mad with desire and happiness!"

I listened with astonishment; I had never known him like that. *Vive amour*, to transform a man thus! Moreover, his language amused me. He had launched his tirade at me with the exaltation of a devotee celebrating the virtues of his idol, very sincere and utterly convinced. I tried nevertheless to provoke other confidences.

"What have you been doing during my absence?" I asked. The ill humor of Captain Le Barze returned to my memory, and I wanted to have an explanation of it.

"What have I been doing?" said René, seemingly surprised by my question. "Nothing worth the trouble of being recounted. No, nothing, except for my increasing amour for Mademoiselle Marie-Thérèse, except soon for my marriage."

"And . . . the other, my dear friend?"

"What other?" he said, more and more astonished.

"Just now, your future brother-in-law, Henri Le Barze, complained . . ."

He stood up abruptly, and a violent emotion colored his face. "Henri Le Barze," he cried, "is a fool and a calumniator. He would have preferred his sister to marry some comrade from the regiment. Too late, my dear Monsieur! Marie-Thérèse will be called the Marquise de Mauréac, my wife!"

He was striding back and forth in the room, expressing his anger by means of disordered gestures; however, he calmed down and came back to sit beside me.

"Bah!" he said. "Let that malevolent man talk! My past life can defy calumny, and my conduct to come will confound my accuser. I won't return to Paris again. Henceforth, I want to live with my wife in her dear land of Bretagne."

"Ah! I understand you, ambitious man! The general council first, deputation afterwards."

"Neither one nor the other. Yes, I'm ambitious, but only for happiness. My father-in-law has just bought a vast domain for his daughter, Le Menée, a wild tract of land where the melancholy of pine and larch-woods extends. We're due to visit it tomorrow, and you'll be in the party . . . Oh," he continued, with a sigh, "it's there that I'd like to bury my treasure like a miser. You recall the delightful line of a poet: 'If I had an arpent of land, mountain, vale or plain . . .'[1] Well, I too only ask for a clump of trees, but from which all the songs of a nest emerge; only a modest roof, but beneath which the slumber of a little child smiles and murmurs! Such is my dream, friend; that's all the ambitious René desires!"

Dawn was already paling the sky. He took his leave of me, and shook my hand.

"As for you, Victor, on the day when you come to visit us at Le Menée, you'll find something that will charm you more than the nest, the roof, the bird or even the child . . . a tumulus, Monsieur Scholar. Yes, in a corner of the park, I'm told, there's a superb tumulus."

---

1 The oft-quoted line is from "Rêves ambitieuses" by the Lyonnais Parnassian Joséphin Soulary (1851-1895)

The tedium of the journey had fatigued me, and I slept until a late hour of the morning. The first appeal of the bell for the morning meal extracted me from my slumber. I dressed in haste and went downstairs.

I was awaited in the drawing room. On entering, I perceived Corentin Le Barze, who was arguing with his clergyman, and, standing next to an open window, Maurice and Marie-Thérèse. Oh, they were not making speeches, much less arguing. They were silent. René was holding the young woman's hands pressed in his, and they were both letting their gazes wander in the azure of the sky. The captain had not yet arrived. I went to salute the master of the house, and then approached the lovers.

Marie-Thérèse was no longer a very young woman; she must have been over twenty-five and had coiffed Saint Catherine. In spite of the enthusiasms of my friend René, nothing about her gave the illusion of a little Breton fay. Tall and slightly thin, but nevertheless graceful, in spite of the superb torsades of her black hair and her beautiful periwinkle-blue eyes, I did not find her pretty. Her facial features were irregular, the nose strong, the mouth too slack, further widened by two little wrinkles hollowed out at the corners of the lips. At that moment, she was smiling, but the smile must not have been the habitual companion of that face, so fugitive did it seem, and so dolorous did it appear to me.

The young woman detached herself gently and came toward me.

"How glad I am to see you at Bruyère," she said to me, "you whom I've known for such a long time."

"Me, Mademoiselle?"

"There isn't a day when Monsieur de Mauréac . . ." She hesitated momentarily. ". . . René," she continued, blushing slightly, "doesn't talk to me about you. Oh, you have a veritable friend in him."

"And he's a noble heart," I replied, inclining.

She uttered a little joyful laugh and her eyes shone with pleasure. Yes, certainly, she loved him.

"Did you hear your friend's compliment, René? He proclaims you a noble heart. But doctor, what a light head! Would you believe that he hasn't yet offered me his engagement ring? He's even capable of forgetting the wedding ring on the big day?"

René took all that banter in good part and stammered excuses. The ring was to be made from a model, but the jeweler in the Rue de la Paix was late. He had been harassed with indignant letters, but he was in no hurry. Too many orders, no doubt. At the moment, in Paris there was a fury of betrothals! Marie-Thérèse listened, very amused by those reasons; cheerful, but slightly malicious.

The second appeal of the bell interrupted that chatter, and a domestic announced that the meal was served.

"Where's Henri, then?" asked Monsieur le Barze. "In Auray I'm sure. Too bad! *Tarde venientibus ossu.*[1] Would you care to offer your arm to my daughter, Monsieur Rameau."

"We went into the dining room. In the middle of the table in a crystal centerpiece, a bunch of white lilacs was blooming, the classic bouquet of engagements.

"The sweetest to the sweetest," murmured the Reverend Powell, gallantly.

Mademoiselle Le Barze responded with a burst of laughter. "Pardon me, dear Monsieur, but in the guise of a compliment you're addressing the funeral oration of Ophelia to me! It's very amiable on your part; nevertheless, I feel very alive, and Hamlet's indifference won't kill me."

She had said that while looking at Monsieur de Mauréac. The latter thought he ought to make an assault of quotations and turned to his fiancée.

---

1 Of the late the bones are left.

"Sooner doubt that the stars are fire, than doubt . . ."[1]

"No, not that oath," she said, becoming suddenly sad and serious. "Hamlet was lying, and you have never lied, René . . . no, never, have you?"

"Oh, that Shakespeare—or, to put it better, that Bacon!" cried Monsieur Le Barze, who appeared to me to be rather embarrassed. "As soon as you're united, my children, I'll translate him in verse."

A constrained silence followed that threat from one poet to another. The Oxford fellow was the first to break it; he addressed himself to me.

"My friend Le Barze has revealed to me, Monsieur, that you also are a fervent Celtomaniac."

"Fervent, no. Bossuet has said: 'Faith must have conviction in it.'"

"All our divines have reasoned in the same way. No, you don't believe, I'm certain of it, that your Kymri were constructors of dolmens? For myself, in your cairns, galgals and tumuli I discover the industry of a race of vanished men: quaternary man, perhaps tertiary, older than the mammoth and the cave-bear; an ape-man, very prognathous, very dolichocephalic, carnivorous, anthropophagous; a demi-brute, the anthropoids of the Neanderthal grotto, the penultimate proof of human transformism: out grandparent, in a word . . .

"You're smiling, Monsieur, because beneath my clergyman's black levite and white cravat you glimpse a materialist and a Darwinian? Oh, that belief in transformism only came to me late. I was a missionary in Natal in the company of Colenso, the illustrious Bishop Colenso.[2] I was sent to convert the Ovampo and Bakuba Kaffirs, to reveal to them that they had emerged

---

1 The actual quotation is "Doubt thou the stars are fire . . . but never doubt I love," but René is probably quoting from a French translation, which I have back-translated.

2 John Colenso became Bishop of Natal in 1853, and traveled across Zululand in 1859.

from the breath of God and were not the work of the gorilla, in which they gloried. Well, I proclaim, Monsieur, that it was me who was converted . . . myself and my bishop. Alas, I've seen so many humans!"

"Admirable! You have remained, however, my dear Monsieur, the priest of a church salaried by your State."

"Yes, a priest, certainly, but of the broad church."

"So broad that it can contain, I see, Christians, deists and even atheists!"

"It is, indeed, very broad," muttered the broad-churchman, swallowing a mouthful of white Bordeaux. He raised the wine to the level of his right eye, remarked the transparency, and declared it "capital."

"My dear Powell," protested Monsieur Le Barze, "your thesis on the constructors of the megaliths is unsustainable. The human debris that has been found has nothing apelike about it; the skulls are conformed like yours and mine. Go to the museum of Vannes."

The reverend champion of the anthropoid ancestor imbibed a few drops of the "capital" Sauterne and addressed a disdainful moue to us. "Oh, I expected the argument. For me it has no value, pure nonsense. Your poor France isn't a land of liberty, like good old England. I'll explain. In Vannes you have a prefect; that prefect obeys an Emperor; that Emperor is under the authority of a Pope. The excavations are therefore made to lie; the skulls are substituted; the fraud is certain, the *Times* has said so . . . oh, if I were there!"

"You shall be there!" cried Monsieur Le Barze. "And you shall see with your own skeptical eyes. Today, in a little while, we shall visit a domain that I have just bought for my daughter, Le Menée . . . for the two of you, my children," he added, turned toward the fiancés. "By the way, René, do you know that I've made a curious find this very morning? I've discovered, by studying the title-deeds of the property, that Le Menée belonged to your family for a time."

"To my family!" said René, in a tone of profound surprise. "I was absolutely unaware of it. Before the Revolution, no doubt?"

"Before and after. It was acquired toward the end of the reign of Louis XVI by your grandfather, the Président à la Tournelle, a magistrate of the old robe, not very tender to his clients, according to the chronicles, the last defender of torture in our Parlement de Bretagne. Confiscated in 1793 and put up for sale as national property, Le Menée did not find a purchaser and was bought back at a rock-bottom price, as the deeds show, by your father."

"By my father!"

"Yes, under the Consulate, in the epoch of his return to France. But in 1814 Le Menée passed into other hands."

"Strange! Very strange!" murmured Monsieur de Mauréac. "A curious discovery, Monsieur . . . yes, yes, very strange."

I looked at him, astonished by the sudden alteration in his voice; I was struck by his pallor. As if he wanted to avoid my eyes, however, he leaned toward his neighbor and began to say a thousand amorous trivia to her.

"Well, my dear Powell," Monsieur Le Barze continued, "on that property there is a magnificent tumulus. It has not been explored, I can answer for that. I've summoned a crew of diggers. They will excavate it; the monster will be eviscerated, and perhaps . . ."

A joyful exclamation interrupted the sentence. "What! Everyone's eating without me! Bonjour, Father; bonjour, my little Mariette!"

Captain Henri had just irrupted into the room. He kissed the young woman on both cheeks and then bowed ceremoniously to his future brother-in-law.

René bowed in his turn, but did not offer his hand. The captain sat down at the table and began devouring avidly.

"What news, Henri?" asked Monsieur Le Barze, desirous of cutting short that little mute scene.

"Nothing very new, Father. Yesterday evening, in Vannes, with a former comrade rediscovered in the garrison, I went to the theater. A successful play was being performed, but I had to leave before the end; I nearly missed my return train."

"Is it good, the play?"

"Pure ineptitude. And the actors, a touring troupe, an accumulated bric-à-brac of petty hams."

"Were there many people in the hall?"

"A full house—a final performance. Tomorrow, the whole band of jokers sets forth for Lorient. Anyway, if your heart bids you, you can hear them this evening in Auray."

"In Auray?"

"Yes, at the Hôtel de l'Europe. A great fête and a marvelous concert. Choice morsels from all the French bellowers: false notes and varied howls, five francs a ticket. The whole town has been in a state of excitement since this morning. The principal artistes from the capital arrived this morning in four omnibuses. What an entrance, Messeigneurs, and what a reception! The president of the choral society made a speech. An hour later, didn't they have the idea of taking the boat and going for a pleasure trip to Belle Isle? I watched the departure—it was epic! But they'll be back for the soirée; a matter of sniffing the ocean breezes and granting themselves three jolly hours of sea-sickness. Well, when one has never known any other waves than the tarry waves of the Son of the Night, it's alluring . . . Let's see, dear Father, shall we go to their little fête this evening? Who knows? Perhaps we'll find some amusement there."

"No thank you, certainly not," replied Monsieur Le Barze, who seemed annoyed by those vulgar pleasantries. "I know their repertoire. Every morning for ten days my coachman has woken me up whistling their folderol, and just now, to my profound amazement, I heard it sung at the top of his voice by one of my peasants. An epidemic of stupidity!"

"Oh yes, the couplets of Mademoiselle Mignon-Chérie . . . an abominable saw," said the captain, sniggering. He had placed his fork on the table and was looking fixedly at his future brother-in-law. "A nasty little face, that girl, and devoid of talent. I've heard a lot about her. The donzelle is from around here; she's been recognized. Glad to inform you of that detail, Monsieur le Marquis de Mauréac."

René turned slowly toward the maker of enquiries and looked him up and down haughtily. For a few moments the two men challenged one another with their eyes. Finally, Monsieur de Mauréac said, in a trenchant voice and a solemn tone: "I've already declared it and I repeat it for the last time: I don't understand you. On my honor, I don't know that young woman."

"However . . ."

"Monsieur le Marquis de Mauréac," cried Marie-Thérèse, "your family motto has always been: *Disdain and pass on*. Yes, and it's engraved on the ring that I perceive on your hand. Give it to your wife, then, that proud motto, and put her engagement ring on her finger!"

Both of them stood up. Very emotional, René took the young woman's hand, slipped the ring on to it, and then, with a passionate movement, raised it to his lips. And as he bent down, Marie-Thérèse seized his head and, blushing deeply, deposited a long kiss on the forehead.

"There! I don't believe them," she said. "I don't believe them, because I love you!"


# XII


The meal finally ended, and everyone went down into the garden. In front of the château's façade two men were waiting, two robust Bretons wearing the black coats with velvet trimmings of the region of Vannes.

"Bonjour, Master," they said, taking off their broad-brimmed hats. "The boat is ready."

"It's you, lads?" replied Monsieur Le Barze, whose gaiety seemed extinct. "Will the day be fine, Léonnec?"

"Fair enough," replied Léonnec, a thickset mariner with broad shoulders, "but it's necessary to hurry, isn't that so, Jean-Louis. The Loch is lowering rapidly."

"We'll descend with the ebb tide," added the other, "but if the rising tide catches us, we'll have to land no matter where."

"*En route*, then!" cried Marie-Thérèse.

She took possession of her fiancé's arm and drew him toward the river. I joined them. Monsieur Le Barze, his son and the Englishman followed us at a distance. In the muddy water of the Loch, a large sailboat was swaying, moored at the bank.

"Go aboard first, René," said Marie-Thérèse. "Offer me your hand to take the difficult step.

Monsieur de Mauréac quit his companion's hand, but instead of running to the boat he asked: "So we're going to visit Le Menée?"

"Of course. Our residence henceforth, our paradise. It's doubly dear to me now, since your family has lived there and their memory might still fill it."

René placed himself in front of her and seemed to want to bar the way. "Let's not go there Marie. Let's seek elsewhere for that shelter, that paradise of our amour—but not at Le Menée. I'm afraid!"

"Afraid? My God, of what?"

He did not reply.

"What childishness, René! Do you want to afflict my father? He's just bought that domain expressly for us. Poor father, so joyful to feel me near to him, always under his kisses!"

Our three companions had caught up with us.

"What! No one's embarking?" asked Monsieur Le Barze, addressing his daughter.

"Father," replied the latter, laughing, "Monsieur your son-in-law is afraid . . . of the wicked fays of Le Menée and the malign little korrigans. Oh well, we'll be quits for singing them the seven days of the week, above all without forgetting Sunday; otherwise, they'll carry us all away. Let's go visit their abode!"

And she leapt lightly into the boat.

"Korrigans, among the Gaels, Korbirs or Kabires among the Phoenicians," Monsieur Le Barze said to us then, "the powerful dwarfs, grandiose smallness, the emblem of intelligence stronger than force itself! So much the better if they're found at Le Menée. En route, my children!"

A few minutes later the anchor was lifted, the sail was hoisted, and we went down the river.

It is severe but truly superb, the landscape that unfurls its sadness along the two banks of the Loch d'Auray. Sometimes the river broadens out like an arm of the sea, stretching out as far as the eye can see the sheet of its waters, variegated by foam; sea-mews and black-backed gulls skim the undulations of the waves and cast their shrill plaints and savage cries into the spray. Sometimes, and abruptly, it narrows. The Loch precipitates then, noisy and tumultuous, between two promontories of massive rocks, from which the enormous arrows of maritime pines launch forth or the secular crowns of parasol-cedars spread out; that all-dark verdure makes a strain on the glittering redness of the sandstone, which appears flamboyant in the sunlight. And up above, on the accumulation of those rocks, bleak châteaux and taciturn manses shelter their solitude and melancholy in the shadow of fir-woods . . .

O Bretagne, miserly nurse of your children, what beauty there is in your superb misery, and how I love your desperation, when the sky weeps over your granite and the storms moan in the harmonious lamentation of your old oaks!

We glided mutely through the drowsy murmur of the waters. The heat of the day was overwhelming, and the midday sun burned us with its rays. Henri went to sleep, as did the Reverend Powell, and sitting beside me, Monsieur Le Barze contemplated his daughter, enveloping her with his tender gaze. Marie-Thérèse and René were sitting in the front of the boat; the young woman had inclined her head on her companion's shoulder, and the two of them, exchanging glances were matching smiles, plunged in the silent sensuality of great happiness.

As for me, I was mulling over a thousand confused thoughts. The name of Mignon-Chérie, pronounced a little while ago, and the insolent pleasantries of Captain Le Barze has amazed me. What had happened, then during my absence? Had René had a caprice for that vicious and stupid chit? Get away! No, the Marquis de Mauréac did not know that young woman; he had sworn it on his honor before us!

Suddenly, the prow of the boat rose up, rearing on the wave. At the same time, the sail flapped, to fall back along the mast.

"Damn!" exclaimed Jean-Louis, who was at the tiller, "the tide is coming in again and the wind has turned."

"Impossible even to make headway," added his comrade. "We'll have to land."

"Are we still far from Le Menée?" asked Monsieur Le Barze.

"About two kilometers."

"Well, lads, one last effort and let's gain ground!"

"So be it," said Jean-Louis. "To the oars!"

They hooked their oars and began to row. The tide was rising rapidly, and the current broke with dull groans against the hull of the boat, white with foam. The two men rowed in cadence, but in spite of their steely muscles, they only advanced slowly. Mauréac, abandoning the front of the boat, had placed himself at the tiller. The great Atlantic swell irrupted into the estuary with a savage din . . . and the oceanic birds, racing in swirls, tore the air with their sonorous cries. The waves beating the shore began to cast dolorous sobs into the air.

A voice rose up in the middle of that formidable concert of nature; the voice of one of our boatmen, drawling and nasal, started intoning a horrible folderol:

"Enter my do . . ." (a stroke of the oar) "my dodo . . ." (another stroke of the oar) "my domain . . ." (a vigorous pull).

"Enough, my good friends, or sing us something else!" cried Marie-Thérèse, who stood up, shivering.

"Excuse us, Mademoiselle," replied Jean-Louis, "but in Vannes it's all the rage."

"And comes to us from Paris," added Léonnec.

"And since when," replied Marie Le Barze, "Have our lads of Morbihan, the grandsons of Georges' soldiers, dared to soil their mouths with such filth? It's a sin, that, my brave lads! Well," she went on, becoming excited, "I want to sing you a song, a true one for the men of Bretagne. It will give you heart and reinforce your muscles."

The young woman was standing up, leaning against the mast, her left hand gripping the rigging. The wind, which was whipping her face, had colored it vividly; her eyes were sparkling and her unfastened hair was falling in black undulations over her shoulders. The young provincial had disappeared and before me I had a truly lovely creature, of a strange and savage beauty.

"The *Albatros!*" she said, in a slow voice; "a story of our Chouanerie of Moribhan; a ballad in Breton verse by Monsieur Corentin Le Barze, my father; French translation by his daughter. Listen, all of you . . ."

And she began:

"Shine my eyes, vibrate my voice, sing O my heart, I want to speak of the *Albatros.*

"Out there in the river of Auray, toward the Passes Locmariaquer; that corner of Bretagne of which the soil is all made of human dust; where under the funerary dolmens, while their souls voyage in the space of worlds; sleep the bodies of the old Celts, the Brenns with flint knives; and necklaces of jade, enormous debris in enormous tombs! Heavily, on her anchors, the *Albatros* sways . . .

"Shine my eyes, vibrate my voice, sing O my heart, I want to speak of the *Albatros.*

"Heavily, on her anchors, the *Albatros* sways; her masts have been cut, the bird is without wings henceforth. Why do you seem so ashamed, poor ship, ashamed of yourself? You once skimmed the waves, elegant and rapidly; now, sunk in the mud, you are no more than a pontoon; a floating jail inhabited by prison guards!

"A floating jail inhabited by prison guards! And inside, numerous and ferocious, are barracks of blues; blues, veterans of Bonaparte, the harvester of peoples; Bonaparte, that man greater than human, as great as Death; and inside are heaped up the captives of war; the faithful of the King of France, the émigrés, our Messieurs!

"The faithful of the King of France, the émigrés, our Messieurs! They are there, for the prisons of Vannes are overflowing and the people murmuring; they are there, awaiting their judgment, a judgment which is advancing and is death! Thrown into the gulfs of the abyss, in the roar of the ocean; a dot lost in space . . . who can deliver them? Who? 'It will be me,' said Sans-Pareil . . ."

A violent shock agitated the boat. Monsieur de Mauréac had let go of the tiller and was marching toward Marie-Thérèse.

"Shut up, Marie; for pity's sake, shut up!"

He grabbed her arm and twisted it brutally. Mademoiselle Le Barze uttered a cry of pain and amazement.

"Shut up, Monsieur? Why? Sans-Pareil was named the Marquis de Mauréac, René, and he was your father!"

But without responding, René had collapsed on a bench, and, inclining his head, he covered his face with his hands.

A profound silence succeeded that strange scene for a long time. Finally, the voice of a boatman was heard: "Here's Le Menée; we can disembark."


# XIII

To our left, on the bank, stood a pavilion in the style of Louis XVI, a sort of hunting-lodge, of dainty appearance, lost in the sinister desolation of the region. A lawn framed by chestnut trees extended in front of the façade. The house seemed deserted and abandoned for a long time. Grass had disjointed the steps of the perron, and a host of plants, shoots of the surrounding trees, were growing along the walls, pitted in many places by cracks.

Our boatmen landed and everyone disembarked. René tried to offer his hand to his fiancée to help her out of the boat, but she refused. The pleasure trip was definitely taking a lugubrious turn. Monsieur Le Barze, increasingly anxious, did not breathe a word, and Reverend Powell followed in his tracks without saying anything. Marie-Thérèse, now sad and taciturn, affected to keep away from Monsieur de Mauréac; she was walking beside her father, suspended from his arm. After them came Captain Henri, who was whistling a military march, amusing himself by cutting branches extending over the path with his cane. I drew nearer to René, who was a long way in the rear, and scolded him, as my old amity gave me the right to do.

"Well then, Monsieur Neurotic, what's got into you?" I asked.

Without making any reply, he turned his back on me and drew away. I went to rejoin Monsieur Le Barze.

"This, then, is Le Menée," the latter sad. "Once, on the site of this park, Celtic alignments must have stood, a few dracontiums. Menhirs extended, serpents of stone, across a heathland that the woods cover today. The granite coils have disappeared; only the name Menée—field of stone—remains. *Lapides ipsi clamabunt!* The present proclaims the past!"[1]

He turned round; René had just touched his shoulder.

"Monsieur Le Barze," he said, in a strained voice, "are you sure, perfectly sure, that Marquis Charles de Mauréac once lived in this place?"

"Your father? Sure that he lived at Le Menée, no; but that he bought it, yes. I have the deed of sale . . . well, yes," Monsieur Le Barze went on, "I'm certain that the marquis, your father, lived here a long time ago. It's here that Napoléon's police must have kept him under surveillance; it's from here that, one Christmas Eve, he departed to steal the *Albatros*."

---

1 The quotation—the stones proclaim—is a common saying.

"Oh, my God . . . my God!" René repeated. "It was here!"

We had reached the little manse; the guardian was waiting for us, surrounded by a whole crew of diggers.

"My friends," Monsieur Le Barze said to them, "go and wait for us by the galgal. We'll join you before long."

"And above all, don't start digging in my absence," added Monsieur Powell. "I always dread some trickery!"

"Let's go with them," said the captain, laughing. "That way, you can supervise them yourself."

The two of them drew away.

"We'll visit the house first," said Monsieur Le Barze, climbing the steps to the landing. "Here's the vestibule, and this is doubtless the drawing room."

The room we had just entered, high and vast, was illuminated by glazed doors pierced in the other façade, which overlooked the park. Outside, that park extended its solitude as far as the eye could see. A morose and savage sadness weighed upon that rebellious nature, which the human hand had never been able to master, and which now, abandoned to its own devices, had covered it with the formidable force of its infertile fecundity. A devastated green carpet extended into the distance, enclosed at its limit by thick woods of age-old firs. Beyond the expanses of grass, a broad avenue was prolonged in the blackness of the woods, and through that open bay, the blue sky could be glimpsed, the glaucous sea and, in the opal of the horizon, the yellow dunes of Locmariaquer. A hillock of pyramidal form cut into the depths of the landscape: the tumulus.

The primitive style of the drawing room had been cruelly deformed; honest bourgeois, proprietors of Le Menée, had dressed it in accordance with the taste of the period. A superb garnet wallpaper overlaid on the paneling was displayed garishly, but damp had stained it with mildew, and it was hanging down in places, unstuck. René seized a piece of that paper and ripped it; beneath the paper delicate woodwork showed, sculpted panels in which Pompadour shells were elegantly mingled with neo-Grecian pearls, in the style of Louis XVI.

"Ah! I recognize it," he murmured.

"What vandalism!" cried Monsieur Le Barze. "My children, I shall restore Le Menée to its primordial state. Everything will be repaired in its style; before long, our Morbihan will possess a Trianon again!"

He went out in order to visit the upper floors. Marie-Thérèse took a few steps behind her father, but, seeing that Mauréac was not following her, she returned to the drawing room, and, while sulking, affected to converse with me. An interjection from René interrupted our colloquium.

"Here, against the wall," he said, seemingly talking to himself, "there was a sofa, armchairs and chairs in Beauvais tapestry. I can see them . . . yes, quite clearly. The subjects were taken from La Fontaine's *Fables*: the wolf and the lamb, the pigeon and the vulture."

"What an imagination, Monsieur," murmured Marie-Thérèse, mocking him—but in such a tender voice.

Without responding to that attack, he ran to a little door fitted into the woodwork, and opened it. "I recognize this too!" he continued, with a bizarre laugh. "It's there, in that room, that they hid . . . the men!"

He closed the door again violently, traversed the drawing room again and stopped in front of the fireplace: a large white marble fireplace. "And there it is, the hearth where, in the icy December night, the logs of oak were burning and the brushwood cackling! Oh, the sinister flame . . . oh!"

He leaned on the mantelpiece, putting his hands together in a gesture of despair.

Meanwhile, seemingly wanting to avoid her fiancé, Mademoiselle Le Barze was observing him with an anxious gaze. She approached him and said, very softly: "What's wrong, Monsieur de Mauréac? Are you suffering?"

"I'm suffering . . . cruelly."

"So close to your physician, Monsieur? To your friend!"

"An entirely mental dolor . . ."

"So close to me, René? Ah, since you're carrying within you a powerful chagrin, regrets, perhaps some remorse, tell me! We'll suffer together, and your burden will be less heavy."

"Remorse?" he said, raising his head. "Not for me!"

She contemplated him, pensively. "Go on! I've understood . . . your father? Yes, your father! They had hearts of steel, the men of those days. But René, is a child responsible for the iniquity of his parents?"

"Yes," he replied, forcefully. "Bound by their glories, he is also bound by their sins."

"What a terrible philosophy!"

"A religious dogma, Marie. God has informed us of that himself."

"The ancient law . . ."

"The eternal law! Hereditary atavism, sharing the indefinite responsibility!"

They fell silent for a few moments.

"For a long time, I doubted it," said Monsieur de Mauréac. "Even now I doubt it still. But finally, I'm going to know . . . I want to . . . I have to know! Then, oh then, I'll confide my secret to you, and you, Mademoiselle, will decide my fate."

"What exaltation! You're making me tremble!"

"All my family have played pitilessly with human life. My ancestors, by virtue of a hereditary charge, were torturers of men. And my father! My father, more implacable than any of them! I'm afraid of myself."

"My God! What are you counting on doing, then?"

"Perhaps entering religion: to expiate myself a family crime as yet unexpiated, and to annihilate forever the name of Mauréac, soiled with blood."

He seized the young woman's arms and drew her toward him. "But you, Marie, whatever might happen, receive my oath! At the foot of the cross, or at your knees, I swear to love you—always, always, always!"

"And I," replied Marie-Thérèse, becoming excited in unison, "will not let you escape me, even at the foot of the cross! What does your family history matter to me? Is it the titles of our ancestors that I'm marrying in you? No, it's you—you alone, my beloved. It's you, my dear husband!"

Then, in a surge of reckless passion, René de Mauréac wrapped his arms around the waist of the adored woman, and clasped her to his heart for a long, long time. Shivering, the young woman finally pulled away, and, very pale, fled from the room.

"Oh, my friend," cried René. "Happiness doesn't kill; otherwise, I'd have died at her feet."

The arrival of Monsieur Le Barze cut short those effusions; Marie-Thérèse came back in with him.

"Doctor," she said to me, smiling, "it's me who wants to be his physician henceforth . . . and I shall be able to cure him, that poor suffering friend, by means of amour."

"So the peace is made!" added Monsieur Le Barze, having become joyful again. "In that case, my children, let's go to the galgal now!"


## XIV

The daylight was already in decline. Rapidly, we crossed the lawn in order to pass under the branches of a long avenue of fir trees, and came to a halt on the strand.

Before us a low mound rose up, built by human hands, of transported earth and stones, one of the tumuli that Celtic archeologists call galgals. A dense vestment of grass, moss and ivy covered it with verdure. Constructed on the edge of the river, it extended its mass as far as the tide-line, and for a long time the big equinoctial waves had been eroding its base.

Beyond it, the broad depths of a marvelous landscape were deployed. The Loch d'Auray, having reached its mouth, mingled its rapid deposits there with the miry waters of the Morbihan and the estuary, "the little sea of Morbihan," extended its undulating sheet as far as the eye could see. Numerous islets—more than three hundred—emerged from the tumultuous marshes of that interior sea, including the Île des Moines, populated by granite masses brought from far away, which had been able to stand for centuries, the mysterious industry of humans who were still even more mysterious; the Île d'Arz, swept by the winds, so ravaged by Death that all the women there wear her colors and dress in mourning; and, further out to sea, the narrow reef of Gavrinnis, which filled in its funerary mount, its sepulchral mountain, entirely: an emblem of Life launching forth from the abyss, the daughter of Death.

Facing us, on the opposite shore of the river, the thatched roofs of Locmariaquer were displayed in the sea mist, an old necropolis where so many humans of the Stone Age had wanted to be buried, as if to have their eternal slumber lulled by the eternal lamentation of the ocean. Finally, on the horizon, confused with the hummocks of the dunes, the strangled pass of Port Navale appeared, and in the distance the green immensity of the Atlantic.

We were impatiently awaited around the tumulus. The Reverend Powell, very angry but still full of cant, was taking out his watch every quarter of an hour and looking the captain in the eyes. "Time is money," he grumbled. For his part, Henri Le Barze riposted to the adage of Yankee wisdom with a few good oaths of the best Algerian vintage. As for the diggers, they had set down their tools and, lying on the grass, were gazing at a point on the horizon, arguing. In the distance, in fact, in the great expanse of the ocean, a thick trail of black smoke could be seen drifting between the sky and the sea.

"What's that, my friend?" asked the captain, while Monsieur Le Barze was apologizing for our long delay.

"That, Monsieur," replied a workman, "is the *Saint-Yves*, the steamboat coming back from Belle Isle. It's going to enter the Port Navale pass."

Henri Le Barze lit a cigar and addressed his father. "There's the boat, already, that is bringing the actors of the Folies-Comiques back to us. Up in flames, my plans for this evening's concert! I won't be able to get back to Auray until much too late."

"They won't get there before nightfall themselves," observed one of the men.

René de Mauréac turned his eyes toward the murky swirls of smoke and, drawing away from Marie-Thérèse, he headed toward the strand.

"*Sursum corda!*" cried Monsieur Le Barze. "Let's begin!"

At that appeal, the workmen stood up, picked up their tools, and grouped around the galgal.

"To the east! Let's attack the tumulus from the eastern side," commanded the clergyman Powell. "It's facing toward the nascent dawn that the Bushmen, those survivors of simian humankind, bury their dead. To the east; dig to the east."

"To the west!" riposted Monsieur Le Barze. "The west is the cardinal point preferred by the Aryans. Study their progressive migrations. Westwards, always westwards."

The conflict between the scholars, both very excited, was threatening to become envenomed. Captain Henri was greatly amused by that learned quarrel; in the meantime the bewildered diggers leaned on their spades, listening.

In the distance, the *Saint-Yves* had crossed the mouth of the Morbihan, and now, cutting across the estuary, was advancing toward us at full steam. Motionless, René watched it approaching.

"Come on, my dear little Father," said Marie-Thérèse, coaxing the old archeologist. "A little abnegation. Let's give our guest the glory of a discovery."

"So be it!" replied Monsieur Le Barze, with an ill grace. "Let our friend commence—he won't find anything!"

On the indications of the Reverend Powell, the workmen attacked the tumulus from the east. Their picks struck the hillock in cadence, the debris thrown backwards, but no trace of a sepulcher appeared: not a single bone.

Suddenly, Monsieur de Mauréac approached swiftly. He seized a pick-ax and with a thrust of the arm, buried it in the earth.

"Bravo, René," said Monsieur Le Barze. "You too, bitten by the demon of archeology! A noble passion!"

Monsieur de Mauréac made no reply, but, bent over, he dug and dug, furiously. Each of us had abandoned our work and we all gathered around him. He was digging, still digging. Suddenly, there was a dull sound: something grated on the iron of the implement. The searcher stopped dead. He straightened and, green-tinged, shivering in every limb, he extended his arm toward the hole.

"Don't come any closer! No . . . no . . . ! There's nothing here . . . nothing there!"

But the Englishman had already thrown himself to the ground, and with his fingers and fingernails, he was scratching and sweeping.

"Hip, hip, Hurray!" exclaimed Monsieur Powell.

Then something terrible appeared to our eyes. It was a hideous skeleton, human debris frightful to behold. The wide-open mouth was filled, stuffed, with leaves and dry grass; the convulsed trunk was twisted upon itself, and the arms and legs were folded, braced against the soil as if they were trying to break the grip of their tomb. Shreds of cloth still dressed those lamentable remains; a few wisps of blonde hair were still adhering to the summit of the head.

"Oh, my God, what's that?" stammered Monsieur Le Barze, terrified.

"That," I said, taking the floor, "is the remains of a human being who lived in our days. Its inhumation is almost recent; the nature of the soil in which it reposes has preserved it almost intact."

I leaned over the skeleton and studied it for a few minutes.

"A woman, Messieurs, still young. Oh, but notice, there, near the sternum, that large rip. The woman has been murdered. And look, the position of the body proves to us that the unfortunate woman must have been buried alive."

"Yes, alive!" replied René de Mauréac's voice, like an echo.

A profound silence was established between us, and all of us, bent over the frightful object, looked at it.

At that moment, a confused rumor, bursts of laughter and joyful songs, rose from the river. The *Saint-Yves* had entered the Loch d'Auray, and following the line of buoys, was making its way along our bank. It was about to pass before the tumulus. Captain Henri, abandoning his position, ran to the shore.

"Pooh! I've had enough of your digging," he said. "Ah, here's something less funereal—our actors! They're cheerful!"

The artistes of the Folies-Comiques did, in fact, seem very cheerful. The landscape of Morbihan doubtless reminded them of all the poetry of a backcloth or a stage-set; they were singing nocturnes and barcaroles. One of them had intoned the rondeau of *Zampa*,[1] as the others, taking up the chorus, threw the well-known platitudes to the surroundings: "Tender youth, come to your boat, traverse the waves . . ."

At that sound, René de Mauréac, kneeling next to the skeleton of the woman, got to his feet slowly; slowly, he took a few steps toward the strand, and then he started to laugh.

The *Saint-Yves* was making rapid progress. It was now possible to make out every passenger on the deck: men in jackets and soft hats, women in traveling costume. Several of them had theater opera-glasses and were examining us curiously. Henri Le Barze, an habitué of the wings of the theater in Vannes, recognized them all and affected to name them:

---

1 Ferdinand Hérold's comic opera, first performed in 1831. The eponymous protagonist is a pirate; after placing a ring on the finger of a statue, which he accidentally animates, he attempts to marry a young woman he has demanded as a ransom; the animate statue fails to prevent the marriage, but soon drags Zampa down to hell, in an obvious parody of Mozart's *Don Giovanni*.

"There's the dugazon, a good girl" The ingénue, the vaporous Mademoiselle Pervenche! The déjazet, a bad little monkey. Hats off, Messieurs, to the noble father . . ."

Very calm and very dignified in the midst of the merrymaking troupe, wedged into his beautiful black frock-coat, Monsieur Guzman, the stage-manager and chevalier of the Order of Nicham was strolling. The tenor intoned his second verse, soon repeated in chorus: "To your voice the echo says, patience and constancy, for your turn will come one day."

With an abrupt movement, René de Mauréac resumed his march and only stopped when he reached the water's edge. The *Saint-Yves* was about to pass in front of us. The barcarole having finished, everything was silent aboard. Suddenly, the shrill voice of one of the actresses vibrated in the silence:

"Hey, Mignon-Chérie, pretty Mignon! Look over there! Your marquis!"

"Yes, yes!" cried ten other voices, "the marquis! Bonjour, Monsieur de Mauréac!"

And the boat went past.

I approached René, and could not repress a gesture of amazement. Pale, with a frightful pallor, his body thrown forward as if he were about to launch forth, his mouth agape and his eyes immeasurably wide, he watched the *Saint-Yves*, which was already plunging into the rising evening mist.

At that moment, Marie-Thérèse came to plant herself in front of him, quivering.

"So, Monsieur the Marquis de Mauréac, you've lied to me!"

She snatched the armoried ring from her finger—her engagement ring—and in a mordant voice, with a scornful smile on her lips, she said: "Take back your promise, Monsieur; you can go to rejoin the one that is claiming you!"

# XV

The autumn went by, and over the slumbering winter earth, according to the image of the old poet, "its mantle of wind, cold and rain" extended.[1]

Having returned to Paris, in the calm of my quotidian life, my work was advancing rapidly, and the good leaves of a first volume were already heaped on my table. While closing my ears to the noises from outside, however, I was very assiduous at the sessions of the scientific societies, and frequently took the floor there.

One day, when I had occupied the tribune of the Académie de Médecine and carried off my oratory success, I saw one of my colleagues running toward me, an assiduous auditor of our learned controversies. It was the young physician, Monsieur Cordier, whom I had once attached to the person of Lieutenant-General de Mauréac, and with whom I maintained amicable relations.

"My dear master," he said to me, "I looked for you a little while ago at the amusing ceremony at Saint Thomas Aquinas. You weren't there."

"What ceremony?"

"The marriage of Monsieur René de Mauréac, of course."

"He's married!" I cried, stupefied.

And as our conversation was troubling the silence of the Académie, I went out with my young colleague.

"What! He's married . . . and without informing me!" I repeated, utterly surprised.

"Doubtless he didn't dare to consult you, dear Master. But how could you be unaware of the news? All Paris has been occupied with it for a week."

I confessed without any shame that, a simple Parisian bourgeois, not a Wallachian, Yankee or Brazilian, I was not part of "All Paris." Monsieur Cordier took a morning newspaper from

---

1 The line is from "Le Printemps" by Charles, Duc d'Orléans (1394-1465)

his pocket, one of those rags that are absurd when they are not infamous, and which coin money with the scandals of the day.

"Read that note, then, Monsieur Cenobite," he said, handing it to me.

The note, almost an article, printed at the head of the Theater News under the signature Arlequin, was a truly impertinent redaction. It was thus conceived:

> *A marriage in the artistic world. Today will be celebrated at the church of Saint Thomas Aquinas, the union that we were the first to announce of one of our most scintillating stars of operetta with a gentleman bearing one of the great names of France. Monsieur le Marquis René de Mauréac is marrying Mademoiselle Mignon-Chérie, the adorable resident of the Théâtre des Folies-Comiques, well known in the city and even in the suburbs. Folies-Comiques if you wish, but in such an occurrence, it is certainly not the charming artiste who can be accused of criminal folly. Our compliments to the new marquise.*

"What do you say to that?" my young colleague went on, folding up the venomous sheet. "No prejudice, Monsieur le Marquis! Talk about old families finishing well!"

"Were there many people at the wedding?" I asked my moralist.

"No one from the family or friends, oh no! In any case, few invitations. On the other hand, the whole flock of Parisian theater-land. It was a hubbub, a charivari of the least edifying kind. People chatted and sniggered, and climbed on chairs in order to see better. I could have thought that I was at a café-concert, the Funambules or the Bal Mabille. Certainly, from the heights of Heaven, his last dwelling, the lieutenant-general . . ."

With that, my young friend, without finishing the classic text of Monsieur Scribe, shook my hand and went away.

I stood there, quite astounded. Was it possible? Not even invited to that wedding! A witness to oaths exchanged at Bruyère, had I become so odious, then, to Monsieur de Mauréac? Would my presence at that ignoble marriage have made him blush? Or rather, was the memory of Marie-Thérèse weighing upon his conscience like a remorse?

While talking to myself I had turned into the Rue Saint-Dominque. A long file of carriages was parked outside the Hôtel de Mauréac, and in the courtyard I perceived the animated coming and going of servants. Impelled by curiosity, I went in. Immediately, Monsieur Baptiste, the old concierge, came running toward me, lifting his arms.

"Oh, Monsieur . . . ! Oh, Doctor . . . ! What an adventure!"

"Yes, what an adventure, Monsieur Baptiste. And what a marriage!"

"Poor man!" the discreet servant contented himself with replying.

I was indecisive, not knowing what to do. Should I go away? Was it necessary, on the contrary, to go upstairs, to place myself in front of my forgetful friend abruptly, salute him silently and withdraw? I listened to that counsel of anger and I penetrated into the house.

The stairway, strewn with flowers, was decorated with shrubs in pots and rare plants. Joyous rumors and bursts of laughter arrived from the first floor, people were amusing themselves greatly and profusely up there. I went up. The doors were open and the drawing room was overflowing with people. Yes, my young friend had told the truth; the all and sundry of the little Parisian theaters had descended on the Hôtel de Mauréac. I spotted messieurs with clean-shaven faces, ladies with white-plastered faces illuminated with red. And the costumes! Velvet, satin, lace and diamonds! The dining room had been transformed into a buffet, and heaps of cakes and sandwiches were piled on a table, with bottles of Champagne, fish and galantines: a superb luncheon-diner! Everyone was feasting avidly, having a ball and uttering risqué quips between mouthfuls. I paraded my gaze around; Monsieur de Mauréac was not there.

The new marquise was in the drawing room, leaning against the fireplace; several of her friends surrounded her, forming a circle. It really was the same thin creature that I had glimpsed a year before, fainted on the boards of the Folies-Comiques: an insignificant face, ugly rather than pretty, the face of a grisette, the nose too short and the mouth too wide . . . but what admirable blonde hair! She was clad in her wedding dress, and beneath the lace of her veil, her face, laden with white make-up, stood out wanly, like that of a corpse. I approached her and saluted her; she scarcely inclined her forehead, doubtless absorbed by her thoughts. She seemed to me to be strangely nervous.

"Don't leave me!" she said to the friends who were surrounding her. "I'm afraid!"

"Come on, Marquise, come on, my Mignon-Chérie, you're not being reasonable," responded the handsome Monsieur Guzman, the stage-manager decorated by Nicham. "The bad quarter of an hour has passed . . . you know, the little ceremony at the church. People sniggered a little, it's true; one was slightly jeered, agreed, but are you any less a marquise? As for the rest . . ."

"I'm afraid," Madame de Mauréac repeated, invariably.

"Afraid of what?" demanded a tall young woman dressed up like a reliquary.

"Of him, Pervenche."

"Oh, that! Afraid of a man!" riposted Mademoiselle Pervenche, who pirouetted on her heels and headed for the buffet, where I followed her. In front of a glass of punch and a slice of *foie gras*, a young and pretty monsieur with a monocle screwed into his eye was shifting his weight from one foot to the other. Little actresses were smiling at him; others were pointing at him and naming him in a whisper: "That's Arlequin! You know, Arthur Dupont, who signs himself Arlequin, the one who writes the theater column in the *Jocrisse*." Mademoiselle Pervenche headed toward Monsieur Arlequin and tapped him on the shoulder familiarly.

"You know, my dear, it isn't polite, your piece this morning. Poor Mignon isn't content. On no, why did you have to say, like that 'well known throughout the city and even in the suburbs'? One doesn't defame little women like that."

"What about my conscience?" replied Monsieur Dupont, alias Arlequin, very solemnly.

"Your conscience? What are you doing here, then, Monsieur Virtue?"

"What about my profession?" responded Monsieur Arlequin again, swallowing another glass of punch.

In the crowd I also perceived my septuagenarian vaudevillian, one of the authors of *Pékin à Paris*, the celebrated Bon Papa. He bowed very humbly to the theater reporter, who extended his fingertips to him.

"Returned to the days when kings married shepherdesses," he said, indicating the marquise. "Poor child, how pale she is. What emotion!"

"This isn't a première for her, though," observed the reporter of the *Jocrisse*.

A burst of laughter saluted that new harlequinade.

"Anyway, why is she marrying?" muttered an old actress, painted vermilion like an aurora. "For nearly a year the kid and I have been making the tables turn every evening. Well, the spirits aren't reassuring. Yesterday again, they were advising against the marriage."

"Naughty spirits!" sniggered Monsieur Arlequin, with his mouth full.

"But that Mignon," the duenna went on, "didn't want to listen. To all our arguments she only had one response: 'It's necessary . . . it's necessary . . . !'"

"Bon Papa," Mademoiselle Pervenche interrupted, cutting through her comrade's mimicry, "what about your epithalamium?"

The old author paraded his gaze around, and then, with a chagrined expression: "A little more patience, Mesdames. The marquis hasn't returned yet."

"He's been preparing his entrance for two hours," said the duenna in a low voice. "A well-ordered household!"

"Time's going by and I'm performing this evening," declared Mademoiselle Pervenche. "Too bad, I'll risk it."

She ran to Madame de Mauréac. "Marquise! Petite! Will you authorize the audition of the epithalamium? Yes, you will? Let's go. One, two, three . . . curtain."

Monsieur Guzman, the stage manager, rapped three times on the parquet, and Bon Papa came to stand in the middle of the room; a noisy acclamation filled the house and extended outside. And from above, arranged against the wall in their crimson and ermine, the Presidents de Mauréac contemplated all that.

I noticed then that the lieutenant-general's portrait was no longer among them.

"What's the tune of your epithalamium?" asked the stage-manager, who had sat down at the piano.

"*La Robe et les Bottes*."[1]

"Old hat!" said Mademoiselle Pervenche, disdainfully.

"*Le Cid* has also become 'old hat,'" riposted the author, red with anger.

Everyone calmed down. Monsieur Guzman played a few chords on the piano, and the quavering voice of Bon Papa began to sing: "God of songs, Momus, take your bells . . ."

For myself, I had threaded my way to the door, and without taking my leave of Madame de Mauréac, I slipped away.


## XVI

I had already traversed the courtyard and I was about to leave the grounds when I heard myself called mysteriously. Baptiste, the concierge, was running after me.

"Monsieur le Marquis is asking for you," he said. "My master would be very glad to see you."

---

1 *La Robe et les bottes, ou un effect d'optique* (1810) is a vaudeville by Michel Dieulafoy and Nicolas Gersin.

"What? He's here, then?"

"Monsieur le Marquis retired to his apartment as soon as the ceremony was over." And the old domestic added, raising his arms to the heavens for a second time: "Oh, Doctor! The unfortunate man!"

I followed him. He guided me via a service stairway all the way to René's bedroom—the same bedroom where Lieutenant-General de Mauréac had lived his infirm and solitary life for such a long time.

Night had fallen and two lighted candles were barely illuminating the somber room, but a large fire was burning in the fireplace, the flames of which projected their glare, alternating with shadow, on the walls. Behind one of the doors, in the drawing room, the rumors of the fête were audible, and the tremulous voice of the old author sent us, at intervals, the couplets of his epithalamium.

Monsieur de Mauréac was stretched out in an armchair near the fire, under the portrait of his father. That portrait was now in his bedroom, suspended between two superb panoplies. Those trophies were rare weapons: naval officers' sabers, Japanese swords, Annamite daggers, Javan krises, and, in the one on the left, shining against the wall, a magnificent khanjar in a silver sheath.

On seeing me, René inclined his head and invited me to sit near him.

"Thank you for your kind visit," he said, rather solemnly. "You, at least, haven't imitated the others, who seem to be treating this house as a leper colony."

"I was unaware of your marriage," I replied, in a piqued tone. "You had forgotten to inform me."

"Forgotten? No . . . but what was the point of consulting you? You would doubtless have lavished me with advice, remonstrations, objurgations, threats . . . how do I know? And I wouldn't have listened to any of it—no, none. I had to get married, to marry that woman . . . yes, marry her. It was necessary . . . it was necessary!"

Mauréac fell silent momentarily.

"Don't believe, at least," he went on, "that I'm the victim of feminine wiles, the imbecilic dupe of some coquette's intrigue. No, thank God, I have a solid mind and a highly-placed heart. My dear, even she didn't want this marriage. You refuse to believe me? She didn't want it! Oh, it wasn't without a struggle that she consented to be my wife. She disdained my amour; she rejected my name. But in the end, war-weary, she gave in. I triumphed over her resistance . . . and now she's mine, only mine!"

A dolorous sob escaped his breast.

"Yes, she's mine," he cried, "and yet she doesn't love me. But I love her madly with a furious desire . . . desperately! Why . . . why? Everyone tells me that she's ugly, devoid of intelligence and vicious! Vicious! No matter, I love her and I'm jealous of her . . . jealous . . . jealous!"

He got up and paced back and forth in the room, agitatedly. Out there, behind the door, in the drawing room in fête, the piano fell silent; now the old man of letters was declaiming a madrigal; each of its verses reached us quite clearly.

> *When Venus, escaped from the cold kisses of the wave,*
> *By wringing her hair created the rivers and streams,*
> *If the amorous blonde had seen your blonde tress,*
> *She would not have dared to emerge from her cradle.*

Monsieur de Mauréac stamped his foot, went white with anger, and turned toward me.

"Oh, I can read your thought and I've understood your gaze! I ought, according to you, to have spared the glories of my name, the memory of my father . . . the memory of my father! . . . the ignominies of such a fête! Yes, certainly; if I had listened to my desires, on emerging from the church, I would have taken the beloved far away . . . far away . . . to the land, if there is one on earth, where one loves forever! With what happiness, enveloping her in my arms, I would have hidden her from all eyes! But no, I couldn't; I had to stay here. I'm fighting a duel tomorrow."

I got up in my turn.

"What are you saying, René?"

He made me sit down again, and came to stand in front of me.

"I'm saying that I'm fighting a duel tomorrow. It was fatal. For a fortnight, all affronts and all outrages have been pouted upon my wife in a cowardly fashion. This morning, a filthy newspaper, a blackmail rag has grossly insulted the marquise . . ."

He showed me, displayed on a table, the prose of the pretty Monsieur Dupont.

"Once, one would have thrashed the poltroon, the author of such ignominies, but today the rod is no longer in fashion, and as for my sword, I wouldn't soil it with the saliva of a Monsieur Arlequin. No, in order to impose respect and silence on everyone, I've been obliged to choose my adversary, and I've chosen. He's a soldier, an officer like me. I'm fighting a duel with Monsieur Henri Le Barze."

"Captain Henri!"

"The same. The Le Barzes, petty provincial bourgeois, coveted my title of marquis; they wanted to decorate themselves with the heritage of my family. You know them . . . that demoiselle Marie-Thérèse, a young woman who makes verses and speaks Greek? I was occupied with her, it's true; I even courted her a little . . . perhaps too much. But from there to a marriage, an entire abyss. Well, those honest folk, chagrined, have found it amusing to play a scene from Molière, the little scene of the forced marriage; they sent me the brother. Here, read what this braggart has dared to write to me this morning . . ."

He handed me a letter signed Henri Le Barze, which only contained two lines:

> *Monsieur,*
>
> *I happen to be in Paris and I have learned from a newspaper of your glorious marriage. Your conduct is that of a clown.*

"On receipt of that epistle," Mauréac continued, "I didn't hesitate. The captain of turcos must pay for all of them. I accepted his challenge and sent him my witnesses. Agreement has been reached and tomorrow, at eight o'clock, we're fighting. I didn't want to wait another day to chastise an insolent for all the insolences."

He had become very calm again, and had resumed his place by my side. I remained silent, my heart wrung by anguish. The discourteous, almost indecent fashion in which he spoke about poor Marie-Thérèse revolted me. As for the duel with the brother, it seemed to me to be abominable. At all costs, I had to prevent it. But how? A sudden idea sprang to my mind . . . I had found it!"

"This combat is impossible," I said, coldly.

"Impossible! Why? It will take place tomorrow, in the Bois de Clamart, with pistols, fifteen places and aimed. I shall kill the man."

"Or the man will kill you."

"Well then, my dear and sweet marquise will know how much I love her."

"How much you love her? And you want to condemn her, scarcely married, to be a widow?" I paused. "A widow . . . and free," I added, slowly

With an abrupt start, René stood up. "A widow and free!" he cried. "What do you mean? Damn it, I understand you. A widow and free!"

He resumed his march, with a jerky step, across the room.

"So, no more duel, René. The affair can be arranged. I'll take charge of it."

He made no response, and continued his silent march; sometimes, he stopped, and exhaled a sigh: "A widow and free!" Finally, the fever appeared to calm down, and Mauréac came to sit down beside me.

"I'll arrange everything," he told me. And, smiling: "No, the marquise will neither be a widow, nor free."

Joyous outbursts of voices coming from the drawing room cut into our conversation. The Bon Papa was intoning a drinking song, and everyone was repeating his refrains in chorus:

*Sing, old wine; women, laugh jolly*
*Crazy are those who aren't in their folly!*

René bounded, exasperated.

"Adieu, Victor. I'm going to throw all those people out."

He launched himself toward the drawing room and opened the door violently. A confused clamor greeted his appearance.

"Here he is . . . ! Here he is . . . ! Finally!"

Standing next to the singer, Madame de Mauréac was chatting at that moment with one of her comrades. At the noise, she turned round; and suddenly, throwing herself backward, she uttered a piercing scream. René marched straight toward her. Then, recoiling step by step, the young woman went to huddle, shivering, in the most distant corner of the drawing room.

Monsieur de Mauréac caught up with her and stood there for a moment, contemplating her. Then he stretched out an arm, seized her hand, drew her to his lips and deposited a long kiss on hers.

Bravos burst forth from all sides, and jovial laughter applauded that little amorous comedy.


## XVII


My day was lost to work. I therefore resigned myself, on quitting the house in the Rue Saint-Dominique, to making various visits deferred for a long time. I was invited to dinner in a friend's house; I succeeded, however, in escaping quite quickly and I returned home at about nine o'clock.

To my great surprise, I found, deposited on the table in my study, a package sealed with the Mauréac arms, which had been brought during my absence. I opened it; it contained a large envelope closed with five black seals, and my anxiety increased when I read on the envelope these few words:

*To be read without delay and thrown into the fire if I am killed tomorrow. The explanation of my marriage with Anne-Yvonne Gallo. René.*

Anne-Yvonne Gallo! And the packet dropped from my fingers. What! That woman was not called "Mademoiselle Chérie," and that name was only a pseudonym, a stage name? Naïve imbecile that I was not to have suspected it! Anne-Yvonne Gallo, the neophyte in the house of Elias, the magnetic subject! But then, what was the frightful and mysterious power of that man? "You will follow her step by step in her life," he had ordered . . . "You will love her, you will love her, pitilessly rejected by her . . . until the day when you will take her for a companion, for a wife . . ." And everything, yes, everything, had just been accomplished!

I remained confounded for long moments, stupefied, no longer believing in myself, almost disposed to tear up my work, henceforth futile. No, never had I experienced such cruel anxieties!

That evening, contrary to my habitude, I had to go out. There was an intimate reception at the Ministry of Public Education, and I feared that my absence would be remarked. Nevertheless, before putting on my black coat, I still had an hour of solitude before me, and I resolved to take advantage of it. I shut myself away in my library and, placing the armoried package on a table, in the light of my lamp, I broke the seals of black wax.

A wad of loose sheets escaped from the envelope; it was a journal written entirely in the hand of René de Mauréac. It was undated, without any mention of the day, or even the year. But my astonishment immediately changed into a veritable fear; this is what my eyes had perceived at the head of the first page:

> *Seen at Ben Tré in the house on the arroyo. Seen again more clearly during the funeral vigil, near my father's body.*

Then, evoking an even more recent past, I remembered. I recalled my terrors of the preceding year: The Hôtel de Mauréac in mourning, the deserted staircase, the large drawing room, so vast in the night. And again I head, behind the closed door, the desperate moans, the angry words, and then the long and lugubrious silence. Was that, then, the moment when, in a formidable confrontation between the living and the dead, the journal had been written? I sensed a frisson of fear running through my veins.

When my emotion had calmed down slightly, I began reading the strange manuscript.

. . . . . . . . . . . . . . . . . . . . . . . . . . . . . . . . . . . . . . . . . . . .

Ben Tré, my new residence for three days. Oh, the horrible place, with its bamboo piles plunged into the mud of the Mekong! The shivering of the fevers, the Annamite dysentery gnawing at your entrails! Everywhere the gaze can extend, the yellow waters of the great river and the ice-fields, from which a host of green plants emerges, variegated with scarlet. The "wintering season" has commenced. The sky is leaden; and atrocious heat sets fire to your head and burns your blood. And it rains, and rains Under the torrents of water that fall from the clouds, the earth foams and seems to be boiling. Ennui overwhelms me, and I sense the first symptoms of nostalgia. Yes, this is my last campaign. Before long, the return to the homeland, and afterwards, the marriage so much desired. O Marie, dear Marie-Thérese, it's always toward you that my thought flies, toward you that my desires are borne!

And my father? Let's get rid of that image. Why, then, for some time, whenever I think about my father, do bizarre ideas come to assail and torment my heart. My father! As far as the memories of my life go back, I always see him the same, nailed to his armchair by an unknown disease, his head inclined, his eyes extinct, never speaking. Is his thought dead and is his tongue truly enchained? No, he can talk . . . he talks! Many a time, watching near him while he sleeps—and what frightful slumbers are his!—I've surprised words among the murmurs of his lips.

Why those words, always the same? "Noël, France and honor!" He has vague memories of his old feats of arms. Often, he sees again "the Breton heath, the desolate fields, the muddy river, the bellowing sea." And he hears . . . he hears the bird cries of the night of the Chouans, clamors of hatred, and also desperate sobs. He speaks of "a deserted house and a beloved woman," perhaps too beloved . . . of a . . . oh no, I haven't head anything! Deliria of an old man, without doubt; thoughts that are buried in childhood! Why does that God, whose soldier he was, for whom he wanted to fight and suffer, not finally grant him the grace of deliverance, the benefit of death?

. . . . . . . . . . . . . . . . . . . . . . . . . . . . . . . . . . . . . . . . . . . . . . . . .

My orderly has just come in; he's brought me the mail from Saigon, my official correspondence. Nothing important . . . Ah! a circular from the Admiral-Governor. Very amusing, that circular; a whole diatribe, a veritable anathema launched against opium.

What magnificent prose! "The substance that distills folly . . . the poison that extends over intelligence the night of the tomb . . ." They are, my word, literate in the grand style, Messieurs the official writers in the bureaux of Cochinchina. What a draconian penalty! Withdrawal of employment for an officer smoking opium, demotion to sub-officer; sixty days in prison for a soldier. That's too harsh, much too harsh. Isn't it cruel to punish thus the poor people whom military service sends to die in these accused climes, and who, in the enervation of their solitude, strive to evoke the dream of absent beloveds? Furthermore, a waste of paper. There isn't, so far as I know, any opium smoking in my command at Ben Tré . . .

What if I'm mistaken, though? Yesterday, while exploring the environs of my new residence, I glimpsed in the distance, hiding under the bamboos on the edge of an arroyo, a house of sinister aspect. A yellow paper lantern, its sign, denounces it to passers-by—it's an opium den. I'll have it put under surveillance . . .

Opium! A literate Chinaman I knew in Shanghai said to me: "What would the earth be without the flower, the flower without the perfume, the perfume without the essence, the essence without the poison?" He also said: "What would life be worth without the ideal, the ideal without the dream, the dream without opium?" A philosopher scarcely sensible to the realities of down here, my friend the Chinese literate.

Is he so very wrong? It's affirmed that under the action of opium the human creature is doubled, that the spirit, freed from matter, launches itself toward infinity, no longer knowing the extent of space or the heavy immobility of time: all the chains of our miserable life. He sees, he hears, he understands, he knows . . . O Marie-Thérèse, dear beloved, so far away and yet still so near . . . Yes, but it's also recounted that the proof is terrible, that the blissful dream is sometimes succeeded by atrocious visions, and that even the terrors of death are less cruel than the anguish of the new dream . . . What does it matter? Has another sage not said: Suffering provoked and voluntary is also a voluptuousness . . . ?

. . . The rain has stopped, but the day is declining. Before night, the twilight-less night of the tropics, falls abruptly, let's go out; I want to refresh my blood, burned by fever, in the sea breeze. The sky is implacable; not a breath of air, not a ripple on the waters . . .

Damn! I've gone astray and night has suddenly taken me by surprise. Along in the narrow causeway that snakes and ramifies among the arroyos, I've lost my way . . . What's that house that I

104

glimpse over there? Why does it seem to be hiding, mysteriously, in this solitude . . . ? Ah, I recognize it. Above the door, the yellow paper lantern. It's here . . . it's the accursed house, the opium den! Let's pass on . . . quickly, let's pass on . . .

. . . I thought I was alone; I was mistaken. Furtive shadows glide in front of me, plunging under the awning of the cagna and disappearing. The wretches! Oh my God, but where am I myself? How have I followed them? What force has pushed me this far? O human liberty, superb phrase, which human pride repeats relentlessly, if you really exist, what insoluble problem are you, then? Certainly, this morning, I was scarcely thinking about the intoxications of opium . . . why were they forbidden to me?

. . . A sordid hovel; ignominies of dirt and stench! The room is dark, scarcely illuminated by the smoky redness of a candle. No one is looking at me, no one is paying any attention to me. Strange scents rise to my brain; an insipid and sickly odor, like that of melting caramel. In a corner of the room, however, I can distinguish a young Annamite boy sitting at a table; he looks at me brazenly and salutes me, In front of him are scales, a heap of shells and a jar in which a viscous jelly in trembling. "*Mossé!* Silver weights against weights of opium." I throw him a piaster; the boy puts it in the pan of his balance, takes a shell, fills it and weighs it. I seize the opium; I have it, the dream . . . !

. . . In the shadow, a hand has posed on my arm; I'm guided. A curtain moves aside; I'm in another room now. Total silence, but plenty of people. Against the wall is a bed, and mats framed by curtains form as many alcoves. On the mats are the smokers, and beside each man, a woman. "Mossé Mossé!" Someone's calling me. One of the women, some Annamite prostitute, beckons me to approach. She's hideous to see, with her wrinkled yellow face and her skin pitted by filthy scars. "Mossé! Mossé!" She's raised herself up on one elbow and is smiling at me; I perceive with disgust her long teeth blackened by betel. Oh, it's ignoble! What if I were to run away from this place?

". . . Mossé, someone's going to take your place!" I've lain down on the mat next to the woman. She's holding a bamboo pipe; she takes a steel needle and plunges it into the opium twice; her hand extends the paste over the bowl of the pipe, lights a little lamp and presents it to me.

I try to give her a piaster; she refuses. "No money, opium!" With what bitter desire and what ardor of covetousness she pronounced that word: *opium!* Pooh! The noxious drug! Come on, come on! A little energy! Let's shake off this torpor! Let's escape this stinking steam-bath . . .

. . . . . . . . . . . . . . . . . . . . . . . . . . . . . . . . . . . . . . . . . . . .

. . . Ah! The sea breeze has just risen! Finally! Its warm frissons have wrinkled the motionless waters and its caress has glided lightly over my face. What freshness, what repose, what ineffable enervation of myself! Through the open windows all the scents of April arrive in gusts; the garden is exhaling the perfumes of its lilacs and its violets. Marie-Thérèse, darling beloved, let's lean on this balcony . . .

Look, the moon is deploying her pallor over the odorous lawn; the splendor of her rays seems to be diamond-tinting the green needles of the fir-wood, and out there, in the depths of the mysterious pathway, look, the waves are scintillating like moving crystal . . . Come closer, my friend . . . close to me . . . closer still. Place your forehead on my shoulder, abandon your hand to mine; and now, silently, let's listen to the great silence of the night talking. Let's plunge our two beings into the voluptuous harmony of that dormant nature. Allow your soul and mine, confounded, to be annihilated in an indescribable ecstasy! Lulled by the languor of these enchanting evening, let's savor the great amour, the great happiness, the great repose . . .

. . . A gust of glacial wind has curbed the quivering crowns of the larches. The north wind is moaning; the leaves, burned by the frost, are detaching and dying! Snow! The lawn, so flowery just now, deploys its long shroud all the way to the blackness of the sister forest; under the moon's rays, the fir-wood shines, powdered with frost, and out there, at the extremity of the frightening pathway, the dull murmur of ice-floes rises, carried away by the ebb-tide, which the flux is bringing back to batter the strand. April has passed so soon for us, my love, and December has fallen upon us so rapidly . . .

. . . The sound of a bell traverses space at that moment—the Christmas bell: midnight mass. How soft and melancholy that distant voice is, singing *Venite adoremus*. The chimes arrive more rapidly; the voice, more sonorous, becomes urgent; it implores, it appeals, it commands: *Venite, venite, adoremus!* No . . . the sound is weakening, decreasing, dying . . . silence! Let's close that window, Marie; the winter wind has chilled me. Let's get closer to that fire, the joyous flames of which are illuminating my room . . . God! Where are you, then, my love? How have you escaped from my arms, impalpable phantom . . . light mist?

. . . I'm not alone in the room. A man, sitting in the armchair, is warming himself at the brands in the fireplace; he's agitated, nervous, impatient. At times, his eyes interrogate the clock and he stamps his feet in anger. He has got up and gone to the window, on the lookout, listening. He stands there, close to me, almost touching me . . . and he hasn't perceived me! For him, I'm invisible, incorporeal, a void in space, nothing.

He . . . oh, it's my father! My father? Yes, but still young and exactly similar to the portrait of him that I know so well. How handsome he is, my father, with his pale face, his brilliant eyes, his black hair, his slim figure and the elegant vigor of his entire body! Arrogant, superb, and so disdainful . . . ! Now he's striding back and forth in the room with a jerky step, stopping, resuming his march, very anxious. Sometimes, he opens a little door fitted in the woodwork; he smiles and makes an amicable gesture. A murmur of stifled voices, whispering, is audible behind the door . . . Men are hidden there!

. . . Someone has just come in: a woman . . . she isn't pretty; very young, but paltry and sickly; very simply dressed. Her stance is modest and her manner fearful; half-peasant and half-bourgeois . . . oh, what superb blonde hair! It shines, like gold, under a white bonnet . . .

My father has gone toward the woman rapidly.

"Anne-Yvonne! At last!"

He takes her by the hand and returns to sit down in his armchair. The woman remains standing: so humble, so timid . . . ! With what passion she is contemplating my father! She speaks; her voice is drawling and nasal, her language vulgar and incorrect, like that of a country girl.

"You summoned me, my tender seigneur; here I am! However, I have a very sick child in the house, and the bell will invite me to midnight mass shortly. But alas, what do my child and the salvation of my soul matter to me? I love you, my dear seigneur . . . oh, I love you!

. . . My father has paled slightly and he suppresses a frisson.

"Yes, I know . . . I know! I too, my poor Yvonnette, I love you . . . very much."

"Not enough! Oh, if I could die for you!"

. . . She puts herself on her knees before him, putting her hands together . . . My father turns away and says nothing . . . Finally, smiling, and in a tender voice: "Let's reserve the words of love, darling, for another rendezvous . . . what I have to say to you at the moment is too serious . . . I'm going to risk my life!

. . . The woman, still on her knees, looks at my father anxiously

"Jesus! You're frightening me, my beloved seigneur!"

. . . He goes on: "For two days, in order to avoid the ice-floes in the river, the *Albatros* has been changing position; she's been brought closer to the coast, and is no more than a cable away from the shore. Anne-Yvonne, how many soldiers are there on the pontoon?"

. . . Very pale, the woman stands up and starts to tremble.

"Monsieur Gallo, dear seigneur . . . Captain Gallo, my husband, commands forty men.

"I knew that; I have the names of the sailors and the soldiers. But tonight, Christmas Eve, there won't be twenty-five on the *Albatros*. Half the men are on land, without permission and on the spree: midnight mass, and then the tavern until dawn for them; the other half will be celebrating with eau-de-vie, probably all dead drunk. Thus, scarcely twenty-five argonauts, in their cups . . . and more than fifty prisoners. Englishmen, yes . . . but also Frenchmen, and among them, a number of my friends, my relatives: noblemen, seigneurs—your messieurs! They're awaiting their judgment and will be shot . . . do you understand? Shot!"

"Undoubtedly, my dear seigneur, since they had taken up arms and were combating in English uniforms."

. . . My father has retained an angry gesture; he gets up in his turn.

"Listen, Yvonnette, and understand. You're intelligent, almost a lady; you must understand. The events are grave. The king—your king—is going to return to Paris. The other, the usurper, the Corsican, Bonaparte, is beaten; his last army has been wiped out at Leipzig; three hundred thousand allies of Louis XVIII are in France at this moment; before long, the white flag will be floating over the Tuileries. But it's necessary that all the faithful come running with the same surge, Personally, I've received from my princes the order to act, to form Georges' old bands again and to rouse Bretagne; I must obey. They have sent me, at the same time, a colonel's brevet. Well, I want to merit my rank and earn my epaulettes. Tonight, I'm stealing the *Albatros*; I'm delivering my friends, and tomorrow, at their head, I'm throwing myself into the heath. You'll come to join me there."

. . . The woman shakes her head.

"No, dear seigneur, for I'm not a trollop, a whore who runs the high roads. I won't come."

. . . My father has bitten his lip and is having great difficulty containing the anger that is overtaking him; his voice is less tender, his tone drier.

"So be it! You'll stay at home, but now, it's necessary for you to prove your love to me. You know, undoubtedly, the password that will permit us to board the pontoon? You're remaining silent . . . yes, you know it. You're going to tell me . . . better still, you'll come with me. I have friends here, in my park, good local lads, true Bretons devoted to God. With them, we'll climb into a boat. You'll place yourself at the prow, clearly in sight. We'll row, approach without making a sound. At the first 'Who goes there?' you'll summon Captain Gallo, your husband . . . you'll cry to him that his child is dead and that you've come to find him. Then we'll board . . . then, '*Vive le roi!*' Then, the *Albatros* is ours."

Yvonne Gallo has gone paler still . . . but she has raised her head, her eyes are shining and she starts to laugh.

"Really! You're very cruel, my dear seigneur!"

"Anne-Yvonne!"

"Yes, yes . . . I know in my turn. Anne-Yvonne is a wanton, a creature, a hussy whom no one respects any longer. Well, Monsieur, listen to me. I've betrayed for you the love of a gallant man; I've surrendered to you his honor as a husband . . . but God hear me, I won't surrender to you his honor as a soldier."

. . . Each of those words causes my father's face to redden. The woman has looked him in the face, disdainfully, even provocatively . . . and now Anne-Yvonne bows her head; tottering, she leans against the wall; a sob lifts her breast; she weeps.

"Oh! Wretch! He didn't love me!"

. . . But almost immediately, she wipes away her tears.

"Adieu, Monsieur. I'm returning to my sick child."

. . . She heads for the door. In two bounds, my father has got there ahead of her. He bars her path, closes the door, locks it and takes out the key.

"You're my prisoner, Yvonne Gallo!"

"Let me go, Monsieur . . . I want to go!"

. . . My father seizes her by the arm and drags her brutally into the middle of the room.

"The password, Anne-Yvonne!"

"I don't know it!"

"You're lying! Every evening, since your son fell ill, your husband confides the password to you, in order that you can go to warn him if the child is in danger . . . you told me so yourself."

. . . The woman emits a burst of furious laughter.

"And that's why you've suborned me! Monsieur de Mauréac, you have no honor!

. . . My father shrugs his shoulders; then, in a loud voice: "My honor . . . is my king!"

. . . With an abrupt movement. Yvonne Gallo has pulled free. She runs to the door and shakes it furiously. The door resists. "Oh, the coward, the coward!" She launches herself toward the window, but suddenly stops, frightened . . . men have just slid behind her. They take possession of her and shove her back into the room. What sinister bandits! They have deformed the features of their faces with silk masks and have pulled down their broad-brimmed hats. The whites of their eyes stand out, terrifying, against the blackness of those bestial faces . . . Yvonne Gallo, mouth agape, rolls terrified gazes over those men, sweat pearling on her brow, and a cry escapes her lips: "The Chouans!"

. . . One of the men approaches Monsieur de Mauréac, and in a very familiar manner, says: "You won't go to the end alone, Sans-Pareil . . . we'll help you."

. . . The bandits heap up dry heather and straw in the fireplace. The flame springs forth, and a bright light illuminates the room . . . Yvonne Gallo has understood.

"Jesus! My God . . . they're going to burn me!"

. . . The men start joking.

"It's a good night to take the chill off, my girl. A nice Noël fire!"

. . . One of the Chouans, a short and thickset fellow with an evil face speaks to her: "You don't know me, Anne-Yvonne, but I know you. Your old man, Captain Gallo, tortured me relentlessly when I was on Belle Isle, among the refractories. Two years ago, the executioner struck me with his cane . . . I'm getting my revenge."

"Yes, yes, Mâche-Balles is right," clamor the others; "her husband is an executioner. Let's avenge ourselves!"

. . . They lift up the woman, who resists; they force her to sit in an armchair, and push it toward the fire. Monsieur de Mauréac, as white as a shroud, comes forward.

"In the name of Heaven, Anne-Yvonne, give us the password and you're free!"

She looks him up and down, haughty and scornful. "Coward! Miserable coward! And that's a colonel, that!"

. . . Monsieur de Mauréac goes on: "For pity's sake . . . pity for you, for me, I implore you . . ."

. . . But one of the men, the deserter from the penitentiary, cuts him off and says, very insolently: "Enough, kind heart! When one doesn't have the bravery that civil war demands . . . one doesn't have it!"

. . . My father tries to protest; he's insulted.

"My friends, what you're going to do is infamous . . . yes, infamous."

. . . Clamors drown out his voice.

"Shut up, Sans-Pareil . . . or sing something else."

"I'm in command here!"

"Obey first!"

"I'm your leader!"

"Not yet . . . we need a pledge!"

. . . My father falls silent, alas. He has surrendered her. Alas, alas! That is it, then, his pledge.

With a violent shove, the Chouans have pushed Yvone Gallo against the flame. Two men press down hard upon the miserable creature's shoulders; the others extend her legs into the fire, all the way to the knees. Anne-Yvonne utters a terrible scream. She resists; she writhes; it's frightful and it's ignoble . . . Odors of burned flesh and wool spread through the room. The men start joking.

. . . Between two screams, the unfortunate woman begs: "Jesus! Jesus! They're going to kill me! Mercy, my good messieurs, mercy! You're not wicked, you! No, no . . . I don't recognize you . . . I swear it! I haven't recognized you . . . ! God! God! Let me go . . . I have a sick child, so ill! There are some among you who have children. And then, remember your mothers, when you were very small . . . Ah! Ah . . . ! I'm dying: a priest! 'France and honor!' Bandits . . . ! Bandits . . . ! Bandits . . . !"

"Enough!" commands Monsieur de Mauréac. "We have the password: 'France and Honor!' Now let her go."

"No," ripostes Mâche-Balles. "Now, take her to the strand."

. . . Out there, at the extremity of the avenue of firs, the waves are unfurling over the shore; the tide is rising, and in the silence of the icy night, her voice moans more lamentably still. The moon is veiled, as if in mourning; the sky seems to be posing on the sea, all heavy with snow, and in the grayness of the moving mists. The mast-less pontoon can be glimpsed: the *Albatros*. There is no light aboard, and no sound. Sometimes, a big wave strikes its side; then it rises up, the wood creaks, and the *Albatros* launches a savage cry to the wind.

. . . Here come the men, the Chouans. They emerge from the depths of the fir-wood and stop on the strand. Near the shore there is a hillock, a mound all white with frost; the troop goes to huddle in the mystery of its shadow . . . They place a burden on the ground: the unconscious woman . . . and then hold council. One of them separates from the group, goes into the water and brings back a boat moored nearby.

"Anne-Yvonne! Anne-Yvonne!"

Snow is thrown into her face . . . She opens her eyes, looks, remembers, and tries to flee. Heavily, she falls back to the ground. Her feet are nothing but wounds . . . the flame has penetrated the bones . . . Monsieur de Mauréac has leaned over her; his face brushes that of the woman, who turns her head and repels him with her fist.

"Anne-Yvonne, I beg you, help us! Anne-Yvonne, you'll be rich, very rich . . . if you want, half my fortune is yours!"

She replies to him with the same scornful laughter as before.

"Yes, yes, my beloved seigneur . . . yes, handsome colonel . . . I'll help you!"

She pulls free . . . crawls over the snow . . . reaches the boat . . . clings on to it, and then, in a vibrant voice: "France and honor! Beware, Gallo! The Chouans!"

. . . Nothing budges aboard the *Albatros*; they have not heard . . . and suddenly, the gleam of steel blade has glistened in the night, a knife has come down; the woman has fallen.

"Ah! They've killed me . . . filthy dogs!"

. . . Oh, that's not my father! That's not my father . . . ! He is kneeling down; he lifts the head of the dying woman; he's weeping . . . and the agonizing woman, whose hand has just been moistened by a tear, turns extinguishing eyes toward the weeping man and very softly, between two gasps, says to him: "I'm dying for you, Monsieur . . . and I'm in a state of mortal sin! Will God want to pardon me? Myself, I pardon you . . . only remember that little Yvonnette is leaving behind a little child."

. . . . . . . . . . . . . . . . . . . . . . . . . . . . . . . . . . . . . . . . . .

The journal had a lacuna at this point. The end of the abominable drama was not related: the burial under the galgal of Anne-Yvonne, still breathing, still alive. Nor did the story say how the blonde tress had been cut by Monsieur Charles de Mauréac, bewildered and perhaps also threatened with death himself. But Colonel Sans-Pareil must have recovered very quickly the sang-froid of great audacities, for that same night, the *Albatros* had been boarded and captured.

The manuscript nevertheless continued, in a different ink, written in a later epoch, evidently after the events accomplished at Bruyère and a short time before the scandalous marriage.

✳

The *Albatros* was stolen. Her commandant was able to escape with a few men and swim to shore. He was to have been killed on the ship. Perhaps, in a moment of weakness, the old soldier had perceived the image of the young woman with the blonde hair and heard the sigh of the little sick child.

A fortnight later, a court martial condemned to death Joseph Gallo, captain of the veteran coastguard, guilty, said the charge-sheet, of having, on the night of the twenty-fourth and twenty-fifth of December 1813, liberated his prisoners and deserted his post in the face of the enemy. The unfortunate man was shot by a firing squad . . . But Marquis Charles de Mauréac disdained to grant the supreme wish of the dying woman and accomplish the clause of his pardon; he did not collect the orphan. Had he even understood? In order to win his game he had risked his head . . . what did the stakes of others matter to him? O civil war, annihilator of consciences, inspirer of unscrupulous crimes and remorseless sins!

Reduced to the most abject poverty and under the weight of the family shame, Gallo's child, having become a man, descended from one fall to another all the way to prison: the son of the tortured woman died in the smock of a detainee. That is what my father has done, and the world had recompensed him; he had obtained from men all glory and all honors! But from God? I have discovered the granddaughter of Yvonne Gallo—what must I do in my turn?

. . . . . . . . . . . . . . . . . . . . . . . . . . . . . . . . . . . . . . . . . . .

The granddaughter of Yvonne Gallo . . . that young woman with the blonde hair that I bumped into on the road of my life. And what if, perchance, that was Anne-Yvonne herself? Certain theosophers, I'm told, teach a terrible dogma: the soul exhaled by a body in a state of sin must submit to reincarnation, to purify itself by suffering, and, from proof to proof, rise up again toward its God. Where, then, have I read that doctrine, and who revealed it to me? I no longer know . . . Anne-Yvonne, poor creature, so loving, what if I've found you again?

. . . . . . . . . . . . . . . . . . . . . . . . . . . . . . . . . . . . . . . . .

No more doubt. It's her, it's really her. Otherwise, why would Providence, which abandons nothing to chance, the Eternal Now—who taught me that name?—have made her surge forth before me like that? Yes, yes, it's you, dear soul in pain; I'm certain of it. I shall accomplish my duty. Oh, what clamors of reprobation men will utter against me!

. . . . . . . . . . . . . . . . . . . . . . . . . . . . . . . . . . . . . . . . .

Duty? Is it really duty that is driving me? Or rather, is it not the folly of a bestial passion? I love that young woman with a savage ardor! I want her! I shall have her . . .

. . . . . . . . . . . . . . . . . . . . . . . . . . . . . . . . . . . . . . . . .

Passion that fills my entire being, shall I call you love or hatred? I don't know. But I'm struggling desperately against you. Sometimes, I have the furious revolts of a slave; immediately, I have the degrading cowardice of one . . . oh, if I could only rid myself of this possession! If only I dared to reclaim you, my heart, my soul, my self . . .

. . . . . . . . . . . . . . . . . . . . . . . . . . . . . . . . . . . . . . . . .

Finally! United forever! She will live my life and die if I die!


## XVIII


Ten o'clock was chiming on the church of the Foreign Missions when I finished reading the manuscript, very pensively. One thing, among so many frightening things, that terrified me above all, was the obstinacy of Mauréac in fighting a duel and his obsession that he would be killed: the subscription he had put on the envelope of his letter told me enough about the state of his soul. I resolved to attempt a supreme effort, the next day, at the earliest hour. If necessary, I would go with him to the terrain. But what an annoyance for a man of my character, and in my situation!

116

While cursing those unexpected and imminent ennuis, I got dressed in order to go to the ministry; the reception must already be well advanced. I had put the final touches to my costume, and attached one of my commander's medals when a violent blast of the doorbell suddenly made me jump. Soon there was a second, even louder, and then a third; at the same time, someone hammered on the door of my apartment. My valet de chambre looked at me, bewildered, not daring to budge.

"Go and open the door, then," I said to him. "But I'm not in for anyone."

He went out. I waited for a few minutes, and as he did not come back, impatiently, I lifted the tapestry that closed my cabinet. There was someone in the antechamber: a shrill and imperious voice was repeating: "He's at home! I know he's at home!" Almost immediately, precipitate footsteps crossed the next room, and I recoiled, seized by alarm. I had recognized the Marquise de Mauréac.

Her face convulsed, her eyes haggard, her hair disordered, she came in like a madwoman. A fur pelisse enveloped her; she let her mantle fall and appeared to me, still clad in her wedding dress. On the white satin of her dress I perceived splashes of blood. I looked at her, mute with surprise.

Finally, however: "You, Madame?"

But she: "Quickly, quickly, Monsieur! Hurry! Perhaps he isn't dead!"

"Dead? Who?"

"Him!" And in a low voice, she added: "I've killed him."

The stupor of novelty took away my power of speech; nevertheless, I regained possession of myself.

"My God! What's happened? Speak . . . speak!"

She rolled wild eyes, and the words emerged from her mouth in a hiss.

"I don't know, Monsieur . . . I swear to you that I don't know! Here it is! The soirée had ended; everyone had gone, my friends, even the domestics. What time it might have been I don't know.

He . . . that man . . . my husband . . . took me to his bedroom then . . . you know, the room where a large painting can be seen, the portrait of an old marquis with such an evil look . . . his father, I'm told. I was trembling all over. He took me in his arms . . . oh, but so brutally . . . oh . . . oh . . . I was scared. He's always scared me, that man . . . yes, scared me, Monsieur, and horrified me at the same time . . . and I ran away . . . He ran after me and caught up with me in the drawing room . . .

"He took me back to his bedroom and, embracing me again, pushed me against the wall. He put his hands on my shoulders and held his face very close to mine . . . so close that I felt the bite of his teeth on my cheeks and the burn of his breath! And for some time, he looked at me silently; then, in a voice that he tried to make soft, he said: 'Anne-Yvonne, tomorrow, because of you, I'm fighting a duel . . .'

"I didn't say anything; I was petrified by fear. He went on, in a louder tone: 'I'm fighting . . . and I'll be killed.' I still didn't say anything. Suddenly, he burst out laughing—oh, what laughter . . . what laughter! And as if he had read the most secret depths of my thought . . . yes, certainly, he must have seen . . . he shouted: 'Well, you won't be either a widow or free!'

"He seized my head with both hands, and while kissing me, he squeezed my neck; he wanted to strangle me. Look—you can see the marks of his fingernails! I struggled . . . I bit the hands that were strangling me and they let go . . . I leapt across the room . . . there were weapons shining on the wall: a long knife with a silver sheath . . . I grabbed it . . . the man, the madman, shouted again: "No, you won't be a widow!" and he ran at me . . . then I struck . . . yes, I struck! He uttered a huge sigh, and fell down. That's it! Quickly, oh, quickly, Monsieur! Perhaps he isn't dead! Let's get there before the police . . . Save him . . . save me!"

She threw her mantle over her shoulders and ran outside. I followed her. Ten minutes later we arrived, running.

# XIX

Everything was asleep in the Hôtel de Mauréac, dark and silent; the noise of the struggle had not woken the domestics. I went upstairs and traversed the drawing room. The door of the bedroom was wide-open, and the lamp that was still burning illuminated a frightful spectacle.

René was lying on the carpet, unconscious but still breathing. A thin trickle of blood that was oozing, drop by drop, between his clenched teeth, immediately made me dread an internal hemorrhage. Beside him I perceived the hilt of a long blood-stained dagger, the same khanjar with the silver sheath that I had noticed glittering in the panoply a little while before; the weapon had broken in the wound. As Monsieur de Mauréac fell, beneath the portrait of his father, he had tumbled into the fire; already the flame had bitten his legs to the bone.

I rang vigorously and woke the house; the domestics came running. With infinite precaution, René was deposited on his bed. His garments were cut and I examined the wound.

I judged it mortal; the case was desperate. Nevertheless, I applied an initial dressing, preferring to wait for daylight before attempting such a delicate operation as reopening the wound and sounding it; in any case, I judged the operation superfluous; my poor dear patient would not support it. But I prescribed aspersions of fresh water over the face and prolonged frictions in the region of the heart; at the same time I attempted the old proof of "Mayor's hammer": an iron hammer dipped in boiling water and applied to the moribund's epigastrum: I wanted the wounded man to come round and to pardon. Perhaps he would have sufficient grandeur of soul to declare before witnesses that he had struck himself, thus sparing his beloved wife the horrors of a judiciary pursuit.

A slow half hour went by. Finally, a pink tint colored Mauréac's face; he moved his head feebly; He recovered consciousness. René paraded his gaze around him.

"What a dream!" he said. "What an abominable dream!"

A movement of his body wrung a cry of pain from him, and he put his hand to his wound.

"It's true then," he said. "I was stabbed in my sleep. Who?"

I approached the bed and said in a low voice: "René, your soul was always so noble . . . forgive! Be generous again . . . don't accuse her."

He opened wide astonished eyes. "It's you, Victor? What do you mean? I don't understand. Then, with a heart-broken smile: "How well I did to invite a physician to my wedding. My wedding! Poor Marie-Thérèse, this will delay our happiness for a long time!"

He raised himself up slightly; he was still gazing, seemingly unable to recognize anything.

"Where am I?" he asked. "How have we quit Le Menée so soon? I no longer remember . . . but where am I, then? Oh, my God! That portrait . . . here . . . at Bryuère!"

His eyes had just perceived his father's portrait.

"Who has dared to bring that here? Take that thing away!"

In a corner of the room, huddled in the shadow, the Marquise de Mauréac was standing, shaken by a nervous tremor. René extended a finger toward her.

"Who is that woman? Why is she here? Look—dressed in white! One might think her a bride. Some local young woman, no doubt. Has she at least wed the boy she loves?"

And that was all . . . He became anxious, nervous, searching avidly with his gaze for someone who was not there. He drew me toward him, and imploringly, he stammered: "Marie-Thérèse? Where's Marie-Thérèse? For pity's sake, someone go to fetch her . . . someone wake her up . . . quickly, quickly . . . oh, let her come! I'm going to die."

He fell silent for a few moments, and a gleam of joy illuminated his face. "Oh, Marie, Marie," he said, "I felt your heart quivering against mine just now, and my forehead still retains the freshness of your kiss!"

He fell backwards; he was unconscious again. And I, fearful and mute with stupor, listened to the man for whom the accomplished and distant past was still only an instant away from the present moment.

Light finally dawned in my mind and I understood. I had before my eyes a terrifying case of morbid psychology: a suggestion of amour imposed on the heart of a man already in love, but elsewhere—in consequence, a doubling of his consciousness, even of his entire being. In the grip of the will of Elias, René de Mauréac, a weak mind in a weak body, had bowed down before the law that, in the struggle for existence, causes all animate matter to buckle: the law of the strongest. He had then becomes something frightful and nameless, living intermittently two entirely contrary lives: a heart full of delicate tenderness and aspirations toward the ideal when he was himself; a brute with bestial appetites when he was not himself . . .

And while a thousand precise memories now presented themselves to my memory, with a sad smile I repeated the words of *Genesis*: "The Lord God formed man of the dust of ground and breathed into his nostrils the breath of Life, and the man became a living soul"[1] Alas!

Meanwhile, the sick man was dying; his agony had commenced, and a rattle stained with blood was already strangling in his throat. Pensively, I was still by his bedside, when I felt him draw me toward him gently. I leaned over his face; he spoke,

"Day is dawning," he murmured. "At the little church in Bruyère, the ringing bell is announcing the morning mass. Her! It's her, Marie-Thérèse! I can see her! I'm moving closer, I'm standing beside her . . . her forehead is inclined between her hands; she's praying; she's plunging entirely into God . . . But no, she's just raised her head. What pallor! How changed she is! Oh! A tear is shining in her eyes! She's weeping! Yes, yes, she's weeping! She loves . . . Marie, Marie, you still love me!"

---

1 *Genesis* 2:7.

Those were his last words. He died at daybreak, in the rapture of an amorous languor, in all the bliss of ecstasy and second sight. Never, in the course of his miserable existence, had the poor boy felt a calmer happiness, a more peaceful voluptuousness. His last breath escaped in a last sigh.

※

There Professor Rameau's strange story concluded. But a hand other than his own had added in the margin of his manuscript this commentary, even more bizarre:

Atavism . . . the shared and indefinite responsibility of an entire family before God, in accordance with what is written in the Decalogue: *I am a jealous God, visiting the iniquity of the fathers upon the children . . .*[1]

And further on: *O immanent Justice! It is patient, since it is eternal.*

---

1 *Exodus* 20:5. The additional quote is not exact, but back-translated from Thierry's French.

# THE MASK
## A Milesian Tale

## PART ONE

Men are so necessarily mad
that it would be mad, by virtue
of another twist of insanity, not
to be mad.
(Pascal, *Pensées diverses sur
religion*, LXXXVIII)

To the Reverend Joshua Osborne D. D. M.A.
President of the Society for Psychical Inquiries,
editor of *The Old and Modern Sphinx*

In accordance with your desire, very honest Monsieur, I am addressing to *The Old and Modern Sphinx* the two fragments of a story found by my eminent colleague Dr. Labastide among the papers of Monsieur le Vicomte Raoul d'Hérival. I certify, in addition, the absolute authenticity of the manuscript.

Dr. Evariste Monteil.
Medical Correspondent
of the Parisian newspaper *Le Molière* [1]

---

1 The Molière play that the author has in mind in this eccentric attribution is undoubtedly *Le Médecin malgé lui* (1666), featuring the drunken woodcutter Sganarelle, who poses as a physician.

P.S. And now, dear Monsieur, at the moment when I am delivering to your interesting collection these pages—bizarre to say the least—of the most fantastic of romances, permit me to formulate a very personal reservation.

As a man of science, and of very positive science, never, absolutely never, have I wanted to admit a single one of the audacious theories of your "spiritualist" metaphysics; I cannot, therefore, see in the divagations of the visionary Hérival anything other than a simple case of morbid insanity. His priestess Callista, Hermes the thaumaturge, his mask and their marvelous adventures are, in my humble opinion, as many phantoms born in a sick mind, and the child of the religious dementia whose renewal is presently dishonoring the last days of a rational century.

No, I am not one of yours, and when I observe with sadness the ravages exercised by the increasing contagion of your mystical doctrines, I can only repeat with a philosopher: "Mysticism, the last thrust of a cowardly despair of human reason."

Simple Response of Rev. Joshua Osborne
and the Spiritualists
The Editors of *The Old and Modern Sphinx*

The story is assuredly veritable, a lived drama of dolor suffered, individuals having existed, objective and real; a curious example of two-second incarnations, submitted inexorably.

Yes, cowardly or bold, our mysticism testifies our desperation of human reason; and we intend to believe in the absurd in the name of absurdity itself. The absurd is not, as Bonald[1] pretends, an evidence of error, but a maddening "unknown," the future verity not yet discovered.

---

1 The conservative social philosopher Louis de Bonald (1754-1840), a stern believer in the supreme authority of the Scriptures and the infallibility of the Catholic Church.

*Being of beings*, Rousseau was obliged to write one day, *the most worthy usage of my reason is to annihilate itself before you.*

Here commences the manuscript found among the papers of Monsieur Raoul d'Hérival.


# I


. . . And the cruel ceremony is completed, for my atrocious, torturing nerves . . . finally! For myself, I am at the end of my strength, exhausted of courage and smiling energy . . . In any case, what have I come to do at this wedding mass? What strange need for suffering pushed me toward this church?

In the narrow nave of Saint-François-de-Sales the murmuring crowd had formed a hedge; and suddenly, with a pompous din, the organs intoned the betrothal chorus from *Lohengrin*: *Joyous lovers, may our wishes accompany you. Adieu* . . . The nuptial cortege emerged from the sacristy.

Standing in the first rank of the spectators—O impotent and anguished rage!—I saw the new bride advancing on her husband's arm, quivering with emotion, radiant with happiness. . . . *Joyous lovers, may our wishes accompany you* . . . My wishes! My wishes! Wretched me! Under the undulating whiteness of her lowered veil, at a slow pace, she approached, and I stretched out my head toward her, begging and hoping for the alms of a gaze. No, without raising her head, my beloved passed by, indifferently. They both descended the steps of the portal; they both climbed into the carriage . . . *Adieu, adieu*, the organ repeated—and carrying both of them away, already enlaced, the carriage drew away.

Utterly enervated, I fell back in my seat, not daring to leave. An unworthy weakness; but I was afraid of ironic glances, mocking handshakes and salutations. Gradually, however, the whispering crowd flowed outside. The cackling and the flirtations became less noisy; their last rumors faded away; I finally found myself alone in the deserted church. Then, shaking off the dolorous stupor of my bewilderment, I decided to leave.

The Rue Brémontier had now recovered its customary solitude. Under the bitter bite of the winter wind all the guests had fled, and there were no more carriages. It was cold, very cold, that day—oh, I remember it so well, a foggy afternoon in January—and scarcely was I outside the church than I felt chilled to the marrow. I tried to walk, to head for the boulevards, but my legs were unsteady and I was staggering, as if overcome by drunkenness. Annoyed by such a malaise, and desiring to get a grip on myself, I interrogated the street with my gaze. Where could I warm myself up, and recover consciousness of myself?

At the corner of the Avenue de Villiers I perceived a café, apparently clean, where the gas was already lit, and the windows, shining under crystals of frost immediately attracted me. Exhausted by fatigue and shivering with fever, I dragged myself that far. I went into the hall and then collapsed in front of a table.

*Oof!* It felt good there, in the moist warmth and the demi-silence!

"Waiter!"

What should I ask for now?

"A glass of raki, waiter, and Egyptian cigarettes."

Although I had never lived in the Orient, I had always been fond of those Levantine treats. And my dream had once been to enjoy a voluptuous idleness in the lands of the sun . . . out there, beside an azure sea caressing its shores, in one of those harems populated by the storytellers of the Thousand-and-One Nights, to the murmur of jets of water falling back into alabaster basins, lulled all day long by the strings of an amorous marabba. A dream, alas, even more vain than my other dreams, but a charming absurdity, the mirage of which had often traversed my slumber.

126

The waiter contemplated me, amazed. "We don't have either raki or Egyptian cigarettes, Monsieur. Our clients never ask for them."

Of course not! In that estaminet with a billiard table, that domino palace for the usage of Batignolles . . . it was therefore necessary to be content with a large American and a nauseating caporal. I lit a cigar and soon plunged back into the bitterness of my dreams.

Well, yes, a stifling chagrin was weighing upon my heart. The young woman who had passed before me just now, indifferent and belonging henceforth to another, I had loved, loved too much. Having pleased her—I'm sure of it—I had asked for her hand in marriage, and had been cruelly rejected. Why? My age? But I still felt very young, forty at the most; only a few gray hairs showed at my temples. My idle life? So what? I was so rich! For several weeks, however, the parents of my beloved had encouraged my pursuit, authorized my courtship; and I had conducted myself as a perfect gentleman, no less than a fervent lover. Bouquets bringing the subtlest perfumes of Nice every morning, gifts already, the engagement ring, the first adornments of the wedding-basket . . . and then one day, all the jewels and lace had been sent back to me—yes, brutally, my promise retuned, without any serious explanation, without any plausible motive, without the slightest pretext. "You're a charming cavalier, my dear Monsieur d'Hérival, but our daughter wouldn't be happy with you." Her, not happy with me—me, whose entire life had been nothing but a dolorous sob cast toward the unknown of grand amour!

Too humiliating an affront; and, while chewing my frightful demi-London I uttered a disdainful burst of laughter.

"To the devil with the stupid members of that family! Dense and vulgar bourgeois! Let's not think about it any longer."

On a table nearby there was a pile of newspapers. I stretched out my arm and took one from the pile at random. Let's see what is playing today in our little Parisian theaters. I felt lugubrious;

perhaps the frivolities of an operetta would divert my chagrin. Or rather, no, some fashionable dance-hall—the Casino, the Moulin Rouge—might procure me a dazzling adventure for the night. Oh, that night! I sensed it coming, full of insomnia, sadness, heartbreak and crazy anger. No, I would not spend it alone, alone with the nightmare of my thoughts; I needed an adventure, a stupefying adventure. Self-degradation? So be it—but at least, for a few hours, forgetfulness. My eyes were moist with tears, and I couldn't read. With an angry gesture I wiped my eyes.

Come on, enough tears! You know the dictum: *Jeanne lost, find Jeanette*. Search then, and ye shall find.

Aha! I could read quite well now. Hold on, what was this?

*This* was a newspaper absolutely unknown to me: a kind of religious gazette, of an aspect simultaneously forbidding and burlesque. A vignette illustrated the first page: the portrait of a meager woman, her body imprisoned in a sheath without pleats, wearing rings on her ankles, and on her head, in the manner of a diadem, a vulture with falling wings. Two heifer's horns surmounted that headdress, gripping a disk, doubtless some crude astrological emblem. Dangling from her left hand the lady was holding a cross of bizarre form, while her right was raised, like a Byzantine icon, as if blessing. Beneath the figurine, in large letters, a name was printed: ISIS.

Isis! I examined the pretentious caricature curiously. Bah! That was you, Madame Isis, the celebrated Egyptian? That deformed ugliness, that face designed in profile, the ruminant eyes of whom were looking me in the face? Not very seductive, my dear . . .

At the same time, I scanned the text of the newspaper. Oh, somniferous, distilling the heaviest of ennuis: a whole abracadabra of big words, sonorous insanities and incomprehensible articles: The Eternal Now; The Thrice Great; The Spur of Karma; Death the Cradle of Life; and *blah blah blah* . . . enigmas, logographs, conundrums, of which I did not understand any. I pushed the fastidious grimoire away.

And time went by. Stretched out on a divan, drinking in avid gulps, sending the noxious smoke of the national tobacco toward the ceiling, I had resumed the course of my dreaming. Certainly, I was still suffering, but I would be able to cure myself; I . . . oh! Why was she looking at me like that, with a horrible grimace, the thin woman with the blessing right hand? Again I picked up the vignette, and, since she was looking at me brazenly, that Isis, I looked at her in my turn. Then I noticed a legend, an amphigoric charade, enveloping the image of the divinity like and aureole.

*Come to me*, it said, *you who are tortured by the dolorous enigma; come also you whom the eternal fear pales. My child, I have suffered; I console.*

In truth, what was that? What did that mystical nonsense signify? The dolorous enigma . . . the eternal fear . . . amour and the heart of a woman? Life or death? Annihilation? Immortality? Alas, they are too numerous down here, enigmas, with their fears. And that appeal? Why that appeal cast toward me like a challenge? "My child, I have suffered; I console."

Very intrigued, I turned the jargonizing logogriph back and forth. Who wrote it, then? Where was it printed? What was the address of its offices? Nothing. Unsigned articles, no mention of a proprietor or editor, not even a subscription price. In the last line, however, a mysterious indication: *Montmartre. At the Isiac Sacrary, in the Asylum of the Repentant*. My surprise turned to bewilderment; I rapped the table to summon the waiter.

"What is this astonishing newspaper?" I asked. "Do you know it?"

The waiter, a fop with superb judiciary side-whiskers, shrugged his shoulders.

"A simple rag, Monsieur. A woman came yesterday and distributed a whole parcel. She even went on to make a little speech about it. I threw her out."

"Some salvationist?"

"No; she talked about a host of new saints, not those of Monsieur le Curé, I assure you. Claptrap."

"Nice, your preacheress?"

"Horrible. A carnival mask—a she-monkey dressed as a nun: white cotton robe, first communion veil. And then . . ." The individual with the bearing of a public prosecutor caressed his chin. "And then, Monsieur, it's unbelievable: a former ballroom tart. Because of her ugliness, several of the clients recognized her."

"Damn! What a road to Damascus! I would have liked to hear her."

"In truth, she spoke well. Aplomb and elegance! Oh, you would have laughed; one of our messieurs, the local municipal councilor, replied to her."

I disapproved with a gesture. What was the point of abusing a poor woman who doubtless believed that she was accomplishing a duty. Very intransigent, freethinkers in the Plaine Monceau!

The voice of a customer asking for a beer interrupted my imbecile's stories; he quit me to go and serve the client. Four o'clock chimed; I settled up, and left, feeling comforted.

## II

Dusk was now falling—a January dusk, with a lacerating cold, a low funereal sky and heavy, motionless clouds. In the bitterness of the air one sensed the suspended snow. A menacing nimbus had formed to the north of Paris, enclosing glacial and imminent torments in its blackness; the day would not end without a sudden downpour.

On the sidewalk of the avenue I consulted myself momentarily. Ought I to go back to my lodgings? My word, no. It scarcely attracted me, my old house in the Rue Vaneau, and for the moment, I wanted to flee its overly solemn ennui. Better to go to my club, to play cards until seven o'clock, dine there at my ease, and see thereafter. So I headed for the Madeleine.

Was it an effect of the snowy heaviness of the atmosphere? Again, spleen—abominable spleen, my habitual torture—had invaded me. Morose, I went at a slow pace, brooding blackly, annihilated in the absorption of my thoughts. Not very charitable my thoughts, while recalling the emotions of the morning, I saw once again the nave of Saint-François-de-Sales and heard its organ snoring. What! Even more banal than a Wesleyan edifice, that faubourg church. Wretched choir, detestable music. And what costumes all those bourgeois wedding guests wore! Oh, very genteel, of course, the café in which I had made the acquaintance of the divine Isis. "My child, I have suffered; come to me; I console." Where, then, do you console, Madame? At the Isiac Sacrary in Montmartre. Assuredly, I had misread,

The deafening roar of a crossroads suddenly obliged me to look around. What! The Place Moncey, the first foothills of the Butte! What a bizarre itinerary, and incredible distraction! Night had fallen rapidly; the shop windows were illuminated, and on the sticky causeway, the yellow reflection of the street lights was already glistening. I looked at my watch; it marked five o'clock. Well, I wouldn't go to my club; I was too dirty, too muddy. Yes, but what was I going to do until it was time for dinner?

My decision was soon made. Wander at random, of course; walk, walk more, and fatigue the beast. I've always loved those vagabond strolls through my great Paris, that disquieting receiver of the Unknown.

En route! The discordant racket of omnibuses deafened me; I turned left and pressed my pace toward the silence.

Oho! What's this?

Under my feet something somber, taciturn, sinister and grim was displayed: a kind of foggy garden with aligned trees, from which sickening odors of rotting vegetable waste rose . . . Good, I recognized it; the bridge of the Avenue Caulaincourt, Montmartre cemetery. Fine raw material for meditations. Leaning on the parapet, I let my gaze fall upon the slumbering necropolis. In the opacity of the fog, I divined the funerary pathways, their borders of pretentious chapels, thousands and thousands of edicules, which, like hayricks after the harvest, seemed to spring forth from the darkness. What terror, Death! What a quivering sensation of the irreparable and annihilation!

A little mocking laugh made me jump suddenly, and then turn my head. A woman had just passed close to me, and perhaps the sight of the contemplator of tombs had seemed amusing to her. She drew away slowly, dragging her hesitant steps, and seemed to want to provoke me to follow her. Awakened by her snigger, I had quit the parapet of the bridge, and—why?—I started studying the gait of that indistinct form. In the floating vapors that the cemetery exhaled toward us, she seemed to be dressed entirely in white: white, the fabric or straw of the grotesque hat that coiffed her hair, and white also the dress, the disgraceful sheath, that imprisoned her figure: doubtless an illusion; a deceptive effect produced by the mist.

Then, as if she had sensed my gaze, the woman stopped dead; swiftly, she turned around, and, without a word or gesture, seemed to be waiting for me. Some prowler of the exterior boulevards, apparently; I didn't budge. A long minute went by—very long—and the woman finally drew away, but even more slowly. One last time I saw her turn around, look, and wait; then her phantom disappeared in the gray veils of the dense fog.

Yes, some vagabond prostitute trawling the locale. I had resumed my course, still going straight ahead, plunging myself into the pacifying solitude of the lost quarter. And while walking I thought about the woman, the wanderer in the dusk, scarcely glimpsed but so provocative. Her image glided lightly by my side and I imagined the dolorous abjection of her existence: the sidewalk, Saint-Lazare, the hospital bed, the amphitheater . . . Unfortunate, wretched woman, what had you come to accomplish down here, and, suffering flesh, what a cruelty of God to have imposed life on you!

The avenue that I was following, traversing vague terrains, was bordered by wooden fences, and those enclosures displayed hosts of posters in garish colors with crude decorations. One of them soon attracted my attention. It was surprising: a long polychromatic sheet illustrated with monstrous designs: men with the faces of jackals, women with the heads of lions, ibises, hawks and dogs—and in that hideous frame, the image of my goddess: *My child, I have suffered; come to me, I console.*

The enigmatic prospectus was lavished abundantly, violating passers-by and assaulting their eyes. By all the sphinxes in Egypt, then, people worshiped Isis in the vicinity of the Moulin de la Galette?

A penetrating sting of cold cut short my witticism; it was snowing. The menacing nimbus that weighed upon Paris had just burst, and was tumbling in avalanches. The snow, at present, was falling in closely-packed flakes, enveloping me with its swirls, blinding and choking me. Paralyzed, I looked around: no refuge. To the left, the ground descended steeply, arduous escarpments to the right, in front and behind the avenue that unfurled, deserted. Where to huddle?

Suddenly, I distinguished in the distance—but so far away— the redness of a light. It traversed the opacity of the night bloodily, and, like a beacon seemed to be sending me a silent appeal in the torment. . . . a shelter . . . I hastened my steps . . . I started to run; breathless, I reached the seductive glow.

At the corner of an unknown side-street, I finally stopped in front of a dimly lit shop, which was nevertheless gleaming strangely in the darkness. Its door stood ajar. I pushed it.


### III


It was a sordid shack, with a low, cracked ceiling and walls eaten away by mildew, exhaling the stink of abject poverty. An oil lamp, sizzling and crackling, infected it further with its smoke. As soon as I had crossed the threshold, I thought that I was suffocating. On the beaten earth, the only floor of the sinister hovel, scrap iron was accumulated, rubbish and verminous old clothes; my chance shelter must be the hut of some rag-picker.

There was no one there. Behind a glazed door, however, in a kind of back room, candlelight was trembling, and two human silhouettes were designed on the panes. They were arguing, or even quarreling. Their voices reached me distinctly; one nasal, the other guttural—and they were uttering insults in English.

"Well then," said one of them. "Twenty-five pounds for the mask."

No response.

"Fifty!"

A burst of laughter, then a reply: "Not a bit; you shan't have it."

"Eighty, then, a hundred, two hundred guineas."

"Damn! Nothing."

At that moment, the door that separated us opened; my presence had been perceived.

"Who's there?" cried the nasal voice in French. The two hagglers came in at the same time.

The one who spoke to me was a fellow of dreary and eccentric appearance, broken, exhausted and wrinkled; an old man, more than septuagenarian, with a bushy beard, a hooked nose, long black eyes buried beneath the brushwood of their brows, and thick black hair falling in corkscrew curls: everything about him denounced a Jewish second-hand dealer. Sordidly clad like a Levantine merchant, he was wearing a ragged brown caftan, with a red Egyptian fez on his hairy head.

The other was a monsieur about sixty years old, tall, thin and stiff, his figure still very straight. His regular, coppery red face seemed to be that of a man of the Orient, but the hard, cold gaze of his green eyes, the stiffness and compassed cant of his appearance accused him equally of a British origin. His face was closely-shaven, but terminated under the chin with an ample beard tinted black, square in form. At that moment he was bareheaded, and in the light of the lamp his entirely bald head also seemed to me to have had a razor passed over it; one might have thought that he was sporting an enormous monastic tonsure.

"What do you want?" asked the second-hand dealer.

I responded with a few apologetic words: the snow, the desire to find a shelter, the . . .

Abruptly, the phrase I had commenced was cut short; I had just perceived an object in the man's hands that had immediately captured my attention.

On a panel of oblong form was the portrait of a young woman, a painting surprising in its verity, albeit of a rather naïve artistry. The delicately rounded oval of the face, the very correct forehead and nose, and the mass of brown hair enlaced with bandlets, recalled in their design the most gracious figures of Pompeiian frescos. A dainty mouth reddened with carmine was parted by a smile—but what a smile!—and large dark eyes observed you, disquietingly. The expression of the gaze was indescribable, simultaneously malicious and ingenuous, tender and mocking. An enchantress . . .

To what school could such a beautiful study belong? Very ancient, no doubt, for leaning toward the panel, I believed that I recognized a painting in wax. Meanwhile, the Jew had deposited it on the counter, and, my body inclined toward the marvelous apparition, I was ecstatic; an immense desire to possess that image had just passed through my heart.

"What a masterpiece!" I exclaimed. "Is it for sale?"

"It's bought," said the Englishman. "Bought by me,"

The man in the caftan shook his head, and said in his drawling voice: "A lie! The beautiful lady is still for sale."

"I already have the coffin," replied the other. "I have the mummy. I want the mask."

A further snigger replied to him.

"No, Sir Archibald! No and no, for I hate you."

A glimmer of anger illuminated the eyes of the individual thus repelled.

"Sacrilege! Don't separate that which the tomb has united!"

"Sacrilege yourself" riposted the Jew. "Yes, sacrilege and four times impious, you who, out there, by means of spells, have stolen from the true God so many of our sons of Israel."

"They were given to Isis; Isis will keep them."

"Isis! You make me laugh, you and your idols kneaded with the mud of Mesram! Go, go, suborn simple hearts, evoker of demons, the school of fire demands you, and in the valley of Josophat, when the Eternal roars. I will denounce you to Judgment.

"Leave your impotent Yaveh there!" cried the Englishman. "His reign is over, and the days of the Christian god are already counted. The times will be accomplished. No more tyranny in heaven or earth, peace to consciences! Now our exiles are returning, the symbolic Eons, the demiurges emanating from the fecund Unity . . . Isis! Isis! Isis! Perpetuity of life through death, you will all understand the Eternal Now!"

His arm elongated by a hieratical gesture, the baronet with the shaven head and the Egyptian beard resembled some preacher of an unknown god. The absurdity of his speech was that of a charlatan, but his sincere and vibrant voice declared all the conviction of an apostle.

During that fine discourse, the little Ben-Yacoub, the Talmudizing second-hand dealer, stamped his foot in fury.

"The insensate is blaspheming! *Raca, raca!* No, the prophets could not have lied; Israel will resume her heritage, the kingdoms will belong to Juda. And the sweet wine will pour from the mountains, milk and honey will flow from the hills."

He picked up the painting I had coveted in both hands.

"You, Monsieur," he said to me, "since this pagan woman pleases you, I cede her to you."

I took a few gold coins out of my purse—all that I had on me—and laid them on the counter; the patriarch pocketed them swiftly.

"Pooh!" he said. "Eighty francs for such a masterpiece, a funerary mask found at . . ."

"Stolen!" interrupted Archibald, furiously "Robbed from her tomb. The Arabs had emptied the sepulcher, and you have shared their infamous booty. Receiver, I've been searching for you for two years—beware of the police."

"Beware of them yourself," riposted the tradesman.

He handed me the portrait, and for a second time, mocked: "Pretty, pretty, the impure Mesramite! She's yours: the idolater shan't have her."

I took possession of the panel, and I turned to leave. The Englishman barred the way.

"I want that dead woman . . . I want her."

"Oh, my dear sir! I want, I want . . ."

"Her icon is necessary to me."

"I'm very sorry, but I'm keeping her."

"It's a matter of saving a soul!"

"A noble project, Monsieur, but I'm saving myself: I'm going to dinner."

With a brutal movement he grabbed my arm and squeezed it as if in a vice. "French humor? Hear me well; I'll silence it. I have spoken: I want it; willingly or by force, I shall have it."

I got ready to sustain a regulation pugilism; a boxing match without a referee and without betting, but the extravagant individual suddenly calmed down. His fingers relaxed. He stood aside to let me leave.

"I cannot spill blood," he said, solemnly, "nor even commit violence; I would be afraid of incurring the inexpiable impurity. Take away your larceny, then. But be careful: I am watching, and my god chastises."

An arch-madman, that fellow! With a few dry words I sent him back to his padded cell, and then, carrying away my find, I launched myself outside.

The snow was no longer falling; even so, I started to run— what if the sectarian of Isis decided to give chase? At such an hour, a hand-to-hand combat with such a colossus scarcely seduced me. While running away, I turned my head sometimes . . .

No, he was not following me; but in the distance, in the wan profundity of the penumbra, I perceived him; I could distinguish his tall corpulence clearly. Standing on the threshold of the shop with his arms folded, he was watching me. Oh, the bizarre illusion of the snowy whiteness! Even larger than before, he seemed to me to be enveloped by an aureole, and his entire body seemed to be emitting a luminous phosphorescence. A simple fatigue of my eyes, I thought; I had not been able to sleep for such a long time.

No matter; I hastened my flight, and, still running, I had soon reached the swarming crossroads of the Place Moncey again. There were carriages there. I stopped a coachman. "Ninety-one Rue Vaneau—quickly, please."

Half an hour later, in possession of my purchase, I was finally sitting in my apartment.


## IV


Still stirred by such a troubling adventure, I dined with a meager appetite: a repast improvised by a peevish cook, and Monsieur Baptiste playing the most insupportable of Frontins;[1] my unexpected return had disrupted some pleasure party. I went into my bedroom before dessert.

No, I no longer wanted to go out. In spite of my gallant words, I was now resolved to stay by the fireside, and better still, to provoke sleep by means of insipid and scholarly reading. A certain phrase, in any case, by which the two maniacs had qualified my find intrigued me, as an enigma. "The Mask," Archibald had cried; a "funerary mask," the second-hand dealer had repeated. Why that name given to such a vivid and graceful painting?

---

1 The wily valet Frontin had been a stock character in French vaudevilles since the seventeenth century.

On the mantelpiece of my fireplace I had set it against the mirror, and extended nonchalantly, my feet in my slippers, I was soon consulting a voluminous encyclopedia.

Mask . . . let's see! Aargh, two columns: a hundred lines of microscopic text! Mask, false face. Corruption of *Masca*, Medieval Latin . . . witch . . ."

"Bah! You, a witch, lovely?"

I lifted my head toward the young woman. Her velvet eyes immediately caressed me; she smiled amorously with her roseate mouth. Yes, certainly, seductive, bewitching . . . truly a witch!"

I resumed my investigation and plunged deep into a pedantic mishmash.

"It is to ancient Egypt, to the land of Khem, that creator of all human industry, that the first and ingenious idea of the mask belongs. It was first employed for the conservation of mummies. The tricheutes (*cf* Tricheute), marvelous embalmers, covered with a thin layer of gold the faces of corpses of high status— kings, queens, priests, scribes and warriors—desiccated by natrum, enveloping them with an adherent muslin; then, over that apparatus, a plaster mask was cast, which was gilded in its turn: a venerable practice, a triumphant struggle against destruction. Whereas Ben Israel, the inferior Semite . . ."

At that point, scornful insults addressed to the people worshiping Jehovah, and a beautiful dithyramb in honor of the Pharaohs: "Seigneurs of the Vulture and the Uraeus." I skipped fifty lines in order to resume my reading further on:

"After the Macedonian conquest and during the Latin occupation, the pious custom changed. It was the epoch in which Hellenism triumphed, and with it the genius of Greece. There was more gilding, of the prepared faces of the dead, although it was still rare, but the usage of the plaster mask disappeared almost everywhere; the subtle Alexandrian, that other zealot of plastic beauty, had doubtless judged it inelegant and barbaric. The fashion then spread of burying with the mummy a portrait of the person it was desired to honor and placing the icon beside the face; it was another mask: a mask respiring life. Some of these paintings, astonishingly conserved, have a remarkable refinement and reveal unknown masters to us (*cf art.* Graaf Museum). A holy and curious destiny of that noble Egypt! Thus, the divine art of Parrhasius and Apelles was combined with the sacred rites of the ancient embalmers, descending into the tomb with it, enabling the dead to revive forever."

The article was signed "Blumenthal," Aha! Blumenthal, my former teacher: Antonius Blumenthal, today one of the potentates of science, a member of the Institut and a curator at the Louvre Museum. I ought to have divined the signature merely by the sublimity of the style. Well, tomorrow, I shall go to launch my scholarship once again into the midst of your papyri and inform myself as to the value of my acquisition.

Ten o'clock chimed; I loaded my fire, buried it under the ash, and then, overwhelmed by fatigue, I went voluptuously to my bed. From my alcove I perceived the image of the beautiful Egyptian; she seemed animate and palpitating. And that morning I had been proposing to myself to go womanizing! But I had her, my amorous woman, the desired companion, the enchantress of my night . . .

Once again I looked at the dear creature, I blew a kiss to her from my fingertips; finally, a headache overtook me, I extinguished my lamp and went to sleep.

Suddenly, I woke up with a start. Someone had just slid into the space between the bed and the wall, and was standing beside my bed . . .

No, nothing: a nightmare. And I closed my eyes again . . .

But yes! I was sure of it: there . . . there! Someone! Eyes that were observing me attentively; a very light breath caressing my hair . . .

Alarmed, I raised my head, and by the last glimmer of the embers I glimpsed . . . on the mantelpiece: the portrait, the mask, the woman, the "pagan." Her gaze was sparkling, strangely luminous; it was throwing sparks at me, a dazzling incandescence . . .

What! Was I going mad? I lit a candle and, dressing in haste, I approached the sparkling object; it was immediately extinguished . . . a dream! No matter; my desire to sleep had passed; I would not go back to bed. Extending myself in an armchair, I took hold of the bewitching portrait with both hands.

"Well, yes, Mademoiselle, the man in the caftan had judged as a perfect connoisseur . . . pretty, you were pretty, with your large astonished eyes, your smile so charged with sadness, and all that perfume of chaste candor emitted by your person! A young woman?

The alluring mouth appeared to elongate rather ironically.

"Your lips, a nest of kisses, my dear! Modest and so enticing! Seductive and desirable . . . of, how much more so than that little bourgeoise married this morning, my momentary caprice. In the time of your conquests, I would have pampered, loved and adored you above all others; I . . .

The mouth with the carmine moue parted slightly, mockingly. "Yes, yes, my good monsieur; I believe you; I know it."

Truly, she amused me, the coquette.

"A confession, my unknown woman. Very quietly, confide me your name."

Approaching my candle, I then perceived, thinly traced, a few letters of the Geek alphabet—perhaps a name: kappa, alpha, lambda, lambda, iota, sigma, tau.

"Kallist! Very beautiful! Oh, yes, very beautiful! And for a long time I remained lost in my contemplation, talking to the portrait, listening and understanding her responses.

A discreet knock on the door extracted me from my fascination. Baptiste came in. Daylight was filtering through the silky thickness of my curtains, and the clock marked nine o'clock. I had spent my entire night in intimate conversation with Callista.

# V

Callista—a lovely name, in truth, but not at all Egyptian: a pure "Hellenic vocable," as Blumenthal would have said.

It was not unknown to me, that name; I had even read it somewhere—but where?[1] Marvelous stories happened to a Callista. My God, I'm not a scholar by custom, and the memories of my classical studies are blurred today by distant mists; I interrogated my memory in vain; it remained uncertain and cloudy. All morning, that day—the last of my tranquil days—went by thus in obstinate research: lexicons and dictionaries were impotent to inform me. But also, what an absurd obstinacy in wanting to know whether my smiling ingenue had been able to play a role in the world's past. I imagined it, nevertheless, and stubbornly.

War-weary, I summoned my domestic. "Baptiste, I'm going out and won't be back until late. You have your evening free. Don't forget to prepare the night-light for my return."

I intended to go, first of all, to pay a visit to Blumenthal. The dear fellow had addressed to me the day before, his most recent lucubration. *Amorous Women in Ancient Egypt*, a morsel of bawdy archeology that I had found delectable. Such learned politeness demanded thanks, and the opportunity was propitious to integrate the omniscient Antonius on the subject of my Callista. I even had a momentary desire to take the beauty's mask with me—but no! When I quit the Louvre Museum I planned to go to my club and then to the theater, and my companion would have caused me embarrassment. In any case, is it not imprudent to awaken certain kinds of covetousness? Such extravagant an-

---

1 Possibly in a French translation of the oft-reprinted *Callista: A Sketch of the Third Century* (1826) by John Henry Newman (later Cardinal Newman), a dramatized version of which, signed J. de La Magdelaine, was published in Paris in 1886. The eponymous character is of Grecian descent in an African colony of Rome, but she is not a courtesan and ends up as a Christian martyr.

ecdotes are recounted about these antiquaries! I was becoming miserly with my treasure, jealous of my conquest . . . so the Egyptian remained a prisoner in my bedroom.

My friend, the illustrious Antonius Blumenthal, was German, but, having lived in France for thirty years, like so many of his countrymen, he had been naturalized as French. His mind nevertheless remained Germanic, disdainful of the non-thinking foreigner, Teutonic and pedantic, although putting on graces and heavily jovial. We had known one another for a long time. When still young he had worn the robe and had come, tonsured, from some seminary in Munich; intransigent maternal piety had chosen him for me as a tutor. My poor father had died then, having been ill for a long time in a sanatorium, and my mother, an ardent Catholic, was directing my education on her own. The fashion in those days, in right-thinking families, was to confide youth to the moralities of the soutane, and by Saint Louis of Gonzague, a Bavarian soutane seemed a guarantee of austere and learned virtue. In consequence, installed with me in my private schoolroom, the illustrious Blumenthal had taught me many things: Latin, Greek, English, German, rhetoric, history, mathematics and philosophy, also initiating me into the confused mysteries of the Kantian criticism that he crossed with Fichte and transcendental idealism. In brief, Pangloss flanked by his Candide; Mentor and Telemachus,

Superfluous precautions, alas! Between two syllogisms, Mentor liked to be playful, to indulge in frivolity, *nugas verborum, quin etiam et rerum.*[1] He ate well, drank dry, courted the chambermaids and, when he was drunk, secretly translated for me some priapism on the part of Catullus or unexpurgated bawdiness from Horace. Apuleius above all, and the marvelous adventures of his Lucius,[2] delighted my mind and tickled my senses. O Lalage with the sweet smile, Lydia the harmonious

---

1 This Latin improvisation is somewhat frivolous itself, referring to jokes, verbal and otherwise.

2 In his *Metamorphoses*, better known nowadays as *The Golden Ass*.

singer and you, Fotis, the ancilla expert in amorous philters, how I dreamed about you, my beauties, during the insomnias of my sixteenth year! The most evident result of such a noble education had been my perpetual failure in the baccalaureate; hence the desolation of my mother and the dismissal of Abbé Blumenthal. Starveling Abbé Blumenthal! He was then a poor fellow, hard-working and needy, chasing from dawn to dusk a wage of three francs, an examiner in ecclesiastical boarding schools, a dirty polisher if young dunces. He vegetated miserably; by degrees I lost sight of him.

Twenty years later, his name, printed in a newspaper, had caught my eye. Blumenthal, in the most exclusive of our periodicals, was writing the archeological news. No longer a soutane-wearing schoolteacher, no longer a priest, no longer even a Christian, but a fervent rationalist, he was possessed of omniscience—knowing Hebrew, Syriac and Sanskrit—an Assyriologist and an Egyptologist, a polemicist and a journalist: an "eminent thinker." In addition, a personality: "Blumenthal (Ottfried Antonius)," said the *Dictionary of Contemporaries*, "Born in 1825 at Donauwoerth (Bavaria), curator at the Louvre Museum, member of the Académie des Inscriptions et Belles-lettres. One of the glories of French science." Of French science! *Den teufel auch!* And now, consecrated as a great man, the former haunter of taverns was an ardent haunter of salons.

One evening, I encountered him in the home of a Sinologist marquis, a giver of superb concerts, and immediately, in spite of the enormous shock of his graying hair, his weeping willow moustache and his frock-coat decorated with a red ribbon, I recognized my rogue priest.

"You!"

"Me, *alumne!*"

He had once called me his *alumnus*. Our amity was soon reforged. From then on I frequented him gladly. Sometimes, I took him for a blow-out in the Restauration, and he invited me to dine in his modest apartment in the Latin quarter and fed me the cuisine of his "Cleopatra." Why "your" Cleopatra, libertine Antonius?

A good fellow anyway, he was ambitious without being nasty, even scholarly, but of pretentious science with fits of buffoonery. Pen in hand, that handler of canopic jars loved to have fun. His latest volumes, in particular, bore rare titles: *The Immodest Rhodopis; or, The Beauty with the Rosy Cheeks; a Glance at the Courtesan, Architect of the Pyramids; Amorous Women in Ancient Egypt*, etc., etc. Some at the Institut waxed indignant at these learned frivolities, and one day the Assyriologist César Benloëwe, another German brother but a son of Israel, had called all the unfortunate Blumenthal's octavos an "infamous ripopée."[1]

For myself, the savant badinage of my illustrious friend seemed delectable; and while a carriage carried me toward the Louvre Museum I recited happily a superb morsel from his recent pamphlet: "Yes, too prudish and sometimes unpleasant, the morality of our ancient Egypt, the land of Ramses, never understood the veritable hetaira, the glorious sensuality of Greece. One would, however, have loved to hear the murmurs of amour mingling with the lamentations of the citharas celebrating Osiris, terror and death." A very gallantly expressed thought, my old Pangloss, but truly, what need of Aspasia had the land that had produced Callista?

Four o'clock was about to chime when, my carriage having taken me to the Louvre, I penetrated into the Pavillon Sully.

"Monsieur Blumenthal?"

"He must be out."

"No, he isn't out."

Without quitting his armchair, the functionary in green livery and a bicorn hat muttered, while stretching himself: "As you wish. Let's see, cabinets of the curators, Staircase A, in front of you, three floors. The open gallery; then turn left, right, left

---

1 The pejorative term *ripopée* is flexible in meaning, referring primarily to a mixture of different wines concocted from dregs, but by extension to other kinds of mixtures of disparate things, including disreputable mobs.

again; corridor along the river, door number fifteen. Out there, one of my colleagues."

*Oof!* Staircase A, a hundred steps, and how steep! Now the open gallery, overhanging a host of masterpiece paintings, canvases piled up six meters from the floor, only perceptible to telescopes and crushing in their nimbus the glorious dust: the apotheoses of the Louvre.

"Messieurs," cried someone below me, "we're about to close, we're closing."

It was the time when, in winter, they try to get rid of the numerous dilettantes of our public heaters. I hastened my steps. Left, right, left again, the corridor along the river. That corridor never ended: an obscure tunnel, low and strangled, nauseating, funereal and fantastic. Night was already falling; I could no longer see there; in the end, I called out. No one. The "colleague" on duty must have gone down; he too was pushing the public out; he was "closing."

Cabinet number fifteen? There it is!

With a discreet hand, I knocked twice, and waited; no response. In veritable bureaucratic French, then, the illustrious Egyptologist was "out." Already cursing, I was about to retire when the sound of a voice stopped my retreat. I listened for a few seconds; the voice spoke, fell silent, and spoke again, sometimes followed by a joyful little laugh: Antonius, assuredly . . .

I opened the door and went in.

He was alone. Leaning over a vast desk, Blumenthal, his magnifying-glass in hand, seemed to be absorbed in the examination of several documents. In front of him, a long yellow sheet extended, frayed and torn, in shreds, like a lace rag. And, prostrate, wallowing over that indefinable object, the corpulent body of the master was quivering. At the sound of the door he raised his head, recognized me and addressed an amicable gesture to me.

"Ach! My Telemachus, in the Louvre! What propitious deity brings us? Knef the vivifying, or the ingenious Thoth, the pseudo-Mercury of the ignorant Latins?"

His lips tried to smile at me but his eyes belied his politeness. He was evidently annoyed; I was disturbing him.

"A moment's patience," he said. "I'm finishing the examination of a papyrus; a Saïtique papyrus. So you understand . . ."

Without completing his sentence he inclined his head for a second time toward his logogriph. I knew my man; without protesting I took a chair and waited. The daylight was declining rapidly and, in order to decipher better, Blumenthal was stretched out over his desk. All I could see of him as an enormous back from which the unkempt tangle of his hair spread.

There was a long silence . . .

Suddenly, his voice rose up, accompanied by a bizarre snigger.

"By Venus, my lad, what an agreeable existence! Palace of a Zenobia; jewels of a Soemias; suppers of a Vitellus! Oh, the too-fortunate rogue!"

"Dear friend," I asked, "what are you reading that's so recreative?"

He turned heavily in my direction, and then said, blissfully: "A prodigious discovery, the most admirable of finds: a Greco-Egyptian romance!"

"Greco-Egyptian! Damn!"

"Yes, a Milesian tale from the time of the Syrian Caesars, author unknown, but as fabulous as Apuleius, more astounding than Lucian himself. Very lewd, of course . . . I'll quote passages at the session of the five Académies."

"A little fête under the Cupola, then? I'd like to be there."

"You shall be. You'll receive your ticket before long, north tribune, distinguished place, in spite of the draughts. I would have liked to send you a center, but with this Pingard . . ."[1]

"Thanks. What does the prodigious romance recount to us?"

He got up and slapped me on the shoulder jovially.

"I've baptized it *The Amours of Kallistè*."

---

1 Julia Pingard (1829-1905), whose more famous father and grandfather had also served as chief usher at the Institut.

A bizarre coincidence! I could not suppress a start of surprise.

"Callista? Yesterday I deciphered that name on a fantastic mask. Don't laugh; I'm passionate about Egyptology. I should have called you about my acquisition, but . . ."

"No, keep your mask, your pseudo-mask. A portrait on a panel, I'll wager: Egyptian decadence, alteration of national customs, Greco-Latin. Very interesting, sometimes those nice trinkets, but almost always apocryphal, alas. They're manufactured in hundreds today. Old new mystification, for the use of Cook's tourists, the stout John Bull and worthy Brother Jonathan. Furthermore, a hetaira, your Kallistè."

"A courtesan, my Callista?"

"Kallistè, dear child; please spare yourself the solecism."

"Callista seems prettier to me. I'll maintain Callista."

"A sustainable opinion. The A would then be an Eolico-Dorian form, and I once revealed to you the delicate refinement of Eolicism . . . Yes, certainly a hetaira, the name provides it. All those dicteriad demoiselles liked to call themselves thus: 'very beautiful.' *Nomen venusticum.* Kallista, eh! Already the lisp of our loose women: that would be curious and very suggestive. But the slut of whom I speak, mine, was named Kallistè."

He uttered a deep sigh of triumphant vanity; then, returning to his papyrus: "An idea! I have my title: *The Expiation of an Amorous Woman* . . . nice, isn't it? Alluring for my colleagues, enticing for the ladies . . . I'm hesitant, though: joking in the heart of the Institut de France."

"Horror, Monsieur Blumenthal. Is it amusing, your tale?"

"Worthy of Boccaccio, my dear, Museaus, Wieland or Mérimée. Idealo-naturalistic and mystico-philosophical: a pure masterpiece. Would you like to know how, in the days of Eliogabal, a 'little beauty' of Alexandria was lodged? Listen."

He rang to ask for his lamp; the attendant was still absent.

"Never at his post, that fellow," Blumenthal grumbled, "but protected by the cousin of a minister, ergo unsackable."

With both hands, like a celebrant handling his God, he picked up a sheet of papyrus and took it to the window in order to read better.

"This is the description of Kallistè's apartment; savor this treat for me; I'll translate word-for-word: 'A sanctuary even more divine than a temple of Aphrodite, the bedroom was a marvel. Amorous paintings, frescoes to the glory of Cythera, decorated the walls; the onyx of eight columns supported a ceiling in vivid colors. The silkiest brocades, woven in the fabulous land of the Serices, covered the mosaics of the floor . . .'

"Mosaics, marbles of Numidia, soft silk carpets! An entire *penetcale Voluptatis*, eh, *licher Freund*, it must have been good to practice one's devotions there! I'll continue: 'There, among the statues sculpted in Paros marble and the ivory simulacra of the Garamantes, stood a solid silver bed, and there . . .' *Hmm, hmm . . .* 'And there, ephebes or old men, senators of the city, magistrates, exegetes, archidicastes, and, among others, the old augustal prefect Valerius Afer . . .'"

Blumenthal interrupted himself, and clicked his tongue noisily. "Ho ho—pornographic, the rest. I'll pass, my child."

"No, why pass, dear master?"

"Rascal! Ach! What procuress chic, *hush hush*, as our petty newspapers say. But patience! The old Egyptian morality is watching; in spite of heady Hellenic weaknesses, it will resume its rights, it is affirmed, it triumphs . . . one day, our Kallistè dies. Dramatic adventure: she is murdered."

"Murdered!"

"Yes, just like a simple baronne of the Marboeuf quarter. The murderer is a slave, a certain Parmenon, who, seeing a ring on the finger of his mistress, seizes a butcher's knife and . . ."

"The wretch! To steal it, no doubt?"

"Not at all, ingenuous soul. My romance is less banal. A crime of passion, if you please: murder by jealousy . . . oh! What's the matter my dear? A tarantula-bite?"

I had risen to my feet, prey to a violent emotion—why?—and was marching back and forth, gesticulating.

"Unfortunate Parmenon! How he must have suffered, the poor slave! He was in love!"

"And he was loved."

"How he must have suffered!"

Antonius Blumenthal uttered a cynical burst of laughter.

"There, there, calm down, excessively sensitive heart. A simple fiction, Raoul; an astonishing tale, but a tale. He was in love, the imbecile, and the tortures of impotent jealousy are here described *magistrali calamo*. Hear and admire. The demanding Parmenon, the inappropriate Parmenon, makes scenes; the amorous fool insults and threatens: 'What, my Kallistè! To my young embraces you prefer the senile caresses of the augustal! Oh, wretched me: you more wretched still! A dolorous rage makes my blood boil; tears swell my eyelids. Fall, my tears, flow, blood of my soul; and may you extinguish the fires that are consuming me!'

"*Stupendum*, isn't it? 'O tears, blood of my soul . . .' A reckless Africanism, yes, but what fine antitheses in the passion! One could believe one were reading Apuleius, the subtle and amusing rhetor I translated for you in secret, *alumne*. Do you remember?"

Calmed down somewhat, I had resumed my seat.

"Do I remember? I could quote you various passages by heart. But please, what became of Parmenon?"

"The lictors took charge of that; he was crucified. The author tells us that in too few words; on the other hand, he talks to us at great length about Kallistè's afterlife."

"Undoubtedly, while the poor slave was writhing in Gehenna, the prostitute was given a scandalous funeral?"

"Magnificent: a first-class embalming. But wait. For her, the bad time commenced right away. The soul of the deceased traverses the Amenti . . ."

"The Amenti? I know that name."

"Yes, the mysterious abyss in which the incessant harvest of death is heaped up. The excessively amiable slut was summoned to judgment. Harsh, very harsh, the sentence that condemned her: 'Then, the One who was, who is and who will be—the Unnamable; the One from whom all emanates, in whom all is absorbed, the Creator of all Creation, the Being of Beings, the primordial Unity, via the mouth of the powerful Eon, bearer of the scepter that protects and the whip that chastises, spoke thus: *Because, human essence, superior to the brute, you have contented yourself with the existence of the brute and retrogressed toward it, in order that you can purify your soul and, you who have caused weeping, can wash away the stain by means of your tears, when the hundreds of years of the sothic cycle have revolved, you will be reborn on earth. From abjection reentered into abjection, hideous to all, an object of repulsive disgust in those who seduce you, but still conserving vivacious the hearth of your intelligence, you will fight again the rude battle against yourself. Your absorption in my Light will be the price of your victory: struggle and triumph. But if, returning to the evil life, you . . .*'"

Sudden and violent, a knock on the door made me shudder. Almost immediately, the door opened.

"Monsieur Antonius Blumenthal?" an imperious voice demanded.


## VI


Night had now fallen; in the sky, the crepuscular grayness had faded; the first stars were already beginning to shine, and, rising above the horizon, the moon was extending her nascent pallor toward us. In the doorway, I glimpsed a man of broad corpulence and tall stature. He was not alone. Behind him, in the shadow of the corridor, a woman dressed entirely in white was effaced, indistinctly. Singular apparel, on a day of rain and muddy snow!

"Who are you?" asked Blumenthal. "I'm no longer receiving; it's too late."

Followed by his companion, the man took a step forward, and then closed the door.

"Who am I?" he said, solemnly and emphatically. "My name is Sir Archibald Williamson; I am also known as Hermes the Egyptian."

"Hermes the Egyptian?" growled Blumenthal. "Personally, I only know the Trismegistus."

"You shall know me," riposted the other, imperturbably. "Africa and Asia have learned my name; it is for Europe now to know who I am."

Alarmed, my friend Antonius had just sat down again, and, with a protective gesture he extended his hands over his papyrus. As for me, I had recognized my Protestant preacher of the previous day, the firmly dismissed lover of the funerary mask.

There was rather a long silence.

"Monsieur and illustrious doctor," Archibald resumed, pompously, "you have before you a priest of Isis."

"Bah!" said the Egyptologist, becoming mocking. "A priest of Isis in trousers and dinner jacket? Why aren't you decked out in linen?"

"I am a priest of Isis," the imperturbable individual went on, "and furthermore, a neoplatonist. I have lived for a long time in familiar commerce with Plotinus, Porphyry, Iamblichus and Proclus; I have practiced the holy *Book of the Dead* and penetrated the celestial profundities of the Orphic poems. I wanted to know; I know."

"More fortunate than Montaigne, then, Reverend.[1] I congratulate you."

Without reacting to the pedantic epigram, Archibald continued: "I have come, Monsieur, to reveal again to forgetful Europe

---

1 Montaigne's philosophical refrain, which became a kind of motto, was "What do I know?"

the Great Mystery, the mystery of life and death. At this hour of agonizing Christianity, we shall resume the ancient combat against it. It is necessary; it is necessary that all the old religions are reborn. Today, Brahmanism, Buddhism and the religion of the Druids have their apostles and neophytes among you. Why, then, should the 'good goddess,' whose sanctuaries once covered the entire world, not rediscover zealous devotees? Divine and completely human, she is also one of the first Eons born of the Absolute Consciousness, of the multiple, productive, inexhaustible Unity, of Being in itself and outside itself—the God without formula, the Essence, the Unnamable, the Eternal Now."

"After all, why not?" opined the ex-abbé Blumenthal. "I don't see any inconvenience in that. In your place, however, I would have chosen a more attractive femininity: Callipygia, for example. A sad face, your symbolic Isis with her cow's horns."

"An overly delicate esthetic," replied the other, disdainfully. "The Zeus-Ammon of the Hellenes and the Moses of the Israelites were horned, Monsieur, very horned. And besides, your first Nazarenes, according to Tacitus, worshiped the ears of a donkey."

"That's true; hurrah for the *keratophore*," sniggered the learned Antonius. "I concede you Isis. However, Monsieur Theosopher, know that my only God is the modern God, Z multiplied by X. I'm inconvertible."

"I'll convert you," declared the astonishing visitor, tranquilly. He paused briefly, and drew nearer to the skeptical Blumenthal. "I'll arrive, Monsieur, at the purpose of my visit. A theurgical periodical, *The Old and Modern Sphinx*, has announced to its readers the discovery of a papyrus that you intend to publish imminently."

"Indeed. A Milesian tale, a romance that . . ."

"It isn't a romance, but a confession of the afterlife, a page of veritable and lived history."

My friend, the worshiper of the algebraic God, stirred in his armchair; the assertion of the priest of Isis contradicted his theory. "Not a romance?" he cried. "A veritable history, this account of the amours of Parmenon and Kallistè . . . ?"

Hermes interrupted him. "Names given by the Greeks, the subtle Akaioushas. In his naïve language the man was named Pakrour, the murdered woman Ahmes."

"How do you know, Monsieur?"

"I even know where they both came from: he was a child stolen by the Ethiopians from Philae, our isle with eight hundred sanctuaries; she, alas, had deserted her temple at Tentyris."

"Kallistè?"

"Callista. The Roman Valerius Afer, her entitled lover, wanted to Latinize her name."

"Nonsense! You don't know the document."

"The courtesan's mummy has told me everything," Archibald declared, phlegmatically.

At that moment, my attention was attracted by the strange white-clad companion who was standing beside the mystifying individual. A woman? Yes, according to all appearance. In the gleam, presently diffuse, of the lunar rays, she seemed almost diaphanous, advancing as soon as he advanced, and when he stopped, becoming immobile. Her figure seemed to float, undulating, but I could not make out her face; a veil—was it really a veil?—covered it entirely.

The good Monsieur Blumenthal had not perceived anything, because, still fidgeting, he addressed the mage, confessor of mummies: "Monsieur, monsieur, I don't like bad jokes. You may withdraw."

The Englishman did not flinch. "And the poisoned ring?" he said. "The gift of the augustal prefect—do you possess that? No, it's in my hands. Confide your papyrus to me. I need it for our mysteries."

"Confide my papyrus to you! A State papyrus, the jewel of our museum!"

"In order to bring forth the Light!" cried Williamson. "It recounts the sins of a sacrilegious soul, a renegade priestess, a being condemned to the torturing inferno of the second life. I have rediscovered that soul, the reincarnate expiatrice, and I need to. . . ."

"A buffoon!" clamored Blumenthal. "*Donnerwetter!* By all the devils, get out!"

"So you refuse."

"I refuse."

"Ah! Be careful! I've brought down stronger . . . I can annihilate whoever hinders me."

And, turning round, Hermes the Egyptian looked at me. In the demi-obscurity of the room, he had recognized me. The incredulous Blumenthal responded to him with a burst of laughter.

Was it an illusion? But it seemed to me that, silently, the form had glided across the room; it approached my friend and, leaning over his shoulder, was examining the papyrus. To my surprise, the irascible archeologist did not even turn his head.

Meanwhile, Sir Archibald continued speaking. "Keep your manuscript," he declared, haughtily. "I know, now, that it's useless to me; you don't possess the original."

"What are you saying? Impostor . . . you dare to say . . ."

"I'm saying, poor Monsieur, that your version must be incomplete and truncated. In any case, even if it were more exact, you don't have the key to that enigmatic and lamentable story. And then, know that, in spite of your locks, my familiar spirit will collate."

"Are you going to get out, Monsieur Socrates!" howled Blumenthal. "I'll throw you out myself!"

He launched himself toward the bell-cord and started ringing frenziedly. It was a superfluous appeal; the attendant was definitely absent. The scene was becoming both sinister and farcical. Blumenthal became demented, cursing and raging; the most comical insults in dead and living languages escaped his doctoral lips one by one.

"Vile pastophore, tympanizing arch-gael, tintinnabulatory schnapphahn, damned humbug, histrion, trickster, mountebank! Empty the place!"

For a moment I feared some burlesque brawl. With a simple shove of the hand, the colossal Archibald could have knocked the raging and shrill corpulent little man down. But no; under the deluge of invective his tall stature had stiffened scornfully. Now he headed toward the exit door, very slowly—and very slowly, the indescribable form followed him step by step. Finally, they disappeared.

"The brazen charlatan!" exclaimed Blumenthal, as soon as the door had closed.

"Yes, certainly," I replied. "A sâr, a farcical necromancer. I've already encountered him, but without his companion, the indiscreet little comrade."

"What comrade?"

"The girl-friend, of course. The female visitor, just now."

My old Pangloss, who was putting his arms in the sleeves of his overcoat, ready to leave, stopped dead.

"I beg your pardon; I don't understand. What female visitor?"

"The young woman who accompanied him."

"Lubricious individual!" my private tutor sniggered. "With you, always women, women everywhere!"

He had taken my arm, and we walked through the obscure maze of the corridors without exchanging a word. At the bottom of the staircase, under the glare of the gaslight, he fixed me with his gaze.

"So, you've encountered that man before?"

"I already told you—yesterday, but without the young woman."

"Don't joke . . . what young woman?"

"The acolyte, the demoiselle dressed in white."

"A demoiselle? Dressed in white? You've been asleep, my dear."

Right! Was he teasing, indulging his Bavarian sense of humor? My leaden jester had once been accustomed to such persiflage. Without getting annoyed, I shrugged my shoulders. "Me, asleep? She leaned over your shoulder, brushed your face; she even examined the papyrus."

Blumenthal let go of my arm. "My child," he growled, "your libertine life is fatiguing you. Go and get some fresh air, and go to bed afterwards. Seven o'clock! My dinner is going cold; I'll be scolded by Cleopatra. *Au revoir, nebulo*; but in future, be more sober."

And he drew away rapidly.


# VII


The old madman! For several seconds I followed him with my eyes; he was trotting along, almost running, hastening toward his Latin Quarter; soon he plunged into the darkness of the Pont des Arts, and I lost sight of him.

The eccentric fellow had cheered me up momentarily, but when he had gone, I became morose again. To begin with, what was I going to do with my evening? I had traced out a plan in advance: dinner at my club, read a few newspapers there, perhaps play cards, and then, at about ten o'clock, put on a jacket, and take an orchestra armchair in order to ogle the ballet-dancers in *Aïda*:[1] The sets of *Aïda* were truly magical: the pharaoh's palace, caressed by the sun, the blue immensity of the river; the sphinx concealing all the secret temples, colossi of pink granite meditating under the fans of tall palm trees: dazzling. Too shrill, though, the fanfares, the unpleasant charivari of trombones; I would rather have had flutes, harps and citharas. And besides, people loving, detesting, ranting, threatening, condemning and expiring in sharps and flats—what absurdity! When the frenzy

---

1 Giuseppe Verdi's lavish Egyptian opera *Aïda* was premièred in Paris in 1876, and was enormously successful there, as it had been elsewhere.

of amour grips you and tortures you, one kills without phrases, and one dies thereafter.

My watch marked seven o'clock. I had plenty of time to dine at the club, so I headed for the Avenue de l'Opéra.

Well, yes, Blumenthal was right; my head was spinning and I needed some fresh air. The evening was cold but bright, scintillating with starlight; weather propitious for my dear idling. Lighting a cigarette, I set forth for the boulevards . . .

Blumenthal! Truly the moralizing fool made me laugh! "A young woman? Dressed in white?" All white, triple blind man, light, graceful and so dainty . . .

Hold on! Over there, ahead of me—that man with the neck of a drum-major, wasn't that my other eccentric, His Eminence the priest of Isis, Archibald Williamson, Hermes the Egyptian?

The gaslight of the shop illuminated us as if in broad daylight; I could observe at my ease; I observed . . . what a vigorous fellow! Athletic torso, dominating head, and yet handsome. He was alone now, without the busy little friend, the inquisitive reader of the papyrus. He too, a strolling monseigneur, was wandering idly, trailing his noble bulk, boldly staring at the passers-by. He intrigued me, damn it. Only a few paces separated us. I followed him.

At that hour of the commencing night, the Avenue de l'Opéra was noisy, filled with busy rumors. It was the joyful moment when the workshops of the seamstresses were closing, and from the houses where couturiers and milliners live, apprentices were escaping, errand-girls and grisettes. Cheerful and pert, they gathered in groups under coaching entrances and the last conversations ran their lewd course.

Suddenly, Williamson veered toward a group of those chatterboxes. I heard a cry, and the girls scattered like a flock of sparrows.

He went on.

Two of them, however, had remained in place, astonished and motionless, inclining their upper bodies toward the man and watching him draw away. I approached, and then addressed the younger of the two, a pale and chlorotic blonde: "The old ape. Did he frighten you?"

Without replying, she clung to her companion's arm. "What a brute! He struck me in the heart. Tell me, Louisette, do you know him?"

"No, do you?"

"He claims to know me."

"I've seen him before, though—but where? I've forgotten."

"How harshly he commanded me!"

"And me even more harshly!"

"Are you going to wait for him tomorrow? He's going to come back."

"No, I don't want to, I . . . I . . . yes, yes, I'll obey!"

Dragging themselves along, heavily, with an unsteady step, the two girls drew away. And yet—I was sure of it—Williamson had not spoken to them.

Briskly, I resumed his pursuit, and had soon caught up with him. At the junction of the boulevards he was standing in front of a gaslight display, a flamboyant advisement for a theater or restaurant . . . no, for a music hall: *This evening, at the Moulin Rouge.*

What a wily individual! Had he divined me, following in his tracks? Undoubtedly, for he turned his head, and his arrogant gaze met mine. Seized by alarm, I threw myself backwards. But the apostle had already resumed his tranquil march, and, crossing the road, he went into the Rue Auber.

Sopped dead by that glance, slightly confused by my indiscretion, I examined the glittering advertisement. It was burning strangely, that gaslight. Sometimes, when a gust of air curbed and depressed the flame, only the blue letters could be seen—such a lovely sapphire blue!—and sometimes, leaping up provocatively, it twisted, with the murmurs and crackling of conflagration . . .

*This evening*, it said to me, *this evening, at the Moulin Rouge.*

A hand was placed on my shoulder. Uttering a cry, I shuddered . . . no, thank God, it was not that man.

"What the devil are you doing there?" a familiar voice asked me. "Are you rhyming to the moon; have you fallen into ecstasy?"

With a violent effort I succeeded in getting a grip on myself . . . Salignac.

"What, it's you, my dear . . . my God; I was looking . . . I was admiring, I . . . oh, what a fortunate encounter!"

Certainly, a fortunate encounter; for, left to myself. I would have started pursuing the Egyptian again. I therefore exchanged the customary salutations and compliments. He was, in any case, a very pleasant fellow. Monsieur de Salignac: not too boastful for a Provençal, an enthusiastic gambler, drawing five and almost always ruined; I like him as much as anyone, of course.

"You're my prisoner," he said, "today is bouillabaisse day at Chez Sylvius; come on, I'll take you."

I allowed myself to be drawn away, and two minutes later we were penetrating into the odors of garlic.

The restaurant was already crammed with numerous diners; the saffroned scorpion-fish had attracted its devotees, men of the Midi for the most part, lovers of bourride, revelers in Neptunian pâtés and palates fond of fetid brandade. Azaï and the Canebière, emigrated to Paris, rushed to the oily cuisine that evening. And among the diners there were many of the female sex, virtuosos of the Pigalle quarter or the Montée des Martyrs, princesses of mid-level gallantry, talking loudly with strident laughter, in garish dresses, adorned like Madonnas and made up like Polchinelle: "an entire basket of madcap hetairas," Blumenthal would have said.

"A rather vulgar society," Salvignac murmured. "But on the other hand, here, the wine of wines. Yes, Monsieur, Châteauneuf-du-Pape. We're going to ask for the best bottle: you can tell me what you think of it."

There was an unoccupied table near the entrance; two places were set thereon, and the waiter presented us with the day's menu. Salignac took possession of it.

"Now, my good man," he said, "feasting, then debauchery! And first, let's order the nectar that contains all the rubies of the sun."

Dithyrambic, the Avignonnais: a felibrige troubadour, another Roumanille; personally, quite indifferent, I approved the confidence. So much verbiage stunned me, and gradually, I let myself sink into my dreams. I saw Blumenthal again and his papyrus; I listened to him describing the chamber of Callista—of Ahmes the renegade—the African onyx of the columns, the solid silver bed: a fatiguing obsession . . . And Parmenon—the desperate Pakrour, the murderer for the sake of amour? Oh, detestable courtesan, who even debauched your slave!

At that moment, the door of the cabaret was opened slightly, timidly at first, and then flung wide. I turned my eyes in that direction.

## VIII

A woman came in.

She was very thin, about twenty-five years old, with a paltry figure, sickly in appearance. Pale, etiolated and cadaverous, with blonde stringy hair, at first sight I thought her very ugly—repulsively ugly. Beneath a sloping forehead, the brow ridges extended ridiculously; the eyes, sunk into those rings of flesh, seemed to have been bored with a drill; the nose, too short, vulgar and squashed, was tucked up by two bestial nostrils; and in that prognathous face, almost no chin, but an advancing mouth, obscene lips with the hiatus of a chimpanzee grimace. The muzzle of an ape—or, rather, a relic of an ossuary. One might have thought, on seeing that macabre monster come in, that it was a grotesque apparition. Oh, a disquieting gaze: luminous, speckled, casting sparks at us!

She was neatly dressed, but without elegance. A disgraceful sheath, pale gray cotton, enclosed the skeletal body, and the white protrusions of a long veil framed the hideous face. At first I thought she was some shop-girl dressed up in the pretentious accoutrement of a bourgeois soirée. The waiter who was serving us judged her similarly, for he looked her up and down disdainfully. Sylvius et Cie did not usually receive such paltry clients. Indecisive, and perhaps frightened by the glare of the lights, the rumor of conversations, the vulgarity of the prostitutes and all their cheap jewelry, the new arrival seemed to hesitate.

A voice, that of a pretty doll, a noisy slattern feasting at a nearby table exclaimed joyously: "Oh la la, that's delightful. Look: a skeleton who wants to have dinner."

The inept quip had been pronounced loudly, and the lady's gallants started laughing. At the shock of the insult, the woman in the white mantilla had blushed; I saw her totter weakly; but almost immediately, the cavities of her eyes lit up, and with a resolute step she marched straight toward the offender. Stationing herself in front of the people who were mocking her, she raised her head and put her hands together.

"Brothers, and you, my sisters," she commenced, "in the name of the Eternal Now I have come to reveal to you the Great Mystery. Voyagers, terrestrial voyagers, too forgetful souls, think of your Karma . . ."

"What does this frightful muzzle want with us?" asked the restaurant owner, who came running, bewildered.

"Some salvationist, no doubt," replied one of the waiters. "It's the hour when those crackpots come to annoy the clients."

"A salvationist? No, I don't recognize the uniform . . . anyway, none of those jokers in my place. Someone throw her out."

Meanwhile, the woman continued:

". . . Death is only a renewal of life, and life a form of expiation. O my companions in pilgrimage, and above all, you, my sisters in the proof, our purgatory is down here. We only die in order to be reborn, again and forever, until the final purification of our soiling. Woe betide the insensate, then . . ."

162

"My girl," Monsieur Sylvius said to her, "you can't stay here; go preach outside."

"What twaddle," sniggered the slattern. "She's boring us with her good God."

The woman approached swiftly and extended her hand toward the sinner. "Poor soul, you have known that God, then, since you insult him! I too, Madame, was as beautiful as you, as adulated as you . . ."

An insulting burst of laugher departed from the joyful tables; quips and jeers began to rain down from all directions on the deformed and ugly woman.

"Beautiful! Adulated! What a wretch! A gargoyle! Oh, that mask!"

Oh yes—that mask!

Go on, get out," a waiter enjoined. And he seized the recalcitrant woman by the arm. Without any apparent effort, she freed herself from the grip and pushed the aggressor away. Ironic bravos welcomed that pugilistic gesture;

"What a fist!"

"A Hercules in skirts!"

"An ape-torpedo!"

"To the fair!"

"To the Folies Bergère!"

They were having great fun at Chez Sylvius that evening.

Disdainful, insensible to the gibes as well as the threats, the preacher continued speaking: "Yes, like you I was beautiful, adulated like you. Out there under the sun of golden javelins, near the sea with blue songs—what memories!"

She paused briefly, searching for words, like a child trying to remember some lesson.

"What memories . . . more ornamented with amorous offerings than a temple of Aphrodite, the bed-chamber shone like a sanctuary . . ."

"Numa, Ernest, Alexandre!" howled Monsieur Sylvius. "Get hold of that madwoman for me and throw her outside!"

". . . The onyx of twelve columns with capitals of bronze supported a ceiling decorated with lascivious paintings . . ."

The three sturdy lads had precipitated upon the woman, and a repugnant hand-to-hand struggle began. They had seized the unfortunate woman, either by the waist or the arms, shaking her and lifting her off the ground. She fought, repelling the assailants, and still she continued, still reciting:

"There, among the statues making the alabaster live, among the green smiling simulacra in Indian jade, stood a bed . . ."

The entire room was now on its feet; some approving and some condemning the ignoble violence.

". . . A silver bed, embellished with gold, sparkling with gems, iridescent with marine pearls. And there, ephebes or old men . . ."

Abruptly, she stopped, seeming to have lost the memory. Stronger now, the three men pulled, dragged and shoved her toward the door.

I had launched myself forward, and I was abusing the waiters: "Boors that you are, brutalizing a woman like that! Let me talk to her."

At the sound of my voice, she turned her head sharply; her gaze met mine, and suddenly, uttering a shrill scream, she threw herself backwards. Then, stretching the mask of her face toward me like some ferocious beast, step by step, the frightful creature recoiled slowly. Finally, they put her out of the door.


IX


"What a villainous crowd," sighed Salvignac. "How I regret having brought you here!"

For myself, I was silent, stupefied. Who was that bold preacher to whores, and how could she have known about Blumenthal's manuscript? She had quoted an amusing passage from it, altering it, to be sure, at pleasure, but her prose seemed to me to be more florid, spangled with romantic variants. Yes, what was this bizarre case? And extravagant thoughts whirled in my brain . . . Maladroit of me, perhaps, not to have followed the illuminate! With a little cunning, perhaps I would have learned the key to the enigma, and—who knows?—diverted my incurable spleen momentarily.

But no, I stayed, bored, with the boring Salvignac, and his Provençal feast was prolonged endlessly. Neither the bouillabaisse nor the Châteauneuf-du-Pape had the virtue of awakening my verve. I only spoke in monosyllables, but at every moment the importunate babble of my companion came to extract me from myself.

"A little culinary eclecticism," he said. "Let's vary the vintages. Chambertin, Sommelier!"

"No, thank you, not for me. I must already be drunk, for . . ."

"So much the better; 'wine furnishes speech to the most mute'—and without reproach, you have the eloquence of a carp this evening. What are you thinking about, then?"

"Salvignac! A single word. The woman a little while ago, that monster with the head of a chimpanzee, the skeleton with the death mask who . . ."

He interrupted me, filling my glass: "Horrible, the gorgon; a hysteric escaped from the Salpêtrière."

"Agreed, but what poetry in her discourse! How she was able to describe the magical palace and the ophite of its colonnades, the population of statues, the masterpieces of forgotten Praxiteles, having made the ivory and the Paros marble live, love and suffer . . ."

The joyous laughter of my Amphitryon cut off my speech.

"O gentle dreamer! Alas, she didn't say anything as charming. Her voice drawled a heap of common things, mystical nonsense . . ."

"But yes, yes! Remember: the ceiling decorated with lascivious paintings, the solid silver bed where . . ."

He pressed my hand gently. "Good, good, I've guessed it: my Châteauneuf-du-Pape! What a bewitching and inspiring wine. Furthermore, I concede that the farce was screamingly funny, but I'm quite blasé about spectacles of that sort. I've witnessed similar comedies many a time in England. In London, charlatan founders of religions pullulate. Once, the sidewalk was sufficient for their preaching; today they introduce themselves into places of entertainment, bars, restaurants and especially ballrooms: the 'dancing academies' . . . oh, nothing like the Académie Française, I assure you. When one of these missionaries has slipped into some den of perdition, he preaches, he declaims, he hectors, he torments; soon, the response is made to the sermonizer that whether he likes it or not, the public will expel him. I remember one evening at Cremorne Gardens, a dance hall, the Moulin Rouge of hypocritical Albion . . ."

"The Moulin Rouge . . ."

And with a start, I stood up. "Excuse me, my dear friend . . . I need to quit you: urgent business."

Salvignac looked at me, bewildered. "Urgent business? At ten o'clock in the evening?"

I stammered incoherent pretexts; he laughed at my trouble and was amused by my stammering.

"Come on, be sincere: an amorous rendezvous."

"Oh, amour!"

"A gallant adventure, I'm certain of it: you can't sit still. Adieu, then, fortunate Don Juan, and may divine Eros be favorable to you."

But already, without listening any further to that pretentious loquacity, I had launched myself into the street.

. . . And now, at the summit of the Rue Fontaine, the Moulin Rouge loomed up before my eyes. Agitating inflamed sails, it was turning, turning silently, in a very smooth, rhythmic, inviting movement; and I contemplated that scarlet thing, shifting so madly: the convulsion of those arms that were soliciting me. *This evening, at the Moulin Rouge!* What if I were to go in? No, too late, it will soon be half past ten . . . what does it matter? Why hesitate? This evening, this evening, at the Moulin Rouge . . .

I went in.

The ballroom was in a frenzy at that moment; the brass instruments of the orchestra were enraged, and in the Temple of Commotion, the dancers were leaping obscenely and furiously. In tightly-packed ranks, a libertine rabble was surrounding the quadrilles, and from that imbecile mass lewd remarks departed, and noisy applause. As soon as I went in, a weight of insupportable ennui, a heavy disgust with all things and oneself seemed to descend upon me. Without seeking to see the gymnastics of the national cancan, familiar with them in any case, and similar to a beast in a cage, I immediately started wandering around the hall.

A sickening spectacle, that public ballroom. What promiscuity in vice: men of the world and bumpkins, low prostitutes and grand courtesans, valets escaped from the servants' parlor and masters escaped from the drawing room—the master more vulgar here than his domestic. Oh, if one of those missionaries that Salvignac had mentioned to me were abruptly to surge forth in that bacchanal, one of those converters who . . .

Suddenly, I stopped, confounded; I had just perceived the preacher of the Sylvius restaurant.

She was no longer clad in her monastic sheath, but in a garish dress, faded finery that reeked of the Temple square or the second-hand clothing store. On her head, no white mantilla but a hat with a feather; and shining in her ears, on her bosom and on her ungloved hands, vulgar jewelry, tinsel and paste. All the elegance of a streetwalker displaying herself in excess of the demoiselle . . . and yet, yes, still the same. One by one I recognized the points of simian hideousness: the sloping forehead, the advanced brow-ridges, the bestiality of the mouth—in sum, the frightful mask . . . Her!

Sitting, or rather collapsed on a bench, she gave the impression of watching and waiting. Five or six "gigolettes" on the arms of their gallants, formed a semicircle around the she-monkey, and, each of them pointing at her sinister muzzle, they were noisily spouting insults or crude jokes. Silent, but frightfully pale under the downpour of ignoble gibes, the unfortunate woman tried to smile, while putting her hands together.

Sometimes, however, a desolate rictus contracted her face, and then she extended her fingers against her face, as if to hide the repulsive ugliness; perhaps she was weeping. And sometimes, again, a poignant anxiety succeeding the dolorous shame, she turned her head back and forth, seeming to search the turbulent crowd. Very intrigued, I approached the group and went to sit down at one of the neighboring tables. Immediately, the woman straightened up; a sudden blush lit up the chlorosis of her cheeks, and, extending her face in my direction, she began staring fixedly. An unpleasant gaze! In the meantime, grossly formulated gibes continued falling in profusion.

"It's her," said one of the ladies. "I recognize her; it's the preaching lemur of the brasseries and music halls. Disappeared, rediscovered. Hey, my beauty, off to the Jardin des Plantes!"

"Salut, Sister Cunegonde," said another comrade. "Have you come here to beg for the parish? A funny parish, Mesdames: the Expiatrices of Montmartre."

The Expiatrices of Montmartre were undoubtedly well known in the Martyrs' quarter, for long joyous laughter flowed from all the made-up lips.

"Oh, divine Aspasia, Phryne, Flora, Ninon d'Enclos," cried a sigisbeo with the mane of a poet, "confide to me your lustful amours, snows of yesteryear, past felicity!"

He must have had a sickness of elegy, the fellow. But, impassive now, the sufferer no longer appeared to hear anything. Her eyes were shining, her breast heaving, panting, and her mouth open, she was looking at me brazenly. Meanwhile, the orchestra had just launched into a riotous polka.

"One last rigadoon!" cried one of the demoiselles. "Next the American; it's getting late!"

At those words—"It's getting late"—like an automaton moved by a spring, the seated woman got up abruptly. I saw her run at a precipitate pace toward the exit; but suddenly, her entire body pivoted on itself; she uttered a cry—like a scream of pain— and then, heavily, with spasmodic frissons in her shoulders, she headed in my direction. Then, taking a chair and placing it next to mine, the strange creature let herself fall into it.

"Bravo, bravo! Beware of conversion!" cried the troop of whores, soon dispersing through the ballroom.

We remained alone, the woman and I, in a tête-a-tête. A minute or two went by silently.

"Bonsoir, Monsieur," she said finally. "Am I indiscreet?"

"Indiscreet? Why so, my dear Madame?"

Again, her dark eyes examined me; then, stammering fearfully: "You can't place me, then? Well, I recognized you immediately. What a fine spectacle, a cemetery at nightfall!"

Nonplussed, I begged her to explain.

"Do you remember, Monsieur . . . yesterday evening, at about six o'clock, before the snowstorm?

Ah, very good! The memory returned: my reverie on the Pont Caulaincourt and the nocturnal walker. What a memory: the young woman, the silhouettes and the passing shadows!

"In truth," she said, becoming bolder by degrees, "how did I recognize you? I don't know. It was foggy, you were some distance away, and I wasn't even able to see your face. However, it's really you, I'm certain of it."

"Very flattered. In my turn, dear demoiselle, I've just recognized you."

"You've noticed me."

"Elsewhere. Where? Guess." I paused briefly, and, observing her—God what ignominious ugliness!—I added: "This evening, I admired you in your holy apostolic functions, at the hour of the sermon at Chez Sylvius."

She made the grand gesture of an actress. "I know . . . in that infamous brothel of Mammon and Azathoth—less filthy, however, than this one."

Stiff and sharp, "brothel of Mammon and Azathoth" to describe a restaurant fashionable among the theater crowd and elegant society. She went on, becoming excited: "And it was you who surged forth nobly to defend me—you, Monsieur!"

"In truth, Mademoiselle, I would have liked to protect you, to constrain the sniggerers to shut up."

"What would be the point? Hideous and repulsive to everyone, I am—it's necessary that I be—an object of derision or horror. But the insults are my delight; affront is voluptuousness to me. Under the slaps of the harshest outrages, under the jeers and the humiliations, I bless my God; sometimes, people strike me; I bless her again."

Enthusiasm inflamed her face, her voice was rhythmic, sonorous, cadenced; the abject hideousness had disappeared. I drew closer.

Suddenly, she advanced her head, looked at me fixedly, and then put a hand on my shoulder. "It's getting late," she murmured. "Take me away."

I had to suppress an insulting start, a mute expression of sensual disgust. What a metamorphosis, and the cynical pleasantry! But she, persisting with a tearful audacity, said: "I don't even have a room to offer you. Yours—take me home with you."

I could not believe my ears. Damn! A funny existence! At seven o'clock a deaconess; at midnight, a whore. I sensed myself shaking with laughter, a laughter of my entire being

"No," I said to her, moving away her hand. "Look elsewhere. My apartment isn't a night shelter."

She blushed, quivering, and lowered her head with a deep sigh. Why was she sighing like that? Anyone else—oh, I know those demoiselles—would immediately have retired, riposting with an insult. What was this living enigma? A parasite in search of supper and rest? A vagabond without shelter? One did not lodge by night, then, among the Expiatrices of Montmartre? I was bewildered, but firmly resolved to send her away. For a moment, the apostolic speech-maker had interested me; aversion for the repulsive ferret took hold of me again. What a monster!

"What! Not even a room to offer me? Sad, sad! So, no more magical villa, enchanted abode, frescos and mosaics? No more amorous couch where gallants of all ages . . ."

A lugubrious burst of laughter—the laughter of a convulsive idiot—interrupted me. At the same time, with a furious grip, the woman put her hands together and wrung them.

"It's getting late," she stammered. "Come on, come on, take me away."

Bah! We were talking familiarly now. But no . . . and peace! The ignoble supplication, this time, made me feel sick. Get out! To the monkey house! Besides which, if I talked any longer to such a marmoset, I felt that I would become ridiculous. What if my friends at the club had seen me? I called the waiter, settled my bill and got up.

"All my regrets respectable demoiselle, and a pleasure to see you again."

The lady immediately followed me.

"Your home! Your home! For pity's sake, your home!"

Without responding I drew away swiftly and lost sight of her. For an hour I walked around the ballroom; I admired the casualness of the quadrilles; idling with the idlers, I encouraged; I applauded certain immodesties. Finally, having had enough of cavalier solos, I thought about retiring.

Yes, the ape was right; it was getting late; but I did not feel any lassitude. The sonorities of the orchestra, the hysteria of the dancers, and the libertinage of the hall had stimulated me. It was in a sprightly fashion that I put on my pelisse in the cloakroom, and I went out humming a tune.

# X

"*Beautiful night, O night of amour* . . ." At a glance, I interrogated the sky: not a cloud; its blue-blackness was scintillating, flamboyant with stars.

"A carriage, Bourgeois?"

No . . . in this dry weather of luminous frost, under the bitter splendor of a winter sky, to walk for a long time and prepare for slumber is a true pleasure for me. I love to fatigue the beast, in order to become drowsy thereafter. Without replying to the coachman, I wrapped myself up in my fur and, still singing, began to go down the steep hill of the Pigalle quarter.

"*Beautiful night, O night of amour* . . ." An enervating obsession, that nocturne from the *Tales of Hoffmann!* The orchestra, to a languorous rhythm, had been playing it as a waltz, at the exact moment when I had repelled the woman; the immodest suppliant had clung to me thereafter; since then I had not heard anything else. Enough! I looked at my watch. One o'clock in the morning! Let's go, Monsieur Noctambulist, pick up your heels! It's a long way to the Rue Vaneau; a whole voyage, but hygienic . . .

Monologuing thus, I reached the boulevards. They were not yet asleep, noisy and agitated under the gaslight, traversed by the silhouettes of suppers of both sexes, rogues and ruffians. There, I consulted myself. Should I stop for a Neapolitan? It was getting very late . . . there, the words that the preacher had repeated: another obsessive refrain . . . Yes, too late; and I set forth along the Avenue de l'Opéra . . .

"*Beautiful night, O night of amour* . . ." Less rumor here; passers-by were becoming rarer. Half the street-lights extinct already; no more electric lamps: a dubious obscurity.

Ah! The place where Williamson frightened the two girls. What a sinister buffoon, that half-breed, doubtless a cross between an Englishman and an Egyptian woman. Priest of Isis? Pontiff of the Eternal Now? The brazen joker. Paris will always be a safe haven for charlatans, messiahs, the founders of Buddhist cults and other abusers of weak brains. If I were in charge of the police, what a clear-out I'd have of the whole heap of neo-Christs. However, he must possess formidable secrets, that individual . . . the custodian of Callista's mummy.

Callista? Well, yes, my enamored companion of last night; I'd almost forgotten her. Soon, I'll see her intoxicating smile again, the dainty pearls of her nacreous teeth, the soft and troubling caress of her great velvet eyes. You, a courtesan, you? More alluring, then, than a Laïs or an Aspasia! A fortunate rogue, Parmenon!

"*Beautiful night, O night of amour . . .*" Silence now, and solitude. Profound and slumbering, the garden of the Tuileries exhaled the bitter scent of the mossy trees, their rotting vegetable debris; and on the grass of the borders, yesterday's fallen snow was glittering like diamonds of frost. Truly, it's too abandoned, this path through the lawns. No *sergent de ville*, and yet, in these dark corners, prowlers and lurkers, menacing cut-throats . . .

I hastened my march . . .

Parmenon, insensate Parmenon! Pakrour the grim assassin! How were you able to strike with your knife, your ignoble butcher's knife, the quivering flesh that solicited you? You were in love, you were jealous, that was your excuse. Oh, when amour grips the heart with its dementia, the beast in man roars and bites, more brutally than the brute.

"*Beautiful night, O night . . .*" Someone went past me: a woman. She was moving very quickly, heading toward the Pont Royal. Enveloped in a white waterproof, the fleeting shadow drew away, thin and paltry; soon I could no longer see her . . . yes, though, at the entrance to the bridge she had slowed down, now she was walking level with me on the opposite sidewalk. Why was her mantle shining so brightly? A fatigue for my eyes; I turned right . . .

Again, the moving silence of a solitary quarter . . . the Rue Bellechasse: extinct, obscure, heavily asleep. Under the portals of coaching entrances, concealments of terror! On the clock of

Sainte-Clothilde, quarter to two chimed. Certainly, I was wrong to refuse the offer of the marauding coachman; this voyage was interminable, and . . .

Ah! So she was still following me, the vagabond, the after-midnight street-walker, running when I hastened my course, slowing down when I slowed down. Shaving the walls, she glided soundlessly, and in the enveloping shadow of the houses, I distinguished the gray mantle and its phosphorescence floating and undulating . . .

Finally the Rue Vaneau; my lodgings, my bachelor pad! At such an hour, my domestic must have gone to bed, but the night-light was waiting for me, lit in my bedroom. Yes, its light was filtering through the gap in the curtains.

What! That whore again, still obstinate in pursuit!

I crossed the road and stopped outside my door. The other stopped. Furious, I shouted to her: "What do you want? Go on your way."

She advanced her head toward me and I uttered a cry: the woman from the Moulin Rouge!

But with a bizarre laugh, she said: "You said *au revoir*, Monsieur; here I am."

I was confounded, without a word or a gesture to send her away. She continued: "You're not going to leave me in the street, I suppose? It's getting late; let's go in."

What a change in her language! The voice was no longer tear-ful; she sniggered, rather impertinently, and the words hissed, ironic, harsh and imperious. A princess of the Parisian gallantry would not have spoken differently.

"Let's hurry," she said. "Go on ahead; I'll follow you."

With one arm extended toward the bell, I looked at the adventuress. Frightful, in truth, but attractive; terribly ugly, but superb and who fascinated . . . yes, who fascinated me. What energy of will there was in that creature! "Your home, your home, Monsieur!" Well, in spite of my rebuffs, was she not about to force my door? I have always admired will-power; I submit to it;

I incline before it. In addition, what an amorous caprice for my person! An homage, rather flattering even in a woman of that species!

Strange appetites were beginning to torment me. Magnificent and desirable! Unhealthy burns gradually inflamed my blood; the ardor to enlace, to slap, to crush the bones of the skeleton, to press my lips upon that death-mask . . .

Her eyes stopped on my eyes; the unknown woman seemed to be following the movements of my thought, setting aside its tumults, mastering resistance. Sure henceforth of her victory, she smiled, uncovering for me, mockingly, the dazzling whiteness of her teeth. Oh, those teeth! Why had I not noticed them before? Worthy of being broken, one by one, of being arranged on the crimson velvet of a jewel-case. And that gaze . . . above all, that gaze! Exciting, voluptuous, impure, so warmly lascivious.

"You find me pretty now," she said. "Many others have also been in love with me."

Many others! With a reckless surge I seized her waist.

"Come, beauty, come! It's getting late; let's go in."

In my turn I repeated the phrase, the exasperating refrain.

In the house, the gas had been extinct for a long time, and for two or three seconds I was obliged to grope in order to find my candle. When it was lit, my companion was no longer with me, but I heard her going up the stairs, marching with assurance through the darkness. I ran to catch up with her; she was waiting, snuffling like a hunting dog, on the landing of my apartment.

"What, you know where I live?" I asked her.

No response, but a slight tremor of impatience; the sound of her fingers scratching and scratching against the closed door.

"So, witch, or to put it better, bewitching!"

The same astonishing silence; the stamping of the feet became more spasmodic.

"Daylight will soon appear," she murmured, finally. "Open it, please, open it."

"Oh, daylight! Not for another four or five hours, beautiful unknown."

The pretentious term "beautiful unknown" made her snigger strangely.

"Unknown? Do you think so, Monsieur? Believe me, we know one another, I swear to you."

An estimable relationship, in truth, and of which I could be proud! While talking, I had opened the door.

"Let me guide you, my dear . . . yes, yes, that's the way. What divination! At the end of the long corridor is my bedroom."

"I know . . . I still know."

"A magicienne, in that case, my white lady?"

And again I tried to put my arm around her waist.

"But first, charming lady, we're going to have supper; I'll ring for my domestic."

She repelled the brutal caress forcefully . . . and suddenly her face decomposed; her features distended; her eyes launched a gaze of wild stupor at me: the same anguished gaze of an agonizing beast that the deaconess had darted at me, in Sylvius' restaurant.

"No," she said, "I can't delay. 'Before daylight,' I was told."

I didn't understand, but vague anxieties slowly overtook me. What imprudence, on my part, to have brought that girl home, and above all, what ignominy! A return to reason chased away my desire; I was ashamed; I was afraid.

Now, step by step, from room to room, I followed the alarming visitor. She went on and on like a somnambulist, heading for my bedroom. Her hand lifted up the door-curtain, and her entire body slipped through it.

Under the unpolished globe of blue crystal, the night-light spread its discreet pallor, a mysterious dawn, like an obscure twilight.

"Daylight!" cried the woman. "And I haven't obeyed!"

With a violent recoil, I threw myself backwards. A madwoman! She was a madwoman.

Nailed to the threshold by fear, I wanted to flee; my feet had turned to lead. Slowly, the menacing apparition advanced into my bedroom, and then stopped. I saw her, panting, turning her head this way and that, parading her gaze everywhere, seemingly searching with her eyes, searching, ferreting in the gloom. Terrifying . . .

Over there, in the hearth, a few brands were still burning; rays of yellow light were reflected from the mirror, and over there, standing on the mantelpiece, shining . . . shining . . . shining, was the Egyptian painting: the mask of Callista . . .

Suddenly, there was a shrill cry, a trident clamor.

And that woman, in two bounds, hurtled toward the shiny object. "Ah!" Clenching the fingers of rapacious hands, she clasped the portrait . . . lifted it up . . . leaned over the fire . . . looked . . .

And then a lamentable sigh rose up in the silence; and then one word, only one:

"Me!"

## PART TWO

At this point, the strange narration of Raoul d'Hérival is abruptly interrupted; a sudden and profound lacuna is found in the communicated manuscript. Perhaps the ingenuous story of Evariste Monteil, and, above, all the curious journal of his colleague, Doctor Labastide, will serve to fill it in:

The Story of Evariste Monteil
Medical correspondent of the Parisian newspaper *Le Molière*
Consultations Tuesdays from 2-6 p.m.

17 Rue de Babylone

On the twelfth of January 1890, at seven o'clock in the morning, someone rang my doorbell loudly. The scientific editor of an important periodical, and quite well known in society, I had gone to bed rather late the previous night. I was therefore still asleep, reposing under the eiderdown: *Sex horas dormire sat est juvenique senique; do septem pigro . . .*[1]

Now, without having ever felt the troubling afflictions of old age—*importuna senectus*—I am no longer very young and I have always been one of those idlers reproved by Salerno. The ringing of the doorbell had woken me up and it was while cursing that I saw Martine come in, my laborious and devoted Norman. She came to announce to me, in ancillary terms, that Monsieur Baptiste, Vicomte d'Hérival's valet de chambre, was asking for my assistance, very frightened, and imploring my Aesculapian aid. His master, the man affirmed, was in danger of death.

Although I am no longer of an age or a personal situation to run after clients in the chill of dawn, knowing the duties of a physician, I did not hesitate. Monsieur d'Hérival belongs to a family esteemed in Cotentin, my homeland; he possesses a tidy fortune and, figuring then among my social acquaintances, he sometimes consulted me as a friend. I would have liked to interrogate the bearer of the message, but he had already gone. I therefore dressed in haste, dispatched a summary collation—*prandere adversus morbos scutum*—and rendered swiftly to the Rue Vaneau.[2]

As soon as I entered I observed a disquieting disarray in the house. A crime, the staff were certain, had just been committed there; the vicomte had been murdered. It was a bad business. On the landing of his apartment, an elegant entresol, several

1 This is a slight distortion of an oft-quoted dictum usually credited to the Medieval Schola Medica Salernitana, in Salerno, recommending the allocation of seven hours per day to sleep and seven to idleness.
2 The flippantly-improvised Latin phrase advises that eating opposes stomach-aches

servants were waiting for me: the Monsieur Baptiste who had come to fetch me, the cook, the concierge and others. Four or five domestics for a single master: an important client.

"We've been careful to leave the body as we found it," those imbeciles declared. "Perhaps it will be necessary to inform the commissaire of police."

"Yes, but later. It is for science to speak first; let us proceed methodically. What has happened?"

"This, Doctor," said the orator of the band, the fine-talking Monsieur Baptiste. "This morning, when I came down to do my work, I was very surprised to discover the door of the apartment wide-open. Furthermore, Monsieur's bedroom was illuminated; his night-light was still burning there. I approached, quietly. Monsieur le Vicomte does not like to be woken up before nine o'clock—and, well, I recoiled in fear. The poor man was lying on the floor, as white as a sheet, exactly like a dead man. He was no longer breathing; his hands were folded against his heart; I even thought I could see—I saw—several bloodstains on his fingers. A cadaver, Doctor, a veritable cadaver! Beside him, on the carpet, was a knife, whose point . . ."

"It was the woman," interjected the concierge.

"What woman?"

That person, a Cerberus of a janitor, self-important and solemn, struck a noble attitude of outraged modesty.

"What woman? Oh, not much: a demoiselle of the night that one had the imprudence to bring us yesterday evening. What a scandal! A house where a counsel of the appeal court lodges! But what can I do? Monsieur le Vicomte is the owner of the building, and it's not for us to watch over his morality. Anyway, I'm certain of it, it was her, it was the woman. Entered at two o'clock in the morning, left almost immediately."

That initial enquiry concluded—it was indispensable to me to enlighten my medical religion, *naturam morborum ostendunt inquisitiones,*[1] I headed for the bedroom.

---

1 Another item of satirically-improvised Latin referring to the ability of symptoms of death to answer questions.

"Let's see."

He appeared to me, at first glance, to be a fellow whose goose was cooked, with no need of rhubarb or an emetic. His body lay inert, blocking the threshold of the door; the murderer must have stepped over him in order to leave. Monsieur d'Hérival was dressed in his town costume, enveloped in an ample fur, and his hat had rolled into the corridor when he collapsed. Monsieur Baptiste's declarations were, moreover, exact; the night-light was still sizzling, ready to go out, and the cadaver's hands were folded over his heart. Immediately, I observed a few scratches, evidence of a struggle, but traumatically negligible, mere grazes, scarcely having brushed the epidermis. On the carpet I perceived an open knife, which I picked up—a miserable "jambette" with the point blunted a long time ago, one of the popular clasp-knives sold in bazaars for a few sous. No, that could not be the "instrument of the crime"—but in truth, was I in the presence of a crime?

My initial impression was beginning to be modified. There was no trace of blood, either on the parquet of the corridor or Monsieur d'Hérival's clothing. Thus, it was probably not a murder, but rather a vulgar cerebral hemorrhage, a foreseeable result of the libertine existence that the unfortunate victim led. However, there were none of the familiar signs of apoplexy: no deviation of the facial muscles, hideous contractile grimace or mucosity at the lips. All animate life seemed to me to be extinct; the face, of a waxy pallor, was motionless; the eyeballs frightfully dilated, the mouth dry and closed. I could not hear the sound of any exhalation of breath. I tried to interrogate the pulse, but the two hands folded over the breast resisted my efforts; cadaveric rigidity already. I bent down to listen to the heart but the fur of the pelisse prevented me from perceiving the diastole. Finally, I asked for a mirror, and almost immediately, it was lightly misted: the man was still alive.

At hazard, I had brought my lancet. A convinced admirer of the ancient masters, I am a faithful believer in the philosophical theory of inflammations; I have always combated the heresiarchs and defended *mordicus* our old orthodoxy: bleeding and purges. I therefore ordered the domestics to undress Monsieur d'Hérival and deposit him on his bed. They set to work, but, to my surprise, the invalid's arms refused any movement. Their contracture could not be released; one might have thought that they were nailed to the thorax. Very strange, in truth: a curious pathological case.

"Well, cut the garments."

Someone went to fetch scissors, and for half an hour they cut and sliced. Like a mannequin, insensible and rigid, the body allowed itself to be handled. Finally, it was laid bare, then carried heavily to the alcove. The dubious daylight of a winter morning did not illuminate the entresol room sufficiently; I needed a brighter light.

"Draw back the curtains," I ordered, "and open the window."

I hoped that a brief sensation of cold might bring about a salutary reaction; I was not disappointed in my expectation. A current of air traversed the room, and immediately, I observed a slight movement; the contracted fingers relaxed. I succeeded in parting them, and then cut away the last scraps of cloth plastered against the breast. Aha! What was that? A bruise?

In the pericardial region I had just perceived a bloody redness, as bizarre in appearance as in character. One might have thought it a profound stigma imprinted in the whiteness of the skin by a broad point, a chopper or butcher's knife: a recent wound and still red. The wound was nevertheless not apparent; the epidermis had not even been broken. I took hold of the knife picked up from the floor; it did not match the stigma. Furthermore, there was no rip in the subject's clothing; their thickness ought to set aside even the hypothesis of a possible contusion. What was it, then? An effect of fear? The reflex and mysterious action of the mental on the physical? Perhaps. Numerous examples came to mind, and I saw it as an admirable subject for an article; I had to write my next Sunday chronicle.

In the meantime, my lancet between my fingers, I was very perplexed. The case was unusual, and moreover, two illustrious professors were dueling in my thought. Certainly, the adventurous Broussais would not have had any hesitation; but the shrewder Trousseau would have abstained;[1] his prudence condemned hasty solutions. That day, he was my guide, and the dangerous lancet went back into its sheath. For the moment in accordance with non-classical methods, I prescribed revulsives: sinapisms at the extremities, cold compresses on the forehead, and continual frictions throughout the body.

"Does Vicomte d'Hérival have a habitual physician?" I asked the loquacious Monsieur Baptiste.

"I don't know of one. He's never ill."

"Too bad: absence of malady, abstention from physician."

"He often talked about you, Doctor; he praised . . ."

"An elite mind, your master. My cares will not be lacking, but his general condition appears grave. It will be necessary to inform the family."

"Monsieur no longer has any relatives except for a distant cousin, a captain in the cuirassiers at Sainte-Menehould, a tall bald man whom he sometimes invites to hunts."

"Better and better; we'll write to the tall bald fellow."

Eleven o'clock chimed. That very day, I was having lunch at home at half past eleven with one of my colleagues, the eminent neurologist Marius Labastide. The two of us had formed the project of elucidating *inter pocula* various philosophical questions, and I also felt a furious appetite for learned feasts. Labastide lived at the end of the world, out in the Parc de Neuilly; he must already have set out, and my savant friend sometimes had the fault of formality; it was necessary to run to receive him.

"Observe my prescriptions carefully," I repeated to the domestics. "I'm obliged to leave, but I'll return before this evening."

And I left.

---

1 The references are to Victor Broussais (1772-1838) and Armand Trousseau (1801-1865).

Having arrived slightly early, my colleague had been waiting for five minutes, the *Molière* in hand, absorbed in reading my latest "medical chat." My dear comrade Marius Labastide is—you can take my word for it—the foremost of our contemporary alienists. Having remained very sprightly in spite of his age, still burning with a youthful ardor, he represents for me the generous old man celebrated by Virgil, but the garden he cultivates—I request indulgence for the metaphor—has always been the inexhaustible field of Science. A former intern at the Salpêtrière, once the favorite pupil of Lélut,[1] whose elegant prose and learned badinage he has been able to reproduce, Labastide publishes every year various opuscules of inestimable value. The "madness of genius" has no more secrets for him. Better than a psychologist or moralist, he has penetrated the cerebral profundities of a Tasso or a Pascal, a Goethe or a Jean-Jacques Rousseau. The author of the *Confessions* has become his favorite; he has demonstrated his sublime dementia, and every medical library ought to possess his excellent pamphlet *Genius and Lubricity*.

Genius . . . he has been able to discover it in all the erotic writers: the likes of Catullus and Ovid, Petronius and Apuleius, Boccaccio and Aretino, in the *Satyricon*, the *Decameron* or the *Sonnets luxureuses*, in the entire works of Restif de la Bretonne—what am I saying?—even in the repulsive Marquis de Sade, a genius, it appears, whom it was not possible to "fecundate" at Bicêtre. What can Labastide have wanted to imply by his adjective *fecundate*? I don't know and I don't want to know. Too inventive, in my opinion, perhaps even a trifle systematic, my audacious colleague's theories.

But if his philosophy sometimes shows temerity, the practitioner, on the other hand, acts skillfully. For twenty years, dear

---

1 A pioneer in the scientific study of insanity, Louis-Franscisque Lélut (1804-1877) remains famous for his sensational adventures in "restrospective diagnosis," *Le Démon de Socrate* (1836; revised 1856) and *L'Amulette de Pascal, pour servir à l'histoire des hallucinations* (1846), in which he argued that Socrates and Blaise Psacal were both insane, in order to support the general argument that genius is a species of madness.

Marius has been directing a "house of retreat" at Neuilly, which he has rendered famous. It is there, in the hygienic repose of a Parisian suburb, among the flowers and the cool shade, that he is able to give his clients calm or excitation of the mind, and to attempt experiments on them that are not banal. That house the Villa Riante, is successful; the sagacity of some relatives willingly prolongs the sojourn of certain invalids here, for truly, as in the ancient adage, the mad are treated there in accordance with their madness. A beneficent foundation, but also a commercial society, our Villa distributes very good dividends, seven or eight per cent at each issue: a true investment for the father of a family. I have the good fortune to be a shareholder.

Yes, I have always venerated that philanthropist, that daring researcher of the human problem, that convincing disquisitor; I applaud—not always without reservations—the ingenuity of his methods, and my amity for him will doubtless excuse a digression that is far too long.

The meal was joyful but savant. While discussing a certain novel, the present of a generous patient, I spoke about Monsieur d'Hérival; I described his case, and Labastide, intrigued, declared that he wanted to see him. An hour later, we were in the entresol in the Rue Vaneau.

"No change," Monsieur Baptiste announced to us.

Perfect! Then, preceded by me, my eminent friend penetrated the bedroom; he examined, turned the body this way and that, and from his quivering lips a single word escaped: "Aïdeisme!"[1]

---

1 I have left the author's "Aïdéisme" untranslated at this point, although Labastide must surely have said "aideisme," referring to a complete "lack of ideas" or a cessation of all mental activity. The addition of the accents by Thierry, however, implies a syndrome derived from "Aïda"—which, although neither doctor could know it, might indeed be a wryly accurate assessment of Hérival's mental illness. Thierry continues to insert the spurious umlaut in Labastide's notes, labouring the joke, but I have removed it from the translations therein

Aideism! A variety of Braid's neurypnosis.[1] I might have divined it—but what an assurance of diagnosis! Then Labastide added, pensively: "A very curious subject. Our Villa Riante demands him."

Evidently. I drafted a telegram in haste, which I addressed to the cousin in Sainte-Menehould, the captain of cuirassiers; I told him that it was urgent and asked for instructions. The response was not long delayed, and I ought to transcribe it, in its entirely military laconism:

*Paris from Sainte-Menehould 540.27.1.12.4.15. Lament unfortunate relative. Commit good care Doctor Labastide. Collect. Absolute confidence. Full powers. Case decease inform. We inherit. Captain d'Hérival-Noireterre.*

"Absolute confidence—collect." The family order was formal.

On the evening of the same day, Monsieur Raoul d'Hérival, still aideic, was transported to the Villa Riante. For myself, I had accomplished my task.

Journal of Critical Observations
by M. le Dr. Marius Labastide
Officier d'Académie, Chevalier de Nicham et du Soleil-Levant
Corresponding member of the Phocéenne, the Dracenoise and other scientific societies.
Author of numerous award-winning memoirs.
Director of the Villa Riante

---

1 The reference is to the Scottish surgeon and pioneer of medical hypnosis James Braid (1795-1860), who coined the term "neurypnosis" as a description of the abnormal sleep supposedly induced by mesmerists, although the briefer "hypnosis" was the term that caught on.

## VILLA RIANTE
House of retreat for neuropaths of both sexes
Parc de Neuilly, 133 Avenue Malakoff
Unparalleled establishment, confided to the care of an
illustrious physician,
honored by the sojourn of several political,
artistic and literary celebrities.
Assured reawakening of the brain;
application of the philosophical
method known as "Labastidian"

*Mentem agitat moles* (Labastide, *Spiritualism Refuted*, p. 3)[1]

"Cries of the organism, cry of the soul . . . what is the soul?"
(Labastide, *Genius and Lubricity, passim.*)

. . . . . . . . . . . . . . . . . . . . . . . . . . . . . . . . . . . . . . . . . .
Observation DCLXVII. M. R. de H. (Raoul d'Hérival) 40-45
years old. Anesthesia, apyschia, aphasia, cataplexy and catalepsy;
braidism and aideism.

Entered the Villa Riante 12 January 1890, 9 p.m. Lodged
in the Paracelsus Room, Averroes section, Hippocrates depart-
ment. Put under continual observation, incessant care, expect-
ant medication.

DCLXVII (continued). This morning, 13 January, the orderly
Galien came to inform me that Monsieur Raoul d'Hérival had
suddenly recovered the power of speech. Immediately, I ran to
study the interesting cataleptic. The anesthesia subsisted, but the

---

1 The Latin phrase is a derivative of *Mens agitat molem*, which refers to the
alleged triumph of mind over matter.

aphasia had disappeared. His speech emerged, sometimes stammered and incoherent, but full of an overly imagistic, somewhat Parnassian, poetry. Certain words recurred in that murmur, which the invalid repeated amorously, modulating them, murmuring them, as if ecstatically rapturous:

"Out there . . . under the sun of golden javelins, near the sea of blue songs . . . what remembrance!"

A man of leisure habituated to fashionable beaches, was Monsieur d'Hérival seeing again his winter casinos at Biarritz or Monte Carlo? Was he evoking countries traveled as a tourist, Naples, Sorrento, Venice and the divine Marseilles, my dear homeland? I could not be edified that day. "The sun of golden javelins; the sea of blue songs." Outré, emphatic, redundant expressions, but what a bizarre flight of lyricism in a futile idler, a libertine running after facile Venus! Cacothymia, assuredly: the inexact perception of real sensations. The sun does not hurl javelins, and yet an ancient poet believed that he could see the Olympian archer therein, the argyrotos. The sea does not sing any leitmotiv, but a Wagnerian might want to accompany it on the piano.

Any poet or musician is, in any case, a cacothymic: insanity inhabits them in a latent state. Several of our old alienists, including Moreau de Tours and Brière de Boismont have already noted that curious aberration of the evident—in my opinion, the first symptom of genius.[1] Perhaps, by unpacking the sensorium

---

1 The psychologist Joseph Moreau (1804-1884), known as Moreau de Tours, remains notorious for supplying psychotropic drugs to volunteers—including several famous authors in search of inspiration—as an aspect of his research into the chemically-induced simulation of madness, but he was also notable for his observation of the role played by grief as a precursor of mental illness. The physician François Brière de Boismont (1797-1881) remains famous for his pioneering study *Des Hallucinations, ou Histoire raisonnée des apparitions, des visions, des onges, de l'extase, du magnetisme et du somnambulisme* (1845), in which he suggested that hallucinations were an important aspect of the psychological history of humankind. He also published *Du Suicide et de la folie suicide* (1856)

of Monsieur d'Hérival, one can find there at the Spurzheimian pole[1] some excessive development of the organ of *supernaturality* (cf Spurzheim. *Loi naturelle de l'homme*; I have commented on that work elsewhere. Germer Vaillière, 1878.) We shall have to wait for the autopsy.

✳

DCLXVII (continued). What a truly unusual and rare case of its species! I remain almost astonished by it.

Today, 14 January, neglecting my other inmates, I installed myself by Monsieur d'Hérival's bedside. At first, the condition of my subject appeared to be the same. My sleeper lay motionless, enchained by a general ankylosis; his mouth continued to talk, stammering and thick; the brain was still secreting delirium—but what delirium! The patient believed himself to be a character in an antique comedy; he said he was a slave, *famulus*, in the house of a courtesan, and gave himself the servile name of Parmenon. Classical reminiscences, memories of school? A hypothesis scarcely plausible in a futile clubman, assuredly illiterate. I need to verify that, however. Possessor of an interesting library, I had two Latin comic writers brought and began to leaf through their scurrilous buffooneries. Yes, first to search for every primal cause in its causality and divine the logic of the apparent illogic has been and always will be the habitual procedure of my method.

"Parmenon" *id est* "servant attached to his master" says my Variorum edition—Elzevir, 1644. Attached to his master: a paleontological rarity, in truth; a poorly domesticated species, disappeared irredeemably. In Plautus, no character of that name; on the other hand, three Parmenons in the work of Terence. But how to choose between them, which of three fellows was laboring Monsieur d'Hérival's memory?

---

1 The pioneer of what came to be known as phrenology, Johann Spurzheim (1776-1832) included "poles" in his speculative "map" of the brain. The reference cited by Labastide is fictitious.

Suddenly, I notice a tremor on the part of the cataleptic. The body is stirring . . . it agitates . . . the head is raised . . . a cry emerges from the mouth and the arm extends, indicating the window. What's happening, then? I run to the window. Nothing. The Avenue Malakoff extends, solitary; not one human face under the denuded plane trees . . . yes, though! On a bench, in the frost, a woman is sitting, a vulgar slattern who is watching the Villa Riante. I return to Monsieur d'Hérival . . .

The agitation was continuing and augmenting. The eyes were shining, the breast heaving; the arms, tight against the thorax, seemed to be embracing some invisible mistress. And soon, coaxing, velvety and harmonious, sighing with an infinite tenderness, the voice, in long sobs, made itself heard.

"Alas, my Callista . . . my adored, alas! Can you prefer senile caresses to my young embraces? Wretched me—you, more wretched still! A dolorous rage is making my blood boil; tears have swollen my eyelids . . . fall, my tears, flow, blood of my soul, and may you extinguish the fire that is devouring me!"

But suddenly, another cry. For a second time, the hand extended, suppliant; a lamentable sigh, then the head slumped backwards, the body resumed its cadaveric rigidity . . . Very intrigued, I returned to the window; the woman had disappeared.

I was bewildered. To whom, then, were the flame of that gaze and the despair of such sobs addressed? To the humble creature sitting outside the house, that street-corner beggar-woman? Like a beast in rut, had the male scented the female through fences and walls? Perhaps . . . but in that case, DCXLVII was one of my cherished erotics, a precious subject of study; I would be able to make a collaborator of him!

Having returned to my study, I began to meditate. Everything about that bizarre client of my friend Monteil seemed to me to be worthy of a passionate examination. A vulgar boulevardier, a socialite stranger to the Muse, becoming so abruptly poetic! A poet in continual progress—yesterday a simple modernist, today antique in the manner of Horace. Oho! That was genius—but genius in need of fecundation!

And let no one, in reading me, mistake the range of that word "fecundation." Certainly, I have never nurtured the foolish project of transforming the Villa Riante into a factory producing Sophocles and Molières, Platos and Aristotles. That ambitious design would be too risible, and, a physician of the insane, they would lodge me at the Petits-Maisons. No, but like those bold seekers of the Middle Ages who, carrying out their experiments in leprosaria or royal charterhouses, discovered the attachments of certain muscles, and learned to know the bone structure of the skeleton, I would like to seize from life the action of the brain while it secretes thought. I can manipulate efficaciously so many of these *animae viles!* Condemn me if you wish, I don't care. My life, and my very honor, to transcendental Science! "I bandage," Ambroise Paré liked to say, "God heals." Thus, it is for God—if the "non-negligible hypothesis" happens to be a reality—and for God alone to cure; personally, I study. And damn it, the physiologists of young America have dared many others. Forward ho! Like them, I intend to march; I want to run, and no one will have the power to stop my momentum.

Now, of all the cerebral inflammations, the cephality of the metaphysician and that of the litterateur have always appeared to me to be the most interesting to study. How does the sensorium of a Socrates or a Pascal form and develop? Two proven madmen—Lélut has established that conclusively—the philosopher with the demonic counselor and the Jansenist with the amulet— but two geniuses. How and why? An exasperating problem that it is necessary finally to elucidate. "Genius, incoercible atom," said the great Diderot; I will add: a fecundatable atom. One of my peers, Moreau de Tours, tells us that in a young hysteric he was able to procreate a more penetrating style of mystical magic than the prose of Fénelon or François de Sales. Why should I not obtain similar products.

Yes, my duty is presently traced: tomorrow, in case DCXLVII, the Labastidian method.

DCLXVII (continued). The Labastidian method! In one of my pamphlets, which has become popular (dare I say without false modesty), bearing an audacious deviation from holy routine, I have cried:

"What gives a nightingale its trills, a lion its roar? Sexual altruism. What puts ardor, audacity, energy and talent into the human heart? Feminine attraction. What am I saying? From exacerbated Eros, the spark of genius sometimes springs forth. Beatrice dies and Dante conceives the idea of the *Divine Comedy.* Madame de Houdetot coquettishly refuses herself, and the excited sensualism of a Jean-Jacques also gives birth to the *Nouvelle Héloïse.* Poetic inspiration almost always comes from erethism . . . Oh, if only one could provoke it, even constrain to genius the supposed genius brain, what a therapeutic innovation, and what a benefit for our humanity!"

Those conclusions, I know, once generated some noise in society, and my new method is summarized in its few lines. Rational, original and so philosophical! The Académie des Science Morales, however, refused to crown my memoir, and my recent candidature for the Académie de Médicine was denied its vote. A theoretician, certain jealous individuals said of me. Yes, Messieurs, but we are all theoreticians, the innovators, the bold laborers of our revolutions! Furthermore, in spite of your criticisms, I persist in my experiments. *Etiamsi omnes, ego non.*[1]

That day, however, 15 January 1890—a date memorable in the history of my life—I got up perplexed. A doubt tormented me. I was firmly resolved to attempt the Labastidian method on DCLXVII, but it is delicate of application, experimental rather than curative. I take a certain subject and I envelop him in passionate effluvia, or, to express myself in banal French, I try to

---

1 Approximately, "Even if everyone else does, I do not"—often used as a motto proclaiming independence.

render him amorous; then, suddenly suppressing the altruistic current—which is to say, the presence of the beloved—I isolate my subject and thus procure him the shock of a fecundating suffering: "Man is an apprentice; pain is his master."[1]

Carefully, then, I note each of the words, cries, gestures and sighs of my desperate individual and I compare them with the creations of the most authentic geniuses: Aeschylus, Shakespeare, Corneille, even Racine, Kean or even Frederick.[2] Alas, how often the furies of Orestes, the jealousy of Othello and the adulterous ardor of a Phèdre or Roxane have appeared to me to be inferior to the formidable roaring of the human beast! I have numerous notebooks filled with stupefying observations. But too often, also, more brutal convulsions than divine poetry.

With Monsieur d'Hérival I had high hopes. And yet, that morning, yes, I got up perplexed. Where could I find the "enveloping effluvia," procure the Elvire whose death made Raphael sigh the stanzas of *Le Crucifix*, the infidel lover who made her lover howl the *Nuit d'Octobre*?[3] In the Hypatia quarter—that of the feminine sex—the experimental material was, at that moment, absent; not one of my habitual inmates, female composers, painters, sculptors, poets or novelists. I had a female economist, a candidate for deputation, but so old, so pretentious, so workaday and so unexciting. Oh, a sad inspirational muse! And also, even if she would lend herself to the experiment, for my part, I would have experienced insurmountable scruples about employing her. I have always conserved intact the prejudice of decorum.

I was extracted from those meditations by two raps on my door. Stammering and timid—I had always frightened him— the concierge of the Villa Riante came into my study.

---

1 The quotation is from Alfred de Musset.

2 The concluding references are presumably to the actor Edmund Kean (1789-1833) and the Prussian king Frederick the Great (1712-1786), both hailed by various commentators as examples of mad genius.

3 The "poetic meditation" *Le Crucifix* by Alphonse Lamartine had been set to music by Adolphe Botte in 1880. Alfred de Musset's poem *La Nuit d'octobre* also became famous in its musical versions.

"Salutations, Monsieur Fagon. You have something to say to me?"

An accomplished bumpkin, the concierge Fagon drunken and choleric, a frank animal, but the man's name had once determined my choice.[1] Oh, it wasn't in that boor that I would ever awaken genius. Very uninteresting, the former gendarme; nevertheless, toward the anterior pole he bears curious protrusions on the head: the organ of locality, I presume. We'll palpate that.

"Monsier le directeur," he said, "it's the woman."

"What woman?"

"An individual who has been hanging around the establishment for a few days. I tried to throw her out yesterday; she only submitted rebelliously. The slut has come back."

"Well, throw her out again."

"In spite of my order, she refuses to go."

"What does she want?"

"To see Monsieur d'Herival."

"DCLXVII! But it's God, if he exists, who has sent her to us!"

I had just started; a flash of lightning had suddenly illuminated my darkness. That "slut" was to be the prey, the exciting altruist who had, in spite of all the obstacles, opened up my estromaniac. And they knew one another!

"Bring her, Monsieur Fagon, quickly!"

"I obey, Monsieur de directeur."

A few moments later, the individual was introduced.

On seeing her enter, I uttered a cry of admiration. The marvelous horror! Maxillary prognathism worthy of the Museum; as dolichocephalic as a Kanak; the apparent cretinism of a Valaisien; all the facial bestiality of the primeval anthropoid. Truly superb, that specimen of simian derivation. Oh, if my illustrious friend Broca had lived long enough to measure that skull![2] With great difficulty, I succeeded in overcoming my emotion.

---

1 Presumably because of its echo of the name of Guy-Crescent Fagon, physician to Louis XIV and director of the royal gardens.

2 The anatomist and anthropologist Pierre-Paul Broca (1824-1880), a pioneer of anthropometry.

Modest and yet assured, the monster stood before me, waiting for me to speak. Her costume, for the season, was bizarre, to say the least. Entirely clad in white, she wore a wretched cotton dress and a long muslin veil, like a nun's wimple, hid her hair. The unfortunate woman must have been cold in that burlesque accoutrement; her eyes—very bright dark eyes—were tearful; marbling effects of cold decomposed her face; her teeth—very pretty teeth—were chattering. And the more I studied her face, the more a recent memory returned to me. Where had I perceived that chimpanzee muzzle before? In what fairground booth? In the display case of what anatomical preparer? Oh yes, I remembered: one evening at Chez Sylvius, a Friday of national bouillabaisse. The woman had slipped impudently into the restaurant, had spouted some nonsense, and the waiters had thrown her out. Doubtless a delirious corporal in the Salvation Army.

After a few moments of mute wonderment, I proceeded to interrogate her.

"For three days you've been prowling around our house . . ."

She interrupted me: "And for three days I've been watching, listening, and waiting."

"I didn't know that. What do you desire?"

"To see him again."

"To see him again? About whom are you talking?"

"You know very well."

"Monsieur d'Hérival?"

"Yes, since that's his name in our second life."

"Second life? Hebrew to me. Be clearer; I don't understand."

"What need have you to understand?"

"An impertinent response. In sum, who are you, what do you do?"

"I expiate."

"A singular métier. What is your name?"

"Redemption."

"A Spanish name?"

"A universal name."

Anger was beginning to take hold of me; was my patience being mocked? "Rubbish! Enough joking. I know you, my beauty."

"Then pray for me."

"You're a Salvationist."

"No, but a humble servant of the Eternal Now."

"The Eternal Now? What's that? The so-called God? Hypothesis."

"Certitude."

"Very good, reverend lady. How do you know?"

"He talks to me."

I jumped for joy, Damn, another one: religious mania. Oh, Pascal was right: "Humans are so necessarily mad that it would be folly, by virtue of another twist of insanity, not to be mad." Yes, all mad. And me? Oh, that's different.

The preacher sister amused me; I thought I could risk a Voltairean sally.

"Bah! He talked to you? Him? The Eternal Now? To the sound of rebecs or ardavalis? Talked with his mouth of shadow or his voice from the abyss? And you've contemplated his august face?"

Following an ancient precept I was humoring the lunatic. Mademoiselle Redemption did not seem to suspect it.

"No, my eyes are scarcely open to the dazzle of Day and a newborn must be spared the Light. But the Supreme Pity deigned to send me one of our protectors, from his divine Eons: the tender and benevolent Isis."

"Isis! The horned head of the Egyptian Museum? You worship Isis!"

I was astounded. What wind of insanity was passing over my contemporaries? The Salvation Army, spiritists, Swedenborgians, Buddhists, Druids, Rosicrucians, Satanists, Chaldean sârs, kabbalists, spell-casting mages . . . and I had before me a proselyte of the cult of Isis! Astonishing!

I remained pensive for a moment. The visitor, however, was beginning to interest me; her bizarre devotion might furnish me with a chapter of a certain volume I was preparing, a long documented work on Contemporary Visionaries, of the genre of Mélanie Mathieu and Bernadette Soubirous.[1]

"How does one converse with Isis?" I asked her.

She seemed slightly hesitant, but the cavities of her eyes soon lit up, a faint redness spread over the hideousness of her face, and my illuminate appeared to obey an irresistible impulsion. Perhaps she hoped to convert me.

"In order to hear the Voice," she said, solemnly, "the soul must first traverse the bitter delights of enôse . . ."

"One moment . . . enôse? Do you mean ecstasy?"

"Yes: the temporary absorption of innumerable creatures in the creative Unity. The rudimentary souls, the animal and even the plant can know enôse.

"Jargon renewed from the Greek, very well! How, then, do you traverse the 'delights' of ecstasy?"

"During nocturnal adoration, in the obsecratory vigil. According to our ancient rites, it's necessary to have fasted for a long time, to have kept vigil repeatedly for three, seven and twelve nights, relentlessly, without weakness, in order better to annihilate our enemy: the beast."

"The body? The whole self?"

"No, the bad part of ourselves. Then it's necessary to be liberated from carnal bonds, to have refrained from ignoble concupiscence. 'I am pure, I am pure,' one must be able to murmur to God without lying."

"A terrible tyrant, your God! He demands the impossible." I shrugged my shoulders, for I have always condemned the dan-

---

1 As a teenager Mélanie Calvat (1831-1904), known as Mathieu, had a vision of the Virgin Mary in the village of La Salette, and claimed to have received a message from her; she subsequently became a nun, and the unwitting prophet of a company of "Melanists." Bernadette Soubirous (1844-1879), who had similar visions at Lourdes, was eventually canonized in 1933.

gerous apostles of absolute continence, the mystical charlatans whose doctrine has for its infallible result mental derangement, sensory aberration and shameful delirium. But bah! The preacher was barely listening to me; joining her hands and inflating her voice, she went on, becoming excited:

"In the silence, in the semi-darkness of the sacrary, by the flame of nine eternally burning tripods from which symbolic scents are exhaled, the soul becomes languid, and then aspires more ardently to love, and more love. In the depths of the chapel, in the shadow populated by religious terrors, stands an alabaster edicule, and it's there that the image of Isis, the powerful and helpful Eon, resides in her terrestrial glory.

"All night long, without weakness, the suppliant who hopes and expects must not quit the radiant face of the Good Mother with her eyes. She is so beautiful, so pleasant to contemplate. Thick hair undulates, blue-tinted, over her celestial shoulders; roses with heady perfumes crown her head; a brilliant disk surmounts her forehead, which soon becomes a splendor, a dazzle of light. Her robe, a snowy cotton fiber, gradually becomes iridescent; she acquires all the glare of daylight, while, like the night, an adorable mantle in which the stars scintillate falls along her adorable body. In her left hand Isis holds a bronze sistrum, and with her raised right hand she blesses the world . . .

"Now the sistrum agitates softly; an increasing vibration traverses the silence, and, even softer than the chant of our priests, an ineffable harmony penetrates the heart of the kneeling person. O delight! O rapture! Her body totters, seized by an unknown intoxication; she shivers, she swoons, and suddenly falls on the floor as a dead person falls. Immediately, there . . . yes, there, before the soul whose wish has been granted, Isis descends from the altar; slowly, she advances, she approaches, smiling; like a tender mother, she enlaces the imploring child in her arms; with the whiteness of her hands she wipes the eyes moist with tears. "Clement One, is that you, Clement One?" Then, moved by our miseries, propitious and favorable . . ."

"The goddess speaks to you!" I cried, interrupting. "The hallucinate has reached the ninth degree of seraphic love, and can hear God . . . I know my authors."

"Although humbly ignorant, I know too," replied the speechmaker. And, like a schoolgirl who had recited her catechism to me, she started to enumerate the nine ascendant formulae invented by the mystagogues: "Solitude, silence, suspension, inseparability, insatiability, indefatigability, rapture, supreme languor, enôse."

"Perfect! Well, a simple pathological case, my poor friend. Some of my inmates—funny saints, I assure you—have also seen the so-called God. Come and live with us, then, at the Villa Riante."

The worshiper of Isis repressed an indignant frisson; this time my pleasantry had displeased her.

"Take me to Monsieur d'Hérival," she said, dryly. "The Voice has said to me: 'Go to the reincarnate.' I am obeying."

Hérival, a reincarnate! Better and better: the folly of spiritism now. "And what do you want, my reverend lady, with that reincarnate?"

"His cruel memory has become my torture. Once criminal, he is expiating—expiating as much as me. I have come to reveal to him the story of his first life, to take the scales from his eyes, to bring him back to us, and, in accordance with our holy rites, to grant him my pardon."

I wanted a clarification of that sacrosanct nonsense. "So, dear demoiselle, you worship Isis?"

"Filial veneration; the cult of gratitude to the Sister, Wife and Mother; for Woman, Isis personifies Amour."

"A pure symbol, I imagine."

"An attribute of God, a divine emanation: Supreme Pity, softening Supreme Justice . . . a symbol, yes, but a personal and living entity."

"In sum, another Manitou. Isis is now worshiped in Paris, then?"

"Our fallen temples are emerging from their debris; they will rise up again toward the heavens."

"Where do you lodge your goddess? At Bicêtre or Charenton?" A disdainful silence. I went on: "Can one visit the parish of Saint Isis?"

"Our doors are open to you; but open your heart first."

"Sublime! Let's talk a little about Raoul d'Hérival. That monsieur has lived before? He's a reincarnate?"

"Like every human power. Death does not exist; it is only a renewal of life. Eternity of God, perpetuity of his creations."

"In that case, I must have been called Epicurus. Truly, my poor child, you believe in these absurd tales?"

"Who dares to say 'absurd' simply says: 'beyond my reason.'"

"And how many faithful are there in our sanctuaries?"

"You, tomorrow, if the Voice summons you."

"The Voice? Pooh; to convert me it would require more than the discourse of the Eternal Now."

She looked at me scornfully. "Blasphemies! Be more modest, infinitesimal atom engulfed in immensities."

Dear God, some fanatic! Should I confess it; I was dying to ring for an orderly to lock that Marie Alacoque[1] in the Helvetius Room. But no; no illegal acts; I reprove them. Even at the Villa Riante, the law is the law."

Time was pressing, however, it was already the afternoon; one can waste precious time in chatter of that sort. I had the orderly Galien summoned; he arrived very mealy-mouthed.

"Good news, Monsieur le directeur; our invalid is cured.

"Nonsense!"

"Absolutely cured, and he's asking to leave."

I shrugged my shoulders. Asking to leave: an incontestable indication of imminent epimania. I knew them so well, my lads

---

1 The mystic nun Margaret Mary Alacoque (1647-1690) had been beatified when the present story was written but was not canonized until 1920.

and lasses. If you believed them they were all cured, and my laboratory had only to close its doors.

The orderly continued: "Monsieur d'Hérival has all his reason. This morning he woke up very surprised to find himself here. The crisis has disappeared. He would like to talk to you."

"Without listening to him, we'll be able to understand him."

"He's irritated and indignant; he's even threatening to write to the public prosecutor."

"Address himself to the court? What, you, Galien, a former bailiff's clerk, can believe such nonsense?"

"Nonsense as much as you please, Monsieur Labastide, but I fear . . ."

He could not finish. The door opened, and Hérival came into my study. That idiot Galien had not locked the Paracelsus Room—deliberately, without a doubt. I should have mistrusted that residuum of the Parisian legal fraternity.

Very calm, arrogant, almost impertinent, my inmate marched toward me.

"I admire you, Monsieur. So, here I am in a madhouse! Truly, you don't lack audacity. What right do you have . . . ?"

I cut him off. "Look that way momentarily. There, yes, if you please."

And, with my finger, I designated the woman huddled in a corner of the room. He turned his head, perceived her, and suddenly uttered a vibrant clamor: "You!" he cried.

Then commenced a scene—the most marvelous of scenes of insanity. The face of the subject resumed its rigidity of the previous day; his eyes appeared to emerge from their orbits; then they dilated, haggard, blind and frightful, and Hérival began to recite, sometimes speaking and sometimes miming, a fantastic monologue. Again he believed himself to be the slave Parmenon.

I had picked up a pen, and I wrote.

✳

Immobile at first, and then becoming exalted by degrees, the man was furious, grinding his teeth, stamping his feet, clenching his fists. Then, running to the window, he examined the sky for a long time; and he uttered noisy sighs and sobbed, with lamentable gestures. His voice soon became audible—murmuring to begin with, and very confused:

". . . Their kisses . . . the wretches . . . to die . . . oh, to die . . . Amenti, the abyss and its harvest; the scepter that protects, the whip that chastises . . . no matter: kill, die afterwards . . . the dead . . . no one must love among the dead."

Those words only reached me with great difficulty; I dared not transcribe them. The meaning of certain words escaped me: Amenti? The harvest of the abyss? The scepter that protects, the whip that chastises? Perhaps I had misheard. Finally, the voice became more emphatic, more distinct, and I succeeded in comprehending.

". . . Dissipating the evil shadow, the sun will soon reappear to the eyes of the living; already the morning star is paling the horizon. It's the awaited hour! The moment I'm looking out for, when the augustal Valerius Afer extracts himself from Callista's embrace . . . I can hear him.

"'Slave. Open the door to the side street for me; I can't go out through the forum; the men of the night watch might recognize me.'

"Vile and pusillanimous, that old man. I obey. He waddles, adjusting his toga and, striking his thought, said: 'By Hercules, handsome child, Caesar is god but Callista is even more divine! All the pleasures that Mars savored with Venus have been lavished in that couch of ambrosia.'

"Obscene imbecile, with your Latin jargon! Oh, isn't he going to go? No, with his eyes of a lustful beast, he looks me up and down and sniggers: 'Do you know, friend, that in florid May, in Carthage, our ephebes sing a very pretty refrain: *Love now, you who have never loved, and you who will love tomorrow, also love today* . . . I'll obey that advice. Tell Callista that I'll return this evening.'

"Oh, this evening, this evening, crapulous Priapus, you won't see her!

"He escapes, fleeing like a furtive thief; he hastens toward his conjugal roof. Soon, putting on his laticlave, that husband will sit down in his praetory; he'll condemn adulterers, exalt holy decency, invoke the chaste heavens. A magistrate of Rome . . . ! I close the door again . . . in the house, everyone is in repose again; just the two of us, Callista!

". . . Callista? No, Ahmes the renegade priestess of Isis, the escapee from the sanctuary, the virgin become a courtesan. Those Greeks called her Kallistè—very beautiful—and the Roman Valerius had Romanized the name. Is she not the infamous property of that old man, that ignoble maintainer? Oh, yes, too beautiful! For all those men I'm 'Parmenon': Pakrour sounded harsh in their delicate ears. Filthy foreigners! Oh, if that wound could be extirpated from our Egypt by iron and fire! But no, Isis is no longer watching over the land of Khem; she is pleasing herself too much among the dead . . .

"Callista! On you I would have liked to avenge our gods, to punish a sacrilege. You . . . I cannot. Heart of a varlet that only knows how to weep . . . !

"Why, then, after stealing me very young, did the Ethiopian merchants dare to sell me as a slave? Out there on the isle of Philoe, under the sanctifying shadow of its porticos, a poor woman is in despair, calling for me. And why have the magistrates not condemned the theft of a free child? Bandits, these men in togas! They share the product of the theft with the thieves. Their Roman peace! And it's for one of those men, the vilest of them all, that Callista, trafficking her flesh, annihilates her soul and prostitutes our gods. Her body seven times consecrated, a brothel! Our priests, I know, have put on mourning; from our temples a cry of shame has risen. But the priests cannot strike, they cannot incur the inexpiable impurity . . . and then, Hermes must love her in secret . . .

". . . Hermes! What a strange, frightening individual! Priest of the Unnamable, hierophant of the Indivisible. Vainglorious, but so magnificent when he celebrates our mysteries clad in linen! The pallor of his face has always frightened me. Doubtless that man has penetrated the unfathomable abysses from which human beings only return with the whiteness of the tomb; he knows the formidable secret, the secret of Life and Death; he has seen God. Yes, for his eyes have retained a few particles of the increate Light; a dazzling spark, it fascinates, orders and constrains. Yesterday, Hermes looked at me and I have understood . . . it is me who must punish, me who must kill, me who will wash away the stain by means of blood. Let's see: the knife! It's here, hidden under my tunic. The other day, Johannes, the Nazarene butcher, ceded it to me for a few sesterces. A worthy fellow, the Nazarene; chaste and very devoted to his idol. How can he worship the head of a donkey? I'll convert him . . . Good knife! Its large hilt fills the hand; a Syrian blade . . . Let's go up . . .

". . . Wait, Pakrour; and above all, no hypocrisy . . . is it truly our gods that you're intending to avenge? Dare to say it, wretch; be frank with yourself. The renegade, unworthy Callista, you love her and you're jealous. Jealous! Ever since the accursed day when, by a caprice of blasé senses, she took you in her arms, you've loved her and you've suffered; you're suffering and you're tortured; she excites you and amuses you . . . In truth, it's necessary that she dies . . .

". . . Yes, but afterwards? The lictors will whip me; with their burning irons they'll dig into my body; the soldiers will nail me to a cross . . . Veh! A temporary torture, less suffering than my amour. I want to kill her and die thereafter. Die? But the Amenti, the sentence of our gods? Coward, coward . . . you know very well that those gods will acquit you; you're working for their glory. In any case, no one can love any longer among the dead . . . Let's go in . . .

". . . There she is. Exhausted, she's asleep; treading very softly, I approach . . . How charming she is, in the mantle of her outspread black hair, with her long close eyes azured by an aureole, the transparent and lascivious pallor of her face, her crimson-tinted lips, still parted, having given everyone the alms of a smile . . . Oh, impotent rage! That hair, that forehead hose eyes, that mouth—recklessly, lips have posed upon it that aren't mine!

". . . Languidly, a dainty hand hangs down, abandoned. I kneel down: chastely, I brush it with a kiss . . .

". . . What's that? On her hand, on the third finger, a ring! I don't know it . . . a ring of Roman workmanship, like those the illustrious knights of Rome wear. Under the discreet radiance of the vigilary lamp, what fires that ring darts at me! Some new present of your Valerius, seller of amour. I push away your hand. The sleeper awakes; she looks, perceives me, smiles, extends her arms to me: 'Is that you, my Adonis? You, handsome Endymion, slimmest of ephebes, my lord rather than my slave? Come, lovely sparrow, come; offer yourself to my caresses. Lie next to me, cherished giton, sweet catamite, pastime of my ennuis.'

"Gilded blandishments of a courtesan! On how many naïve individuals has she already lavished them? 'Don't talk like that, Callista. Renounce that language; it makes me feel ill. Those words are too reminiscent of the impure Akaioushas . . . Ahmes, the hour is solemn and the gods are listening to us . . .'

"Frowning, she contemplates me, stupefied. But her eye has followed my gaze; she sees me fascinated by the Roman jewel. 'Oh, Cythera, Parmenon is jealous! You'd like that ring, my dove? To offer it to Eros, who is so favorable to you, or to sell it to the Jews? But it's not for you, handsome darling. Valerius has given it to me, and I cherish my Valerius.'

"'I congratulate you, Callista. An old cinaedus, your delights! He's divine, the lover. His Mauritanian skin has all the whiteness of soot.'

"'Envious! Black are violets and black the scabious.'

"'His skull is bald, his sparse hair very gray.'

"'All bald in days of winter Olympus appears to us; and Olympus is the abode of the gods.'

"'Exhausted by age, he walks with a limp.'

"'Zeus also tottered when Ganymede poured the nectar.'

"'Give me that ring, Callista.'

"'What do you want to do with it?'

"'To throw it into the howling waves, the breakers unfurling under the Pharos.'

"'Imprudent, you'd poison Poseidon! Admire, sweet Parmenon, that delicate jewel. Look. The bezel opens and the ring contains a very subtle poison, a maleficent powder, a masterpiece of Thessaly. Valerius obtained it yesterday from More, the redoubtable sage of Larissa. These Thessalian women possess marvelous secrets. They disinter the dead and prepare with their burned bones . . .'"

"'For whom is that poison destined, Callista? For what old man or adolescent whose heritage you covet?'

"This time she sits up, white with anger. 'Evil dog! I ought to have you passed under the whips, marked with fire and then chained in the ergastule. But I have pity; amour has rendered you mad, and I know its frenzy. Know, then that this poison is for me. Now get out of here, barker; you've displeased me. Get out.'

"Again I bow my head; I prostrate myself humbly. 'What enemy threatens you, O clement mistress, my deity? Command: who is it necessary for me to kill for you?'

She has softened, and strokes my face with her rosy fingers. 'Naughty, naughty! Alas, the enemy that threatens me is not one of those you can attain; it is old age. Yesterday, at the two corners of my mouth, the mirror denounced winkles to me. A little more time, and the Chaldean make-up will not be able to hide them, and I dread hideous Chronos. I'm afraid of heavy disdain, abandonment and misery; afraid of the crossroads where the too-public Venuses wander by night . . . yes, the poison is for me—later, much later, but definitely for me. Loved, I want to live; I want to die mourned.'

"'Are you, then, so forgetful of the gods, poor soul close to extinction, that you no longer know the cry of the dead: *I am pure, I am pure!* Listen, my Ahmes, I beg you, listen to me; return to our gods. Out there, on the isle of Philoe, among the eight sanctuaries, stands a temple of Isis—Isis who pardons, and who will pardon you. Would you like me to take you there? Great as your crime is, greater still is the mildness of the Good Mother. Come. Seven times purified in the river, to the sound of golden sistra, to the song of psalteries, under the myrrh and the incense, by the paths strewn with flowers, you . . .'

"'I know all that, eloquent Parmenon: citharas and guitars, the lustral waters and the strewn roses, Isis and the clement smile, even the ecstasy and the stupid intoxication. Yes, I know that, my dear, and it has never charmed me . . . I'd be bored; I'd want new sensations. Me, return to your gods? The gods don't exist.'

"Indignation makes me shudder; the renegade has blasphemed. In spite of myself, I feel the knife and I think of Hermes. However, I remain prostrate; my voice begs again: 'Well, so be it; let's abandon the gods, but leave with me. With me, into a solitude that will be filled by our amour. In my arms, always beautiful, under my kiss, always young, you won't see the old age that frightens you coming. In vain, sun after sun will be extinguished in order to be reborn; only looking at one another, we'll collect the days, we'll savor the hours. Yes, the light is brief; too soon the inexorable night arrives . . .'

"She interrupts me with a burst of laughter—mocking laughter, insulting hilarity. 'You're scarcely inventive, my poor boy. A fastidious speech-maker, even more banal than the others. Twenty times, at my knees, they've said as much, the amorous of rare drachms. What torture! The other evening, it was Menelas, the bucolic poet; he cooed as much as a Theocritus and offered me the cottage, the black bread, the white cheese; I threw him out. Yesterday it was the turn of Phocion . . . you know, Phocion, the bearded philosopher, a cynic. He offered me half of his beggar's wallet; I could easily have taken the entire wallet . . . I'm bored, I'm bored, oh, how bored I am! By Hecate, what a stupid refrain all men sigh! And here's another one, Parmenon, my latest purchase: ten staters of fine gold. I chose him vigorous and robust; he ought to be diverting me, and all I can get out of him is tearful homilies . . . Let's go, on your feet, idler who's exasperating me. Have my bath prepared; you've woken me up, I can't sleep any longer . . . oh, haven't you understood? Get up!'

"I don't budge, still humbly prostrate; but for the second time I palpate the knife. Brutally, she pushes me with her foot. 'By Iacchos, he's drunk! A dozen strokes of the stirrup-leather, soon, and full! Get out, go sleep off your wine in the street. One order, however; Seleucus, the rich Syrian, is due to come today. Run and inform the mimes and flute-players. Seleucus is related to the king; I want to receive him royally.'

"I finally get up, and I laugh in my turn. Then, folding my arms, in a very calm voice, speaking slowly: 'Seleucus won't enter, triple wretch. And as for the augustal, you won't see him again.'

"She rushes at me, furious. 'What are you saying, slapped face? What are you saying?'

"'I'm saying that your sacrileges have finally awakened the gods; that your prostitutions are the shame of Egypt. I'm saying . . . I'm saying that you're going to die.'

"And I seize the knife . . .

". . . Fearfully, she launches herself toward the door; I bar her way. She screams . . . she shouts . . . she howls: 'Murder! Murder!'

"I grab her by the throat and throw her back on the bed.

"'Murder!'

"'Oh, shut up!' And with full fingers I close her mouth. She struggles and bites; her fingernails scratch me; her teeth dig into my flesh. Will I dare to kill her? I hesitate; my arms have become leaden. Is it so difficult to kill, then? The house fills with rumors; others have heard; they're going to come . . . go on, Pakrour, go on, avenge the gods, quickly! Our gods demand it . . .

"The knife comes down; it strikes full in the breast . . . a little blood . . . a deep sigh . . . nothing more . . . why, then, has the cold of steel suddenly traversed my heart?

"'Apostate! Blasphemer! Opprobrium of our temples! Soulless she-wolf! Filthy bitch!'

"I lift my fist to smash it into her face. No, this time I stop . . . How strangely she's staring with her eyes wide-open, menacing, indignant . . . ! Callista, my Callista! Oh! Oh! Pakrour, what have you done, wretch? I loved her . . . I still love her . . .

"I've fled . . . Hiding in the house of the Nazarene, breathless, my heart traversed by the cold of the knife, I've seen the long, slow funeral cortege file past. What magnificence! The sumptuous pomp, all the apotheosis of an imperial majesty, going to find a derisory Olympus. Mourners, musicians, singers of Orphic hymns, even our priests . . . for priestly pity has wanted to descend upon a coffin. Pompously, you have entered the Amenti, poor Callista; Dragged on the hurdle, I shall soon go to join you there. Oh, may the thorns of the harsh road that the dead travel not bloody your feet! And may the grip of the grim conductor of souls not dare to bruise my so-much-beloved! Wretch, wretch, I have not let the moment of repentance pass! What! Without me, my Ahmes, will you be able to traverse the stages of fear? Will you be condemned without me? Will you be reborn without me, to live life again and suffer expiation without me?

". . . I want to die; I want, by delivering myself to the augustal, to writhe under torture and render my last sigh pronouncing your name. Let's go, Pakrour, quickly, to the praetory, quickly, to the cross. The beloved is calling me, here I am . . . ! No, not yet; one last time, at least, I shall contemplate your dear face . . . Tomorrow, I shall abandon my refuge; at nightfall, tomorrow, crawling into the necropolis, I shall slide toward the sepulcher; tomorrow, tomorrow, lifting the shroud and taking possession of the mask, I . . ."

At that point, the voice of the sinister actor became stammering and confused again:

"The lictors! Strike, strike harder; burn and claw my bones; punish more rapidly . . . ! The cross! Ah . . . ! I love, I love . . . One still loves, then, among the dead . . . !"

Abruptly, Monsier d'Hérival collapsed on the floor. Immediately, I bent over him; his pulse was no longer beating; his arms were rigid; the cataleptic slumber had reclaimed the man.

And during that frightful scene, standing in a corner of my study, the woman had watched and listened impassively: not a word, not a gesture. I finally spoke to the bizarre creature; her presence was henceforth unnecessary to me.

"Enough for today, my dear. Go away, but come back tomorrow."

Without responding to me, she marched toward the recumbent body, knelt down, lifted the head, and deposited a kiss thereon.

"Go, your crime has not rendered you criminal in my eyes, and since your sin was only the folly of your amour, poor expiatory soul, be pardoned."

DCXLVII (continued—same day.) The preacher has just left. I had changed my mind and would have liked to retain her for longer; she refused to prolong her visit. So loquacious at first, the lady had become strangely mute, or rather, she monologued in her turn:

"They've deceived me!" she sighed. "They lied. The poor fellow loved."

Did she, perhaps believe herself to be the former Callista? Oh, but then, what a descent into Hell! A sad metamorphosis.

"Come back tomorrow," I said to her. "Tomorrow, at the same time. It's necessary. I demand it."

At a processional pace, without breathing a word, she left, and I had Hérival taken back to the Paracelsus Room. There was one that the Villa Riante had to cage like a white blackbird.

I feel very intrigued. What mysterious link, then, unites those two beings? A secret of the organism, admirable material for imminent discoveries. The late Puységur or the deceased Potet[1] would once have claimed to unveil that enigma for me, and their noisy imitators will doubtless respond to me: "Passive suggestion and simple telepathy. Your somnambulist must have glimpsed, deciphered, read fluently and declaimed as an actor the most arcane thoughts of the credulous devotee who had hypnotized him without him being aware of it." Bold conjectures, Messieurs, pretexts for incessant advertisements for your books and your persons: leave literary charlatanism to the charlatans of letters. As for me—telepathy or not—I have reason to be satisfied. My journal can insert the case of a new insanity: Isis has worshipers in the heart of Paris,

How sadly hilarious the approaching century promises to be, with its mysticism, its renewal of the most degrading superstitions. Are you sleeping contentedly, Voltaire?

DCXLVII (continued). 14 January. Am I sincerely satisfied? On studying the pages scribbled yesterday, I sensed a doubt invading me. Is it truly a work of genius, that Egyptian melodrama with modern sentiments, sprinkled with antique locutions? I don't know. Genius—a very big word, and barbaric too. And then, returned to himself, what a paltry genius, the subject Hérival!

This morning he has woken up feeling well again, and insolent again. I was with him; he recognized me, and said: "By

1 Jules-Denis, Baron Du Potet (1796-1881), also known as Dupotet de Sennevoy, was a renowned mesmerist and homeopath, who also acquired a considerable reputation among occultists for his *La Magie dévoilée et la science occulte* (1856).

what right have you sequestered me here? Be careful, Monsieur, be careful!"

He finally concluded his interrupted abuse of the day before.

I retired disdainfully from the futile conversation. The day has been bad. Monsieur argues, Monsieur cavils, Monsieur waxes indignant, Monsieur talks about the law; Monsieur knows a deputy; Monsieur threatens the court. Tomorrow, if calm has not returned to that agitated individual, I shall take efficacious measures. The Esquirol Cell—it is padded, spacious and very comfortable—will perhaps teach him that a madman is a madman, the cold shower an argument without reply, and the Villa Riante a serious place. Let's wait.

The woman has not returned. She is, however, necessary to me; at all costs, she must be found.

DCXLVII (continued—same day.) I have just reread the delirious verbiage; alas, no trace of latent genius. But what could the erotomaniac have meant by the abominable sentence that he left unfinished:

"Tomorrow, I shall abandon my refuge; at nightfall, tomorrow, crawling into the necropolis, I shall slide toward the sepulcher; tomorrow, tomorrow, lifting the shroud and taking possession of the mask, I . . ."

All bestiality, Darwin has demonstrated to us, still inhabits the human beast, and many a time, dementia and criminality are only remembrances of a brute anterior to the transformed human. Monstrous instincts must therefore be slumbering in this Hérival. Which ones? I shall soon know.

DCXLVII (continued). 15 January. Malediction! The Paracelsus Room is empty; the wretched madman has escaped!

# PART THREE

At this point, Raoul d'Hérival's manuscript resumes.

## XI

. . . . . . . . . . . . . . . . . . . . . . . . . . . . . . . . . . . . . . . . . . . . . . . .

"Midnight, Monsieur," the orderly Galien said to me. "Courage, and let's hurry."

Courage? Of course, I'd like to have it; but my savior was suspect; his criminal appearance worried me.

"Before God, Galien, can you answer for the success?"

"Faith of a former bailiff, before God . . . and for the sake of justice."

And an extortionist too; "for the sake of" five thousand francs in promissory notes that I'd signed.

"En route!"

He shod me in espadrilles, then dressed me in a skullcap, spectacles and an ample apron. Disguised in that fashion I resembled one of Molière's matassins.[1] "*Piglialo su, Piglialo su, Signor monsu.*"

Quietly, Galien opened the door, and we were off.

Look out! Deserted and sinister, the Averroes corridor extended endlessly. Stealthily, we marched in darkness; sometimes the floorboards creaked under our feet: immediate halt.

"As long as the maddest of the mad," murmured my guide, "the only, the unique, the veritable one, is in bed!"

---

1 "Matassins" are Spanish dancers featured in Molière's comedy ballet *Monsieur de Porceaugnac* (1669), from which the nonsensical quotation is taken.

O disaster! He wasn't in bed, the maddest of the mad, the detestable Labastide. At the extremity of the corridor, his door was open, and a ray of light spread over the stairway.

"Who goes there?" shouted the old rogue. "Someone's still prowling at such an hour!"

Boldly, my companion went into the study; I hid in the shadow.

"It's me, Monsieur le directeur . . . me, Galien. You called me?"

Poring over his stacks of paper, the odious maniac was writing. He turned his head in my direction; my costume reassured him.

"And the other orderly, who's he?"

"Pelletier, Monsieur, a comrade engaged this morning. He doesn't know the house and I'm guiding him to his room."

"Ta ta ta, I'm not swallowing that pill. The comrade and you are going to make merry. Galien, I forbade you to quit DCXLVII. I find you in default, my lad: a ten franc fine."

"Oh, my good Monsieur Labastide!"

"And twenty francs if you argue. How is Hérival?"

"At this moment he's fearful and agitated."

"Salutary terror. Is he still thinking of leaving?"

"More than ever."

"We'll calm him down. Has the Esquirol Cell been prepared?"

"Everything is ready."

"Straitjacket and shower apparatus? Good; return to your patient and sleep with one eye open."

Without replying, Galien saluted, and as he went out, the crafty fellow closed the door.

"Now, Monsieur, let's not hang about."

Still following him, I went downstairs, but on the third step my liberator stopped. "Dear Monsieur, I've reflected. The key to the street is eight thousand francs."

"We agreed five thousand."

"A minimal sum; eight thousand francs or tomorrow, the straitjacket: choose."

Scoundrel! Nevertheless, I smiled.

"Agreed. You're my providence, dear friend, and I abandon myself to your honor.

"Another request. The concierge Fagon is alerted; he'll pretend to be asleep. Five little blue vignettes for him, no? The father of a family!"

Swine! I would have liked to caress the ex-ministerial officer with my boot, but I suppressed the desire.

"You have a heart of gold, my good Galien. So be it! Five hundred francs for the father of a family.

"Word of a gentleman, Monsieur? Your promissory notes for the end of the month; the new supplement in an hour. In addition, I'll accompany you."

Now we're in the lodge. He's fast asleep, the interesting Fagon. The sleep of the just! He's even snoring: a conscientious fellow. Galien pulls the cordon . . . Free, I'm free! Adieu, then Villa Riante, where laughter is a gnashing of teeth, adieu!

I take off and throw away my Monsieur Fleurant costume,[1] and I launch myself toward Paris. It's up to the other now to trot on my heels. He's panting heavily and must be out of breath. At the Porte de Ternes a carriage is parked. Coachman!"

"Coachman, Ninety-one Rue Vaneau . . . No Galien, not beside me, on the seat."

The clown obeys, cursing. He'll catch influenza, perhaps bronchitis—and that will be "justice." The carriage pulls away; we're rolling.

Finally, home!

In my bedroom, now, my Galien was obsequious, waiting for his money. Without argument—a d'Hérival knows how to keep his word—I counted out the supplement that he had just extorted, and then asked him: "How are you going to exercise your talents henceforth, Monsieur honest man?"

"In my homeland, at Romagnat, Puy-de-Dôme; I want to open an office there. Vive l'Auvergne! That's where the peasant quibbles and takes proceedings."

---

1 The apothecary in Molière's *Le Malade imaginaire* (1673).

"Perfect, Master Rogue; I hope you'll reap your prison there."

"Well, well, so I'm no longer the savior, the providence, the good friend, Galien with the heart of gold? Always ingrates! But nothing astonishes me; I'm philosophical. One piece of good advice, though, dear benefactor. The night's advancing; believe me, be elsewhere before daylight."

"Leave here? Why?"

"Because they'll come here to recapture you."

"Recapture me?"

"Oh, I know: the law of 1838; tutelary prescriptions, preliminary papers. Don't trust that. Rather reread a certain article 19, on immediate internments. They imprison first and explain later. And between us, you're one of those who can be locked up without fear. So decamp as quickly as possible, Ah, Monsieur le Vicomte and former friend, you're going to traverse palpitating emotions, all the alarms of the rabbit in its warren. But courage! Good feet, good eyes! Send them back empty-handed. Alas, I have great fears for your failure."

Anger stifled me. Was the crook mocking me?

"Insolent fellow, it's me who'll have Labastide locked up, and as for the Villa Riante . . ."

"Oh, my poor Monsieur! A minister among the shareholders!"

Pocketing his banknotes then, the rogue saluted me, like a bailiff whose palm has been greased, and he left.


# XII


I lay down on a sofa, still shivering with so many various emotions, and started to reflect. What adventures since yesterday! A bad dream, a nightmare! What if I reassembled my memories? I had gone—why that stupid caprice?—to the Moulin Rouge; there, a prostitute had accosted me, followed me, pursued me, and then had introduced herself all the way to my bedroom. Perceiving the Egyptian painting, the mask, on the mantelpiece . . . by the way, where was the mask? I no longer saw it. Had it been stolen?

What! Stolen, an object of such great value? Yes, I remembered now. The woman had taken possession of it; I had tried to get it back, but she had shoved me in order to get out, and bang! I woke up in the Villa Riante. How, how? I couldn't remember anything about it; my brain was seething in confusion and my reason was getting lost. In any case, I felt so tired; a curvature in my entire body, shooting pains in the head. Let's go to bed—and I began to undress. No, better to sleep fully dressed, to be ready at the slightest alert. Heavy with sleep, I closed my eyes . . .

Immediately, the woman!

"Me," she had said as she grabbed the portrait . . . You, wretch, you, resemble my celestial Callista? An inept pleasantry . . . After all, why not? I had sometimes discovered admirable beauties in frightful ugliness. In any case, even though not pretty, my thief was attractive. What eyes! Shining carbuncles, two black diamonds . . . "Me . . . !" Yes, yes, I'll be able to catch up with you, you and your mask. The city and the suburbs will be searched: the police . . .

What was that? A noise on the staircase. Get up!

I bounded to my feet and blew out my candle.

In the dark now . . . What an odious trickster, that ignoble Galien. Lugubrious, his jokes. "It's here, Monsieur, that they'll come to recapture you." Here? What about the law of 1838? It ought to protect citizens, since it's the law. Its prescriptions are tutelary; it demands preliminary paperwork. Yes, but article 19! Menacing, that article 19. How dare they decree articles 19?

My resolution was made. In the morning I would go to the Palais de Justice: an annoying visit. I knew a deputy there, a good fellow, a member of my club who plays poker very well, He often wins from me, so he's a friend. People of importance, deputies: all sons, nephews, sons-in-law and cousins of senators or députés. I would tell him about my affair; between the two of us, we could chastise Labastide; the Villas Riante would be shut down, and . . .

Oh yes, a minister among the shareholders! In truth, far too many ministerial shareholders . . .

Daylight!

It had slid, wan and sly, through the gap in the curtains. I opened them a little further. In the street, suppliers, bread-porters, coal merchants and milkmen were stationed, jabbering and gesturing. They must be talking about me. One of them looked at the house; yes, those people were talking about me. A few more moments and Labastide, the orderlies and the com-missaire . . .

"They imprison first," Galien had said to me, "and explain lat-er." Damn it, his advice was good; it was necessary to decamp.

I took a little money from my desk and ran downstairs. At the entrance to his lodge the concierge saluted me and smiled: a nasty smile.

"Monsieur has returned?"

"Yes, a little pleasure trip."

"A registered letter came for Monsieur yesterday. The post-man . . ."

"Tell him to bring it back later."

And I drew away slowly, steadily, with the stride of a propri-etor. At the street corner I hastened my steps; I started running, and . . .

Abruptly, I found myself on the Pont Caulaincourt. How long had I been wandering at random? I never knew, but for hours on end, for it seemed to me that the day was declining. I was calm now . . . very calm.

In any case, during my furious vagabondage, I had been rea-soning and had traced out an entire plan of conduct. Yes, the wisest thing for me to do was to take an evening express at the

Gare Saint-Lazare and take refuge as quickly as possible in my château in Cotentin. There, nothing to fear, farmers who adored me, gendarmes who clinked glasses in my kitchens, a justice of the peace—too radical, that one—I allowed to poach on my land; at the tribunal, a president in advance of decrees to whom I sent the best carp from my river: all, without exception, friends. Furthermore, to defend me, three gamekeepers with three good rifles. So, nothing to fear, and en route for Normandy!

The direct train to Cherbourg not departing until eight o'clock in the evening, I had the leisure to stroll for a while longer. Reassured, almost joyful, I resumed going up the slope of the Avenue Caulaincourt. I felt a ferocious appetite—having fasted since the day before!—but there wasn't a single restaurant in the vicinity where I could sit down. Could I decently eat at the cheap hostelry the sign of which—*For the consolation of families. Rooms for the night*—I perceived in the distance, wedged against the wall of the cemetery?

Bah! Raoul, you'll dine all the better tomorrow, like a gentleman. I therefore went into a bakery, and then, while nibbling I know not what mold, continued walking straight ahead. As I went, I recognized, to the right and the left, the flamboyant posters of Hermes the Egyptian . . .

Why had someone lacerated and dirtied them ignobly, defacing them with filthy inscriptions? They had been almost intact the other evening: what a deterioration in less than a day! Almost everywhere, the eyes of the maternal Isis had been put out. In my turn, I aimed a thrust of my cane at the sinister figure.

"Take that, goddess! In memory of your pontiff and his threats. What an insolent fellow!"

Finally, weary of striking, I continued on my way. Aha! The second-hand dealer's shop, the shack where the Jew had sold me Callista.

# XIII

The wretched shop appeared to have been pillaged. The door was wide open, and there were piles of garments, rags and scrap iron on the pavement. In spite of the biting cold, people—workers or their housewives—were circulating around that rubbish, handling the clothes and weighing saucepans and cooking pots. One might have thought that they were in a village at one of those expositions that precede an auction sale. What! Was he selling his stock, my Levantine in a caftan, the Talmudist? I approached the display, hoping to discover some trinket there.

On the dusty threshold of the hovel, a horrible old woman was standing, a hunchbacked fossil with a Semitic nose, whose tentative gaze was following all the customers.

"Is your boss here?" I asked her.

She examined me with a suspicious eye, and then said, in a tearful voice: "My husband? He's dead."

What did she say? A very prompt decease! I felt a strong disturbance.

"Dead, the Israelite master of this shop?"

The words *Israelite* and *shop* appeared to charm the ragged old woman.

"Did you know him, Monsieur?"

"Yes, certainly, the good old fellow. Last Thursday he was still full of life."

Suspicion returned to the face of the Jewess. "Thursday . . . ? We buried him that day."

"Get away! That day he sold me an Egyptian mask, and . . ."

"The mask!" I thought she was about to attack me, furiously. "Oh, it's you, you, who rolled us over like that! Scoundrel, eighty francs for that treasure worth two thousand!"

"Your husband ceded it to me in order to be rid of it."

"I know, I know! I know the story and all his double-dealing. An idiot, my late husband, who bequeathed me the hospital. Yes, an idiot, idle throughout Yom Kippur, making his grease melt instead of attracting custom; always in his books, never our affairs, wanting to be buried in the Valley of Josophat, poor pullet! Even opening his window during every storm to see the Messiah fall . . . the Messiah! The best of Messiahs is Christian money . . . Yes, yes, an idiot, but a cohen, a rabbi: not a real merchant. He execrated Archibald; the idolater killed him."

"Archibald? The half-breed, the charlatan?"

"He killed him, I tell you; he put a spell on him. That was foreseeable."

A madwoman, apparently, that widow so well consoled; or rather, a wily play-actor. Her patriarch wasn't dead. One can't die and be buried in one day; the law is the law. No, the husband must be far away, kicking his heels in fraudulent bankruptcy, and his plaintive wife was lying impudently. I tried to move away, but she hung on to me.

"So, for eighty francs, you believe you've duly acquired an inestimable object? The justice of the peace . . ."

"Let me go; I no longer have your mask."

"Father Abraham! He's sold it . . ."

"It was stolen from me."

"Stolen? Well, then, its Archibald."

"No, a woman, some sort of Salvationist . . ."

"It's Archibald! No matter what the cost, Hermes wanted that mask; he must have it now. Oh, you don't know Archibald. He employs a heap of women in his service, his vampires. Look, there's one of them prowling around here. Hey! Over there, get away, ghoul! Turn on your heel or you'll receive a stone."

The "ghoul" was a girl about sixteen years of age clad in a gray sheath and the bonnet of a quakeress; she was distributing pamphlets. At the same time, her whining voice advertised a newspaper: "Ask for the *Isis*, the *Triple Isis*, the *Terrestrial Isis*, the *Isis Persephone*, the *Isis Urania*, the *Trismegistus*. Five centimes, one sou."

The workers, connoisseurs of old clothing, took the pamphlets and mocked the patter; Rachel or Rebecca howled, throwing stones; the little crier was not intimidated.

"Buy the *Isis*, purify your hearts, regenerate your souls; five centimes, one sou."

Cheap, human regeneration . . . oh, but I recognized her: the chlorotic apprentice of the Avenue de l'Opéra . . .

Escorted by the abject old woman, I approached the vendor.

"Bonjour, Mademoiselle; what are you selling these messieurs?"

She looked at me brazenly; then, half-seriously, said: "A work of redemption. Read it and come to us."

*Come to us*, I commented: *Come to me*.

"You've quit the workshop, then, capricious girl?"

With a gamine gesture she shrugged her shoulders. "I'm working for my God."

*For my God*: edifying words; but Judith or Deborah started sniggering. "Less fatiguing work than plying the needle. What about your parents, vermin?"

"My mother lives in sin; vice enveloped me; Hermes collected me."

"Hermes? How many skirts of your species does he have, the padishah?"

The starveling made as if to go away; the other woman retained her by her skirt. "Ask her for news of your mask, then, Monsieur."

In fact, why not?

"Madame affirms, dear child, that since the day before yesterday your master possesses a funerary mask, an Egyptian painting that he stole from me."

"I don't understand you, Monsieur."

"Liar!" cried the Jewess. "See—she blushed."

She had indeed blushed, and was making efforts to escape. A circle of idlers surrounded us: gibes, jeers and jokes erupted, and rapidly, I had divined everything—the whole story of my sad adventure. The Englishman had followed me all the way to the Rue Vaneau, and then, informed on my account, had had me followed step by step by one of his "vampires," the woman of the

Moulin Rouge. Well played: but I wanted my revenge. Offering two louis to the wife of the pseudo-deceased, I said: "This is on account, dear Madame; now, leave me alone with this child."

Agar or Esther pulled a face, but she pocketed the money, and I set forth on the heels of the liar.

## XIV

Briskly, she was making herself scarce; I had soon caught up with her, and placed my hand on her shoulder: "Where are you running off to, little one?"

Without seeming indignant at my audacity, the girl looked at me from the corner of her eye. "I'm going to Belleville, big man, to try to sell my rags."

A veritable Parisian sparrow. Laughing, she shook the heavy wad of newspapers that hung over her left arm like a maniple.

"Irreverent, my dear, that word 'rag.' The holy apostolate doesn't seem to fill you with enthusiasm."

"It's a joke, the holy apostolate. Oh, those of us who distribute them on the boulevards are lucky; they might encounter handsome gentlemen like you there, while for me, in these filthy quarters, it's always drunkards and furies."

Then I repeated my question: "Why have you deserted your shop?"

"A proud stupidity—but in apprenticeship one earns so little: four or five francs a week, and then . . . poorly nourished and dry. And Maman lives with a good-for-nothing. He insulted me, called me his kid and took all my money."

"Hence your vocation."

"Oh, vocation! Hermes fascinated me at first; I felt a strong yen for his black eyes and frizzy beard . . . well, I soon got over it."

"A prompt reversion. What does the man do, then?"

"He regenerates the world. With his holy frusquin the old fool builds temples of Isis and shelters for the expiators: a fine crackpot."

"What expiators?"

"The repentant reincarnates."

"Who are the reincarnates?"

"All of us, of course: you and me."

"I didn't know that I was a reincarnate."

"One learns something every day."

"Are they numerous, the souls the apostle purifies?"

"Twenty cells occupied for the moment."

"By women?"

"Yes, but not first-rate: the dregs of the exterior boulevard."

"Magdalens whose virginity he's remaking? A hard enterprise. And my mask?"

The brazen girl burst out laughing. "So why take unknown women home with you?"

"So it has been stolen from me?"

"Stolen, no; the priest will doubtless pay you. Hermes doesn't care about expense."

That explained what my concierge had said about a registered letter arriving the day before. Seized by a scruple, the sacrosanct burglar had sent me a gift: by God, it would be well received.

"One piece of information, my girl . . . the name of the thief?"

"Callista."

Good, another joke. Now I understood the word pronounced by my robber: the mysterious "Me" that had intrigued me so bitterly.

"Callista! A delightful *nom de guerre*—but the true one, the one on her birth certificate?"

"The one papa or mama calls her? I don't know."

"Callista, perfect for putting the police off the track. Let's talk about Callista."

"Oh, she's the beloved, the favorite of the moment. A hag, but she has the vocation; Madame has her vapors, her ecstasies. So, in less than six months, postulant, deaconess, preacher, and in a little while . . ."

"She's alluring enough to merit her favor."

"A funny taste: the face of an ape."

"Bah! My caprice; I'd like to see her again."

"Impossible. Today, very soon, she's going to be consecrated as a priestess again."

"Again? Why again?"

"I don't know; doubtless a way of speaking. Hermes told us 'again.'"

"A priestess, my thief! Well, I desire to see the ceremony."

"Not often! Only our great initiates are admitted into the chapel."

While chattering, the former errand-girl was trotting, and we had descended from the heights of Montmartre. "Now, let's quit one another, Monsieur. They've already punished me this morning and I've had enough of their penances."

Quit her. No, certainly not. A bitter and furious covetousness had taken possession of me for a second time: I wanted Callista. She seemed exciting to me, monstrously pretty, desirable. What! Consecrated as a priestess before nightfall? What a delirious adventure if I could steal her from her pontiff, snatch her from the altar, in order to launch her thereafter into Parisian gallantry. And what a triumph over the vulgar Lovelaces of my circle! Would she go with me? Without a doubt: a starveling whose vocation was merely a means of earning her bread. Hermes had stolen my mask; I would take his vestal; we'd be quits . . .

Except that it was necessary to slip into the cloister. My not-very-fanatical companion was going to serve my designs.

Gallantly, I put my arm around her waist. "In exchange for an offering, could one get as far as the professing sister?"

"Professing? A nice word, you must be an author. No, Monsieur, our priests are incorruptible."

"You hierophants, perhaps . . . but you, Mademoiselle!"

"Leave me alone; I'm not for sale."

Nevertheless, she had stopped, blushing, and her eyes lit up with concupiscence.

"Let's see, darling: two gold pieces, beautiful and ringing true . . . three . . . four, even."

Oh, I was using up my poor coins recklessly. It would come back to me dearly, the mask!

Without responding, the seller of human renovation had turned round; she climbed the escarpments of the Butte again, hesitant but very agitated. Still looking at her, I made the coveted suborning louis jump in my hand, enticingly, thus baiting the hook. And the taciturn Mademoiselle Tortillon[1] looked sideways, sighed, and then hastened her pace. Finally, breaking the silence, she said: "Four yellows? It's still not a May queen's dowry . . . no matter, I accept. Follow me and be sharp."


## XV


Dusk had almost fallen. Under the low floating vapors exhaled by the City, a few street-lights were already lit, and one by one, the red streaks of gaslight stretched away toward Saint Denis in the plain, gradually illuminating the commencing night; but on the far side of Montmartre, in the strangled back-streets under the shadow of the high terraces, everything was still dubious mist, increasing obscurity, and soon thick darkness.

Without speaking we followed an arduous route, muddy and pitted, the pavement and unique gutter of which seemed a last legacy of the most ancient outlying districts. To either side mossy walls rose up, and behind those enclosures the tormented crowns of a few centenarian elms were perceptible. The name of the mysterious back-street I still don't know. Oozing and decrepit, the stones of its borders were crumbling in many places; to the left, especially, the dilapidation was lamentable . . .

---

1 A Mademoiselle Tortillon is a character in Paul de Kock's *Taquinet le Bossu* (1848), but it is possible that Thierry only intends to refer to the girl's thinness by comparing her to a roll of paper used by artists to smudge charcoal drawings.

And, silently, abandoning myself to reveries, I plunged into the blackness of the unknown alleyway.

What was happening within me? I have never been able to understand it. In the times—distant, alas!—of my childhood, when I had been refused some desired treat, I fell into convulsions. What I wanted, I had to have; and I had to have Callista . . .

I suddenly remembered, so clearly!

In possession of her larceny, she had launched forth to flee; I had blocked her path. "You shan't go! You please me; you'll be mine!" Then, before my eyes, there was a flash of lightning: the cold of a knife, full in the heart. An imaginary wound, but what energy in defending her sad honor of a repentant whore . . .

"Me!" Certainly, that morning, again I had only been thinking with terror about my sinister escapade; why, then, was the unexpected suffering of a torturing desire making me run toward another adventure?

A desire? No, and I became ashamed of the ignominy of my thoughts . . .

Oh, Raoul, would you, a gentleman, the child of a Christian mother, dare to accomplish an absurd and cruel infamy? Leave her, the wretched woman, leave her to the absorbing folly of her god. A ridiculous god? What does it matter? Her god! The derisory temple was truly a temple, since it had pity; it was divine, being all forgiveness. Souls soiled by mud, the refuse of our social corruption, the wretches that it picked it . . . yes, but souls! What a crime it was, then, to want to trouble the repentant, to snatch her recovered conscience away from mystical mildness, from quietude, from the sacred slumber of the great forgetfulness. Fortunate are those who can sleep, annihilated in all their being. Oh, if you could only sleep yourself . . . !

Thus spoke the revolts of my reason; and yet I marched, marched recklessly; I wanted to see "her" again. An invisible force propelled me toward her, and I felt a hand placed on my shoulder, a brutal hand, shoving me. Stop? Already, I could not. Like the ship in the old Arab tales, I was drawn, dragged toward the magnet, the reef and its abyss—irresistibly. I have meditated a great deal since then, without being able to explain my dementia . . .

To see her again! Why, why?

A movement of my guide drew me out of that reverie.

"It's here, Monsieur; we've arrived."

She indicated a breach made in the base of a wall; a narrow fissure that one could only traverse by crawling.

"The door isn't very convenient," the girl went on, "but there's no porter. We use it every evening, me and the other expiatrices, in order to get away from the tedium of the expiation."

Those few words from my vicious gamine had returned me to reality. A nasty place, their Pantheon . . . and briskly, I repelled the last return of my scruples.

"Well supervised, my darling, your sacred college of reparatory virgins! Does Hermes know about your escapades?"

"Hurry up! Here one pays in advance."

With the impudence of a bacheloress, the brazen little creature held out her hand; I deposited therein the four louis so coveted. Immediately, thin and supple, she slid through the cat-hole; with difficulty, I followed her. *Oof!* What brambles! What scratches! But I was inside.

I found myself on the edge of a profound lawn enveloped by bushes, a prairie that undulated in accordance with the declivities of the hill. Overlooking the slope was the breadth of a large building, a lugubrious and silent house, green under its mantle of ivy. There was no light yet in its bleak windows, but someone might be watching from the depths of their voluntary darkness. A former convent, by all appearances. Its principal façade overlooked Montmartre—perhaps the Rue de Rosiers of criminal memory, or perhaps some other road. In truth, I have never known where I was introduced into it.

Almost at the bottom of the sloping meadow stood a new building: a temple—or rather a chapel, to judge by its exiguous forms. It rose up in isolation amid the grass powdered with frost, and in the melancholy of the evening, in the enveloping shadow of the mist, it resembled a bizarre stone catafalque. Raised up on several steps, a portico preceded it. The door was closed, but through narrow gaps, over the white snow covering the grass, the symbolic red glow of a mysterious light emerged and spread out distantly. And in front of me, not far from the taciturn monument, twenty small lodgments were spaced out: cells.

"Up there is the college of the initiates," my guide murmured, "down below, their new sacrary; in front of you are the kennels where we lodge, we the repentant, the rabble."

The sight of that amusing phalanstery sprouted in the heart of Paris intrigued me greatly. It was reminiscent in some respects of the dreary Saint-Simonian house at Menilmontant, of which we have all heard such astonishing descriptions. In my youth, I had even known an old physician who had made his debut in life by being a little choirboy in the service of the Supreme Verb, the Manitou decreed by Père Enfantin.[1] In his soprano voice he had once sung hymns composed by Félicien David, while by turns Duveyrier, Talabot, Mony-Flachat, Lachambaudie and other "adjective practitioners," Cécile Fournel and Aglaé Saint-Hilaire, the two "messianic women" waxed the boots, swept the floor and ornamented the august couch of the Father—the "subjunctive theorician," the thrice-holy "verb-priest." A verb-priest—what a sacerdocy! As much and more so than Hermes, that one had been a neo-Christ, an entire "living Law," the servant elect of the "Infinitesimal." And a madman. Nothing is new under the sun, alas, even in madness.

"How do you employ your days?" I asked my neophyte.

---

1 Barthélemy-Prosper Enfantin (1796-1864) became a preacher after the July Revolution of 1830 and became the "supreme father" of a reformist cult notorious for its advocacy of "free love" in opposition to marriage, and for its search for a supposedly-predestined female Messiah, although the forty disciples who lived with him for a short while at his house in Ménilmontant in 1832 were all men. After a period of imprisonment he went to Turkey, and then to Egypt. Following his return to France he became a leading proponent of the Suez Canal.

"Not diverting. At six o'clock in the morning, wake up. One gets up and goes to the audience room where the pontiff is enthroned. Hermes interrogates and hears confessions. *What progress have you accomplished toward the good? Do you sense the vocation, my daughter?* Very sly, the curious fellow; but we're just as cunning, so we lie to him, and happily. Then, the chapel: we sing the office there, a mass in their fashion. Then, hours and hours of meditation; some of us fall in ecstasy. At eleven o'clock, a communal meal in the refectory. The high priest is there but doesn't touch our aliments; the worthy crackpot forbids all animal nourishment; he's a vegetarian. Not too bad, their ratatouille, in spite of the insufficiency of wine. The rattle announces midday; work commences immediately. A priest confides to everyone the newspapers printed in the house—you know, the *Isis*, the little rag—that it's necessary to distribute. Preachers and deaconesses go to preach in public places; it's even claimed that, before sending them to spout, Hermes hypnotizes them. The rest of us, the repentant, wander around the city. That's the best time; on the sidewalk one can make such pleasant encounters. The produce of the sale belongs to the seller, but every evening she has to deposit the money in the hands of the treasurer. Hermes capitalizes our gains in order to form us a dowry and marry us off later. A tidy sum, it appears, which he steals from us. Returned to base before nine o'clock, we have supper. Then another interminable office, a new sermon, more ecstasy. Finally, the purr of the rattle, off to the niche and goodnight. That's it, Monsieur, that's how one purifies oneself."

"Admirable results. But what does the pontiff say if you're caught in default?"

"First he reprimands, and then he punishes the second offence; in the end, he dismisses the hardened. So, this evening, I'm an 'impenitent rebel'; I'm forbidden to attend the 'ceremonies of delight'—the one in a little while, for example—and I'm made to fast too often. A fine business! Tonight, I'll escape again and go to supper with friends, two figurants at the Ambigu; I like artistes . . . now, enough chatter, let's try to get to my room; I'll have the honor of receiving Your Lordship there."

I would have liked to ask her many other questions. Was Archibald in regulation with the police? Skeptical and suspicious, did the Lady of the City approve of such a marvelous enterprise? What could Messieurs the commissaires think of the purificatory refuge and its landlords? But the girl was agitating anxiously.

"Silence, people are on watch up there."

With her head she designated the slumbering edifice, which seemed to be trying to wake up. A few windows had been suddenly illuminated, and were shining in the twilight like searching eyes.

"Follow me, Monsieur."

With precaution, my wily companion started moving along the wall of the garden; we began to circle the enclosure, under the shelter of the bordering bushes. Having reached the level of the chapel I looked . . . yes, a stone catafalque in the Oriental style; a curious miniature of an Egyptian temple, walls constructed in mortar and decorated with garish paintings. In front of the funeral edicule there were steps, and then a peristyle formed by two columns, and behind it, a staircase descending into a crypt.

"The 'hypogeum'—the old joker's cellar," sniggered my companion. "No casks, but mummies. I counted as many as eighteen. Stinking horrors! Come on, Monsieur, enough peering. Get a move on; time's pressing."

Going downhill and then up again, we finally reached the penitents' cells

"Palace number fifteen, mine. Salutations, chaste and pure dwelling. Let's go in."

The palace of my frolicsome expiatrice was a modest room, but pleasant and well-kept. A ray of moonlight that filleted in through the only window soon permitted me to make out all the details. On the whitewashed walls, repeated many times, was an Egyptian rebus, a hieroglyph with a French translation: "I am pure! I am pure!" At the head of the narrow couchette the illuminated image of Isis has been placed. With one hand the goddess was blessing the peoples, her children of the earth; in the other she carried a symbolic vessel, the savior ship in which souls in distress were picked up. Such, at least, was the explanation of my catechist. Also in the cell were two chairs and a table, with several volumes.

"Your pious reading, my pretty saint?"

"Oh la la! Sad romances: *La Fleur mystique*,[1] a load of nonsense; hymns that I don't understand, and the ritual of our offices. I prefer reading my rocamboles."

"An irresistible vocation. Now, let's talk little but well. When can I see Callista?"

"In a little while, I suppose. For a week, at nightfall, she's been taken to the chapel and abandoned there until morning."

"In that case, I can slip in to see her."

"As you wish; today, however, we have something new: our priests are making a heap of mysteries, grimaces and mummeries. What secrets! The great Berenice says that they're going to bury Callista alive. We'll laugh." And she added, mockingly: "A singular taste, Monsieur: the mask of an ape, your adored."

I wanted to protest, but the envious sinner grabbed my arm: "Shut up! Here they come."

I posted myself behind the curtain, and I watched.

## XVI

All the windows of the conventual house had been illuminated abruptly, and its bleak façade was shining in the night. Soon, both battens of the door were opened and a fantastic masquerade emerged slowly . . .

---

1 Not the title of a book, although there is a symbolist painting by Gustave Moreau with that title; the most likely intended reference is to the symbolic mystic rose of the Theosophists.

Was I the victim of a mirage or a dream? Were my abused eyes only perceiving an illusion of my brain? No, I say no; I saw it, in verity, I saw . . .

The cortege approached, baroque, bizarre and solemn.

At the head marched several women clad in white, but so ridiculous in their tunics and tragediennes' peplums. Some were agitating and vibrating the strings of long bronze sistra, others were holding torches or strewing flowers on the ground. Those, according to my neighbor, belonged to the class of trivial repentants; they were expiatrices picked up on the sidewalk, simple reincarnates redeeming their anterior lives as adulterous wives or courtesans. One by one the gamine recognized them and whispered their names: all ancient Cleopatras or former Phrynes—ignoble in appearance today, atrocious and lamentable redemptions.

Then came a discordant orchestra, whose note-crunchers, apprentice Orpheuses and novice Linuses were making the flute grimace or the psaltery whine. At times, the infamous cacophony stopped and the voices of women replied to it, plaintive and psalmodic:

> *I have searched in vain, voyager of earth.*
> *For Isis to whom I aspired, her temple and her heart.*
> *You called me, you say; no, you fled me, my mother;*
> *I could only find you in the depths of dolor.*

Alas, they were speaking the truth. Yes, dolor, dolor—the more profound is your abyss, the more humans need to encounter a God there.

After the tibicians and the citharists, other women filed past, but of higher grade, preachers or deaconesses; those purified of the initial impurity. Sheathed in the falling pleats of their hieratic stoles, crowned with roses, with palms in hand, they advanced stiffly, without any grace, like automata . . . There was an interval; then, in the same rank, three pastophores, also clad in linen, bare-headed, with their heads completely shaved—*brrr*, in that wintry cold! They were shaking the flames of their Egyptian lamps, elegant luminaries in the form of triremes, and seemed to me to be stupidly fanatical . . . Finally, amid torches and candles, in an orb of light, Hermes appeared.

Ornamented like a priest of ancient Memphis, his forehead ringed by a tiara, he was strutting superbly, and the floating amplitude of his symbolic alb trailing over the snowy grass. For such a fine nocturnal fête the man was outrageously plastered with make-up, and the blackness of his dyed beard stood out in contrast over the whiteness of his tunic and pectoral. Not a muscle of his face stirred; one might have thought, to look at him, that he was Osiris going to judge the dead. In his raised arms, the impudent sectarian was carrying a simulacrum of Isis, garlanded with roses; and he held up the idol pompously, exactly as if he were presenting his goddess to the kneeling adorations of the peoples of the world. No, a Pope traversing Saint Peter's, exalted in the gestatory chair, would not have shown himself more impassive or more convincing. An exhilarating puppet!

But what followed the amusing hierophant appeared to me to be a far less jovial spectacle. Buckling under the burden, six men draped in black were sustaining on their shoulders a large and funereal box, evidently a coffin; and behind them was the void, the silence, the night.

The hymns continued.

> *Child you have only yet lifted one of three veils*
> *Hiding from the gaze of my sublime light.*
> *What is your name on earth, O queen of stars?*
> *Active resignation and benevolence.*

Under the pallors spread by the moon, to the moving brightness of torches the bizarre procession went down the hill and up again, toward the chapel; in its entirety it unfurled before my eyes. At that moment, I glimpsed the curtains. In the coffin, amid muslins and bandlets, two bodies were lying side by side; one of them had to be Callista . . .

They passed by . . . and, still moaned to the dissonant charivari, the lessons sighed by the mourners succeeded one another.

> *Isis, I'm afraid, I'm afraid, forgive me if I tremble.*
> *"Child, we shall descend into the tomb together."*
> *"I'm afraid, mother I'm afraid . . ."*

I'm afraid! On that cry of fear, the bloody strophe was cut short. The eccentric procession had arrived outside the temple; an extravagant ceremony, therefore, was about to commence.

"Let's go outside," I murmured to my companion, "and get closer."

"No, no, not me! Those people terrify me . . . are they really going to bury poor Callista alive? Oh, tomorrow I'll be a long way from here."

The mocking assurance of the bold Parisienne had abandoned her; she was trembling. For myself, utterly bewildered by the unexpectedness of such a spectacle, I was determined to see everything, to risk anything. I found, nevertheless, that their "fête of delight" was becoming strangely lugubrious, and I could almost have wished for a sudden intervention by the police.

Quietly, I emerged from my hiding place. A clump of bushes extended protective branches; I moved soundlessly from one hornbeam to another; I succeeded in reaching the vicinity of the chapel. None of the sinister play-actors had perceived me.

The macabre Egyptian parody presented, at that moment, a curious regulated stage-setting. Arranged in a double hedge, deaconesses and preachers were aligned on the steps of the temple; the surplus of the cortege overflowed into the grass. The six necrophores had stopped in the rear; they were standing a few meters away, in the shadow and beneath their coffin. The orchestra had now stopped playing; anxious or meditative, everyone had fallen silent. Then, in the midst of that moving silence, accompanied by his three acolytes, the hierophant went up toward the portico.

"I am pure, I am pure, I am pure!" he cried, in a loud voice.

At that appeal, the door was opened; the interior of the sacrary appeared to the gaze. Decorated with tropical plants and strewn with flowers, it was resplendent with light. At a majestic pace, Hermes went in, but alone. In the center of the edicule, in the reflection of tripods with green flames, rose an alabaster cella surmounted by a porphyry cartouche. The celebrant deposited the idol there, and suddenly fell full length on to the paving-stones, in adoration. Immediately, the sistra were softly agitated, and in muffled murmurs a prayer passed from mouth to mouth. One of the priests who had remained on the threshold recited a prayer that was interrupted at intervals and countered by responses:

"Isis! Isis! Isis! O Trismegistus, thrice great; Eleusine, Persephone, Urania, be propitious . . ."

"Be propitious."

". . . Be propitious. O Thou, foremost of beings emanated from the Eternal Now, Creature creator of humankind, Cause of our causalities, fecundating Nature, Mistress of the elements, First Principle of our centuries, uniform Type of the protectors of our earth; Isis, all divine and yet all human; Isis, who was the sister; Isis who was the spouse; Isis, who was the mother; Isis, who is woman; Isis, human amour; Isis, human suffering; Isis, divine pardon, pardon today . . ."

"Pardon today."

"Listen. A sinner, once renegade of your sublime verities, will go again to appear for Judgment. Reincarnate, she has suffered in accordance with the imposed laws of suffering, and suffering, she has been purified. Be her advocate, therefore, and her protectress; deign to accompany her weakness amid the terrors of the Afterlife; remove from her path the jackal and the howling demons; stand behind the throne on which your Husband sits, he who pronounces the name of the Unnamable; extend your arms; speak for her. In truth, Isis, she has suffered; she is purified . . .

"She is purified."

". . . She is pure now, she is pure. Wretched during her second life, she has never refused her own bread to the wretched; an orphan, she has not tormented the orphaned; and, weeping herself, she has not made others weep. Never has a blasphemy against the rigor of your laws emerged from her mouth. Returned to our temples, she has practiced God, and whoever practices God, Isis, is as if they had never accomplished Evil. Pure, pure, she is pure . . . !"

"She is pure!"

". . . Accept her as a daughter, O powerful Mother, so that in emerging from the darkness she enters the Light, a priestesses for your glory, an elect servant of the Eternal Now . . . Isis, Isis, Isis, O Trismegistus, thrice great; Eleusine, Persephone, Urania, be propitious!"

"Be propitious!"

Throughout the interminable obsecration, the mute immobility of the officiant Hermes before the idol was prolonged. Finally, a frisson appeared to agitate his body; the acolytes approached and helped him to stand up. Sustained by their hands, he dragged himself painfully out of the sanctuary; but he tottered, as if overwhelmed by drunkenness; drops of sweat ran over the fard of his cheeks.

"He has seen God!" cried one of the deaconesses.

"Yes," replied the audacious fanatic, "I have seen God."

Stopping then, on the peristyle, and contemplating his people inclined before his face, like Moses on the heights of Sinai, he extended his hand toward the coffin.

"Ahmes! Callista!" he said, "I have begged for you; for you I have obtained the great pardon. You know now, expiatrice soul, that death is only a renewal of life; enter without dread, therefore, into the life of the tomb. Isis will guide your steps, and, seeing you, the Judge will only have a clement smile. O

236

my daughter, dear child of my tears, beloved of my prayers, descend, joyously, toward the joys of our sepulcher. Submit with gladness to the pacifying slumber of your symbolic death, and tomorrow, throwing off the shroud—the swaddling-clothes of the newborn—get up triumphant in all the victory and all the splendor of your redemption."

He had spoken. Immediately, the men clad in black drew together; three times, followed by fearful murmurs, they made the circuit of the chapel; and when they reappeared on the fourth circuit the coffin-bearers no longer had their burden. The procession formed up again then. Citharas and psalteries recommenced whining; the lamentations of the mourners resounded:

> *The invisible has spoken in his formidable tongue;*
> *The souls of the future and those of the past*
> *Surround me, and I sense my sin crushing me.*[1]

---

1 Author's reference: "Jules Bois, *L'Hymnaire d'Isis*, I, II, II. That strange collection is a ritual of the cult of Isis that certain contemporary "occultists" are attempting to re-establish in Paris at this moment. The enterprise is not new, moreover. An amusing print dating from the Directoire of year VII shows us an Isiac ceremony projected by 'citizen friends and sectarians of the Good Goddess.' The setting is entirely imitated from the famous description found in Book IX of the *Metamorphoses* of Apuleius. It is also to the tale of the African writer, one of the initiates and revealers of the sacred mystery, that our modern apostles of the Trismegistus claim to borrow the rites of their ceremonial.

"Is it not curious to see the mysticism of neo-Catholics and that bizarre neo-Alexandrian symbolism encountering one another in a final result: the deification of Woman? Furthermore, orthodox positivists—the only ones that Auguste Comte ever wanted to recognize—obeyed the same impulsion, and the modest apartment in the Rue Monsieur-le-Prince in which the founder of the Cult of Humanity had erected an altar to the beloved who was the companion of his last days is a place of pilgrimage and a sanctuary of meditation for numerous and devout atheists."

The text referenced is cited in other volumes as a collection of poetry dated 1894, but the Bibkiothèque Nationale has no record of it and it might be a phantom title; "L'Hymnaire de la nouvelle Isis" did appear in Bois' own periodical *Le Coeur* in June 1895, after the present story appeared in the *Revue des Deux Mondes*. Thierry might have seen the poem in manuscript.

Chanting their liturgy they went back up the hill and attained the conventual house. In their primitive order, they all went in: repentants, preachers, pastophores, and finally Hermes. The door was closed on them; their "fête of delight" was complete.

## XVII

The aspect of the vast meadow returned to slumber was, at that moment, strange and truly religious. In the heavens, a sudden opacity of clouds had just veiled the whiteness of the moon; no radiance was descending any longer from on high. But the doors of the chapel were still open; the sanctuary was illuminated by firelight, and its gleam spread out into the distance, penetrating and searching interminable profundities.

I gazed at Isis. Enveloped by torches, in the gleam of the alabaster cells, the variegated image stood out brightly. One might have thought it—was it another symbol?—a helpful beacon shining in the darkness, inviting toward a refuge souls in torment, the shipwreck victims of life . . . Isis the spouse! Isis the mother! Isis the woman! I had to react against my nerves in order not to bend my knee.

In the distance, at the church of Montmartre, nine o'clock chimed. The piercing vibration of the clock caused me to shiver and return to myself. Vague anxiety began to cause me anguish, and terror invaded me. I had renounced my design. What was I to do? Go back to Paris as soon as possible. Yes, certainly, but how, without my guide, in that blinding obscurity could I discover the narrow exit, the hole for crawling animals through which I had been introduced? At a furtive pace I went back toward the cells. No one there! Room number fifteen was locked with a key; my conductress had fled . . .

I went from lodge to lodge, knocking with a discreet hand, appealing in a muffled voice; they were all equally closed. An alarming adventure! I plunged back into the hornbeams.

An hour went by in that anxiety. My eyes aimed at the convent, I observed: windows still illuminated; the uncertain sound of music and songs. Hermes must be continuing his demented ceremonies there . . . How cold it was! And snow was beginning to fall. Slow and heavy, it traversed the denuded branches, burned my face and chilled me to the marrow . . .

Another half-hour . . . in truth, I could not remain under that avalanche. A shelter, a shelter! Again, my gaze turned toward the chapel; but at the first glance, I recoiled in fear. In her flamboyant niche, under the porphyry cartouche, Isis had just moved. The arm that had been blessing before extended toward me with menace; the other, falling back spasmodically, opened its fingers as if to protect the crypt, to defend the deposit confided to its mystery: Callista! The Callista that they had buried alive!

Suddenly, at the top of my head, I felt a sharp pain. It was the hand, the invisible hand, stinging my cranium, sharp and penetrating. It had left me a moment's respite; now it resumed its torture.

*Quickly, quickly, go faster, then* . . . Atrocious dolor. And yet I struggled. No, I wouldn't go. What did that woman matter to me? I didn't know her; I didn't love her; I . . .

*Quickly, quickly, faster!* No, no, I no longer wanted to . . . a purified flesh, buried, almost a corpse!

*Quickly, quickly, faster!* No, no, no, I . . . I . . .

Twelve steps; the stairway descending under the nave had twelve steps. The crypt was barred by a bronze door that must be closed; thank God, I wouldn't be able to enter. I stopped; the hand spurred me on, more forcefully. I threw myself backwards. *Quickly, quickly, go faster!* And against my will, it was necessary to push; I experienced resistance, but I leaned harder. Then, grating and creaking, the door rotated on its hinges; I went in.

At that moment, a strident scream cut through the silence; the scream of a woman, indignant and suppliant. Her voice had resounded up here, in the sacrary. It was prolonged outside, reverberating from place to place, awakening the slumbering echoes of the garden. Who, then, was appealing thus—desperately? The temple, I believed myself to be certain, was deserted; not one worshiper had been left before the idol. In truth, then, who had uttered that appeal?

Frightened, I retraced my steps, firmly resolved to flee. Malediction! The door, pushed by a spring, had closed of its own accord; like a maleficent beast I was caught in a trap . . .

And for a long time I groped and palpated the bronze walls: nothing; it could only be opened by an external pressure. A profaner of the tomb, the tomb had closed upon me.

It was a vast funerary chamber, a second, subterranean temple with the same dimensions as the superior sanctuary. A lamp hung from its vault, antique in its curvature, the crackling wicks of which only projected indecisive gleams, excessively vacillating glimmers. Soon, however, my eyes became accustomed to the gloom and I was able to glimpse, distinguish, recognize and read clearly.

The walls were ornamented with Egyptian paintings, frescos representing the judgment of the dead, and a French legend, translating their hieroglyphs, explained the peripeties of that drama of the afterlife: a powerful tragedy, a palpitating mystery, darkened by terrors but illuminated by divine hopes!

Escaping from her hypogeum one saw a young woman—an impalpable but visible soul—transported toward the formidable immensities that developed, extended and were prolonged "out there." With his sun-bronzed arms, Anubis, the demon with the face of a jackal enlaced the quivering form and dragged it toward the terrors of the Amenti. At every step, infernal monsters, baboons, the Elementals of matter, sought to bar the route of the voyager. "I am pure," she said to them; and upon that magical cry, the malevolent spirits stood aside respectfully. Then, from fright to fright, the dead woman reached the serene country where Osiris, the administrator of life's justice, and sentencer of death, sits in his sad glory.

Sitting on the throne three times most high, having in his hand the whip, flagellator of evil, his forehead circled by a tiara and his legs imprisoned by a tightly-wound shroud, the Eon martyr listened impassively to the tremulous confession. And standing behind that much-beloved, Isis the suppliant extended her arms; she pleaded on behalf of human weakness; she implored the exorable equity.

"I am pure, I am pure!" affirmed the soul on trial. Immediately, the symbolic weighing proceeded, the pyschostasis in which the slave is less heavy than his master, the beggar lighter than the king. On one pan of the exact balance, Horus Areori, the child of celestial kisses, the son of Night and Day, of Chastisement and Clemency, of Osiris who punishes and Isis who pardons, placed the canopic jar containing the actions of that defunct life. In the other, he only placed a feather. The balance oscillated; by turns, hope and dread anguished the soul on trial; would it be condemned to reincarnation?

O joy, the feather sank, heavier than the evil actions; perhaps one tear of repentance had sufficed to wash away many stains . . .

Joyful then, liberated then, the soul flew toward the solar splendors; it went to plunge into the radiant abyss, into the increate light of God, its terrestrial pilgrimage forever accomplished.

Here and there, along the wall, coffins had been set up, doubtless stolen from the soil of Khem, and in illuminated sheaths, grimacing mummies were writhing. Almost all of them had been stripped of their bandages, and were collapsed on themselves, the head lolling, opening their jaws, black with bitumen and natron; they seemed to be dancing a macabre saraband. It was hideous . . . hideous . . . hideous. Labels gave the names and qualities of those various individuals: warriors or artisans, scribes, several priests, two pharaohs . . .

Only one of the boxes was empty, but its inscription bore a stupefying mention: *The courtesan Callista. Hermes has discovered her reincarnate.*

She was not far away, that reincarnate: there, before me, extended in an open coffin, side by side with the mummy, her primitive body, the initial envelope of her soul. By the red gleams that fell from the lamp, I distinguished a mass of muslins sheltering the double face: the two bodies had been united by the same bandages. I leaned over, desirous of seeing more clearly. The strips were covered with cursive writing, words in ligatures, which I recognized as letters of the Greek alphabet. Extensively torn, that papyrus had to be the manuscript, the "confession of the afterlife" that the insolent Hermes had mentioned to Blumenthal.

Yes, I had divined correctly, for among the alphas and the omegas, the sigmas, the deltas and the xis, I read a name repeated many times: kappa, alpha, lambda, lambda, iota, eta, tau, alpha.

I sounded and searched further . . . a painting! A portrait—the Mask, my mask! This, then, was why Archibald had sent the neophyte after me. The mask was necessary to his abominable rites, to his blasphemous parody of a resurrection.

I did not experience any dread, and the spurring hand left me in repose. But a curious desire to compare the two faces excited me vividly. It seemed impossible that Nature copying herself could have employed twice the mold that she breaks at each creation. Sliding my fingers under the loose shroud again, I lifted up one of the heads. Pooh! The first Kallista, the mummy. Cold, very cold, repugnant! I let that thing fall back and disengaged the other face . . .

Suddenly, in the superior sacrary, even more dolorous and more exasperated, a new appeal resounded. It shook the vaults and traversed space. What? It was Isis who was moaning? Insolently, I started to laugh.

Well, yes, she was smiling, exactly similar to the marvelous portrait, the second Callista. The "Me" that she had murmured was not the effect of a subjective illusion the mask reproduced her image.

Feature by feature, line by line, save for the eyes-momentarily closed—I compared them and I rediscovered them all. How had I been able to hesitate at Chez Sylvius? Why, at the Moulin Rouge and during the nocturnal pursuit, had I not recognized such a fantastic resemblance? Stupid blindness . . . Her arms folded over her breast, languid and sedative, the young woman seemed to be reposing chastely, and chastely pursuing the dreams of a cradle. Respectfully, I detached one of the dainty hands and I knelt down . . .

"What is so charming in the mantle of her outspread black hair, with her long-closed eyes azured by an aureole, the transparent and lascivious pallor of her face, her crimson mouth parted, mockingly, to give all the alms of a smile! Callista, my Callista . . ."

And while pronouncing those words, a confused memory of a forgotten reading. I clasped the dangling hand and posed my lips upon it . . .

"Callista, my Callista, how I love you!"

A bitter sensation of cold suddenly made me jump. The door had just grated on its hinges; Hermes advanced toward us, menacingly.

# XVIII

Bare-headed, having left his Osirian miter in his lodgings, he was still clad in the alb, the pectoral and his other finery. One might have thought that, the reiterated appeal of Isis—was it truly Isis who had appealed?—having surprised him in mid-ceremony, the pontiff had come running in haste. At any other moment I would not have been able to repress a fit of mad laughter. That shaved and shiny cranium, those cheeks vermilion-tinted with a hieratic fard, that gigantic corpulence in the costume of a bride—his entire person seemed absurdly buffoonish. And yet, such was the indignant glare of his eyes that I immediately assumed a defensive stance. With one bound I came upright in order to go to meet him. He stopped, haughty and theatrical, and then folded his arms.

"Monsieur," he said, "in our ancient and religious Egypt, the violators of tombs were nailed to the cross; you ought to know something about that."

The joking animal! For what reincarnate did he take me?

"Monsieur," I replied, "in our modern, skeptical and rational France, impostors of your species are locked in the Mazas; you ought to know something about that."

Still very arrogant, Monsieur Archibald shrugged his shoulders.

"Enough boasting, if you please. I hold you in my power. With a single blow I could terminate our quarrel here, and cruelly chastise an infamous crime. My hands—look at them, these hands—would only have to clasp you to throw you gasping on to the stone floor. Over your agony I could close the sepulcher. Who would come to find you?"

And the half-breed showed his colossal fingers, his formidable gorilla wrists.

"But no," he said, becoming debonair, "you have nothing to fear. A priest of the All-Clement, I do not have the right to accomplish bloody work. In the name of the Supreme Bounty, Hermes ought only to beseech and can only persuade. In truth, don't move away like that, Monsieur. Let us rather talk as friends; let us explain ourselves frankly."

A stone bench ran along the walls; he went to sit down on it, and then pointed at the body of the buried woman. "Why have you slipped into our abode, near the coffin of that deaconess?"

The unexpected mildness of such language disconcerted me. I had prepared myself for some violence; no, benign, coaxing, crafty, my charlatan expressed himself with the tender amenity of a fashionable confessor, an amiable Jesuit Father dictating pious advice to the repentances of a moribund. Nonplussed, I could only stammer incoherent responses.

"My God, yes, I loved that woman and I wanted to see her again. Imagining that she was in serious danger, I came down to help her. Furthermore, I intended to stay until the moment when she emerges from this funereal cellar."

And while I excused myself rather piteously, the priest of the "All-Clement" observed me compassionately.

"So, you have witnessed our mysteries and not one fiber has quivered within you; no remembrance has shaken the torpor of your memory! Poor, poor blind and groping soul! But that woman whom you say you love, only having glimpsed her once, why do you love her? The thunderbolt? Elective affinity? Or bestial altruism? Words, confess it, words! What! In the darkness in which your present life is being consumed, no flash, unveiling a past existence, has ever illuminated your heart? Never? How I pity you, Monsieur; your blindness is heart-rending. Yes, yes, I pity you, strayed soul seeking in vain in the night."

While speaking, the good apostle had seized my hands and gently constrained me to sit down next to him.

"Oh, my brother," he said, "my brother in torturing proofs, hear me, repent! Like our symbolic vessel, a disabled skiff, you are going to perish; steer for port; Isis will pick you up. She will reveal to you who you are, she will inform you of the Great Mystery. She will tell you the reason for the relentless agitation of our life, the poignant fits of sorrow in the midst of an apparent happiness, the passions that are instantly ignited by sudden encounters, the aspiration toward the ideal that is incessantly disappointed but never discouraged, and the perpetual sob we utter over our entire self. Voyager, voyager, on the road of life you believe that you are traveling an unknown route, but look: each of our footsteps collides with a memory. Here you were happy, there you suffered. These valleys, these shores, these mountains, this entire country, which seem to open unknown before your march, welcome you like old friends. You know them, then, since your being palpitates at their aspect and your eyes are moist with tears. Look again; those passers-by who sometimes follow you with a long gaze, you have encountered them before. Already, you . . ."

Abruptly, he ceased his homily and turned his head toward the depths of the hypogeum, anxiously.

Throughout that verbiage I had not ceased sniggering. "My dear Monsieur, you're spreading the torrents of your eloquence in vain. Isis and her 'Supreme Bounty' will not have either my person or my money."

"Insolence?" he said, disdainfully. "That is poor recompense for my forbearance. Now, I engage you to leave."

At the same time he had stood up, and he indicated the door, which he had fixed by means of a spring when he penetrated into the crypt.

I did not budge.

"Hermes!" a plaintive voice suddenly murmured. "I have divined the presence. For pity's sake, deliver me."

The plaint departed from the coffin where I had contemplated the recumbent Callista; it was so full of sadness that I approached, very emotional.

"Hermes! Hermes!" repeated the suppliant voice. "Deliver me! The man, the slave so much beloved, is here; I know it. I'm athirst to see him again . . . deliver me."

Archibald had shuddered; he was looking at me now with a hostile expression, and his theatrical gesture showed me the door imperiously.

"Did you hear me, Monsieur? You must go. The initiate has broken the bonds of her mortuary sleep too soon. You are only a profane; go away."

"No, Hermes," moaned the voice again. "Let him stay . . . Pakrour loved, he has repented, and I have pardoned him."

At each of those incomprehensible phrases the theosopher's agitation augmented.

"Go, go then! Is it necessary to employ violence?"

"No, no!" the tearful voice repeated. "Let him stay . . . ! Let him stay . . . I want it!"

Some rude combat must then have begun in the conscience of the hierophant. He raised his hands toward the vault, obsecrating and imploring. "Isis, the peril is imminent . . . help me, Isis . . . !"

Finally, his resolution seemed to be made. "So be it," he said to me. "In any case, expelling you today would be a superfluous precaution. Tomorrow, under the spur of incessant Karma, like a beast in rut, you would come back to prowl around this refuge; I am responsible for souls, and I fear an ignoble scandal. Stay, then . . . Isis, in any case, requires a supreme proof. I obey."

But his speech was ill-assured; the order of the heavens found him hesitant. "It is the last assault of Evil," he sighed. "O Clement One, deign to speak to our child."

What was about to happen? An ardent and new curiosity had taken possession of me.

Effortfully, like a man who is being pushed and who is resisting, Archibald approached the buried woman. He knelt down, and pressed his lips to the dangling hand. For a few seconds he remained as if in prayer, mute and humbly prostrate, perhaps having forgotten my presence . . .

A kiss . . . what, was the burlesque old man in love? Was the image of his goddess not sufficient to fill his heart?

When he stood up, I saw that Hermes had been weeping. A temporary emotion, for almost immediately, resuming authority over himself, the poseur and actor reappeared, melodramatically.

"Ahmes . . . Callista!" he pronounced, in a solemn voice. "In the name of Resurrection, Life and Death, seed of Immortality, abandon the abode of ecstasy, of dazzling enôse; descend again down here."

And three times the hand of the incantator passed over the muscles of the motionless face; three times he blew upon the eyelids sealed by slumber.

"Open your eyes, Callista, look and recognize."

The eyes immediately opened; in a spasmodic fashion, the summoned woman straightened up and looked. She gazed, and then disengaged her head from her shroud.

"Him . . . ! Him . . . ! The beloved of old!" she stammered, smiling.

"Yes, *the man*," replied the thaumaturge. "The reincarnate, an expiator like you; once, one of the sins of your first life; now the obstacle to your redemption. Tell the sacrilegious individual that your body no longer belongs to you; order the tempter to leave your soul in repose; it is no longer his, you have reconquered it."

No response; already, however, delivered from the bindings that enveloped her, Callista had got up. Avidly, I examined her. Svelte, slender, gracefully formed, the postulant was wearing the pleasant costume of the goddess: the white tunic symbolic of chastity; the crown of crimson roses, the emblem of fervor. She came toward us, unsteadily.

"Have you not understood me?" the sectarian enjoined. "Command this man to end his pursuits; reject the impurity. Entirely devoted to your redemption, you rejected his memory, vomited his remembrance. Tell him . . ."

"Hermes," the young woman interrupted, timidly, "do you truly believe what you teach us?"

## XIX

Those few words, pronounced in a very soft voice, appeared to me to have astounded the illuminate; he looked at the questioner, stupefied.

"If I did not believe my doctrine," he said, haughtily, "would I have sacrificed my life to it?"

There was a long silence between them. Through the door, now open, gusts of wind chased snowflakes into the crypt, and the cold was becoming sharp. In a sonorous distance, the clock of Montmartre chimed midnight.

"At the same hour, tomorrow," cried the hierophant, "the last veils of Isis would have been torn for my daughter."

Another silence; Archibald had resumed his place of the stone bench, folded his arms, and seemed to be awaiting some pious response.

"Hermes," asked the postulant, "Why, then, has Isis lied to me?"

"What language! No, a lie cannot soil the mouth from which all verity flows."

"Nevertheless, the goddess lied. Isis dared to tell me that the murderous slave had never loved Callista. Look: he is here."

Turning her head toward me, she designated me. I began to understand. The man, the reincarnate, Pakrour the slave assassin: that was me. True God, what a brilliant civil estate the impudent reciter of nonsense had fabricated for me in the past of worlds! Well—should I confess it?—my character did not displease me, for the stupid invention was about to turn to the opprobrium of the inventor. For the moment, I decided to keep quiet, to observe in simple curiosity the scene that was in preparation, only intervening at a favorable moment. I had, in any case, traced a new plan of conduct: no longer a shameful retreat to my château in Cotentin, but an amusing voyage far from Paris. I would take the priestess, my lover of days accomplished; she was not banal, and her stories would divert me. We would depart together, we would go to Egypt, and go as far as the isle of Philoe. There are magnificent ruins there, according to geographers: eight sanctuaries, once vibrant with orisons and canticles, silent today in the great murmur of cataracts. An interesting excursion, an agreeable mistress. *Quid magis?* Doctor Blumenthal would have cried.

"Hermes," the deaconess interrogated, in a firmer tone, "why did you command me to commit a crime, ordering and imposing the theft?"

The question might have embarrassed another; on the contrary, Archibald stiffened his spine.

"Priesthood demands of a priest the martyrdom of oneself; I had the right to test your vocation."

"My vocation! So, theft yesterday, perhaps murder tomorrow."

"One who dare not risk life and honor for my God is not worthy of her."

"Imprudent, don't talk about honor."

"I was sure of you! Each of your actions has always been a suggestion of my will; all those here, preachers or deaconesses, only speak, preach and act in a state of hypnotic wakefulness, and that night, my invisible presence accompanied you, dear child."

"Truly! Thank you for the solicitude. Do you know that my conscience has condemned you, Hermes? So . . ."

She stopped, hesitant; then, raising her voice, emphasizing and spelling out her words, she said: "Let me depart, Master. I no longer have faith."

Depart? He recoiled, as if struck by an impact. Beneath the make-up moistened by sweat, his face had decomposed, and with a dolorous gesture he extended his hand over his breast. He contained himself nevertheless, even striving to smile,

"Impossible. The vows were pronounced yesterday."

"No matter! Let me depart. Here, everything frightens me: the lies of your gods, the wind of insanity that blows over your house, your criminal abuse of our credulous hearts, your odious practices, your abominable rites—everything, including the infamous comedy of death to which I was obliged to lend myself this evening. I no longer believe . . . I no longer believe; I want to depart!"

The sudden abuse seemed to exasperate the mild but arrogant individual.

"You're lying, for you believe more and better than ever before! Who, then, revealed the existence of the reincarnate to me, if not you? You divined him at Chez Sylvius; at Neuilly you wanted to convince yourself, and you came back to me convinced. Yes, you believe; but the spur of your Karma, the shameful itch of your old sins is soliciting you, and you're wavering. Coward! Coward! You really are Ahmes the renegade, the courtesan Callista!"

The debonair smile had disappeared from the rouged lips and involuntarily, the fanatic unleashed his devout fury. At times, demented wrath made his cheeks tremble or creased his forehead, and at other times, he addressed a suppliant gaze at the rebel.

"Believing or not, I want to leave," the woman declared, excitedly. "Listen to me, and after my confession, you'll no longer retain me. Do you know the history of the soul that you intend to consecrate to your deity? It's lamentable in its trivial vulgarity, but it is the history of us all, of all our neophytes. My father died in prison. My mother . . . oh, let's not talk about her! On her advice, in accordance with her orders, at the age of sixteen I had to surrender myself to the most abject adventures, and for a long time, a long time, I lived vilely among the vilest. But what could I do? No education, no apprenticeship, presenting myself everywhere, rejected everywhere; and the hunger, the hunger that the revolts of the soul don't cure, and which only the body knows!

"Came the day when I encountered you, when, as was your custom, you appeared at my hovel with the hope of recruiting an adept there. You spoke to me, and I, not understanding anything of the martyrdom of my life, listened to you. You told me that, by suffering today, I had to expiate some crime of a former life. Your dogma, Hermes, elevated me; its providential doctrine excused Providence and explained its cruelties to me; it arrested blasphemy on my lips, it rehabilitated God for me. I followed you, and I believed, I believed, I believed.

"You know with what a frenzy of voluntary faith I then became the apostle of your doctrines. For months and months, nothing put me off. Preaching in taverns, in public dance-halls, in all bad places, talking to the rich, sitting down beside the meager beds of the poor, mocked by everyone and often insulted, I wanted to reap an abundant harvest of souls for you. For me, Hermes was a revelatory Messiah; I venerated him as the equal of a God . . .

"Alas, how brief my illusion was! The idol was kneaded from clay; my God was only a man, inclined to fallibility like other men, and the revelatory Messiah only revealed his weakness and his insanity to me . . ."

"Callista!"

". . . No radiance of divine charity illuminated his conduct. He was not able to be humble with us, the humble; his pretended social pity was only contentment with himself. How often have I seen my companions go to him, hoping for the word that elevates, the word that purifies, and return with discouragement in the heart and eyes full of tears . . . ? No, you have not been able to found a religion, and your church will collapse on top of you. Hermes, Hermes, it is not God who fills your sanctuaries but the immensity of your pride!"

"My pride?" riposted the pontiff, dryly. "Yes, I am proud of the work accomplished; many other prophets, although saints blessed by the Eternal, have felt a similar pride. Proud I am . . . but the benevolence that I spread over you, wretched women, why don't you talk about that? Without me, who would welcome you, the refuse of our social corruption? All religions reject you, even that of Jesus Christ."

"The word of Jesus had pity for us."

"Get away! His priests have only made recluses of you, shameful Magdalens. Their refuges are inflexible prisons; withered you enter them, and you emerge still withered. I wash away your corruption forever. What am I saying? In my hands, you get up again consecrated, you can become divine, the living glories of my God!"

"The priests of Jesus are right," replied the deaconess. "Penitence can only be born from humility. To sin, and then to make a parade of one's expiation, is to take God for one's dupe. Ostentation in repentance is a blasphemy."

Confounded by such audacity, the theosopher got up. Never, doubtless, in the seminary of the repentant, had he heard such language. He clenched his fists, as if to crush the rebellion, and rolled his eyes, which he wanted to render terrible; but the fingers came apart, inertly, and in the indignant eyes I thought I perceived a tear.

"Words!" he said, finally. "Big words harvested from your books. It's my fault. In you I developed the intelligence to the detriment of the heart."

"A new error, my master! I'm still ignorant, but the whore you collected, the 'refuse of social corruption,' is now a soul."

Exalted and provocative, she wanted to deliver a new challenge. Hermes avoided rising to the bravado.

"Forgive," he said, making himself very humble, "the words of my anger. Yes, you are a soul, a generous and beautiful soul. And in my apostolate, so full—alas—of disillusionment, I have never encountered a keener intelligence, a heart more worthy of my God."

"No. Karma is stronger than my vocation."

"Less powerful, I affirm, than celestial Mercy."

"It is and always will be the stronger. I need to love."

"To love . . . to love!" cried Archibald, dolorously.

That word—love—had made the old man tremble; the emotion that I had observed reappeared, intense and heart-rending. Under the bite of his desire, then, the insolent preacher of continence suffered like anyone else. A physician of souls, was he ignorant of the fortunate secret of healing himself?

With a reckless movement, his hands tried to seize the hands of the rebel. She pulled away in order to throw herself backwards. But with a voice full of frissons, he said: "To love? You're asking to love, child, when love is all around you? Here, love invites you and solicits you . . . oh, if you could only hear it!"

"I have your confession, then?" sniggered the young woman. "Well, what is chasing me away from your refuge is you, you most of all. Interrogate your conscience, recall to your memory some of your gazes, your counsels, your words murmured in my ear, which I heard all too clearly. Yes, I want to love; but, deceived by your lies, I refuse to be the plaything of your passions. A priest, suborner of his penitents—what ignominy! Don't protest; I'm not the dupe of your indignations. Oh, what a crime you have committed, Hermes, in having robbed me of faith! I believed so ardently, and I felt so happy in believing! That's why I hate you now, and despise you . . . No, no, I won't be your mistress. Have you finally understood?"

Certainly, he had understood, for a sigh like a sob elevated his breast.

"Wretched creature!" he moaned, curbing his head. "Under the obsession of the flesh again! Always and forever Callista!"

At that moment, a confused murmur of human voices reached us. Canticles made themselves heard again; the cortege of the worshipers of Isis must have reformed in order to return to the chapel.

At the still-distant rhythm of liturgical orisons, the hierophant appeared to emerge from his dejection. He straightened up; the blackness of his eyes lit up; under the amplitude of first light I saw him shaken by a convulsive tremor. One might have thought that he had been agitated by the divine frissons of a quaker, when the breath of the Spirit descends into the silence of ecstasized "brethren," coming to chill the body in order to inflame the soul.

"Here they are! Here they are!" he proclaimed. "The office of the last day has commenced. Let us pray, my Callista: God is forgiving you."

Without replying to that objurgation, the deaconess shredded the roses of her coiffure and tore away the veil that swathed her hair. But he, madly stirred by his strange intoxication, went on:

"Listen friend listen to what they're saying: 'Hope even in despair, amour must be a suffering, suffering a sensuality. Do you see? Do you understand? Suffering and sensuality! Yes, I love you, I love you, but with an amour that cannot offer you the bestiality of other men, an amour that is not sensual, immaculate, purificatory and ideal. I love you. Look: vanquished by you, the vainglorious is humiliating his pride, he has bent his knee.

Welcome without disdain such a confession of his weakness, take pity on his despair. I love you . . .

"Every revelatory Messiah requires a companion: do you want to be that inseparable companion of my life? Oh, Callista, my Callista, if you deigned to listen to me, what transports for both of us and what rapture! Nothing, believe me, equals the ineffable joy of the mystical possession. United with one another, but without weakening in the duties of our chastity, scorning the ignominies of the flesh as a degradation of the soul, together we would cross the nine steps that lead to the annihilation of the body, and together we would attain that supreme voluptuousness, the insatiable languor of amour. Then, loving as God loves, by the heart, we would be similar to God . . ."

He paused briefly, lending an ear to the hymns that were cadenced more distinctly.

". . . And then," he continued, "I sense myself becoming very old. Under the harvest of Isis, every day, I buckle more wearily; I need a sister, another self who will glean after me. What a consolation, if I could know that my work is not decrepit! Be my companion; I will associate you with my apostolate; you too will don the tiara, to march as my equal. Immediately, the most profound arcana will be revealed to your eyes. I will inform you of the great mysteries that India, before Egypt, had revealed to me; you will understand how the ascetic acquires the gift of doubling the body and obtaining the ubiquity of a god. Do you know that, even after death, the astral body of a pious Brahmin can always appear and loom up before the face of a living beloved? Oh, if your ingrate abandonment killed me tomorrow, with what rapid flight I would impel myself toward you! Neither distance, nor the dazzle of the Light, nor even— alas—your forgetfulness would prevent me from coming to lean over your face, to intoxicate myself on your breath, to carry you away in my arms and sigh in your ear: 'I loved you! I loved you! I love you still . . . !'"

"He's scaring me," the abjuratrice interrupted. "Take me away, Monsieur."

Hermes had fallen to his knees; violently, he stood up. His gaze was now shining in a sinister fashion; his mouth was hateful, his speech hissing.

"Enough insults!" he cried. "No, I shall chastise . . . Once, in Catholic cloisters, such a sacrilege as yours would have been punished by an *in pace* until death. I will treat you more cruelly, renegade; I surrender you to this man, and it is him who will torture you pitilessly."


## XX


Meanwhile, the cortege was approaching. The mourning lamentations had been succeeded by joyful cantatas, hilarious enthusiasms: "Victory! Victory! Life has triumphed!" To the rhythm of gallops, polkas or Irish jigs, they were celebrating the defeat of sin; they were mocking Death. At the same time, the voices of women were demanding Hermes, demanding their pontiff. Indifferent to those appeals, however, he had headed for the coffin where, amid the muslins, the Egyptian mask was placed, the stolen portrait of the first Callista.

Bewildered by so much insanity, I had turned my eyes toward the fascinating image for several minutes. Upright on the pale undulations of the shroud, she was looking at me so languidly. Her carmined lips were smiling, lascivious and mocking; sometimes, she even addressed provocative winks to me. Oh, courtesan, courtesan of mute speech and clandestine caresses, still wanting and knowing how to tease even in her tomb!

Suddenly, Hermes extended his arm toward her; he seized the charming image, and then, with a dry click, snapped the magic panel in two and fell to his knees, moaning.

A cry of atrocious dolor responded to that savage brutality; fainting, the deaconess came to lean on my shoulder . . .

What a surprise! Was it an illusion produced by the obscure glimmer of the funerary lamp? The face of my new friend seemed to me to be frightfully altered. She had been much more beautiful when she was slumbering tranquilly in her sepulchral bed, under my wonderstruck gaze. Her eyes had sunk into their orbits, and her mouth, so dainty a little while ago, now advanced, bestial and grimacing. Not understanding the rapid metamorphosis, I dissimulated my astonishment.

Very close to the hypogeum, the sacrosanct charivari was raging, in leaping notes. The procession had reached the chapel; one of the pastophores ran to the entrance to the crypt.

"Hermes! The office is about to commence; we're only waiting for you."

"Return to the conventual house and all put on mourning," the old man replied, sadly. "No more songs and joyous canticles, but the stupor of funerals. Death is victorious; your priestess has just abjured her God."

The other withdrew, consternated; soon, uncertain rumors were heard, cries of indignation, and finally footfalls that drew away, heavily cadenced. The noise decreased, became muted, and stifled; then, nothing more.

Motionless, as if paralyzed, the abjuratrice was still leaning on my shoulder, and with a conquering gesture I had put my arm around her waist.

"They've gone back now," I said to her. "Let's depart."

But Archibald blocked our path.

"At least take away, in your apostasy, one last souvenir of our beliefs and your faith."

"What souvenir?" she asked, astonished.

"Callista's ring."

"The . . . the mummy's ring?"

"Yes. Found on the body of your first incarnation, it belongs to you."

The amorous individual had become very calm again, and the growling threats of his dolor appeared to me to have faded away very rapidly. His gaze, however, was sparkling grimly; he fixed it upon us, disquietingly.

"The ring? Why the ring?" the young woman repeated, indecisive and troubled.

Without responding, Hermes leaned over the bier, tore away the last shroud and laid bare the rigid whiteness of the mummy.

The mummy! The marvelous Callista, my dicteriade of the porphyry palace, the lust of a people when, adored by all, she lavished her embrace on all of them . . . out there, under the burning sun near the sea "of blue songs." Horror! Paltry, shrunken, like a filthy fetus, exhaling the repugnant odors of the embalming: an abominable thing. The face was still swathed with bandages, and I could not recognize those lips, donors of so many kisses, covered by so many kisses. But the arms folded over the breast exhibited their hideous nudity, and on one finger of the left hand a ring was perceptible: *the* ring.

It was a gold ring with a large Oriental cornelian stone, one of the knightly rings that, in the days of the Pax Romana the *equites aurium*, the procurators and stewards of Caesar, had worn. The form of the ring was not unknown to me; once before—but where, in some European museum?—I had noticed an exactly similar sigil. A bizarre ornament, which must have bruised the hand of the amorous beauty! Immediately, I imagined—an amusing hypothesis—seeing in that cameo the present of some lover . . .

And the ring glistened; the polished redness of its agate scintillated, reflective in the gloom.

With a reckless surge, the woman ran toward the Egyptian.

"The gift of Valerius Afer," the priest of Isis said to her. "Evoke the memory: remember."

"Yes, yes, I remember . . . I was afraid of heavy disdain, of abandonment, of poverty, afraid of the crossroads where, wandering by night, the . . ."

"Good, your own words, Callista; they were wise; you have a good memory."

"Hermes," she asked, in a very quiet voice, "when Karma is stronger than repentance, the spur of the flesh more powerful than our will, is suicide truly a crime?"

258

"No, for it is an appeal to God."

"Give me that ring, Father!"

And, snatching it from the mummy, she passed the ring over one of her fingers. "Thank you, Hermes, thank you for this testimony of your amour."

"Rather say, poor girl, my pity for you."

At present, nothing any longer denounced in that man the stormy fury that had agitated him. He had recovered full mastery of himself; his speech was affectionate, his smile sympathetic.

Four o'clock chimed.

"The night is about to end," said the hierophant, placidly. "Your prolonged presence here would be a pollution; it's necessary for you to withdraw."

Preceding us then, he guided us personally through the obscure declivities of the mysterious enclosure. The snowy torment had ceased; a low and heavy sky weighed upon the hill; the sacrary of Isis had been extinct for a long time; and silently, over crackling ice, we marched in the darkness. But all along the way I observed Archibald. Why did the whiteness of his robe shine like that, and why did his entire body trail luminous vapors? I had already remarked the phenomenon the other evening when he was standing on the threshold of the Jew's house in the opacity of the fog. Strange, truly strange!

Having reached the bottom of the garden, Hermes opened a door and stood aside in order to let us through. We were about to go out when he abruptly lowered his hands on to the shoulders of the former deaconess.

"One last word," he said. "An order, the last of my orders. Listen, and understand well. The day will shortly be reborn; soon, in whatever impure bed to which your Karma will have impelled you, turn your eyes toward the first light of dawn. Look; and if you are still able to see, wretch, you will see."

I drew my companion away; the extravagant old man closed the door on us. Henceforth, the priestess was mine—mine alone . . .

Yes, but what was I going to do with that fugitive?

# XXI

. . . And the day dawned. Its wan light spread out, uncertainly, in the room of the infamous hotel—the only one that had deigned to open its doors to shelter our amours. Oh, that journey through slumbering Montmartre, over the escarpments encumbered by snow, the back streets winding and intersecting in the silence, in the terrors of the silence! What a memory! And while we walked, the insanities that the comrade pronounced! She was hanging on to my arm and chattering, discoursing, sermonizing, loquacious and stupefying.

"Who are you, then, on earth today, and what, poor friend, is your second life? Fortunate or unfortunate? Unfortunate, I'm afraid, for you too, Monsieur, have to expiate, to suffer . . . How were you able to discover my retreat, to reach me? I don't know, but it doesn't matter. Remembering, your heart has pity. Pity be blessed; no one has ever taken pity on me . . . See, I'm abandoning myself to your honor; I'll be your servant, your slave, your thing; but you'll respect—oh, I implore you!—you'll respect the dolorous flesh of the reincarnate."

Reincarnate? Oh . . . she believed, then, in the abstruse follies that Archibald taught. In spite of her disavowal, she had the faith! But in that case, what a triumph for my vanity as a seducer! And I felt stupidly vainglorious. However, I did not sing victory; the exaltation of my lover and her big words bewildered me.

"Good, good! Calm down, my darling. We'll talk later; first, let's find a shelter."

We rang at four or five hotels; everywhere, wooden faces and inexorable doors. Finally, on the perimeter of the cemetery, I had come across the eatery whose sign I had glimpsed: *For the consolation of families. Rooms for the night.*

A dive: but at five o'clock in the morning, one takes refuge where one can. Immediately, blows of the fist on the shop-front, and a judas-hole that opened

"I'd like a room."

"All occupied except for the sixth."

"We'll take that paradise!"

There, in a verminous closet, a new sermon, more supplications.

"On my knees, I implore you: spare me, Monsieur. In the name of the Eternal Now, don't debase my soul."

"Bah, my dear. The Eternal Now will veil her face."

"Mercy! Mercy for my miserable honor, for my womanly dignity, finally recovered."

No . . .

✳

. . . And the day dawned; penetrating into the high mansard, it spread its first pallors over the tiles of our garret. I raised myself up on my elbow in order to get a better view of the sleep of my modest victim. A ray of light fell directly on to her face . . .

Divine justice! What was that? That monster, that abominable hideousness lying alongside me? Pale, etiolated, cadaverous. A forehead that sloped ridiculously. A nose that was too short, vulgar, squashed, with two bestial nostrils. A protruding mouth and grimacing lips, trying to smile at me. The features of a skeleton, the mask of a corpse escaped from an ossuary!

Frightened, I leapt out of bed and got dressed in haste . . . If I could decamp, slyly, sparing myself all the customary homilies of the excessively eloquent demoiselle, I could settle the bill, the whole bill, at the office of the hotel . . . But no; she was sitting up in the wretched bed and looking at me wildly.

"Monsieur! For pity's sake, Monsieur . . . in the name of the Supreme Bounty, don't abandon me!"

"Another speech! We're no longer preaching, my reverend lady . . . I'm going; adieu."

With a desperate gesture, she held out her hands toward me; then, with the hiccups of a lamentable laughter: "The other was less cruel; he killed."

The other? Who was "the other"? A former acquaintance of my companion? Absolutely unknown, that "other." Oh, yes, Pakrour! The good story . . . !

Her desolation was so heart-rending that I ought to have felt sympathetic; to the contrary. Horrible before, her tearful rictus rendered her grotesque; the mask of Death had become that of an ape. Pooh!

Undoubtedly, she divined the disgust, the repugnant disgust that her monstrosity inspired in me, for she bowed her head and fell silent.

I was ashamed, however, of fleeing in that fashion and, not knowing what to do, I moved restlessly on the spot.

Suddenly, raising her head, the woman uttered a strident clamor: "Hermes!" she cried. "I've killed him! I've killed my only friend, my savior, my holy refuge, my father! Hermes! Hermes! Oh, forgive me . . ."

And she stretched out her hands toward the nascent daylight, put them together imploringly and wrung them, in a crisis of insensate despair. I turned my eyes in that direction.

Through the window, although it was closed, a dense fog had just penetrated into the room. A fog? No . . . floating draperies, stained with blood, and in that misty shroud, a human form, the livid face of a dead man: an apparition, a phantom—Hermes . . . Hermes, menacing . . .

How had the audacious thaumaturge been able to enter?

With a furious surge, I rushed at him . . .

Nothing: a mass of vapors, for I traversed them completely. I turned round. But yes! But yes! A specter! Hermes. Hermes himself! He had approached the bed, leaned over his preacher, and appeared to say something to her. She responded . . .

Again, I precipitated myself upon the spell-caster; everything dissipated.

. . . . . . . . . . . . . . . . . . . . . . . . . . . . . . . . . . . . . . . . . . . . . . . . . . .

Now, my memories are confused, my remembrance too uncertain . . .

In the filthy couchette the young woman was writhing, shaken by atrocious convulsions. The stone of the mummy's ring had rotated, and a few grains of yellow powder were still adhering to it. Poison! The unfortunate woman had poisoned herself . . .

"I'm afraid of heavy disdain, of abandonment, of poverty, afraid of the crossroads where, wandering by night, the . . . ."

I ran to open the door.

"Help! Help! A physician . . ."

Nothing in the house stirred; I went back to the agonizing woman's bed . . .

O surprise! The repulsive ugliness had disappeared, and I recognized Callista—my Callista, with the large velvet eyes, the heady smile and the incorruptible beauty. Falling to my knees, I seized her already-icy hands; passionately, I applied them to my forehead, and for a long, long time I remained thus, seeing nothing, hearing nothing, no longer understanding anything.

A brutal voice extracted me from my annihilation. The room was full of people; policemen interrogated me; they took possession of me.

FINAL OBSERVATIONS
of M. le Dr. Marius Labastide, etc., etc.

February 1890. The subject Raoul d'Hérival has been reintegrated, not without efforts, into the Villa Riante. The examining magistrate wanted to retain him; I had great difficulty getting him out of his hands. What tenacious claws examining magistrates have!

Henceforth, for that agitated individual, the Esquirol Cell, a charterhouse from which he will never escape.

August 1890. Very calm for six months and absolutely incurable. He devotes every day to writing extravagant lucubrations, pretended adventures strewn with fantastic characters. No symptoms of genius . . .

Here, at any rate, is a page of that sort, picked up yesterday in the cell where he lives; I am addressing it with various other fragments to the editors of *The Old and Modern Sphinx*. Better than any treatise of philosophy, these few lines will demonstrate to them the intimate correlation that exists between the erethism of certain invalids and the transports of certain mystics:

"From the expiatory prison where my body is enchained, hoping for and awaiting the imminent deliverance. 'Nothing dies, you tell us, in the perpetual renewal of the worlds. Death is only an evolution of life, life a purifying refinement of the soul by dolor and amour, a progressive ascension, from earth to earth and from star to star, toward the seductive Light into which everything sinks, into which everything is absorbed.' Adorable logic: the law of human perpetuity, a divine emanation of divine Eternity! I want, I would like to believe it . . .

"Oh, Hermes, what if the dogma that your madness taught us was, nevertheless, an entire revelation?"

## A PARTIAL LIST OF SNUGGLY BOOKS

**G. ALBERT AURIER** *Elsewhere and Other Stories*
**CHARLES BARBARA** *My Lunatic Asylum*
**S. HENRY BERTHOUD** *Misanthropic Tales*
**LÉON BLOY** *The Tarantulas' Parlor and Other Unkind Tales*
**ÉLÉMIR BOURGES** *The Twilight of the Gods*
**JAMES CHAMPAGNE** *Harlem Smoke*
**FÉLICIEN CHAMPSAUR** *The Latin Orgy*
**FÉLICIEN CHAMPSAUR**
 *The Emerald Princess and Other Decadent Fantasies*
**BRENDAN CONNELL** *Unofficial History of Pi Wei*
**BRENDAN CONNELL** *The Metapheromenoi*
**RAFAELA CONTRERAS** *The Turquoise Ring and Other Stories*
**ADOLFO COUVE** *When I Think of My Missing Head*
**QUENTIN S. CRISP** *Aiaigasa*
**QUENTIN S. CRISP** *Graves*
**LUCIE DELARUE-MARDRUS** *The Last Siren and Other Stories*
**LADY DILKE** *The Outcast Spirit and Other Stories*
**CATHERINE DOUSTEYSSIER-KHOZE** *The Beauty of the Death Cap*
**ÉDOUARD DUJARDIN** *Hauntings*
**BERIT ELLINGSEN** *Now We Can See the Moon*
**BERIT ELLINGSEN** *Vessel and Solsvart*
**ERCKMANN-CHATRIAN** *A Malediction*
**ENRIQUE GÓMEZ CARRILLO** *Sentimental Stories*
**EDMOND AND JULES DE GONCOURT** *Manette Salomon*
**REMY DE GOURMONT** *From a Faraway Land*
**GUIDO GOZZANO** *Alcina and Other Stories*
**EDWARD HERON-ALLEN** *The Complete Shorter Fiction*
**EDWARD HERON-ALLEN** *Three Ghost-Written Novels*
**RHYS HUGHES** *Cloud Farming in Wales*
**J.-K. HUYSMANS** *The Crowds of Lourdes*
**J.-K. HUYSMANS** *Knapsacks*
**COLIN INSOLE** *Valerie and Other Stories*
**JUSTIN ISIS** *Pleasant Tales II*
**JUSTIN ISIS AND DANIEL CORRICK (editors)**
 *Drowning in Beauty: The Neo-Decadent Anthology*
**VICTOR JOLY** *The Unknown Collaborator and Other Legendary Tales*

MARIE KRYSINSKA *The Path of Amour*
BERNARD LAZARE *The Mirror of Legends*
BERNARD LAZARE *The Torch-Bearers*
MAURICE LEVEL *The Shadow*
JEAN LORRAIN *Errant Vice*
JEAN LORRAIN *Fards and Poisons*
JEAN LORRAIN *Masks in the Tapestry*
JEAN LORRAIN *Monsieur de Bougrelon and Other Stories*
JEAN LORRAIN *Nightmares of an Ether-Drinker*
JEAN LORRAIN *The Soul-Drinker and Other Decadent Fantasies*
ARTHUR MACHEN *N*
ARTHUR MACHEN *Ornaments in Jade*
CAMILLE MAUCLAIR *The Frail Soul and Other Stories*
CATULLE MENDÈS *Bluebirds*
CATULLE MENDÈS *For Reading in the Bath*
CATULLE MENDÈS *Mephistophela*
ÉPHRAÏM MIKHAËL *Halyartes and Other Poems in Prose*
LUIS DE MIRANDA *Who Killed the Poet?*
OCTAVE MIRBEAU *The Death of Balzac*
CHARLES MORICE *Babels, Balloons and Innocent Eyes*
GABRIEL MOUREY *Monada*
DAMIAN MURPHY *Daughters of Apostasy*
DAMIAN MURPHY *The Star of Gnosia*
KRISTINE ONG MUSLIM *Butterfly Dream*
CHARLES NODIER *Outlaws and Sorrows*
PHILOTHÉE O'NEDDY *The Enchanted Ring*
YARROW PAISLEY *Mendicant City*
URSULA PFLUG *Down From*
JEREMY REED *When a Girl Loves a Girl*
JEREMY REED *Bad Boys*
ADOLPHE RETTÉ *Misty Thule*
JEAN RICHEPIN *The Bull-Man and the Grasshopper*
DAVID RIX *A Blast of Hunters*
FREDERICK ROLFE (**Baron Corvo**) *Amico di Sandro*
FREDERICK ROLFE (**Baron Corvo**)
   *An Ossuary of the North Lagoon and Other Stories*
JASON ROLFE *An Archive of Human Nonsense*